Laurell K. Hamilton is the bestselling author of the acclaimed Anita Blake, Vampire Hunter novels. She lives near St. Louis, with her husband, her daughter, two pug and two part pug dogs and an ever-fluctuating number of fish. She invites you to visit her website at www.laurellkhamilton.org

Find out more about Laurell K. Hamilton and other Orbit authors by registering for the free monthly newsletter at www.orbitbooks.net

# CERULEAN SINS

## An Anita Blake,
## Vampire Hunter Novel

## LAURELL K. HAMILTON

orbit

www.orbitbooks.net

ORBIT

First published in Great Britain by Orbit 2003
This edition published by Orbit 2003
Reprinted 2004, 2005, 2006

A CIP catalogue record for this book is
available from the British Library.

ISBN 978-1-84149-201-8

Papers used by Orbit are natural, recyclable products made from
wood grown in sustainable forests and certified in accordance with
the rules of the Forest Stewardship Council.

Typeset in Times by M Rules
Printed and bound in Great Britain by
Mackays of Chatham Ltd, Chatham, Kent
Paper supplied by Hellefoss AS, Norway

Orbit
An imprint of
Little, Brown Book Group
Brettenham House
Lancaster Place
London WC2E 7EN

A Member of the Hachette Livre Group of Companies

www.orbitbooks.net

To J., who says yes more than he says no;
who never makes me feel like a freak,
and who came up with the title for this book.

## Acknowledgements

Thanks to Karen and Bear, who helped me find new places to hide the bodies. To Joanie and Melissa, who helped entertain Trinity when she needed more playtime than a hardworking mommy can supply. To Trinity, who helped me finish this book by being old enough to entertain herself. Every year just gets better. To Carniffex and Maerda, who helped me with research, and who should have been mentioned here books ago. To Darla, without whom so much would go undone. To Sherry, for keeping the place liveable. To Sergeant Robert Cooney of the St. Louis City Police Mobile Reserve Unit, for answering my last-minute questions. He did not have time to read over this manuscript, so all mistakes are mine and mine alone. And, as always, to my writing group: Tom Drennan, N. L. Drew, Rhett McPhearson, Deborah Millitello, Marella Sands, Sharon Shinn, and Mark Sumner.

IT WAS EARLY September, a busy time of year for raising the dead. The pre-Halloween rush seemed to start earlier and earlier every year. Every animator at Animators Inc. was booked solid. I was no exception; in fact, I'd been offered more work than even my ability to go without sleep could supply.

Mr. Leo Harlan should have been grateful to get the appointment. He didn't look grateful. Truthfully, he didn't have the look of anything. Harlan was medium. Medium height, dark hair, but not too dark. Skin neither too pale nor too tan. Eyes brown, but an indistinguishable shade of brown. In fact the most remarkable thing about Mr. Harlan was that there was nothing remarkable about him. Even his suit was dark, conservative. A businessman's outfit that had been in style for the last twenty years and probably would still be in style twenty years down the road. His shirt was white, his tie neatly knotted, his not-too-big, not-too-small hands were well groomed but not manicured.

His appearance told me so little that that in itself was interesting, and vaguely disturbing.

I took a sip from my coffee mug with the motto, "If you slip me decaf, I'll rip your head off." I'd brought it to work when our boss, Bert, had put decaf in the coffeemaker without telling anyone, thinking we wouldn't notice. Half the office thought they had mono for a week, until we discovered Bert's dastardly plot.

The coffee that our secretary, Mary, had gotten for Mr. Harlan sat on the edge of my desk. His mug was the one with the logo of Animators Inc. on it. He'd taken a minute sip of the coffee, when Mary had first handed it to him. He'd taken the coffee black, but he sipped it like he hadn't tasted it, or it didn't really matter what it tasted like. He'd taken it out of politeness, not out of desire.

I sipped my own coffee, heavy on the sugar and cream, trying to make up for the late work the night before. Caffeine and sugar, the two basic food groups.

His voice was like the rest of him, so ordinary it was extraordinary. He spoke with absolutely no accent, no hint of region, or country. "I want you to raise my ancestor, Ms. Blake."

"So you said."

"You seem to doubt me, Ms. Blake."

"Call it skepticism."

"Why would I come in here and lie to you?"

I shrugged. "People have done it before."

"I assure you, Ms. Blake, I am telling the truth."

Trouble was, I just didn't believe him. Maybe I was being paranoid, but my left arm under the nice navy suit jacket was crisscrossed with scars – from the crooked cross-shaped burn scar, where a vampire's servant had branded me, to the slashing claw marks of a shape-shifted witch. Plus knife scars, thin and clean compared to the rest. My right arm had only one knife scar, it was nothing in comparison. And there were other scars hidden under the navy skirt and royal blue shell. Silk didn't care if it slid over scars or smooth, untouched skin. I'd earned my right to be paranoid.

"What ancestor do you want raised, and why?" I smiled when I said it, pleasant, but the smile didn't reach my eyes. I'd begun to have to work at getting my smiles to reach all the way up to my eyes.

He smiled too, and it left his eyes as unaffected as my own. Smile because you were smiled at, not because it really meant anything. He reached out to pick up the coffee mug again, and this time I noticed a heaviness in the left front of his jacket. He wasn't wearing a shoulder holster – I'd have noticed that – but there was something heavier than a wallet in his left breast pocket. It could have been a lot of things, but my first thought was, *gun*. I've learned to listen to my first thoughts. You're not paranoid if people really are out to get you.

I had my own gun tucked under my left arm in a shoulder holster. That evened things up, but I did not want my office to turn into the O.K. Corral. He had a gun. Maybe. Probably. For all I knew it could have been a really heavy cigar case. But I'd have bet almost anything that that heaviness was a weapon. I could either sit here and try to talk myself out of that belief, or I could act as if I was right. If I was wrong, I'd apologize later; if I was right, well, I'd be alive. Better alive and rude than dead and polite.

I interrupted his talk about his family tree. I hadn't really heard any of it. I was fixated on that heaviness in his pocket. Until I found out whether it was a gun or not, nothing else much mattered to me. I smiled and forced it up into my eyes. "What is it exactly that you do for a living, Mr. Harlan?"

He drew a slightly deeper breath, settling into his chair, just a bit. It was the closest thing I'd seen to tension in the man. The first real, human movement. People fidget. Harlan didn't.

People don't like dealing with people who raise the dead. Don't ask me why, but we make them nervous. Harlan wasn't nervous, he wasn't anything. He was just sitting across the desk from me, chilling, nondescript eyes pleasant and empty. I was betting he'd lied about his reason for coming here and that he'd brought a gun hidden on his person in a place that wasn't easy to spot.

I was liking Leo Harlan less and less.

I sat my coffee mug gently on my desk blotter, still smiling. I'd freed up my hands, which was step one. Drawing my gun would be step two; I was hoping to avoid that step.

"I want you to raise one of my ancestors, Ms. Blake. I don't see where my work has any relevance here."

"Humor me," I said, still smiling, but feeling it slide out of my eyes like melting ice.

"Why should I?" he said.

"Because if you don't, I'll refuse to take your case."

"Mr. Vaughn, your boss, has already taken my money. He accepted on your behalf."

I smiled, and this time it held real humor. "Actually, Bert is only the business manager at Animators Inc., now. Most of us are full partners in the firm, like a law firm. Bert still handles the business end of things, but he's not exactly my boss anymore."

His face, if it was possible, went quieter, more closed, more secretive. It was like looking at a bad painting, one that had all the technicalities down, yet held no feel of life. The only humans I'd ever seen that could be this closed down were scary ones.

3

"I wasn't aware of your change in status, Ms. Blake." His voice had gone a tone deeper, but it was as empty as his face.

He was ringing every alarm bell I had, my shoulders were tight with the need to pull my gun first. My hands slid downward without me thinking about it. It wasn't until his hands raised to the arms of his chair that I realized what I'd done. We were both maneuvering to a better position to draw down.

Suddenly there was tension, thick and heavy like invisible lightning in the room. There was no more doubt. I saw it in his empty eyes, and in the small smile on his face. This was a real smile, no fake, no pretense. We were seconds away from doing one of the most real things one human being can do to another. We were about to try to kill each other. I watched, not his eyes, but his upper body, waiting for that betraying movement. There was no more doubt, we both knew.

Into that heavy, heavy tension, his voice fell like a stone thrown down a deep well. His voice alone almost made me go for my gun. "I am a contract killer, but I'm not here for you, Anita Blake."

I didn't take my eyes from his body, the tension didn't slacken. "Why tell me then?" My voice was softer than his, almost breathy.

"Because I haven't come to St. Louis to kill anyone. I really am interested in getting my ancestor raised from the dead."

"Why?" I asked, still watching his body, still treading the tension.

"Even hitmen have hobbies, Ms. Blake." His voice was matter-of-fact, but his body stayed very, very still. I realized, suddenly, that he was trying not to spook me.

I let my gaze flick to his face. It was still bland, still unnaturally empty, but it also held something else . . . a trace of humor.

"What's so funny?" I asked.

"I didn't know that coming to see you was tempting fate."

"What do you mean?" I was trying to hold on to that edge of tension, but it was slipping away. He sounded too ordinary, too suddenly real, for me to keep thinking about drawing a gun and shooting up my office. It suddenly seemed a little silly, and yet . . . looking into his dead eyes that humor never completely filled, it didn't seem all that silly.

"There are people all over the world who would love to see me

4

dead, Ms. Blake. There are people who have spent considerable money and effort to see that such a thing would happen, but no one has come close, until today."

I shook my head. "This wasn't close."

"Normally, I'd agree with you, but I knew something of your reputation, so I didn't wear a gun in my usual manner. You noticed the weight of it when I bent forward that last time, didn't you?"

I nodded.

"If we'd had to draw down on each other, your holster is a few seconds faster than this inner jacket shit that I'm wearing."

"Then why wear it?" I asked.

"I didn't want to make you nervous by coming in here armed, but I don't go anywhere unarmed, so I thought I'd be slick, and you wouldn't notice."

"I almost didn't."

"Thanks for that, but we both know better."

I wasn't sure about that, but I let it go; no need to argue when I seemed to be winning.

"What do you really want, Mr. Harlan, if that is your real name?"

He smiled at that. "As I've said, I really do want my ancestor raised from the dead. I didn't lie about that." He seemed to think for a second. "Strange, but I haven't lied about anything." He looked puzzled. "It's been a long time since that was true."

"My condolences," I said.

He frowned at me. "What?"

"It must be difficult never being able to tell the truth. I know I'd find it exhausting."

He smiled, and again it was that slight flexing of lips that seemed to be his genuine smile. "I haven't thought about it in a long time." He shrugged. "I guess you get used to it."

It was my turn to shrug. "Maybe. What ancestor do you want raised, and why?"

"Why what?"

"Why do you want to raise this particular ancestor?"

"Does it matter?" he asked.

"Yes."

"Why?"

5

"Because I don't believe the dead should be disturbed without a good reason."

That small smile flexed again. "You've got animators in this town that raise zombies every night for entertainment."

I nodded. "Then by all means go to one of them. They'll do anything you want, pretty much, if the price is right."

"Can they raise a corpse that's almost two hundred years old?"

I shook my head. "Out of their league."

"I heard an animator could raise almost anything, if they were willing to do a human sacrifice." His voice was quiet.

I shook my head, again. "Don't believe everything you hear, Mr. Harlan. *Some* animators could raise a few hundred years' worth of corpse with the help of a human sacrifice. Of course, that would be murder and thus illegal."

"Rumor has it that you've done it."

"Rumor can say anything it damn well pleases, I don't do human sacrifice."

"So you can't raise my ancestor." He made it a flat statement.

"I didn't say that."

His eyes widened, the closest to surprise that he'd shown. "You can raise a nearly two-hundred-year-old corpse without a human sacrifice?"

I nodded.

"Rumor said that, too, but I didn't believe it."

"So you believed that I did human sacrifice, but not that I could raise a few hundred years' worth of dead people on my own."

He shrugged. "I'm used to people killing other people, I've never seen anyone raised from the dead."

"Lucky you."

He smiled, and his eyes thawed just a little. "So you'll raise my ancestor?"

"If you tell me a good enough reason for doing it."

"You don't get distracted much, do you, Ms. Blake."

"Tenacious, that's me," I said, and smiled. Maybe I'd spent too much time around really bad people, but now that I knew that Leo Harlan wasn't here to kill me, or anyone else in town, I had no problem with him. Why did I believe him? For the same reason I hadn't believed him the first time. Instinct.

"I've followed the records of my family in this country back as far as I can, but my original ancestor is on no official documents. I believe he gave a false name from the beginning. Until I get his true name, I can't track my family through Europe. I very much wish to do that."

"Raise him, ask his real name, his real reason for coming to this country, and put him back?" I made it a question.

Harlan nodded. "Exactly."

"It sounds reasonable enough."

"So you'll do it," he said.

"Yes, but it ain't cheap. I'm probably the only animator in this country that can raise someone this old without using a human sacrifice. It's sort of a seller's market, if you catch my drift."

"In my own way, Ms. Blake, I am as good at my job as you are at yours." He tried to look humble and failed. He looked pleased with himself, all the way to those ordinary, and frightening, brown eyes. "I can pay, Ms. Blake, never fear."

I mentioned an outrageous figure. He never flinched. He started to reach into the inside of his jacket. I said, "Don't."

"My credit card, Ms. Blake, nothing more." He took his hands out of his jacket and held them, fingers spread, so I could see them clearly.

"You can finish the paperwork and pay in the outer office. I've got other appointments."

He almost smiled. "Of course." He stood. I stood. Neither of us offered to shake hands. He hesitated at the door; I stopped a ways back, not following as closely as I normally do. Room to maneuver, you know.

"When can you do the job?"

"I'm booked solid this week. I might be able to squeeze you in next Wednesday. Maybe next Thursday."

"What happened to next Monday and Tuesday?" he asked.

I shrugged. "Booked up."

"You said, and I quote, 'I'm booked solid this week.' Then you mentioned next Wednesday."

I shrugged again. There was a time when I wasn't good at lying, even now I'm not great at it, but not for the same reasons. I felt my eyes going flat and empty, as I said, "I meant to say I was booked up for most of the next two weeks."

7

He stared at me, hard enough to make me want to squirm. I fought off the urge and just gave him blank, vaguely friendly eyes.

"Next Tuesday is the night of the full moon," he said in a quiet voice.

I blinked at him, fighting to keep the surprise off my face, and I think I succeeded, but I failed on my body language. My shoulders tensed, my hands flexed. Most people noticed your face, not the rest of you, but Harlan was a man who would notice. Damn it.

"So it's the full moon, yippee-skippy, what of it?" My voice was as matter-of-fact as I could make it.

He gave that small smile of his. "You're not very good at being coy, Ms. Blake."

"No, I'm not, but since I'm not being coy, that's not a problem."

"Ms. Blake," he said, voice almost cajoling, "please, do not insult my intelligence."

I thought about saying, *but it's so easy*, but didn't. First, it wasn't easy at all; second, I was a little nervous about where this line of questioning was going. But I was not going to help him by volunteering information. Say less, it irritates people.

"I haven't insulted your intelligence."

He made a frown that I think was as true as that small smile. The real Harlan peeking through. "Rumor says that you haven't worked on the night of the full moon for a few months now." He seemed very serious all of a sudden, not in a menacing way, almost as if I'd been impolite, forgotten my table manners, or something, and he was correcting me.

"Maybe I'm Wiccan. The full moon is a holy day for them you know. Or rather night."

"Are you Wiccan, Ms. Blake?"

It never took me long to grow tired of word games. "No, Mr. Harlan, I am not."

"Then why don't you work on the night of the full moon?" He was studying my face, searching it, as if for some reason the answer were more important than it should have been.

I knew what he wanted me to say. He wanted me to confess to being a shape-shifter of some kind. Trouble was I couldn't confess, because it wasn't true. I was the first human Nimir-Ra, leopard queen, of a wereleopard pard in their history. I'd inherited the leopards when I was forced to kill their old leader, to keep him from killing me. I was also Bolverk of the local werewolf pack. Bolverk was more than a bodyguard, less than an executioner. It was basically someone who did the things that the Ulfric either couldn't, or wouldn't do. Richard Zeeman was the local Ulfric. He'd been my off-again, on-again honey-bun for a couple of years. Right now, it was off, very off. His parting shot to me had been, *"I don't want to love someone who is more at home with the monsters than I am."* What do you say to that? What can you say? Damned if I know. They say love conquers everything. They lie.

As Nimir-Ra and Bolverk, I had people depending on me. I took the full moon off, so I'd be available. It was simple really, and nothing I was willing to share with Leo Harlan.

"I sometimes take personal days, Mr. Harlan. If they've coincided with the full moon, I assure you, it's coincidental."

"Rumor says you got cut up by a shifter a few months back, and now you're one of them." His voice was still quiet, but I was ready for this one. My face, my body, everything was calm, because he was wrong.

"I am not a shape-shifter, Mr. Harlan."

His eyes narrowed. "I don't believe you, Ms. Blake."

I sighed. "I don't really care if you believe me, Mr. Harlan. My being a lycanthrope, or not, has no bearing on how good I am at raising the dead."

"Rumor says you're the best, but you keep telling me the rumors are wrong. Are you really as good as they say you are?"

"Better."

"You're rumored to have raised entire graveyards."

I shrugged. "You'll turn a girl's head with talk like that."

"Are you saying it's true?"

"Does it really matter? Let me repeat: I can raise your ancestor, Mr. Harlan. I'm one of the few, if not the only, animator in this country that can do it without resorting to a human sacrifice." I smiled at him, my professional smile, the one that was all bright and shiny and as empty of meaning as a lightbulb. "Will next Wednesday or Thursday be alright?"

He nodded. "I'll leave my cell phone number, you can reach me twenty-four hours a day."

9

"Are you in a hurry for this?"

"Let's just say that I never know when an offer may come my way that I would find hard to resist."

"Not just money," I said.

He gave that smile again. "No, not just money, Ms. Blake. I have enough money, but a job that holds new interests . . . new challenges. I'm always searching for that."

"Be careful what you wish for, Mr. Harlan. There's always someone out there bigger and badder than you are."

"I have not found it so."

I smiled then. "Either you're even scarier than you seem, or you haven't been meeting the right people."

He looked at me for a long moment, until I felt the smile slide from my eyes. I met his dead eyes with my own. In that moment that well of quietness filled me. It was a peaceful place, the place I went when I killed. A great white static empty place, where nothing hurt, where nothing felt. Looking into Harlan's empty eyes, I wondered if his head was white and empty and staticky. I almost asked, but I didn't, because for just a second I thought he'd lied, lied about it all, and he was going to try and draw his gun from his jacket. It would explain why he wanted to know if I was a shapeshifter. For a heartbeat or two, I thought I'd have to kill Mr. Leo Harlan. I wasn't scared now or nervous, I just readied myself. It was his choice, live or die. There was nothing but that slow eternal second where choices are made and lives are lost.

Then he shook himself, almost like a bird settling its feathers back in place. "I was about to remind you that I am a very scary person all by myself, but I won't now. It would be stupid to keep playing with you like this, like poking a rattlesnake with a stick."

I just looked at him with empty eyes, still held in that quiet place. My voice came out slow, careful, like my body felt. "I hope you haven't lied to me today, Mr. Harlan."

He gave that unsettling smile. "So do I, Ms. Blake, so do I." With that odd comment, he opened the door carefully, never taking his eyes from me. Then he turned and left quickly, shutting the door firmly behind him, and left me alone with the adrenaline rush draining like a puddle to my feet.

It wasn't fear that left me weak, but the adrenaline. I raised the dead for a living and was a legal vampire executioner. Wasn't that unique enough? Did I have to attract scary clients too?

I knew I should have told Harlan no dice, but I had told him the truth. I *could* raise this zombie, and no one else in the country could do it – without a human sacrifice. I was pretty sure that if I turned it down, Harlan would find someone else to do it. Someone else that didn't have either my abilities or my morals. Sometimes you deal with the devil not because you want to, but because if you don't, someone else will.

# 2

LINDEL CEMETERY WAS one of those new modern affairs, where all the headstones are low to the ground and you aren't allowed to plant flowers. It makes mowing easier, but it also makes for a depressingly empty space. Nothing but flat land, with little oblong shapes in the dark. It was as empty and featureless as the dark side of the moon, and about as cheerful. Give me a cemetery with tombs and mausoleums, stone angels weeping over the portraits of children, the Mother Mary praying for us all, her silent eyes turned heavenward. A cemetery should have something to remind the people passing by that there is a heaven, and not just a hole in the ground with rock on top of it.

I was here to raise Gordon Bennington from the dead because Fidelis Insurance Company hoped he was a suicide, not an accidental death. There was a multimillion dollar insurance claim at stake. The police had ruled the death accidental, but Fidelis wasn't satisfied. They opted to pay my rather substantial fee in the hopes of saving millions. I was expensive, but not that expensive. Compared with what they stood to lose, I was a bargain.

There were three groups of cars in the cemetery. Two of the groups were at least fifty feet apart because both Mrs. Bennington and Fidelis's head lawyer, Arthur Conroy, had restraining orders against each other. The third group of two cars was parked in between the others. A marked police car and an unmarked police car. Don't ask me to explain how I knew it was an unmarked police car, it just had that look.

I parked a little in back of the first group of cars. I got out of my brand new Jeep Grand Cherokee, which was partially purchased by money I got from my now deceased Jeep Country Squire. The insurance company hadn't wanted to pay up on my claim. They

12

didn't believe that werehyenas had eaten the Country Squire. They sent out some people to take photos and measurements, to see the bloodstains. They finally paid up, but they also dropped my policy. I'm paying month by month to a new company that will grant me a full policy, if, and only if, I can manage not to destroy another car for two years. Fat chance of that. My sympathies were all for Gordon Bennington's family. Of course, it's hard to have sympathy for an insurance company that is trying to squirm out of paying a widow with three children.

The cars closest to me turned out to be those of Fidelis Insurance. Arthur Conroy came towards me, hand outstretched. He was on the tall end of short, with thinning blond hair that he combed over his bald spot, as if that hid it, silver-framed glasses that circled large gray eyes. If his eyelashes and eyebrows had been darker, his eyes would have been his best feature. But his eyes were so large and unadorned that I thought he looked vaguely froglike. But then maybe my recent disagreement with my insurance company had made me uncharitable. Maybe.

Conroy was accompanied by a near-solid wall of other dark-suited men. I shook Conroy's hand and glanced behind him at the two six-foot-plus men.

"Bodyguards?" I made it a question.

Conroy's eyes widened. "How did you know?"

I shook my head. "They look like bodyguards, Mr. Conroy."

I shook hands with the other two Fidelis people. I didn't offer to shake hands with the bodyguards. Most of them won't shake hands, even if you do offer. I don't know if it ruins the tough-guy image or they just want to keep their gun hands free. Either way, I didn't offer, and neither did they.

The dark-haired bodyguard, with shoulders nearly as broad as I was tall, smiled, though. "So you're Anita Blake."

"And you are?"

"Rex, Rex Canducci."

I raised eyebrows at him. "Is Rex really your first name?"

He laughed, that surprised burst of laughter that is so masculine – and usually at a woman's expense. "No."

I didn't bother to ask what his real first name was, probably something embarrassing, like Florence, or Rosie. The second bodyguard was blond and silent. He watched me with small pale eyes. I didn't like him.

"And you are?" I asked.

He blinked as if my asking had surprised him. Most people ignored bodyguards, some out of fear of not knowing what to do, because they've never met one; some because they have met one and figure they're just furniture, to be ignored until needed.

He hesitated, then said, "Balfour."

I waited a second, but he didn't add anything. "Balfour, one name, like Madonna or Cher?" I asked, voice mild.

His eyes narrowed, his shoulders a little tense. He'd been too easy to rattle. He had the stare down and the sense of menace, but he was just muscle. Scary looking, and knew it, but maybe not much else.

Rex intervened, "I thought you'd be taller." He made it a joke, with his happy-to-meet-you voice.

Balfour's shoulders had relaxed, the tension draining away. They'd worked together before, and Rex knew that his partner was not the most stable cookie in the box.

I met Rex's eyes. Balfour would be a problem if things turned messy, he'd overreact. Rex wouldn't.

I heard raised voices, one of them a woman. Shit. I'd told Mrs. Bennington's lawyers to keep her home. They'd either ignored me or been unable to withstand her winning personality.

The nice plainclothes policeman was talking to her, his voice calm, but carrying, in a low, wordless rumble, as he, apparently, tried to keep her fifty feet away from Conroy. Weeks ago she'd slapped the lawyer, and he'd bitch-slapped her back. She'd then put a fist to his jaw and sat him on his ass. That was about the time the court bailiffs had had to step in and break things up.

I'd been present for all the festivities, because I was part of the court settlement, sort of. Tonight would decide the issue. If Gordon Bennington rose from the grave and said he'd died by accident, Fidelis had to pay. If he admitted to suicide, then Mrs. Bennington got nothing. I called her *Mrs.* Bennington at her insistence. When I'd referred to her as *Ms.* Bennington, she'd nearly bitten my head off. She was not one of your liberated women. She liked being a wife and mother. I was glad for her, it meant more freedom for the rest of us.

14

I sighed and walked across the white gravel driveway towards the sound of rising voices. I passed the uniformed cop leaning against his car. I nodded, said, "Hi."

He nodded back, his eyes mostly on the insurance people, as if someone had told him that it was his job to make sure they didn't start coming over. Or maybe he just didn't like the size of Rex and Balfour. Both men had him by a hundred pounds. He was slender for a police officer and still had that untried look in his face, as if he hadn't been on the job long, and hadn't yet quite decided whether he wanted to be on the job at all.

Mrs. Bennington was yelling at the nice officer who was barring her way. "Those bastards have hired her, and she'll do what they say. She'll make Gordon lie, I know it!"

I sighed. I'd explained to everyone that the dead don't lie. Pretty much only the judge had believed me, and the cops. I think Fidelis thought my fee had insured their outcome, and Mrs. Bennington thought the same.

She finally spotted me over the cop's broad shoulders. In her high heels she was taller than the officer. Which meant she was tall, and he wasn't very. He was maybe five nine, tops.

She tried to push past him, yelling at me now. He moved just enough so that he blocked her way, but didn't have to grab her. She banged against his shoulder and frowned down at him. It stopped her yelling, for a second.

"Get out of my way," she said.

"Mrs. Bennington," his deep voice grumbled, "Ms. Blake is here by order of the court. You have to let her do her job." He had short gray hair, a little longer on top. I didn't think it was a fashion statement, more like he hadn't had time to go to the barbershop in a while.

She tried to push past him again, and this time she grabbed him, as if she'd move him out of her way. He wasn't tall, but he was broad, built like a square, a muscular square. She realized quickly that she couldn't push him, so she moved to walk around him, still determined to give me a piece of her mind.

He had to grab her arm to keep her away from me. She raised a hand to him, and his deep voice came clear in the still October night, "If you hit me, I will handcuff you and put you in the back of the squad car until we're all finished here."

15

She hesitated, her hand raised, but there must have been something in his face, still turned away from me, that said, clearly, that he meant every word.

His tone of voice had been enough for me. I'd have done what he said.

Finally, she lowered her arm. "I'll have your badge if you touch me."

"Striking a police officer is considered a crime, Mrs. Bennington," he said in that deep voice.

Even by moonlight you could see the astonishment on her face, as if somehow she hadn't quite realized any of the rules applied to her. The realization seemed to take a lot of the wind out of her. She settled back and let her cadre of dark-suited lawyers lead her a little away from the nice police officer.

I was the only one close enough to hear him say, "If she'd been my wife, I'd have shot myself too."

I laughed, I couldn't help it.

He turned, eyes angry, defensive, but whatever he saw in my face made him smile.

"Count yourself lucky," I said, "I've seen Mrs. Bennington on several occasions." I held out my hand.

He shook like he meant business, good, solid. "Lieutenant Nicols, and my condolences on having to deal with . . ." He hesitated.

I finished the sentence for him, ". . . that crazy bitch. I believe that is the phrase you're searching for."

He nodded. "That is the phrase. I sympathize with a widow and children getting the money that is due them," he said, "but she makes it awful hard to sympathize with her personally."

"I've noticed that," I said, smiling.

He laughed and reached into his jacket for a pack of cigarettes. "Mind?"

"Not out here in the open, I guess. Besides, you've earned it, dealing with our wonderful Mrs. Bennington."

He tapped the cigarette out with one of those expert movements that longtime smokers use. "If Gordon Bennington rises from the grave and says he offed himself, she is going to go ballistic, Ms. Blake. I'm not allowed to shoot her, but I'm not sure what else I'm going to be able to do with her."

"Maybe her lawyers can sit on her. I think there's enough of them to hold her down."

He put the cig between his lips, still talking. "They've been fu . . . freaking useless, too afraid of losing their fee."

"Fucking useless, Lieutenant. Fucking useless is the phrase you're searching for."

He laughed again, hard enough that he had to take the cigarette out of his mouth. "Fucking useless, yeah, that's the phrase." He put the cig between his lips again and took out one of those big metal lighters that you don't see much anymore. The flame flared orangey red, as he cupped his hands around it automatically, even though there was no wind. When the end of his cig was glowing bright, he snapped the lighter shut and slid it back into his pocket, then took the cig out of his mouth and blew a long line of smoke.

I took an involuntary step back to avoid the smoke, but we were outdoors and Mrs. Bennington was enough to drive anyone to smoke. Or would that be drink?

"Can you call in more men?"

"They won't be allowed to shoot her either," Nicols said.

I smiled. "No, but maybe they can form a wall of flesh and keep her from hurting anyone."

"I could probably get another uniform, maybe two, but that's it. She's got connections with the top brass because she's got money, and may end up having a lot more after tonight. But she's also been fucking unpleasant." He seemed to relish saying the F-word almost as much as smoking the cigarette, as if he'd had to watch his language around the grieving widow, and it had hurt.

"Her political clout getting a little tarnished?" I asked.

"The papers plastered her decking Conroy all over the front page. The powers that be are worried that this is going to turn into a mess, and they don't want the mess to land on them."

"So they're distancing themselves in case she does something even more unfortunate," I said.

He took a deep, deep pull off the cig, holding it almost like someone smoking a joint, then let the smoke trickle out of his mouth and nose as he answered me, "Distancing, that's one word for it."

"Bailing, jumping ship, abandoning ship . . ."

He was laughing again, and he hadn't finished blowing out all the smoke, so he choked just a little, but didn't seem to mind. "I don't know if you're really this amusing or if I just needed a laugh."

"It's stress," I said, "most people don't find me funny at all."

He gave me a look sort of sideways out of surprisingly pale eyes. I was betting they were blue in sunlight. "I heard that about you, that you were a pain in the ass, and rub a lot of people the wrong way."

I shrugged. "A girl does what she can."

He smiled. "But the same people that said you could be a pain in the ass had no trouble working a case with you. Fact is, Ms. Blake," he threw the cigarette on the ground, "most said they'd take you as backup over a lot of cops they could name."

I didn't know what to say to that. There is no higher praise between policemen than that they'd let you back them up in a life or death situation.

"You're going to make me blush, Lt. Nicols." I didn't look at him as I said it.

He seemed to be gazing down at the still-smoldering cigarette on the white gravel. "Zerbrowski over at RPIT says that you don't blush much."

"Zerbrowski is a cheerfully lecherous shit," I said.

He chuckled, a deep roll of laughter, and stomped out his cigarette, so that even that small glow was lost in the dark. "That he is, that he is. You ever met his wife?"

"I've met Katie."

"Ever wonder how Zerbrowski managed to nab her?"

"Every damn time I see her," I said.

He sighed. "I'll call for another squad car, try for two uniforms. Let's get this done and get the hell away from these people."

"Let's," I said.

He went to make the call. I went to fetch my zombie-raising equipment. Since one of my main tools is a machete bigger than my forearm, I'd left it in the car. It tends to scare people. I would try very hard tonight not to scare the bodyguards, or the nice policemen. I was pretty sure there was nothing I could do to scare Mrs. Bennington. I was also pretty sure there was nothing I could do to make her happy with me.

18

# 3

MY ZOMBIE-RAISING EQUIPMENT was in a gray Nike gym bag. Some animators have elaborate cases. I've even seen one who had a little suitcase that turned into a table like a magician's or a street vendor's. Me, I made sure everything was packed tight so nothing got broken or scratched up, but other than that, I didn't see the point to being fancier than you needed to be. If people wanted a show they could go down to the Circus of the Damned and watch zombies crawl from the grave with actors pretending to be terrified of them. I wasn't an entertainer, I was an animator, and this was work.

I turned down Halloween parties every year, where people wanted zombies raised at the stroke of midnight or some such nonsense. The scarier my reputation got, the more people wanted me to come be scary for them. I'd told Bert I could always go and threaten to shoot all the partygoers, that'd be scary. Bert had not been amused. But he had stopped asking me to do parties.

I'd been trained to use an ointment spread over face, hands, heart. The smell of rosemary, like breathing in a Christmas tree, still held a great nostalgic for me, but I didn't use the ointment anymore. I'd raised the dead in emergencies without it, more than once, so it got me to thinking. Some believed it helped the spirits enter you, so the powers that be could use you to raise the dead. Most, in America anyway, believed that the scent and touch of the herbal mixture enhanced your psychic abilities, or helped open them so they'd work at all. I never seemed to have any trouble raising the dead. My psychic abilities were always on line for animating. So I still carried the ointment, just in case, but I didn't use it much anymore.

The three things I did still need for animating were steel, fresh blood, and salt. Though the salt actually was to put the zombie

19

back in the grave once we were finished with it. I'd cut my para-phernalia to the absolute minimum, and recently, I'd cut it down even more. And I mean that "cut" part literally.

My left hand was covered in little bandages. I was using the clear ones, so I didn't look like a tan version of the mummy's hand. There were larger bandages on my left forearm. All the wounds were self-inflicted, and it was beginning to piss me off.

I had been learning how to control my growing psychic powers by studying with Marianne, who had been a psychic when I met her, but had become a witch. She was Wiccan now. Not all witches are Wiccan, and if Marianne had been another flavor of witch, I wouldn't have had to cut myself up. Marianne as my teacher, shared some of my karmic debt, or so her group – read coven – believed. The fact that I killed an animal every time I raised the dead, three, four times a night, almost every night, had made her coven rant, rave, scream, and basically lose it. Blood magic is black magic to a Wiccan. Taking a life for magical purposes, any life, even a chicken's, is very black magic.

How could Marianne have tied herself to someone who was being so . . . evil? they demanded to know.

To help Marianne's karmic burden – and mine, the coven assured me – I'd been trying to raise the dead without killing any-thing. I'd done it in emergencies without an animal to sacrifice, so I knew it was possible. But – surprise, surprise – while it was true that I could do my job without killing anything, I could not do it without fresh blood. Blood magic is still black magic to Wiccans, so what to do? The compromise was that I would use only my *own* blood. I wasn't sure it would work. But it did, for the recently dead, at least.

I'd started out slicing up my left forearm, but that had rapidly lost its appeal, since I needed to do it three or more times a night. Then I'd taken to pricking my fingers. Just a little blood seemed to be enough for those dead under six months. But I'd run out of fin-gers, and my arm had enough scars already. I'd also found that when I practiced lefthanded shooting that I was slower, because the cuts freaking hurt. I would not cut up my right hand, because I couldn't afford to be slower with my right. I'd pretty much decided that, while I was sorry I had to kill a few chickens or goats to raise

20

the dead, the animals' lives were not worth my own. There I've said it, a totally selfish judgment call.

I'd really hoped the tiny cuts would heal instantly. Thanks to my ties to Jean-Claude, master vamp of the city, I healed fast, very fast. The little cuts didn't heal fast. Marianne said it was probably because I was using a magically charged blade to do the cutting. But I liked my machete. Truthfully, I wasn't a hundred percent sure that I could raise the dead with only a prick of blood without a magically charged blade. It was a problem.

I was going to have to call Marianne and tell her I'd failed the Wiccan test of goodness. Why should they be any different? Most right-wing Christian groups hated me too.

I glanced behind me at my audience. Two new uniformed police officers had joined Lt. Nicols and the first officer. The police stood in the middle of the two groups, which had been allowed to come close enough to the grave to hear what the zombie would say. It was way closer than fifty feet, but both parties needed to hear Gordon Bennington, or so the judge had ruled. The judge in question had actually joined us, along with a court reporter and her little machine. He'd also brought along two burly looking bailiffs, which made me think the judge was even smarter than he looked, and I'd been pretty impressed before. Not every judge will take zombie testimony.

For tonight Lindel graveyard was court. I was glad that Court TV hadn't gotten wind of it. It was just the kind of weird crap that they liked to televise. You know – transsexual's custody case; female teacher rapes thirteen-year-old boy student; pro-football player's murder trial. The O. J. Simpson trial had not been a good influence on American television.

The judge said in his booming, court voice, which echoed strangely in the flat emptiness of the cemetery, "Go ahead, Ms. Blake, we're all assembled."

Ordinarily I'd have beheaded a chicken and used its body to help me sprinkle a blood circle, a circle of power, to contain the zombie once it was raised so it wouldn't go wandering all over the place. The circle also helped focus power and raise energy. But I had no chickens at the moment. There was a chance that if I'd tried to get enough blood out of my body to walk even a small circle of power, I'd be finished for the night, too dizzy and too light-headed to do anything else. So what's a morally upright animator supposed to do?

I sighed and unsheathed the machete and heard several gasps behind me. It was a big blade, but I'd found that in beheading a chicken one-handed you needed a big, sharp blade. I stared at my left hand and tried to find a space that was bandage free. I put the top edge of the blade against my middle finger (the symbolism was not lost on me) and pressed. I kept the machete too sharp to risk drawing the blade down my finger. It would be a bitch to need stitches because I'd cut too deep.

The cut didn't hurt immediately, which meant I'd probably cut deeper than I wanted. I raised my hand so the moonlight fell on it, and saw the first dark welling of blood. The moment I saw it, the cut hurt. Why was it that everything hurt worse when you realized you were bleeding?

I began to walk the circle, holding the steel point downward, my bleeding finger flat to the earth, so that occasional drops would hit the ground. I'd never truly felt the machete carving the magic circle through the ground, through me, until I stopped killing animals. It had probably always been like a steel pencil tracing my circle, but I'd never ever been able to feel it over the stronger rush of the death. I felt each drop of blood that fell, felt the earth almost hungry for it, like rain in a drought, but it wasn't the moisture the earth drank, it was the power. I knew when I'd walked the entire circle around the headstone, because the moment I touched the place where I'd begun, the circle closed with a skin-tingling, hair-raising rush.

I turned to face the headstone, feeling the circle around me like an invisible trembling in the air. I went to the headstone, which was at the far end of the circle. I tapped the headstone with the machete. "Gordon Bennington, with steel I call you from your grave." I touched my bloody hand to the cold stone. "With blood I call you from your grave." I moved back to the far edge of the circle, at the foot of the grave. "Hear me now, Gordon Bennington, hear and obey. With steel, blood, and power, I command you to rise from your grave. Rise from your grave and walk amongst us."

The earth rolled like heavy water and just spilled the body upward. In the movies the zombies always crawl from the grave with reaching hands like the ground tries to keep them prisoner, but most of the time, the earth gives freely, and the zombie simply rises to the top, like something floating to the surface of a liquid. There were no flowers to get in the way this time, nothing for the body to trip over, as the zombie sat up and looked around.

One thing I had noticed with not killing the animals was that my zombies weren't as pretty. With a chicken I could have made Gordon Bennington look like his photo in the paper. With only my own blood, he looked like what he was, a reanimated corpse.

He wasn't awful, I'd seen much worse, but his widow screamed, long and loud, and began to sob. There had been more than one reason I wanted Mrs. Bennington to stay home.

The nice blue suit hid the chest wound that had killed him. But you could still tell he was dead. It was the odd color of his skin. The way the flesh had begun to sink into the bones of his face. His eyes were too round, too large, too bare, so they rolled in their sockets barely contained by the waxy flesh. His blond hair was patchy and looked like it had grown. But that was illusion, caused by the shrinking of the meat of his body. Hair and fingernails do not grow after death, contrary to popular belief.

There was one more thing I had to do to help Gordon Bennington speak. Blood. The *Odyssey* speaks of blood sacrifice to get a dead seer's ghost to give Odysseus advice. It's a very old truism that the dead crave blood. I walked across the now solid ground and knelt by his puzzled, wizened face. I couldn't smooth my skirt down in back because one hand was full of machete and the other was bleeding. Everyone got a nice long glimpse of thigh, but it didn't really matter, I was about to do the thing that disturbed me the most since I stopped sacrificing poultry.

I held out my hand towards Gordon Bennington's face. "Drink, Gordon, drink of my blood and speak to us."

Those round, rolling eyes stared at me, then his sunken nose caught the scent of blood, and he grabbed my hand with both of his, and lowered his mouth to the wound. His hands felt like cold wax with sticks inside. His mouth was almost lipless, so his teeth pressed close in my flesh as he sucked at my hand. His tongue

23

whipped back and forth on the wound like something separate and alive in his mouth, feeding from me.

I took a deep, steadying breath, breathe in and out, in and out. I would not be sick. Nope. I would not embarrass myself in front of this many people.

When I thought he'd had enough, I said, "Gordon Bennington."

He didn't react, but kept his mouth pressed to the wound, his hands clutching my wrist.

I tapped the top of his head gently with the side of the machete. "Mr. Bennington, people are waiting to talk to you."

I don't know if it was the words or the tap with the blade, but he looked up, and slowly began to pull back from my hand. His eyes held more of him now. The blood always seemed to do that, fill them back up with themselves.

"Are you Gordon Bennington?" I asked. We had to be all formal.

He shook his head.

The judge said, "We need you to answer out loud, Mr. Bennington, for the record."

He stared up at me. I repeated what the judge had said, and Bennington spoke, "I am, was, Gordon Bennington."

One of the upsides to raising the dead with only my blood was that they always knew they were dead. I'd raised some before where they didn't know that, and that was a bitch, telling someone that they were dead, and you were about to put them back in the grave. Real nightmare stuff, that was.

"How did you die, Mr. Bennington?" I asked.

He sighed, drawing in air, and I heard it whistle, because most of the right side of his chest was missing. The suit hid it, but I'd seen the forensic photos. Besides I knew what a mess a twelve-gauge shotgun makes at close range.

"I got shot."

There was a tension behind me, I could feel it over the buzz of the power circle. "How did you get shot?" I asked, voice calm, soothing.

"I shot myself going down the stairs to our basement."

There was a cry of triumph from one side of the crowd and an inarticulate scream from the other.

24

"Did you shoot yourself on purpose?" I asked.

"No, of course not. I tripped, gun went off, so stupid, really. So stupid."

There was a lot of screaming behind me. Mostly Mrs. Bennington yelling, "I told you so, little bitch . . ."

I turned and called, "Judge Fletcher, did you hear all that?"

"Most of it," he said. He turned that booming voice on overdrive and shouted, "Mrs. Bennington, if you will be quiet long enough to listen, your husband has just said he died by accident."

"Gail," Gordon Bennington's voice was tentative, "Gail, are you there?"

I did not want a tearful reunion on top of the grave. "Are we finished, Judge? Can I put him back?"

"No," this from Fidelis Insurance's lawyers. Conroy stepped closer. "We have some questions for Mr. Bennington."

They asked questions, at first I had to repeat them for Bennington to be able to answer, but he got better at answering. He didn't look any better, physically, but he was gathering himself up, being more alert, more aware of his surroundings. He spotted his wife, and said, "Gail, I'm so sorry. You were right about the guns. I wasn't careful enough. I'm so sorry to leave you and the kids."

Mrs. Bennington came towards us, with her lawyers in tow. I thought I'd have to ask them to keep her off the grave, but she stopped outside the circle, as if she could feel it. Sometimes the people that turn out to be psychically gifted surprise you. I doubt if she was even aware of why she stopped moving forward. Of course, she was holding her hands tight to her body. She was not reaching out to touch her husband. I don't think she wanted to find out what that waxy looking skin felt like. I couldn't blame her.

Conroy and the other lawyers tried to keep asking questions, but it was the judge who said, "Gordon Bennington has answered all your questions in detail. It's time to let him get back to . . . rest."

I agreed. Mrs. Bennington was in tears, and Gordon would have been too, except his tear ducts had dried up months ago.

I got Gordon Bennington's attention. "Mr. Bennington, I'm going to put you back now."

"Will Gail and the children get the insurance money now?"

I glanced behind me at the judge. He nodded.

"Yes, Mr. Bennington, they will."

He smiled, or tried to. "Thank you, then, I'm ready." He gazed back at his wife, who was still kneeling on the grass by his grave. "I'm glad I got to say good-bye."

She was shaking her head, over and over, tears streaming down her face. "Me, too, Gordie, me, too. I miss you."

"I miss you too, my little hell cat."

She burst into sobs at that. Hiding her face in her hands. If one of the lawyers hadn't grabbed her she'd have fallen to the ground.

*My little hell cat"* didn't sound like a term of endearment to me, but hey, it proved Gordon Bennington had really known his wife. It probably also proved that she would miss him for the rest of her life. I could forgive her a few temper tantrums in the face of that much pain.

I squeezed on the wound in my finger and thankfully got a little more blood. Some nights I had to reopen a wound, or make another one, to get the zombie put back. I touched my bloody hand to his forehead, leaving a small dark mark.

"With blood I bind you to your grave, Gordon Bennington." I touched him with the edge of the machete, gently. "With steel I bind you to your grave." I switched the machete to my left hand and picked up the open container of salt that I'd left inside the circle. I sprinkled him with salt, and it sounded like dry sleet as it hit him. "With salt I bind you to your grave, Gordon Bennington. Go and rise no more."

With the touch of the salt, his eyes lost their alertness, he was empty as he lay back on the earth. The ground swallowed him, like some great beast had rippled its fur and he was just gone, sunk back into the grave. Gordon Bennington's corpse was back where it belonged, and there was nothing to distinguish this grave from any other. Not so much as a blade of grass was out of place. Magic.

I still had to walk the circle backwards and uncast it. Normally, I don't have an audience for that part. The zombie goes back in the grave, everyone leaves. But Conroy of Fidelis Insurance was arguing with the judge, who was threatening to cite him for contempt. And Mrs. Bennington was not in a condition to walk yet.

The police were standing around watching the show. Lieutenant Nicols looked at me and shook his head, smiling. He walked over

26

to me as the circle went down, and I began to clean my new wound with antiseptic wipes.

He lowered his voice so the truly grieving widow wouldn't hear him. "You could not pay me enough to let that thing suck my blood."

I half-shrugged, holding gauze over my finger so it would stop bleeding. "You'd be surprised what people pay for this kind of work."

"It ain't enough," he said, an unlit cigarette already in his hand.

I started to give some flip answer, when I felt the presence of a vampire, like a chill across my skin. Out there in the dark, someone was waiting. There was a gust of wind, and there was no wind tonight. I looked up, and no one else did, because humans never look up, never expect death to fall upon them from the sky.

I had seconds to say, "Don't shoot, he's a friend," before Asher appeared in our midst, very close to me, his long hair streaming behind him, his booted feet touching down. He was forced to make a half running step to catch the momentum of his flight, which brought him to my side.

I turned and put myself in front of his body. He was too tall for me to cover all of him, but I did my best, moving us so that if anyone shot at him they'd risk hitting me. Every policeman, every bodyguard had drawn a gun, and every barrel was pointed at Asher, and at me.

# 4

I STARED AT the half circle of guns, trying to keep an eye on everyone at once and failing, because there were too many of them. I kept my hands out from my body, fingers spread, universal sign for I'm *harmless*. I didn't want anyone thinking I was going for my own gun, that would be bad.

"He's a friend," I said, voice a little high, but otherwise calm.

"Whose friend?" Nicols asked.

"Mine," I said.

"Well, he ain't my friend," one of the uniforrns said.

"He's not a threat," I said, pressing my body back enough that I could feel Asher in a long line against me.

He said something in French, everybody gripped their guns a little tighter. "English, Asher, English."

He took a deep shuddering breath. "It was not my intent to frighten anyone."

Not too long ago, the police were allowed to shoot a vampire on sight, just for being a vampire. It had only been five years since Addison V. Clark had made vamps "alive" again, at least to the law. They were citizens with rights now, and shooting them without just cause was murder. But it still happened now and then.

"If you shoot with me in the way, you can all kiss your badges good-bye."

"I don't have a badge to lose." It was Balfour, of course, being tough, but he had a big gun to go with his big talk.

I looked at him. "If you shoot, you better kill me, because you won't get a second chance."

"Nobody's shooting anybody," Nicols said, and I was close enough to hear him mutter, "damn it," under his breath.

He'd moved his gun to point at the bodyguards. "Put the guns down, now." The other policemen followed his lead, and suddenly

28

the circle of guns was pointed away from me, and at Balfour and Rex. I let out a breath I hadn't realized I was holding, and sagged a little against Asher.

He knew better than to have surprised a bunch of humans, especially policemen, by flying into their midst. Nothing freaked people out like seeing vampires do things that were impossible. He'd also spoken in French, which meant he was scared enough, or angry enough, to have forgotten his English. Something was very wrong, but I couldn't question him, not yet. First, get out of the line of fire, then fix the rest.

We were standing so close together that his wavy golden hair brushed against my own black curls. He put his hands on my shoulders, and I could feel the tension. He was scared. What had happened?

The police had convinced the bodyguards to put their guns away. The uniforms divided up and walked the two interested parties back to their respective cars. It left Nicols, the judge, and the court reporter standing near us. At least the court reporter wasn't still typing.

Nicols turned to me, his gun pointed downward, tapping a little against the leg of his slacks. He frowned, eyes flicking to Asher, then to me. He knew enough not to risk staring the vampire in the eyes. They could bespell you with their eyes, if they wanted to. I was immune because I was the human servant of the Master Vampire of the City. Through Jean-Claude I was safe from most of what Asher could do. Not all, but most.

Nicols was obviously unhappy. "Okay, what was so damned urgent that he had to fly in here like that?"

Damn, he was too good a cop. Even though he'd probably dealt very little with vampires, he'd made the logic jump that only an emergency would make Asher appear as he had.

His eyes flicked up to Asher again, then down to my face. "It's a good way to get yourself shot, Mr. . . . ."

"Asher," I answered for him.

"I didn't ask you, Ms. Blake. I asked him."

"I am Asher," he said in a voice that fell on the air like a caress. He was using vampire powers to make himself more acceptable. If Nicols figured out what he was doing, it would backfire. But it didn't.

29

"What's wrong, Mr. Asher?"

"Just Asher," and the voice glided across my skin so soothing. I had some immunity to the voice, but Nicols didn't.

He blinked, then frowned, puzzled. "Fine, Asher, what the hell is the rush?"

Asher's fingers tightened minutely on my shoulders, and I felt him take a breath. I had a second to hope that he wasn't going to try an Obi-Wan on Lieutenant Nicols. You know, *these are not the droids you're looking for*. Nicols was stronger willed than that.

"Musette has been gravely injured. I came to take Anita to her side."

I felt the color drain from my face, my breath caught in my throat. Musette was one of Belle Morte's lieutenants. Belle Morte was the fountainhead, *le sourdre de sang* of Jean-Claude and Asher's bloodline. She was also a member of the Council of Vampires that had a home base somewhere in Europe. Every time council members had visited us, people had died. Some of them ours, some of them theirs. But Belle Morte had never sent anyone, until now. There had been some careful negotiations about Musette coming over for a visit. She was due three months from now, just after Thanksgiving. So what the hell was she doing in town a month and some change before Halloween? I didn't for a minute believe Musette was hurt. That was Asher's sneaky way of telling me how bad things were in front of witnesses.

I didn't have to pretend to be shocked, or scared. My face must have looked like someone who'd just gotten bad news. Nicols nodded, as if satisfied. "You close to this Musette?"

"Lieutenant, can we please go? I want to get there as soon as possible." I was already looking around for my gym bag. I was glad it was already packed. My skin was cold with the thought of what Musette might be doing right now to people I cared about. The very mention of her name had always been enough to make Jean-Claude and Asher go pale.

Nicols nodded again, putting up his gun. "Yeah, go on. I hope . . . your friend is okay."

I looked up at him, and didn't try to hide the confusion in my eyes. "I hope so, too." I wasn't thinking of Musette, I was thinking of everyone else. So many people she could hurt if she had the blessing of the council, or at least the blessing of Belle Morte. I'd learned that council politics meant that having one member as an enemy didn't mean that the others hated you. In fact, many of the council seemed to believe the old Sicilian adage, *the enemy of my enemy is my friend.*

The judge murmured his thanks, and hopes for speedy recovery of my friend. The court reporter didn't say anything – she was gazing at Asher as if mesmerized. I didn't think he'd bespelled her, more like she'd never seen anything so beautiful. Maybe she hadn't.

His hair in the reflected glow of the headlights was truly gold, a curtain of nearly metallic waves flowing like a shining sea across the right side of his face. The hair looked even more gold against the dark brown of his silk shirt. The shirt was long-sleeved and untucked over blue jeans and brown boots. He looked like he'd dressed in haste, but I knew that was how he usually dressed. He made sure that the left side of his face, that most perfect of profiles was what showed to the light. Asher was a master at using light and shadow to highlight what he wished seen, and hide what he did not. The one eye that was visible was a clear, pale blue like the eyes of a Siberian husky dog. Human beings just didn't have eyes like that. Even in life he must have been extraordinary.

You got glimpses of that full mouth, the glimmer of his other blue, blue eye. What he was careful not to show to the light was that a few inches past his eye, trailing in a line nearly to his mouth were scars. Rivulets of scars, where holy water had been poured on that most beautiful of faces. More scars ran down the right side of his body, hidden under the clothes.

The court reporter stared at him so still, as if she'd stopped breathing. Asher saw it and stiffened beside me. Perhaps because he knew that with a flick of his head he could show her the scars and watch that adoration turn to horror, or pity.

I touched his arm. "Let's go."

He walked towards my Jeep. Normally he sort of glided, as if vampire feet never rolled on gravel but floated just above it. Tonight he moved almost as heavily as a human.

Neither of us spoke until we were inside my Jeep. We had the privacy of the darkened car, no one would overhear us.

I buckled myself in while I talked, "What's happened?"

"Musette arrived an hour ago."

I put the Jeep in gear and began to drive carefully over the gravel around the still-parked police cars. I waved at Nicols as we went past, and he waved back, a cigarette flaring in his other hand.

"I thought we hadn't finished negotiating on how many people she could bring over with her."

"We had not." His voice held sorrow so thick you could have squeezed it out, tears in your cup. Jean-Claude's voice was better at sharing joy, seduction, but Asher was the master at sharing the darker emotions.

I glanced at him. He was staring straight ahead, his face very still, hiding whatever he was feeling. "Then didn't she break some treaty or law or something by invading our territory like this?"

He nodded, his hair sliding around his face, hiding himself from me. I hated to watch him hide his scars from me. I found him beautiful, scars and all, but he never quite believed me. I think he thought the attraction was part Jean-Claude's memories in my head, and part pity. There was no pity, but I couldn't deny Jean-Claude's memories. I was Jean-Claude's human servant, and that gave me all kinds of interesting side benefits. One of those benefits was getting glimpses of Jean-Claude's memories.

I remembered Asher's skin like cool silk on my fingertips, every inch of him flawless. But it was Jean-Claude's fingers that had done the touching, not mine. The fact that I remembered the touch of Asher's skin so strongly that even now, I had the urge to reach for his hand, just to see if the memory was real, was just one of those odd things I had to live with. Even if Jean-Claude had been in the car, he wouldn't have touched Asher either. It had been centuries since they'd been part of a ménage à trois with Julianna, Asher's human servant. Julianna had been burned as a witch by the same people that had used holy water to cleanse Asher's evil. Jean-Claude had been able to save Asher, but he'd been too late for Julianna. Neither of the men had forgiven Jean-Claude for his tardiness.

"If Musette broke the law, can't we punish her, or kick her out of our territory?" I was at the edge of the cemetery now, watching for nonexistent traffic.

"If it were another master vampire come so rudely, then we would be within our rights to slay her, but it is Musette. As you are Bolverk for the werewolves, so Musette is Belle's . . ." He seemed to be searching for the word. "I do not know the word in English, but in French, Musette is the *bourreau*. She is our bogeyman, Anita, and she has been such for over six hundred years."

"Fine," I said, "she's scary, I accept that, but that doesn't change the fact that she's invaded our lands. If we let her get away with it, she'll try for more."

"Anita, it is more than that. She is the . . ." he seemed to grope for a word again. That he was forgetting this many English words spoke to how frightened he was. "The *vaisseau* – why can I not think of the English for it?"

"You're upset."

"I am frightened," he said, "but Belle Morte has made Musette her vessel. To harm Musette is to harm Belle."

"Literally?" I asked, as I turned onto Mackenzie.

"*Non*, it is more like a courtesy than magic. She has given Musette her seal, her ring of office, which means Musette in effect speaks for Belle, we are forced to treat her as we would treat Belle Morte herself. This was most unexpected."

"What difference does this *vaisseau* make?" I asked. We were stuck at the light on Watson, staring at the McDonald's and the Union Planters Bank.

"If Musette were not Belle's vessel, then we could punish her for coming early and breaking off negotiations. But if we punish her now, then it would mean that we would do the same to Belle if she came here."

"So? Why wouldn't we punish Belle for entering our territory so rudely, as you put it?"

Asher looked at me then, but I couldn't hold eye contact because the light had finally changed. "You do not understand what you are saying, Anita."

"Explain it to me then."

"Belle is our *sourdre de sang*, our fountainhead. She is our bloodline. We cannot harm her."

"Why not?"

He looked at me full face, letting his hair fall back so that his

33

whole face showed at last. I think he was too shocked at my question to worry about hiding himself.

"It is not done, that is all."

"What is not done? Defending your territory against all encroachers?"

"Attacking the head of your line, your *sourdre de sang*, your fountain of blood, it is just not done."

"And I say again, why not? Belle has insulted us. Not the other way around. Jean-Claude has negotiated in good faith. It's Musette that's been the bad little vampire. And if she comes with Belle's blessing, then Belle is abusing her status. She thinks we'll just take whatever she dishes out."

"Dishes out?" he made it a question.

"Whatever she does to us, she thinks we'll just take it, just suck it up and take it without complaining."

"She is right," Asher said.

I frowned at him, then turned, still frowning, back to the road. "Why? Why shouldn't we treat any threat or insult the same?"

He ran his hands through his thick hair, pulling it back from his face. The streetlights crisscrossed his face in light and shadow. We were stopped at another light with an SUV beside us so that their window was even with ours. The woman behind the wheel glanced at us, then did a double take. Her eyes went round, and Asher didn't notice. I looked at her and she looked away, embarrassed at being caught staring. Americans are taught not to stare at anything that isn't perfect. It's like to look at it is to make it more real. Ignore it, it'll go away.

Asher never noticed as the light changed and we drove off. He was exposing his face to strangers, and not noticing the effect it was having. No matter how angry, no matter how sad, no matter how anything, he never forgot the scars. They dominated his thoughts, his actions, his life. For him to forget like this said more than anything how serious the situation was, and I still didn't understand why.

"I don't understand, Asher. We defended ourselves when council members invaded our territory a while back. We hurt them, did our best to kill them. Why is this different?"

He let go of his hair and swung it back into place like a curtain.

I don't think he was any less upset, it was just habit. "Last time it was not Belle Morte."

"What difference does that make?"

"*Mon Dieu*, do you not understand what it means that Belle is the mother of our line?"

"Apparently I don't, explain it to me. We're going to the Circus of the Damned, right? It will take a while to get there. You'll have time."

"*Oui*." He stared out the window of the Jeep, as if looking for inspiration in the electric lights, the strip malls, and fast food restaurants.

He finally turned to face me. "How do I explain to you what you have never understood? You have never had a king or queen, you are American and young, and you do not understand the duty owed a liege lord."

I shrugged. "I guess I don't."

"Then how can you understand what it is we owe Belle Morte, and how it would be . . . treason to raise a hand against her?"

I shook my head. "That's a great theory, Asher, but I've dealt with enough vampire politics to know one thing. If we let her push us around, she'll see it as a sign of weakness, and she'll push and push until she sees how weak, or how strong we are."

"We are not at war with Belle Morte," he said.

"No, but if she thinks we are weak enough, that might be next. I've seen how you guys operate. The big vampire fish eat the little vampire fish. We can't afford for Musette or Belle to think we're little fish."

"Anita, don't you understand, yet? We *are* little fish, compared to Belle Morte, we are very little fish indeed."

35

# 5

I HAD A hard time believing we were very little fish indeed. Maybe not big fish, but that wasn't the same thing as being very little. But Asher was so obviously convinced of it that I didn't argue.

I did call on my cell phone and leave messages around town about Musette's early arrival. Richard may have been pissed at me, but he was still the other third of our triumvirate of power; Ulfric to Jean-Claude's Master of the City, and my necromancer. Richard was Jean-Claude's animal to call, and I was his human servant, whether we liked it, or whether we didn't. I also called Micah Callahan who was my Nimir-Raj and took care of all the shape-shifters when I was off doing other things. I was so often embroiled in other things, I needed the help. Micah was also my boyfriend, along with Jean-Claude. Neither of them seemed to mind, though it still made me uncomfortable. I was raised to believe that a girl didn't date two people at once, at least not seriously.

I got only machines, and left messages that were as succinct and calm as I could make them. How do you leave phone messages like this? "Hi, Micah, this is Anita, Musette has come to town early, invading Jean-Claude's territory. Asher and I are driving to the Circus now, if you don't hear from me by dawn, send help. But don't come down to the Circus before that unless I call personally. The fewer people in the line of fire, the better." I let Asher leave the message on Richard's machine, sometimes he erased messages from me without listening to them. It depended on how bad a mood he was in that day. Though he'd dumped me, not the other way around, he acted like the wounded party and blamed me for every-thing. I gave him as wide a berth as I could, but there were times, like now, when we were probably going to have to work together to keep all our people alive and healthy. Survival took precedence over emotional pain. It had to. I hoped Richard remembered that.

The Circus of the Damned was a combination of a live action drama with frightening themes; traditional, if macabre, circus performances; a carnival complete with rides, games, corn dogs, funnel cakes; and a side show that would give even me nightmares.

Behind the Circus was dark and quiet. The calliope music that blared out front was a distant dream back here. Once upon a time I'd only come to the Circus to kill vampires. Now I used the employee parking lot. Oh, how the mighty have fallen.

I was actually a few steps from the Jeep, when I realized that Asher was still sitting in the car, immobile. I sighed and went back to the car. I had to tap on his window to get him to look at me. I half expected him to jump, but he didn't. He just turned his face slowly towards me like someone in a nightmare who knows if they move too fast the monster will get them.

I expected him to open the door, but he just stared at me. I took a deep breath and counted slowly. I did not have time to hold his emotional wounds closed. Jean-Claude, my sweetie, was down under the Circus, entertaining the bogeyman of vampire-kind. Asher had told me no harm had come to anyone, yet. But I wouldn't actually believe it until I saw Jean-Claude, touched his hand. As much as I cared for Asher, I did not have time for this. None of us did.

I opened the door for him. Still, he did not move. "Asher, don't fall apart on me here. We need you tonight."

He shook his head. "You must know. Anita, Jean-Claude didn't send me to you because I travel faster than anyone else. He sent me to get me away from her."

"Are you not supposed to go back in?" I asked.

He shook his head again, all those golden waves swimming around his face. His eyes were their normal ice-blue in the dome light. "I am his *témoin*, his second, I must go back inside."

"Then you're going to have to get out of the Jeep," I said.

He looked down at his hands, limp in his lap. "I know." But he still didn't move.

I put one hand on the door and the other on the roof, leaning in towards him. "Asher . . . if you can't do this, then fly to my house, hide in the basement, we've got an extra coffin."

He did look up then. There was anger in his face. "Let you go in there alone? No, never. If something happened to you . . ." He looked down again, his hair hiding his face like the curtain he'd made of it. "I could not live with the knowledge that I had failed you."

I sighed again. "Great, thanks for the sentiment. I know you mean it, but that means you have to get out of the car now."

A gust of wind slapped against my back, too much wind, like the wind Asher had raised in the cemetery. I went for my gun as I dropped to one knee.

Damian landed in front of me. The barrel of the gun was aimed low at his body. If he'd been a little shorter than six feet, it would have been chest high.

I let out a breath slowly and eased my finger off the trigger. "Damn, Damian, you startled me, and that can be real unhealthy." I got to my feet.

"Sorry," he said, "but Micah wanted you to have someone else with you." He spread his hands wide, showing himself both unarmed and harmless. He might have been unarmed, but harmless, never that. It wasn't just that Damian was handsome – a lot of men, dead and alive, are handsome. His hair fell in a straight, silken curtain, scarlet, like a spill of blood. It was what red hair looked like after more than six hundred years of no sun. He blinked green eyes into the lights of the streetlamps overhead. A green that any cat would envy. The eyes were three shades brighter than the T-shirt that clung to his upper body. Black slacks fell over black dress shoes. A black belt with a silver buckle completed the outfit. Damian hadn't dressed up, he'd just been wearing slacks and dress shoes. Most of the vamps that had recently come from Europe didn't feel comfortable in jeans and jogging shoes.

Yeah, he was a treat for the eyes, but that wasn't the danger. The fact that I wanted to touch him, to run my hands up the white, white skin of his arms. That was the danger. It wasn't love, or even lust. Through a series of accidents and emergencies, I'd bound Damian to me as my vampire servant. Which was impossible, I mean vamps have human servants, but humans don't have vampire servants. I was beginning to understand why the Council used to kill all necromancers on sight. Damian was glowing with

38

good health, which meant he'd recently fed on someone, but I knew it had been a willing victim, because I'd forbidden him to hunt. He would do exactly what I said, no more, no less. He obeyed me in all things, because he had no choice.

"I knew I could get here before you went inside," he said.

"Yeah, flying does have its benefits." I shook my head and put up my gun. I had to rub my hand on my skirt to keep from touching him. The palm of my hand ached to caress his skin. He wasn't my lover, or boyfriend, yet I craved his touch when he was near me, in a way that felt disturbingly familiar.

I took a deep breath that seemed to shake just a little. "I told Micah not to send anyone until I'd found out what was up."

Damian shrugged, hands up. "Micah said, *go*, so here I am." He kept his face carefully blank. There was a tension to him that said he was waiting for me to hurt the messenger.

"Touch him," Asher said.

His quiet voice from right behind me made me jump, but at least he'd gotten out of the Jeep.

"What?"

"Touch him, *ma cherie*, touch your servant."

I felt heat climb up my face. "Is it that obvious?"

He smiled at me, but not like he was happy. "I remember what it was like with . . . Julianna." He said her name in a whisper that still carried on the cool autumn air. It startled me a little to hear him say her name, he avoided her name if he could; saying it, or hearing it.

"I'm Jean-Claude's human servant, but I don't feel an overwhelming need to touch him every time I see him."

He looked up at me. "You don't?"

I started to say, *no*, then had to think about it. I did want to touch Jean-Claude when I saw him, but that was the sex, the rush of being a relatively new couple, wasn't it?

I frowned and concentrated on something else. "Does Jean-Claude feel the same need to touch me?" *Like I feel for Damian* went unsaid.

"Almost certainly," Asher said.

I frowned harder. "He hides it well."

"Because to expose such raw need to you would have made

39

you run away." He touched my elbow, a light touch. "I did not mean to give away uncomfortable secrets, but we must show a united front for . . . her, this night. When you touch Damian you gain power, just as when Jean-Claude touches you and Richard, he gains power."

I took a deep breath, let it out slowly. One thing I was almost certain of was that Richard wouldn't be here tonight. He hadn't come near the Circus of the Damned since we broke up. It weakened us that one-third of our triumvirate was missing. He'd promised to come to the Circus in three months' time to greet Musette, but he wouldn't come early. I would bet my life on that, and maybe I was. Who the hell knew what was inside the Circus waiting for us?

I glanced from one vampire to the other, then shook my head. We needed to get inside, and I needed to stop being squeamish. Asher needed it, too, but I couldn't control what he did, only what I did.

I touched Damian's arm, and power flared between us like a breath of wind. I slid my hand down the smoothness of his arm, using everything but the tips of my fingers. The tips of my fingers hurt when they brushed things too solidly. His breath came out in a shudder, as I slid my left hand into his right, squeezing my fingers 'round his. As long as I didn't squeeze too hard, my bandaged fingers were fine. It felt so right to touch him. It was hard to explain, because touching him didn't make me think of sex. It wasn't like touching Jean-Claude, or Micah, or even Richard. Richard and I were feuding, but he could still affect me just by being present. When I could be in the same room with Richard and not feel my body tighten, then I'd know that I was truly out of love with him.

"I don't mind that Micah sent backup."

I felt his hand, his arm, his body give up the tension I hadn't even realized he was holding. He smiled and squeezed my hand back. "Good."

"You've mellowed," a voice behind us called. We all whirled, to find Jason walking towards us over the pavement. He was grinning, proud he'd startled us, I think.

"Damn quiet for a werewolf," I said.

40

He was wearing jeans, jogging shoes, and a short leather jacket. Jason was as American as I was, we liked the casual look. His blond hair was still cut short like a young executive. It made him look older, more grown-up. Somehow without the hair to trail around his face, you noticed his eyes more, blue, the color of an innocent spring sky. The color never matched the twinkle in his eye.

"A little warm for a leather jacket," I said.

He unzipped the jacket in one smooth motion, and flashed his bare chest and stomach, still walking towards us, never missing a beat. Sometimes I forgot that Jason's day job was as a stripper at Guilty Pleasures, one of Jean-Claude's other clubs. Then there were moments like this when he managed to remind me.

"I didn't have time to dress when Jean-Claude sent me out to wait for you."

"Why the hurry?" I asked.

"Musette has offered to share her *pomme de sang* with Jean-Claude, if he'll share me with her."

*Pomme de sang* meant literally, apple of blood, it was slang with the vamps for someone that was much more than simply a blood donor. Jean-Claude had once described it as a beloved mistress except instead of sex you got blood. A kept woman, or in Jason's case, a kept man.

"I thought it was a faux pas to ask to feed on someone else's *pomme de sang*," I said.

"It can also be a great courtesy and honor," Asher said. "You may trust Musette to turn custom into torment if she is able."

"So she's not offering up her *pomme de sang* to honor Jean-Claude, she's doing it because she knows he won't want to share Jason?"

"*Oui*," Asher said.

"Great, just great. What other little vampire customs are going to come up and bite us on the butt tonight?"

He smiled and raised my hand to his lips for a quick, chaste kiss. "Many, I would think, *ma cherie*, very many." He looked at Jason. "As truth, I am amazed that Musette allowed you to leave her presence without sharing blood."

Jason's grin faded. "Her *pomme de sang* is illegal in this country, so Jean-Claude had to decline."

41

"Illegal," I said, "in what way?"

He sighed, looking decidedly unhappy. "The girl can't be more than fifteen."

"And it's against the law to take blood from a minor," I said.

"Jean-Claude informed her of this, which is how I come to be standing out here in the cold."

"It's not cold," Damian said.

Jason shivered. "That is a matter of opinion." He huddled the still unzipped jacket around his bare body. "Jean-Claude doesn't want you to be surprised, Anita, but two of the vamps with her are children."

I could feel my face tightening with anger.

"It's not that bad, they aren't new. At a guess I'd say several hundred years old, minimum. Even in the United States they'd be grandfathered in under the current law."

I tried to ease some of the tension I was holding. I'd let go of everyone's hand, because I had this urge to have my hands free for weapons. There was nothing to fight, not yet, but the urge was still there.

Damian touched my arm, tentative, afraid the anger would spill over onto him, I think. My usual theory was anybody to be angry at was better than nobody to be angry at. I was trying to be better than that, more fair, but damn, it was hard.

When I didn't jerk away, or yell at him, Damian touched my hand, and his fingers light across my skin made me feel calmer. "Do you think Musette brought an underage *pomme* just to see what we'd do?"

"Musette likes them young," Asher said, voice still very quiet, not a whisper but close, as if he were afraid of being overheard. And maybe he was.

I looked up at Asher. Damian's fingers were still moving, lightly, over the back of my hand. "She's not a pedophile, please tell me she's not."

He shook his head. "No, not for sex, Anita, but blood, yes, she likes them young."

Yuck. "She cannot take blood from anyone under eighteen while she's in this country. Doing that can get you an order of execution with your name on it, and I'm the Executioner."

42

"I believe that Musette was carefully chosen by Belle Morte. Belle has other lieutenants that have less objectionable habits. I believe that Musette is an ordeal in the traditional sense of the word. She has been sent by Belle to test us, especially you, I think, you and perhaps Richard."

"Why do we get special treatment?" I asked.

"Because Belle does not know either of you of old. She likes to test her blades before blooding them, Anita."

"I am not her blade, I'm not her anything."

Asher had a patient look on his face. "She is *le sourdre de sang*, the fountainhead of our bloodline. Belle is like an empress, and all the master vampires that descend from her line are kings that owe her fealty. To owe fealty means to owe so many troops to the cause."

"What cause?"

He let out an exasperated breath. "Whatever cause the empress wishes."

I shook my head. "You're not really making sense to me here." Damian's hand was still playing lightly over mine. I think if he hadn't been touching me, I'd have been more upset.

"Belle considers all who descend from her line, hers, thus through Jean-Claude you and Richard belong to her."

I shook my head and started to speak. Asher held up his hand. "Please, let me finish. It does not matter, Anita, whether you agree that you and Richard belong to Belle. It matters only that she believes you belong to her. She sees you as more weapons in her arsenal. Can you understand that?"

"I understand what you're saying, I don't agree that I belong to anyone, but I can see where Belle Morte might think so."

He nodded, looked a little relieved, as if he hadn't been sure what he'd do if I'd continued to argue. "*Bon, bon,* then you must agree that Belle will want to test the metal of her two newest weapons."

"Test how?" I asked.

"For one thing, by bringing an underage *pomme de sang* to America and flaunting it in front of the Executioner herself. If Musette has offered to share *pommes de sang*, then she may also offer to share human servants. It is considered a great honor to do so."

43

"Share?" I asked, instantly suspicious. Damian's fingers had sped up, but I didn't tell him to stop, because anger was tightening my shoulders, my arms.

"Share blood, probably, because most vampires take blood from their human servants. Do not worry about sex, *ma cherie*, Musette is not a lover of women."

I half shrugged. "I guess that's a relief." I frowned. "If she considers me and Richard part of her . . . whatever, then what about his pack and my pard? Does Belle consider our people her people?"

Asher licked his lips, and I knew the answer before he said it. "It would be like her to assume that."

"So Musette and company will be testing not just me, or Richard, but the rest of our people." I made it a statement.

"It is logical to assume so," he said.

I closed my eyes and shook my head. "I hate vampire politics."

"She's not yelling yet," Jason said, "I've never seen her this calm after this much bad news."

I opened my eyes and frowned at him.

"I believe it is Damian's influence," Asher said.

Jason's eyes flicked down to where Damian was playing gently with my hand. "You mean just touching her like that is helping her hold her temper?"

Asher nodded.

I had an urge to make Damian stop touching me, but I didn't, because I was furious. How dare anyone come into our territory and test us? How arrogant! How typically vampire. And I was tired already, tired of the games to come. If Jean-Claude would just let me shoot everyone in Musette's party tonight, it would save a lot of trouble. I just knew it would.

I did make Damian stop playing with my hand by taking his hand in mine and holding it firmly. The edge of my anger softened. I was still angry, but it was distant, manageable. Damn, Asher was right. I hated that. Hated that some new metaphysical bullshit had reached up to force me into closer personal contact with yet another vampire. Why couldn't metaphysics work just once without all the touchie-feelie crap?

Jason was looking at us, an odd expression on his face. "I think we should attach Damian to Anita for the night."

"You think Musette is going to piss me off that badly?" I asked.

"She's not hurt anyone, yet, Anita, not raised a finger to anyone, yet everyone's terrified. I'm fucking terrified, and I can't figure out why. She's this cute little, blond thing, and she's gorgeous like a life-size Barbie doll, with smaller breasts, but hey a man doesn't need more than a mouthful, right?"

"You're over-sharing," I said.

He didn't smile at me. His face was way too serious. "Normally, I wouldn't mind a gorgeous vampire sinking fang into me, but Anita, I do not want this chick to touch me." He looked scared all of a sudden, scared and younger even than his twenty-two years. "I do not want her touching me." He stared up at me with haunted eyes. "Jean-Claude's promised me that Musette isn't one of those vampires who rots all over you. But it doesn't matter, I'm still so scared of her that it makes my stomach hurt."

I reached out my free hand, and Jason came to me. I hugged him and could feel a fine tremble running through him. He was cold, but not the kind of cold that extra clothes would fix. "We'll keep her off of you, Jason."

He hugged me so tight it was hard to breathe, and he spoke with his face against my neck. "Don't promise things you can't deliver, Anita."

I opened my mouth to promise just that, when Asher interrupted. "No, Anita, do not promise safe passage to any of us, not yet, not until you have met Musette."

I drew back from Jason and looked up at Asher. "If I just shoot her dead when I walk in the room what would Belle do?"

He paled, and that's a neat trick for a vampire, even one that's fed. "You cannot, you must not, Anita . . . I beg of you."

"You know that if I killed her tonight we'd all be safer."

He opened his mouth, closed it, opened it. "Anita, *ma cherie*, please . . ."

Jason stepped back from me and made a motion with his hands. Damian was at my back, hands on my shoulders. The moment he touched me, I felt better, not exactly calmer, not even clearer-headed. Because I was right, we should kill Musette tonight. In the short run it would save so much trouble. But in the long run Belle Morte, maybe even the whole council, would come in force and kill us. I knew that. With Damian's hands kneading gently on the tight muscles of my shoulders I could even agree with it.

"Why does Damian's touch make me feel less like killing things?" I asked.

"I have noticed that you seem to gain a measure of calm, an extra layer of thoughtfulness before you pull the trigger when he is touching you."

"Jean-Claude isn't one bit less ruthless when I'm around him."

"You can only gain from your servant what your servant has to offer," Asher said. "I would say that you have helped make Jean-Claude more ruthless, not less, because that is your nature." He looked at the vampire standing behind me. "Damian survived for centuries with a mistress that tolerated no anger, no pride. Her will and her will alone was allowed. Damian learned to be less angry, less ruthless, or she-who-made-him would have destroyed him long ago."

Damian's hands had gone very still against my shoulders. I patted one of his hands the way you'd pat a friend that was hearing bad news. "It's alright, Damian, she can't touch you now."

"No, Jean-Claude bargained for my freedom from her, and I will always owe him a great debt for that. But that has nothing to do with blood oaths or vampiric bonds. I owe him for bringing me out of a terrible bondage."

"If you can keep Anita from doing anything unfortunate tonight, then you will have paid part of that debt," Asher said.

I felt Damian nod. "Then let us go down to the underground, for I know Musette of old and I do not fear her, as much as I fear she-who-made-me."

I turned so I could see Damian's face. "Are you implying that you fear Musette only a little less than she-who-made-you?"

He seemed to think about that for a second, or two, then slowly nodded. "I fear my old master more, but yes, I fear Musette."

"All fear her," Asher said.

Damian nodded. "All fear her."

I laid the top of my head against Damian's chest, shaking my head back and forth, messing up my hair, but I didn't care. "Damn it, if you'd just let me kill her tonight, now, it would save so much trouble. I'm right, you know I'm right."

46

Damian raised my face so I had to meet his eyes. "If you slay Musette, then Belle Morte will destroy Jean-Claude."

"What if Musette does something really terrible?"

Damian looked behind me at Asher. I turned so I could watch the vampires exchanging glances. Asher finally spoke, "I would never want to tell you that under no circumstances are we to slay Musette, because there may come a time when she gives you no choice. I would not have you endanger yourself by hesitating, if that time comes. But I think that Musette will play the political game very well and will give you no excuse so awful as that."

I sighed.

"If you don't handcuff Damian to Anita tonight, she's never going to make it through Musette's little show," Jason said.

"I do not believe that will be necessary," Asher said, "will it, Anita?"

I frowned. "How the hell should I know? Besides, I'm fresh out of handcuffs."

Jason drew a pair out of his jacket pocket. "You can borrow mine."

I frowned harder. "What are you doing carrying around a pair of handcuffs?" I held up my hand. "Wait, I don't want to know."

He grinned at me. "I'm a stripper, Anita, I use all sorts of props."

On one hand it was good to know that Jason didn't carry the handcuffs around for his own love life. On the other hand, I wasn't sure I wanted to know that handcuffs were part of his props as a stripper. What kind of shows were they doing down at Guilty Pleasures these days? Wait, I didn't really want an answer to that question either.

We all trooped to the back door of Circus of the Damned. We didn't use Jason's handcuffs, but I did end up walking down all those stairs holding Damian's hand. There was a growing list of people that walking hand in hand with I would have found roman-tic or titillating. Damian wasn't on the list, more's the pity.

47

# 6

DEEP UNDER THE Circus of the Damned were what seemed like miles of underground rooms. They had been the home of St. Louis's Master of the City, whoever that happened to be, for as long as anyone could remember. Only the huge warehouse above ground had changed. Jean-Claude had modernized the underground, redecorated some of it, but that was all. It was still room after room of stone and torches.

To soften the stone look, Jean-Claude had used huge gauzy drapes to make a sort of tent for his living room walls. The outside was white, but once you parted the first set of hangings the "walls" were silver, gold, and white. Jason had reached out to part the drapes, when Jean-Claude pushed through. He motioned us all back, a finger to his lips.

I swallowed my greeting. He was wearing skin-tight leather pants tucked into thigh-high boots, so it was hard to tell where the pants left off and the boots began. The shirt was one of his typical shirts, something sort of 1700s, with mounds of ruffles at sleeves, and neck. But the color of all that silk was something I'd never seen him in. A vibrant blue somewhere between royal and navy. The color made his midnight eyes bluer than ever. His face was as always flawless, breathtaking. It was, as always, like some wet dream come to life, too beautiful to be real, too sensuous to be safe.

My heart was hammering in my throat. I wanted to fling myself on him, to wrap myself around him like a blanket. I wanted all those black curls to sweep along my body like I was being caressed by living silk. I wanted him. I almost always wanted him, but tonight, I WANTED him. With everything that was happening and about to happen, all I could think of was sex, sex with Jean-Claude.

He glided towards me, and I held out a hand so he wouldn't

touch me. If he laid so much as a finger on me, I wasn't sure what I'd do.

He looked puzzled, and I heard his voice in my head, "What is wrong, *ma petite?*"

I still didn't have the trick of talking mind-to-mind down pat, so I didn't try. I just held up my left hand and pointed at my watch. It was ten to midnight.

Like Cinderella, I needed to be home by midnight every night. I'd told my coworkers that it was a lunch break, and it was, sometimes I even got food. But what I had to feed every twelve hours didn't have much to do with my stomach. No, lower places, definitely lower places.

Jean-Claude's eyes went wide. In my head, he said, "*Ma petite,* please tell me you have fed the *ardeur* already."

I shrugged. "Twelve hours ago." I didn't bother to whisper; the vampires behind the curtains would hear it, so I used a normal tone of voice. It wasn't like I was going to be able to hide the *ardeur* from them anyway. The *ardeur* was one of the side effects of being Jean-Claude's human servant. In another age, Jean-Claude would have been considered an incubus, because he could feed on lust. Not just feed upon it, but cause others to lust after him. It was a way of making more of what you needed. In an emergency, he could feed off of lust and forgo blood for a few days. It was very rare for a vampire to have a secondary power like this. Damian's master had been able to feed off of fear. She'd been what they call a night hag, or mora.

Belle Morte, of course, held the *ardeur.* She had used it for centuries to manipulate kings and emperors. Jean-Claude was one of the few of her bloodline to inherit this particular power. And I was, to my knowledge, the only human servant to ever inherit it from anyone.

When the *ardeur* first awoke in a vamp, it controlled them just like the blood lust, then gradually they learned to control it. Or that was the plan. Since I'd had it, I'd fought like hell so that I only had to feed every twelve hours or so. The feeling didn't have to involve intercourse, but there did have to be sexual contact. All those old stories about succubi and incubi killing people by loving them to death were true. I could not feed off the same person every time.

Micah let me feed off him. Jean-Claude had been waiting to share the *ardeur* with me for years, though he'd thought it would be him doing the feeding, not me. I'd been forced to make Nathaniel, one of my wereleopards, into my own version of a *pomme de sang*. Embarrassing as hell, but it beat the heck out of molesting strangers, which was entirely possible if you fought the *ardeur*. It was a hard taskmistress just like Belle Morte.

The plan for tonight had been to go to my house and meet with Micah, but instead I was here at the Circus. That wasn't bad in itself, because Jean-Claude was always willing. Unfortunately, we had big bad vampires in the next room, and I didn't think they'd wait while we had hot monkey sex. Call it a hunch, but I suspected Musette would be sympathetic.

The trouble was, the *ardeur* wasn't sympathetic either.

The men were all standing around with that, *oh, my god*, silence thick on the ground. We were all looking at Jean-Claude to solve this. "What do we do?" I asked.

He looked lost for a moment, then he laughed, that touchable, caressable laugh. It made me shudder, and only Damian grabbing me kept me from falling. I waited for the *ardeur* to spread to him like the contagious disease it could be, but it didn't. The moment he touched me, the *ardeur* receded like the ocean pulling back from the shore. I felt light and clean, clear-headed. I could think again. I clutched Damian's arm like it was the last piece of wood in the ocean.

I turned wide eyes to Jean-Claude. He was looking very serious. "I feel it too, *ma petite*."

We knew through practice that if Jean-Claude concentrated on controlling the *ardeur*, he could help me control it as well. But when he wasn't concentrating, the fire burned through us both like some overwhelming force of nature.

I felt Damian's sorrow at my cool touch, felt it like a taste across my tongue, as if rain could have a flavor.

I knew that Damian wanted me, in that good ol'-fashioned way that had very little to do with hearts and flowers, and everything to do with lust. He craved me the way he did blood, because to be without me was to die. Damian was over six hundred years old, but he'd never be a master vampire. Which meant that literally his original mistress had made his heart beat, his body walk. Then Jean-Claude had been his animating force, and then, accidentally, I'd stolen him from Jean-Claude, and now it was my necromancy that made his blood flow, his heart beat.

I'd been horrified to find that I had, in effect, a pet vampire. I'd tried to ignore what I'd done, run from it. I'd been running from so many things. But I knew that Damian wasn't one of those things that I could ignore.

If I cut myself off from Damian, he would first go mad, then he would die in truth. Of course, long before he faded away, the other vampires would have had to execute him. You couldn't have a six-hundred-year-old vampire gone stark raving mad running around the city slaughtering people. It was bad for business. How did I know what would happen if I denied Damian? Because I hadn't known he was my vampire servant for the first six months after it had happened. He had gone mad, and he had slaughtered innocents. Jean-Claude had imprisoned him, waiting for me to come home, waiting for me to live up to my responsibilities instead of running from them. Damian had been one of my object lessons that you either embraced your power, or others paid the price.

I looked at Jean-Claude. He was still beautiful, but I could look at him without wanting to swarm all over him. "This is amazing," I said.

"If you would have let Damian touch you like this months ago, we would have discovered it sooner," Jean-Claude said.

There was a time, not that long ago, that I would have resented being reminded of my own shortcomings, but one of my new resolutions was not to argue about everything. Picking my battles, that was the goal.

Jean-Claude nodded, walked over to me, and held out his hand. "My apologies for the earlier indiscretion, *ma petite*, but I am master now, no longer pawn of the fire that burns us both."

I stared at the hand, so pale, long-fingered, graceful. Even without the *ardeur*'s interference, he was always fascinating in ways that I had no words for. I took his hand, while still clutching Damian's arm. Jean-Claude's fingers closed around mine, and my heart stayed calm. The *ardeur* did not raise its lascivious head.

He raised my hand to his mouth, slowly, touched his lips to my knuckles. Nothing happened. He risked a caress of his lips, sliding along my skin. It did make me catch my breath, but the *ardeur* did not rise.

He stood upright, my hand still in his. He smiled, that brilliant smile that I valued, because it was real, or as close to real as he could come. He'd spent centuries schooling his face, his every motion to be courtly, graceful, and give nothing away. He found it hard to simply react. "Come, *ma petite*, come let us meet our guests."

I nodded. "Sure."

He wrapped my arm through his and looked at Damian. "Take her other arm, *mon ami*, let us escort her inside."

Damian settled my hand on the smooth, muscled skin of his forearm. "With pleasure, master."

Normally, Jean-Claude didn't like his vamps calling him master, but tonight we'd be formal. We were trying to impress people who hadn't been impressed by anything in centuries.

Asher stepped forward to get the drapes, Jason went to the other side, and they held the drapes aside for us so we could enter without having to bat at the drapes. There are reasons that wall-hangings over doorways fell out of favor.

The only downside to having an attractive vampire on each arm was that I couldn't go for my gun quickly. Of course, if I had to draw a gun as soon as we went through the door, then the night was going to be a bad one. Bad enough that we might survive this night, but not the next.

# 7

MUSETTE STOOD BY the white brick fireplace. It had to be her, because she was the only little blond Barbie doll in the room, and that's how Jason had described her. Jason had a lot of faults, but describing a woman inaccurately was not one of them.

She was indeed small, shorter than me by at least three inches. Which made her barely five feet tall, if she was wearing heels under the long white gown, then she was tinier still. Her hair fell around her shoulders in blond waves, but her eyebrows were black and perfectly arched. Either she dyed one thing or the other, or she was one of those rare blonds where body and head hair didn't match. Which did happen, but not often. The blond hair, pale skin, dark eyebrows and eyelashes framed blue eyes like spring skies. I realized that her eyes were only a few shades bluer than Jason's. Maybe it was the dark eyebrows and lashes that made them seem so much more vivid.

She smiled with a rosebud mouth that was so red I knew she was wearing lipstick, and once I saw that I knew she was wearing more makeup. Well done, understated, but there were touches here and there that helped a striking, almost childlike beauty along.

Her *pomme de sang* knelt at her feet like a pet. The girl's long brown hair was piled on top of her head in a complicated layer of curls that made her look even younger than she was. She was pale, not vampire pale, but pale, and the icy blue of her long, old-fashioned dress didn't help give her any color. Her slender neck was smooth and untouched. If Musette was taking blood, where was she taking it from? Did I want to know? Not really.

A man stood between the fireplace and the large white couch with its spill of gold and silver pillows. He was the opposite of Musette in almost every way. Well over six feet tall, built like an overly large swimmer, broad-shouldered, slim-waisted, narrow-

53

hipped, with legs that seemed longer than I was tall. His hair was black, black like mine was black – with blue highlights. It was tied in a thick braid down his back. His skin was as dark as skin that hadn't seen much sun in centuries could be. I was betting he tanned with very little effort. He just hadn't had much opportunity to catch any rays. His eyes were an odd blue green, aqua, like the waters of the Caribbean. They were startling in his dark face and should have added warmth and beauty. But they were cold. He should have been handsome, but he wasn't, the sour expression on his face stole all that. He looked as if he were always in a bad mood.

Maybe it was the clothes. He was dressed as if he'd stepped out of a centuries-old painting. If I had to go around in tights, I might be grumpy, too.

Though I had a man on either arm, it was definitely Jean-Claude who led us between the two overstuffed chairs, one gold, one silver, with their piles of white pillows. He stopped in front of the white wood coffee table with its crystal bowl of white and yellow carnations. Damian also stopped instantly, standing very still under the touch of my hand. Jason flopped, gracefully, into the gold chair closest to the fireplace. Asher stood on the other side of the silver chair, as far away from Musette as he could get without leaving the room.

Musette said something in French. Jean-Claude replied in French, and I actually understood that he'd told her that I didn't speak French. She said something else that was a complete mystery to me, then she switched to a heavily accented English. Most vampires have no accent, at least in America, but Musette had a doozy. Thick enough in places that I knew if she spoke too fast, English or not, I wouldn't be able to understand her.

"Damian, it has been long since you graced our court with your presence."

"My old mistress did not care for the life of the court."

"She is an odd one, your mistress Morvoren."

I felt Damian's body react to the name like he'd been slapped. I stroked the top of his hand the way you'd soothe a worried child.

"Morvoren is powerful enough to compete for a council seat. She was even offered the Earthmover's old place. She would not even have had to fight for it. It was a gift." Musette was watching Damian, studying his face, his body, his reactions. "Why do you think she refused such a bounty?"

Damian swallowed, his breath shaky. "As I said," he had to clear his throat, to finish, "my old mistress is not one for court life. She prefers her solitude."

"But to give up a seat on the council without a battle to risk, that is madness. Why would Morvoren do that?"

Each time she said the name, Damian flinched. "Damian answered your question," I said, "his old master likes her privacy."

Musette turned those blue eyes to me, and the flat unfriendliness of the stare made me half wish I hadn't interrupted.

"So, this is the new one." She walked towards us, and it wasn't just gliding, it was a sway of hips, there were high heels under the skirt. You didn't get that sashay without them.

The tall dark and scary man moved behind her like a shadow. The young girl stayed sitting in front of the fireplace, her pale blue skirts spread around her like they'd been arranged. Her hands were very still in her lap. She looked arranged, too, as if she'd been told *sit here, like this*, and she would sit there, like that, until Musette told her to move. Definitely yucky.

"May I present Anita Blake, my human servant, the very first I have ever called to me. There is no other, there is only she." Jean-Claude used his hand in mine to sweep me outward away from the coffee table, and incidentally, Musette. It was almost a dance move, as if I was supposed to curtsy, or something. Damian followed the movement, making it look like a very graceful game of crack the whip. The vampires bowed, and, caught between them, I had little choice but to do what they did. Maybe there was more than one reason that Jean-Claude had put me in the middle.

Musette swayed towards us, her hips making a dance of the billowing white skirt. "You know the one I mean, Asher's servant, what was her name?" There was a look in those blue eyes that said she knew damn well what the name was.

"Julianna," Jean-Claude said, voice as neutral as he could make it. But neither Asher nor he could say Julianna's name without some emotion.

"Ah, yes, Julianna, a pretty name for someone so common."

She'd come to stand in front of us. The tall dark man stood behind her, menacing by his very size. He had to be damn close to seven feet tall. "Why is it that Asher and you choose such common women? I suppose there is something comforting about good, sturdy, peasant stock."

I laughed before I could think. Jean-Claude squeezed my hand. Damian went very still under my other hand.

Musette didn't like being laughed at, that was plain on her face. "You laugh, girl, why?"

Jean-Claude squeezed my hand tight enough that it was just this side of pain. "Sorry," I said, "but calling me a peasant isn't much of an insult."

"Why is it not?" she asked, and she looked genuinely puzzled.

"Because, you're right, as far back as anyone can trace my family tree I have nothing but soldiers.and farmers. I am good peasant stock and proud of it."

"Why would you be proud of that?"

"Because everything we've gotten, we've made with our two hands, the sweat of our brows, that kind of thing. We've had to work for everything we have. No one has ever given us anything."

"I do not understand," she said.

"I don't know if I can explain it to you," I said. I was thinking it was like Asher trying to explain to me what you owed a liege lord. I had nothing in my life that prepared me to understand that sort of obligation. I didn't say that out loud though, because I didn't want to bring up the idea that I owed Belle Morte anything. Because I didn't feel I did.

"I am not stupid, Anita, I would understand if you would explain yourself clearly."

Asher moved from behind, to the other side of us, still as far as he could stay from Musette, but it was brave of him to draw attention to himself. "I attempted to explain to Anita earlier what one owes a liege lord, and she could not understand it. She is young and American, they have never had the . . . benefit of being ruled here."

She turned her head to one side, disturbingly like a bird just before it takes a bite out of a worm. "And what has her lack of understanding of civilized ways to do with anything?"

A human being would have licked their lips, Asher went still, quiet. (Hold still enough, and the fox won't know you're there.) "You, lovely Musette, have never lived where you were not subject to a lord, or lady, or where you did not rule others. You have never lived without knowing the duties one owes one's liege."

"*Oui?*" she made that one word cold, so cold, as if to say, go on, dig yourself a deeper hole to be buried in.

"You have never dreamt of the possibility that being a peasant, owing no one, would be a freeing experience."

She waved a carefully manicured hand, as if clearing the very thought from the air. "Absurd. 'Freeing experience,' what does that mean?"

"I believe," Jean-Claude said, "that the fact that you do not understand what that means is Asher's exact point."

She frowned at them both. "I do not understand, thus it cannot be that important." She dismissed it all with a wave of dainty hands. Then she turned her attention back to me, and it was frightening. I wasn't sure what it was about the mere gaze of those eyes, but it chilled the marrow in my bones.

"Have you seen our present to Jean-Claude and Asher?"

I must have looked as confused as I felt, because she turned and tried to motion behind her, but all I could see was her very large human servant. "Angelito, move so she may see." Angelito? Somehow the name, "little angel" didn't fit him. He moved, and she finished the motion towards the fireplace.

It was only the fireplace with its painting above it, then something about the painting caught my eye. It was supposed to be a painting of Jean-Claude, Asher, and Julianna in clothing à la the Three Musketeers, but it wasn't. If there hadn't been new and strange vampires in the room, I'm sure I would have noticed it sooner. Oh, yes, I would have noticed it sooner.

It was a picture of Cupid and Psyche, that traditional scene where Cupid asleep is finally revealed to the candle-wielding Psyche. Valentine's Day has robbed Cupid of what he was in the beginning. He was not a chubby sexless baby with wings. He was a god, a god of love.

I knew who had posed for Cupid, because no one else had ever had that golden hair, that long, flawless body. I had memories of what Asher had looked like before, but I'd never seen it, not me, myself. I walked towards the painting like a flower pulled towards the sun. It was irresistible.

Asher lay on his side in the painting, one hand curled against his stomach, the other hand flung outward, limp with sleep. His skin glowed golden in the candlelight, only a few shades lighter than the foam of hair that framed his face and shoulders.

He was nude, but that word didn't do him justice. The candlelight made his skin glow warm from the broadening of his shoulders to the curve of his feet. His nipples were like dark halos against the swell of his chest, his stomach was flat to the grace of his belly button as if an angel had touched that flawless skin and left a delicate imprint, a line of hair dark gold, almost auburn, traced the edge of his stomach, and ran in a line down, down to curl around him, where he lay swollen, partially erect, caught forever between sleep and passion. The curve of his hip was the most perfect few inches of skin that I'd ever seen. That curve drew the eye down to the line of his thigh, the long sweep of his legs.

I remembered with Jean-Claude's memories what the curve of that hip had felt like under my fingertips. I remembered arguing about whose hip was the softest, the most perfect. Belle Morte had said that the lines of both their bodies were the closest to perfection she'd ever seen on a man. Jean-Claude had always believed that Asher was the more beautiful, and Asher had believed the same of Jean-Claude.

The artist had painted white wings on the sleeping figure, so detailed they looked as if they'd be soft if you could touch them. The wings were huge and reminded me of renaissance pictures of angels. They seemed out of place on that golden body.

Psyche was peering around the edge of one wing, so that it shielded her upper body, yet revealed a shoulder, the edge of her body, down to that first curve of hip, but most of her was lost behind Cupid's body. I frowned up at the picture. I knew that shoulder, the curve of the ribs under that white skin. Though traced with golden candlelight, I knew the line of that body. I'd expected Psyche to be Belle Morte, I'd been wrong.

I looked past the long black curls that didn't so much hide the figure as decorate it, and the face peering around the candle's edge was Jean-Claude's. It took me a second to be sure, because he seemed more delicately beautiful than normal, until I realized that he was wearing makeup – that centuries-old version of it, anyway. Things had been done to soften the line of his face, make his lips more pouting. But the eyes, the eyes were unchanged, with their black lace of lashes and that drowning deep color.

The painting was too large for me to stand next to the fireplace and see it all, but there was something about the eyes of the Cupid figure. I had to move close to see that they were open a mere slit, enough to show the cold blue fire that I'd seen when the hunger was upon Asher.

Jean-Claude touched my face, and it made me jump. Damian had moved back, giving us space. Jean-Claude traced the tears on my cheeks. The look in his eyes said clearly that I was crying tears for both of us. He couldn't afford to appear weak in front of Musette. And I couldn't help it.

We both turned to Asher, but he was standing as far away as the room would allow. He had turned away, so that all you could see of his face was that golden fall of hair. His shoulders were slightly hunched, as if he'd been struck.

Musette came to stand on the other side of Jean-Claude. "Our mistress thought, since you are together again as of old, that you would enjoy this little reminder of days gone by."

The look I gave her around Jean-Claude's shoulder was not a friendly one. I saw the girl who was her *pomme de sang* on the other side of the couch. I hadn't even been aware she'd moved away from the fireplace. If the bad guys had wanted to take me out, they could have done it, because I had seen nothing for a few minutes but the painting.

"The painting is our guest gift to our host, but we have a more personal gift just for Asher."

Angelito moved up beside her like a dark mountain, a much smaller painting in his hands. There were remnants of the paper and twine that had covered it like a discarded skin on the floor. It was half the size of the other, but obviously in the same style, realistic, but in glowing colors, hyperrealistic, very Titian.

The only light in the painting was firelight, the glow of the forge. Asher's body was colored gold and crimson with the reflected firelight. He was nude again, the edge of the anvil hid his groin, but the right side of his body was bare to the light. Even his hair was tied back in a loose ponytail so that the right side of his face couldn't be hidden. His arms were still strong as they pretended to forge the blade that lay on the anvil, but the right side of his face, the right side of his chest, his stomach, his thigh, were a melted ruin.

These were not the old white scars that I was used to seeing, these were raw, red, discolored, angry lines, like some monster had slashed and gouged at his body. I was suddenly overwhelmed with a memory that was not mine.

*Asher lying on the floor of the torture room, freed of the silver chains, the men who had tormented him slaughtered around him, in an explosion of blood. He reached out to us, his face . . . his face . . .*

I swooned, and Jean-Claude and I fell in a heap on the floor, because I was experiencing directly what he was remembering.

Damian and Jason moved up beside us, but Asher stayed well back. I didn't blame him in the least.

## 8

"ASHER, COME AND see your gift," Musette called.

Damian was already on the ground beside me, his hands on my shoulders, fingers digging in. I think he was afraid of what I would do. He should have been.

Asher's voice came strained, but clear, "I have seen that particular gift before. I know it well."

"Do you wish us to return to Belle Morte and tell her you did not appreciate her gift?"

"You may tell Belle Morte, that I have gotten exactly what she wished me to get out of her gifts."

"And what is that?"

"I am reminded of what I was, and of what I am."

I got to my feet, Damian still with a death grip on my shoulders. Jean-Claude rose gracefully like a puppet pulled by invisible strings. I would never be that graceful, but tonight it didn't matter.

Musette turned back to Jean-Claude. "We have given our gift to you, Jean-Claude, and to Asher. We await our guest gifts."

His voice was empty, so bland it was like listening to silence. "I have told you, Musette, our guest gifts are weeks away from completion."

"I'm sure you can find something to stand in their stead." She stared at me.

I found my voice, and it wasn't bland. "How dare you come here three months early, knowing we won't be prepared, and make demands on us?" Damian was clinging to my back a little frantically, but I was polite, for me. After what she and Belle Morte had just done, I was downright kind. "Your rudeness will not be used as an excuse to force us to do anything we don't want to do."

Damian's arms slid over my shoulders so he was cradling me against his body. I didn't fight it, because without his presence I think I would probably have struck her, or shot her. Which sounded like such a good idea.

Jean-Claude tried to smooth things over, but Musette waved him aside. "Let your servant talk, if she has something to say."

I opened my mouth to call her a heartless bitch, but it wasn't what came out. "Did you believe that gifts worthy of such beauty could be hurried? Would you really take some poor substitute in the place of the magnificence we had commissioned?"

I stopped talking. All of our men were staring at me, except Damian, who was hugging me for all he was worth.

"Ventriloquism," Jason said, from the other side of Jean-Claude, "it's the only answer."

Jean-Claude nodded. "A miracle indeed." Then he turned to Musette. "All, save one, pales before your beauty, Musette. How could I offer anything less than something beautiful to grace your loveliness?"

Her gaze turned back to me. "Is she not a beauty to equal mine?"

I laughed. Damian's arms tightened enough that I had to pat his arm so I could keep breathing comfortably. "Don't worry, I've got this one covered." I don't think anyone believed me, but I did, honest. "Musette, I know I'm pretty, I can admit that, but compared to the otherworldly triplets here, I am not the most beautiful person on our side."

"Triplets," Jason said, "why do I think I'm not included in that threesome?"

"Sorry, Jason, but you're like me, we clean up nice, but with these three standing here we are out of our league."

"You include Asher in the three beauties?" Musette said.

I nodded. "If you are cataloging beautiful people and Asher is in the room, then he always makes the list."

"Once, *oui*, but not now, not for centuries," she said.

"I disagree," I said.

"You lie."

I looked at her. "You're a Master Vampire, can't you tell when someone's lying, or telling the truth? Can't you feel it in my words, smell it on my skin?" I watched her face, those beautiful but frightening eyes. She couldn't tell if I was lying, or not. I'd only met one other Master Vamp that couldn't tell truth from lie, and that was because she was lying so badly to herself that truth would have gotten in her way. Musette was blind to truth, which meant we could lie through our teeth to her. That had possibilities.

She frowned at me and waved it all away with those tiny well-manicured hands. "Enough of this." She was intelligent enough to realize she was losing part of this argument, but she wasn't bright enough to know why. So she was moving on to something she thought she could win.

"Even Asher with his ruined beauty is more lovely than you are, Anita."

It was my turn to frown at her. "I think I already said that."

She frowned again. It was like she had been sent with certain lines to say, and I wasn't making the replies she'd expected. I was throwing her performance off, and Musette didn't seem to enjoy improvisation.

"It doesn't bother you that you are not more beautiful than the men?"

"I had to make peace with being the homely one of the group a long time ago."

She frowned so hard it looked painful. "You are a very hard woman to insult."

I shrugged as much as I could with Damian's arms still wrapped around me. "Truth is truth, Musette. I've broken the cardinal girl rule."

"And that would be?"

"Never date anyone prettier than you are."

That made her laugh, a surprised burst of sound. "*Non,* non, the rule is never to admit it." The smile faded. "You truly have no . . . difficulty with me saying I am more lovely than you."

I shook my head. "Nope."

She looked completely lost for a moment, until her own human servant touched her shoulder. She shuddered, took a deep shaking breath, as if remembering who and what she was, and why she was there. The last sign of laughter faded from her eyes.

"You have admitted that your beauty cannot rival mine, thus taking blood from you would not be a gift worthy of replacing the bauble that Jean-Claude is having made for me. You are correct, also, about your wolf. He is charming, but not as charming as the three of them."

I suddenly had a bad feeling about where this was headed.

"Damian is somehow yours. I do not understand it, but I can feel it. He is yours the way Angelito is mine, and you are Jean-Claude's. As Master of the City, Jean-Claude cannot be drink for the taking, but Asher belongs to no one. Give him to me for my guest gift."

"He is my second in command, my *témoin*," Jean-Claude said, still in that empty, means-nothing voice, "I would not lightly share him."

"I have met some of your other vampires this night. Meng Die has an animal to call. She is more powerful than Asher, why is she not your second?"

"She is another's second and will be going back to him in a few months."

"Why is she here then?"

"I called her."

"Why?"

The real reason was that while I was off doing my soul-searching Jean-Claude had needed more backup. But I didn't think he'd share that. He didn't. "A master calls home his flock periodically, especially if he thinks they will soon become masters of their own territory. A last visit before he loses the power to call them."

"Belle was most perturbed that you rose to Master of the City without that one last visit, Jean-Claude. She woke speaking your name, saying that you had struck out on your own. None of us thought you would ever rise so high."

He gave a low, sweeping bow, and she was standing so close that his hair almost brushed her skirt. "It is not often that anyone so surprises Belle Morte. I am most honored."

Musette frowned. "You should be. She was most . . . unhappy."

He stood slowly. "Why would my rise to power make her unhappy?"

"Because to be Master of the City is to be beyond the ties of obligation."

Ties of obligation seemed to mean more to the vampires than it did to me, because I felt them go all quiet. Damian was so still

64

around my body that it was like he wasn't there at all. Only the weight of his arms let me know he was still clinging to me. The beat and pulse of his body was gone, tucked away somewhere deep inside.

"But Asher has not risen so high. He could still be called home," she said.

I glanced at Jean-Claude, but his face was utterly blank, that polite nothingness that meant he was hiding his every reaction. "That is, of course, within her purview, but I would need some notice before Asher was called away. America is less settled than Europe, and fights for territory are much less civilized." His voice was still empty, emotionless, nothing mattered. "If my second were to simply vanish, others would see that as a weakness."

"Do not worry, our mistress is not going to call him home, but she admits to being puzzled."

We all waited for her to go on, but Musette seemed content to let the silence stand.

Even with Damian hanging on to me, I broke first. "Puzzled about what?"

"Why Asher left her side, of course."

Asher moved up closer, though still keeping a much greater distance between himself and Musette than the rest of us. "I did not leave her side," he said, "Belle Morte had not touched me in centuries. She would not even watch entertainments where I was . . . featured. She said I offended her eye."

"It is her prerogative to do with her people as she sees fit," Musette said.

"True," Asher said, "but she bid me come to America with Yvette as my overseer. Yvette died, and I had no more orders."

"And if our mistress ordered you home?"

Silence, ours this time.

Asher's face was as empty of emotion as Jean-Claude's. Whatever he felt was hidden, but the very blankness of both their faces said that it did matter, and it was important.

"Belle Morte encourages her people to strike out on their own," Jean-Claude said. "It is one of the reasons her bloodline rules more territories than any other, especially here in the United States."

Musette turned those beautiful pitiless eyes on him. "But Asher

65

did not leave to become a Master of the City, he left to have revenge on you and your human servant. He wanted to extract payment for his beloved Julianna's death."

See, she had known the name all along.

"Yet, here your servant stands, strong, well, and unharmed. Where is your vengeance, Asher? Where is the price Jean-Claude was to pay for his murder of your servant?"

Asher seemed to close in upon himself, so very, very still. I thought if I blinked, he'd have vanished altogether. His voice came distant, empty. "I found that, perhaps, I had blamed Jean-Claude in error. That, perhaps, he too mourned her loss."

"So," she snapped her fingers, "like that, all your pain, your hatred is forgotten."

"Not just like that, *non*, but I have learned many things that I had forgotten."

"Such as the sweet touch of Jean-Claude's body?" she asked.

The silence this time was so thick I could hear my blood roaring in my ears. Damian felt like a ghost against my body. All the vampires, I was sure, were wishing themselves away.

Either Jean-Claude and Asher had been doing it behind my back. Which was not impossible. But if not, to answer the question truthfully would be bad.

Jason caught my eye, but neither of us dared even shrug. I don't think we were sure what was going on, but that it would end some place painful was almost certain.

Musette swayed around Jean-Claude, to stand closer to Asher. "Are you and Jean-Claude a happy couple, once more, or," here she looked at me, "is it a happy ménage à trois? Is that why you did not come home?" She pushed past Asher and Jean-Claude, making them move back, so she could stand in front of me. "How can the touch of such as this compare to the magnificence of our mistress?"

I think she'd just implied that I wasn't as good in bed as Belle Morte, but I wasn't entirely sure that's what she meant, and I didn't care. She could insult me all she wanted. Insulting me was less painful than so many other things she could be doing.

"Belle Morte is sickened at the sight of me," Asher said, finally, "she avoids me in all things." He motioned at the painting that

Angelito was still holding up. "This is how she sees me. How she will always see me."

Musette swayed her way back to stand in front of Asher. "To be least among her court is better than ruling anywhere else."

I couldn't help myself. "Are you saying it's better to serve in Heaven than rule in Hell?"

She nodded, smiling, seemingly oblivious to the literary allusion. "*Oui, précisément*. Our mistress is the sun, the moon, the all. To be parted from her, only that is true death."

Musette's face was rapturous, glowing with that inner certainty usually reserved for Holy Rollers and television evangelists. She was, indeed, a true believer.

I couldn't see Damian's face, but I was betting it was as carefully blank as the rest. Jason was staring at Musette as if she had sprouted a second head, an ugly, spiky second head. She was a zealot, and zealots are never quite sane.

She turned to Asher with that radiance still suffusing her face. "Our mistress does not understand why you left her, Asher."

I did. I think everyone in the room did, except maybe for Angelito and the girl who was still standing on the other side of the couch where Musette had put her.

"Look at the painting of me as Vulcan, Musette, see what our mistress thinks of me."

Musette didn't bother to look behind her. She gave that Gallic shrug that meant everything and nothing.

"Anita does not see me that way," he said.

"Jean-Claude cannot look at you without seeing what was lost," she said.

"The time when you could speak for me, Musette, is long past. You do not know my heart, or my mind, you never truly did," Jean-Claude said.

She turned to him. "Are you truly telling me that you would touch him, as he is now? Be careful how you answer, Jean-Claude, know that our mistress has seen deep into your heart and mind. You may lie to me, but never to her."

Jean-Claude was quiet for a time, but finally he told the truth. "We are not currently together in that way."

"See, you refuse to touch him, as she refuses to touch him."

I loosened Damian's arms enough so I could move more easily. "Not exactly," I said, "sorry, but it's my fault that they aren't a couple."

She turned to me. "What do you mean, servant?"

"You know, even if I was, like a maid, I know enough about polite society to know that you don't call a maid, simply, maid. You don't call a servant, servant, not unless you truly have never interacted with servants." I folded my arms across my stomach, looking puzzled on purpose. Damian's hands stayed lightly on my shoulders. "Is that it, Musette? Are you not an aristocrat, after all? Is it all pretend, and you simply don't know any better?"

Jean-Claude gave me a look that she couldn't see.

"How dare you!" Musette said.

"Then prove you are noble, address me at least like someone who has truly had servants."

She opened her mouth to argue, then she seemed to hear something that I couldn't hear. She let out a long breath. "As you like, Blake, then."

"Blake is fine," I said, "and what I mean is that I'm not entirely comfortable with this bisexual thing. I won't share Jean-Claude with another woman, and definitely not with a man."

Musette did that head to the side movement again, as if she'd spied the worm she intended to eat. "Very good, then Asher has no tie to any of you. He is merely your second."

I looked from one vampire to another, only Jason looked as confused as I felt. The vamps were acting like a trap had been sprung, and I didn't see it yet. "What's going on?" I asked.

Musette laughed, and it wasn't anywhere near as good a laugh as Jean-Claude or Asher were capable of. It was just a laugh, a vaguely unpleasant one, at that. "I am within my rights to ask for him as my gift for tonight," she said.

"Wait," I said, and Damian's hands tried to pull me back in against him, but I wasn't moving this time. "I thought you agreed with Belle that Asher isn't pretty enough to have sex with anymore."

"Whoever said anything about sex?" Musette asked.

Now I really was puzzled. "Why else would you want him for the night?"

She laughed then, head back, very unladylike, a bray of sound like a hound baying. I hadn't said anything that funny, had I?

Jean-Claude's quiet voice came into the silence that followed that laugh. "Musette's interests run to pain more than sex, *ma petite*."

I looked at him. "You don't mean dominance and submission where you have safe words, do you?"

"There is no word in any language that I have ever heard screamed that would dissuade Musette from her pleasures."

I licked my suddenly dry lips. They lie about that moisturizing lipstick. Your lips still dry out when you get scared. "Let me test my understanding. If Asher was your lover, or mine, or anyone's, then he'd be safe from her?"

"*Non, ma petite*, Asher would only be safe if he belonged to you, or me. Lesser powers cannot protect those they love."

"But because we're not doing him, he's free meat?" I asked.

He seemed to think about that for a time. "That is accurate enough, *oui*."

"Fuck," I said.

"*Oui, ma petite, oui*." A thread of tiredness had finally broken through his empty voice.

I looked at Asher, and he was hiding behind that shining hair again. What was I supposed to say, that if I hadn't been so squeamish this wouldn't be happening? I'm sorry I have issues with my boyfriend doing other men. I'm sorry I have issues with me doing other men. Why was I always being made to feel guilty because I wasn't having sex with more people? Wasn't it supposed to be the other way around?

Musette held her hand out to Asher. He stood there for a second or two, then he took her hand. He looked back once at Jean-Claude, a shine of eyes in all that hair. Jean-Claude never reacted, as if he were trying to pretend he wasn't there.

I moved forward, only Damian's fingers digging into my shoulders brought me up short. "We are not letting her do this," I said.

"She is Musette, and Belle Morte's lieutenant." Jean-Claude's voice had gone small and distant.

Musette didn't take him through the drapes into another room. She stopped a few yards away, not even that close to the "walls."

69

She turned Asher to face her, then she drew a knife from her white skirts, and plunged it into his stomach before anyone could react. Asher could move faster than the eye could follow, but he made no move to protect himself. He just let her sink the knife home, grinding it until the hilt met his skin, and she couldn't push it in any farther.

I had my gun out of the holster, and Jean-Claude grabbed my hand. "The knife is not silver, *ma petite*, when it is removed he will heal almost instantly."

I looked up at him, straining to raise the gun, and making some progress. Thanks to his own vampire marks, I was stronger than I should have been. "How do you know it's not silver?"

"Because I have played this game with Musette before."

That made me stop trying to bring the gun up. I went quiet in his hands. Their hands, I should have said, because Damian's hands were plastered to my shoulders. Only Jason hadn't joined in trying to hold me back. From the look on his face I think he wanted to help me, not hinder me.

I looked past Jean-Claude to see Asher still standing, his hands to his stomach where blood blossomed across the skin of his fingers. The brown of the shirt was dark enough to hide the first rush of blood. Musette put the knife to her delicate mouth and licked down the blade.

I knew through Jean-Claude's memories that vampire blood gives no sustenance. You cannot feed from the dead, not in that way.

Asher looked at us. "It is not silver, *ma cherie*, it will not kill me." His breath was cut off in his throat, as Musette plunged the knife in a second time.

The world swam in streamers of colors. I closed my eyes for a second and spoke in a low, careful voice. "Let go of me, Damian." The hands at my back dropped away instantly, because I'd given a direct order. I opened my eyes and met Jean-Claude's gaze. We stared at each other, until his hand dropped, slowly, away. His voice echoed like a whisper in my mind, "You cannot kill her for this."

I put my gun back in its holster. "Yeah, I know." I couldn't kill her, because she wasn't trying to kill Asher, but I would not stand

here and watch him be tortured. I would not, could not, do it. I'd
once thought that arm-wrestling vampires was a bad idea. She was
stronger than me, even with Jean-Claude's marks, but I was also
betting she wasn't trained in hand-to-hand fighting. If I was wrong,
I was about to get my ass kicked. If I was right, well, we'd see.

# 9

MUSETTE MADE NO move to protect herself. Angelito stayed with the other men across the room. It was as if neither of them saw me as a threat. You'd think with my reputation, vampires would stop underestimating me. But dead or alive, there are always fools.

I could feel myself smiling, and I didn't need a mirror to know that it wasn't a nice smile. It was the smile I got when I'd been pissed off too much and I'd finally decided to do something about it.

Musette made a big show of licking the knife clean, while Asher stood in front of her and bled. She licked it like a kid with a Popsicle on a hot day – got to lick carefully, but quickly, or it drips down your hand, and you lose some of it. Her eyes were all for me, the show was all for me. It was as if Asher didn't matter at all to her. Maybe he didn't.

She had actually turned back to plunge the blade home a third time, when I was within touching distance. I don't know what she thought I planned to do, because she seemed totally surprised when I grabbed her hand. Maybe she expected me to fight like a girl, whatever the hell that means.

I pushed my shoulder into her, and she tottered backwards on her high heels. I hooked my heel behind hers, and my foot swept her leg out from under her. She fell backwards, because I helped. I rode her body down to the ground, turning the knife in her hand with mine, and when she hit the floor, I plunged the knife home. I leaned my knee into the back of our hands and felt the blade come out the back of her body.

I whispered to her, "It's not silver, you'll heal."

She screamed.

I didn't so much hear Angelito move as feel him. "If you come over here, Angelito, I will force this blade up into her heart, and it

72

won't matter if it's silver, or if it's not. I'll shred her heart before you can cross the room."

The far drapes opened and vampires spilled into the room, some ours, some hers. I don't know what would have happened, but I heard the far door open, behind the drapes. I heard a lot of movement, and I almost tore the blade up through her, not at all sure the metal was strong enough to take the strain. With a better blade I could have dug for her heart, with this one I wasn't sure.

A split second before I tried it, I heard a sound that raised the hair on my arms. The sound of hyenas hunting. It's a hell of a lot creepier than the howl of a wolf, but that joined with it. I knew the moment I heard the noises that it was our cavalry coming, not Musette's.

I didn't look behind, because I didn't dare take my eyes off the vampire I had pinned to the floor. But I felt the crowd surge behind me, felt the neck-ruffling power of shape-shifters filling the room like an electric cloud.

The touch of so many of them with such tension called my own beast like a snake in my gut to writhe and flow inside my body. I wasn't a shape-shifter, but through Richard and my tie to the wereleopards, I had the closest thing a human being could have to their very own private beast.

It was Bobby Lee, who was actually a wererat, that came forward enough for me to see him. His Southern drawl always sounded so out of place in a fight. "You planning to kill her?"

"I'm thinking about it."

He knelt on one knee beside us. "You think that's the smart thing to do?" He glanced up at the vampires on the other side of the room.

"Probably not."

"Then maybe you should oughta ease up there, before you gut her."

"Micah send you?" I asked, eyes still on Musette's pain-filled face. I was happy to see her hurting. I didn't usually enjoy causing pain to anyone, but I just didn't mind hurting Musette.

"He didn't send any of your leopards, 'cause you told him not to, but he contacted the other leaders, and here we are. If you're not going to kill her, girl, you should probably let her go."

73

"Not yet," I said.

He didn't ask again, but stood up near us, like the good body-guard he was.

I spoke directly to Musette, but I made sure my voice carried. "No one comes into our territory and harms our people. No one, not the council, not even *le sourdre de sang* of our bloodline. Everyone tells me that when I speak to you I'm speaking to Belle herself, well, here's the message. The next one of her people to harm one of our people is dead. I will take their heads, their hearts, and I'll burn the rest."

Musette found her voice, at long last, though it was strained, and a little afraid. "You would not dare."

I leaned into the blade, a little bit more, made her grunt with the force of it. "Try me."

The pain in Musette's face faded, vanishing like someone wiped it away, and her blue eyes began to darken. I rode the knife into her while Belle's pale brown eyes swirled to the surface, the dark overwhelming all that blue, until Musette's eyes were the color of poisoned honey.

I'd seen Belle do this trick once before, but it had been in a mirror, and my own eyes. Fear drove through me like a blade, chilling my skin, bringing my heart into my neck like a trapped thing. Fear can either chase back the beast, or call it. This fear calmed it, dampened it, so that that rising power sank away, leaving me alone, and scared. It wasn't a vampire trick that made me want to let her go and run away. I'd felt Belle move through my own body, and I never wanted her to be able to do it again. If I took Musette's heart with Belle inside her, could I kill them both? Probably not, but God, it was tempting.

Belle's voice came without a trace of fear, or strain. If the knife hurt her too, it didn't show. "Jean-Claude, have you taught her nothing?" The voice was not Musette's, it was deeper, richer, a low contralto. The irreverent thought that she'd give really good phone sex crossed my mind.

Jean-Claude started gliding towards us. He motioned for Damian to follow, and the red-haired vampire fell into step behind him. Jean-Claude came to kneel beside us and motioned Damian to do the same. They both bowed their heads, carefully out of reach.

74

"Musette overstepped the bounds for a visitor to my lands. You would not tolerate such treatment of one of your own people. I have learned well the lessons you taught me, Belle Morte."

"What lesson is this?" she asked.

"Tolerate nothing. No hint of disobedience. No breath of revolution. No insult is tolerated. I admit that I forgot this in the rush of fear that Musette brought with her. The thought of insulting you, even indirectly was unthinkable, but I am no longer your creature. I am a Master of the City now. I am my own creature, and Asher is mine now. I will be what you brought me up to be, Belle, I will truly be your child. I will let *ma petite* be as ruthless as she likes, and Musette will either learn better manners, or she will not be coming home to you ever again."

She sat up. With the knife plunged through her body, she sat up, and I could not keep her pinned down. The movement pushed me backwards enough to brush against Damian. He touched my back, and when I didn't tell him not to, he touched my shoulder.

Belle even dropped Musette's hand away from the knife, so that my hand held it in place. But she showed no pain, in fact she ignored me to look at Jean-Claude. I began to feel silly with my bloody hands and the knife still stuck in Musette. No, not silly, superfluous.

"You know what I would do to you if you harmed her," Belle said.

"I know that according to our own laws, the laws you helped enact, that no one is allowed to simply enter a territory without negotiating safe passage. Musette and her people are here three months before we gave them permission to enter, which means, in effect, they are outlaws, and have no rights, no safety. I could slaughter them all and council law would be on my side. You have too many people on the council that fear you, Belle, they would think it a good joke."

"You would not dare," she said.

"I will not allow you to harm Asher, not anymore."

"He is nothing to you, Jean-Claude."

"You are the most beautiful thing I have ever seen, magnificent in your lust; I am humbled by your power, awed by the political maneuvering that you do so effortlessly. But I have been long

75

away from you, and I have learned that beauty is not always what it seems, that lust is not always better than love, that power alone is not enough to fill the bed or the heart, and that I don't have your patience for the politics."

She reached out a slender hand towards him. "I showed you love such as no mortal ever could."

"You showed me lust, mistress, sexual appetite."

"*Oui, amour*," she said, her voice sultry enough to cause goose-bumps on my arms.

Jean-Claude shook his head. "*Non*, lust, not love, never love."

A look passed over her face, like a badly designed mask moving liquid under Musette's skin. It reminded me uncomfortably of watching the beast glide under the skin of a shape-shifter before it springs forth. If she changed into Belle completely, I was trying for her heart while I had the chance.

"You loved me once, Jean-Claude."

"*Oui*, with all my heart and all my soul."

"But you do not love me now," her voice was soft, there might even have been a trace of loss.

"I have learned that love can grow without the touch of sex, and that sex does not always lead to love."

"I would love you again," she whispered.

"*Non*, you would possess me again, and love is not about possession."

"You speak in riddles," she said.

"I speak truth as I have come to know it," he said.

Those pale honey-brown eyes turned to me. "You have done this. Somehow, you have done this."

I was beginning to feel positively silly with the knife still in Musette, but I was afraid to take it out, because I was half expecting Belle to stand up and say, *aha, that was what I was waiting for*. So I kept the blade in and tried to think what to do. Staring into those pale brown eyes it was hard to think, hard not to either run away or try and kill her. If I can't run from my fears, I have a tendency to try and kill them. It's a strategy that's worked so far.

"What have I done?" I asked, and my voice showed the strain. Damian's hands kneaded gently at my shoulders, not so much a massage, as a reassurance that he was there, I think.

"You have turned him against me," she said.

"No," I said, "you did that all on your own, centuries before I was born."

That liquid mask moved under Musette's skin again. If I touched her face I thought I'd feel things underneath that should not have been there. "I took him to my bed, what more does anyone desire of Belle Morte?"

"You showed him what your love was worth when you cast Asher out of your bed."

"What does Asher's fate have to do with Jean-Claude's love?"

That anyone who knew the two of them could ask that was amazing. That the vampire that brought them together could ask that was both frightening and sad.

"You need to leave now, Belle," I said.

"Why, what have I said to upset you?"

I shook my head. "The list is too long, Belle, we don't have all night, let me hit the highlights. Go away, for now, please, just leave. I'm tired of trying to explain color to the blind."

"I do not understand what that means."

"No," I said, "you don't."

She stared up at me. Her hand came up as if to touch my face. "If you touch me," I said, "I'll see if Musette can survive without her heart."

"Why is the touch of my hand worse than the touch of our bodies one against the other?"

"Call it a hunch, but I don't want you touching me on purpose. Besides it's not your body, it's Musette's. Although I'm not sure about that, so call me cautious, and just don't touch me."

"I will see you again, Anita, I promise you that."

"Yeah, yeah, I know."

"You don't seem to believe me."

"Oh, I believe you, I just can't get too worked up over it."

"Worked up?" she made it a question.

"She means she cannot get too upset about your threat," Jean-Claude said.

Belle looked back at me. "Why can you not?"

"I've had a lot of vampires threaten me, I can't panic every time."

77

"I am Belle Morte, member of the council on high, do not underestimate me, Anita."

"Tell that to the Earthmover," I said. He'd been a council member that had come to town once upon a time. He'd died.

"I have not forgotten that Jean-Claude slew a council member."

Actually, I'd slain him, but why quibble? "Just go, Belle, please, just go."

"And if I choose to stay? What will you do? What can you do?"

I thought about several options, most of them fatal to one or both of us. Finally, I said, "If you want to keep this body, fine. It's not my body. It's not even my vampire. You want it, knock yourself out."

I leaned back from her and jerked the knife out. There was no way I was leaving a weapon on Musette. She was too likely to take the blade out and stick it in me. The blade pulling out brought a gasp from Belle that plunging it in hadn't.

She grabbed my wrist, as if to keep me from hurting her, but I should have known better. Some small, screaming part of me knew I was still kneeling on the carpet in Jean-Claude's living room, but the rest of me was in a dark, candlelit room. The bed was large and soft, mounded with pillows as if it would rise up in a soft cushioned wave and engulf me. The woman pressed into all that softness lay in a bed of her own dark hair, her eyes a solid golden brown fire, like staring at the sun through a piece of colored glass. Belle Morte stared up at me, her pale body naked. The glory of her spread before me, nothing hidden. I wanted her, wanted her as I'd never wanted anything else in my life.

I came back to myself, with a gasp. Jean-Claude held my other hand in a death grip. Damian was a weight against the back of my body. Jason stood over the rest of us as we knelt. His hands were on Jean-Claude's shoulder, and against the side of my neck, above Damian's hand. I could feel the pulse in my neck pounding against the pulse in the palm of Jason's hand.

I could smell the musty scent of fur, the rich, almost eatable smell of the forest. It was the smell of the pack. The werewolves that had come to guard our back had stepped up through the crowd. I could feel the wolves ranged behind me, feel them like there was an invisible thread between Jason, me, and them. Jean-Claude's ties to the wolves were direct, they were his animal to call. He didn't need Richard's beast to call the wolves. I needed a surrogate wolf to bind me to them. Richard should have been at our back, but he wasn't. If Jason had not been there to be our third, then Belle might have raised the *ardeur*, drowned us in memories of her sweet flesh. Flung us out into the room and turned my Mexican standoff into an orgy.

But Jean-Claude gave me his control through the press of his hand; Damian gave me his desperate reserve through his body molded against my back; Jason fed the pulse of the pack into the bend of my neck. We were not merely a triumvirate of power; through Damian's addition, we were more. And that more was stronger than Belle Morte trapped in Musette's body. If she'd been here in person, it might have been a different story, but she wasn't. She was way the hell in Europe somewhere.

A howl broke out behind me, and another, and another. Jason threw his head back, making a long clean line of his throat. A howl trembled from his mouth, to join with the chorus behind us. The sound rose and fell, one wolf's note dying off, another taking up the call, until the sound rose and fell like music – lonely, trembling, amazing music.

I met Belle's pale brown eyes and found them full of fire, like staring at flames through brown glass. It did remind me of her eyes in the memory she had chosen, but it was just a memory. There was no bite or pull to it now. The *ardeur* lay quiet, held behind the bars we had forged for it, from sheer force of will, and months of practice.

"The last time you rolled the *ardeur* over us, it was new to me. It's not new anymore," I said.

Something flowed under Musette's skin. It was like watching a second face roll underneath her skin. Again, I half expected Belle to burst out through Musette's body like some kind of shapeshifter. But the rolling shape stopped, and those dark fire eyes stared into mine.

"There will be other nights, Anita," she said, in that low, almost purring voice of hers.

I nodded. "I know."

With that she vanished. Musette fell back onto the floor into a . . . dead faint. Her vampires rushed forward. The wolves stayed at my back, the werehyenas stepped up, the wererats drew guns, and Bobby Lee said, "Don't queer our shot, gentlemen."

The werehyenas hesitated, forming two groups one to either side of the vampires. Our vampires peeled off from Musette's and eased through the crowd of wereanimals. "Nobody moves, nobody gets hurt," Bobby Lee said.

"Let them fetch their mistress," Jean-Claude said.

Some of the shape-shifters looked his way, none of the wererats did. We had this much backup not because Jean-Claude had a tie to any other animal except the wolves, but because I'd made friends. The wererats and werehyenas were here for me, not him.

"Ease down, Bobby Lee, let them get Musette. I certainly don't want to have to take care of her."

The men and women, wererats all, with their guns nicely pointed, moved back in two lines so the vampires had to walk between them to reach Musette. Angelito had joined them, but Bobby Lee motioned him back with a wave of his gun barrel. Angelito was imposing, but he was also one of the few humans among them. I wasn't sure the big man was the most dangerous person on their side. A little girl of seven or eight with dark curls cut short around an angelic face flashed dainty fangs and hissed at me. An older boy who looked like a young twelve, or an old ten, picked Musette's shoulders up, raising her limp figure off the ground as if she weighed nothing. He didn't flash fangs, he just looked at me with dark, unfriendly eyes.

A male vamp in a dark conservative suit got Musette's feet, though he made no move to take the small woman from the boy. I knew the male vamp could have carried her easily, but he didn't argue with the boy. The boy didn't lack strength, just height, and leverage.

They carried her back to Angelito, who took her from the others. Musette looked tiny held in his long arms. There were people in the room who had thicker arms than Angelito. The werehyenas were bodybuilders, but there was no one on our side that had the length and size of Musette's little angel.

Jean-Claude stood, drawing me to my feet. Damian moved as I moved. Jason, too. "We have rooms prepared for all of you. You will be escorted to them, then we will leave guards outside your doors, for the protection of all concerned."

Bobby Lee was still holding his gun nice and steady on the vamps. "Anita?" he made my name a question.

"I don't want them wandering around without guards on them, so yeah, sounds like a good idea to me. You guys able to stick around that long?"

"Honey-child, I would follow you to the ends of the earth. 'Course we can." He laid the Southern accent on thick enough to walk across.

"Thanks, Bobby."

"Our pleasure."

"Meng Die, Faust, you know the way to the rooms, show our guards where to go." Meng Die was lovely, delicate, with perfectly straight black hair cut just above her shoulders; her skin was like pale porcelain. She would have looked like a perfect China doll if she hadn't liked wearing skintight black leather most of the time. The leather sort of ruined the image. She was a Master Vampire, and her animal to call, I'd been surprised to learn, was the wolf. Strangely, this didn't make her any more attractive to the wolves or me. She was just too damn unfriendly.

Faust was not much taller than Meng Die, but he didn't make you think delicate, just short. He was cheerfully attractive – like the boy next door if he happened to be a vampire – and had dyed his hair a dark wine-burgundy. His eyes were the color of new pennies as if the brown had a touch of fresh blood in it. He was a Master Vampire but not strong enough to ever be Master of the City, or at least not hold on to it. A weak Master of the City is usually a dead one.

Meng Die and Faust led the way through the drapes and the far corridor beyond. Musette's vamps went next. The wererats and the werehyenas brought up the rear. The drapes swished closed behind them. We were left alone with our thoughts. I hoped everyone else's thoughts were more useful than mine, because all I could think was that Belle wouldn't like being given her hat and shown the door. She'd find a way to make us eat the insult, if she could. Maybe she couldn't, but she was over two thousand years old, according to Jean-Claude. You didn't survive that long without

81

knowing things, things that would make your enemies run scream-ing. The council member we'd killed had been able to cause earthquakes simply by thinking about it. I was pretty sure Belle had her own special tricks. I just hadn't seen them yet.

## 10

LESS THAN AN hour later Jean-Claude and I were in his room, alone. Damian was one of the guards outside our door. We'd split our vamps up among the wereanimals so that, hopefully, the bad vampires couldn't use mind tricks on the wereanimals without the vamps knowing it. We'd done the best we could do, which had actually been pretty damned good. The *ardeur* was still in hiding. I wasn't questioning it, just grateful.

Jean-Claude's large four-poster bed was draped in blue silk, mounded with pillows in at least three vibrant shades of blue. He traded the drapes and pillows to match whatever color the sheets were, so I knew without looking that the sheets would be blue silk. Jean-Claude did not do white sheets, no matter what they were made out of.

He was sitting in the room's only chair, slumped down, hands crossed over his stomach. I was sitting on the rug that he'd put beside the bed. The rug was actually fur, thick and soft, and somehow just by touch you knew it had once been alive. We'd both been strangely reluctant to go to bed. I think we were both afraid the *ardeur* would rise, and we weren't ready for it.

"Let me test my understanding," I said.

Jean-Claude looked at me, moving only his eyes.

"Tomorrow night, if Asher is still nobody's, will they be within their rights to ask for him?"

"Not as they did tonight, no, you have made that impossible now, unless they can take him by force."

I shook my head. "I've been around enough vamp politics to know that if you stop them from doing one thing, they'll do something else, not because they want to, but because it will cause you pain."

He frowned at me.

I sighed. "Let me try that again. Here's the deal, what are they within their rights to ask from us, while they're here?"

"Hunting rights, or willing donors, lovers – the basic needs to be met."

"Sex is a basic need?"

He just looked at me.

"Sorry, sorry. So I understand the willing donor part, they've got to eat. But the lovers, what does that mean, exactly?"

"It would be déclassé to demand lovers for the servants, so Musette's lady's maid and butler are not to be worried over. The two children are special cases. The girl is physically too young, she does not think of such things. The boy is a problem. Bartolomé was precocious, which is why Belle sent Musette to take him."

I stared at him. "Please, tell me that Musette never had sex with the kid?"

He seemed suddenly tired, rubbing his eyes with his fingertips. "Do you wish the truth, or a more pleasant lie?"

"The truth, I guess."

"Belle Morte can smell sexual appetite, it is one of her gifts. Bartolomé may look like a child, but he does not think like one, nor did he when he was human and a true boy of eleven going on twelve. He was the heir to a great fortune. Belle wanted to control that fortune. He was also notorious in an age when noble sons were allowed almost any indiscretion with women who were not of noble blood."

"Explain that," I said.

"He looked like a child, Anita, and he would use that innocent face to maneuver women into compromising situations. By the time they realized that they were in danger of abuse, it was often too late. More than that, he threatened to accuse them of being the aggressor. There was no such phrase as child molestation in that century, but everyone knew it happened. Children were often married as young as ten or eleven, so the people who had such tastes could satisfy their needs within the marriage bed, until their spouses became too old for their tastes, then they would look outside their marriage, or by that time their own children might be old enough."

I stared at him. "I don't think I wanted to know that last part. That is beyond disgusting."

"*Oui, ma petite*, but it is still true. A fortune as large as Bartolomé's would normally be Belle's task. She would never leave such monies, or lands, or titles, to anyone else. But she is not a lover of children, no matter how grown-up they may be, so she cast it to Musette. Who, as you now realize, will do anything our mistress bids her do."

"I got that impression."

"So, yes, she seduced, or allowed herself to be seduced by the boy. Belle gave her a touch of the *ardeur* and Bartolomé was enraptured. Belle did not mean to bring him over to us as a boy. She meant to wait until he grew older, but Bartolomé was thrown from his horse. He had crushed his skull, and was dying. His next brother was only five, and Belle would have no hold on him. She needed Bartolomé, and so she bid Musette finish him."

"How did he feel when he woke up?"

"He was happy to be alive."

"How'd he feel when he finally realized he'd be a little boy forever, no matter how precocious?"

Jean-Claude sighed. "He was . . . unhappy. Bringing children over is forbidden for a reason. Musette did not make Valentina one of us. Belle found that one of her Master Vampires was a pedophile and had brought over children to be his permanent . . . companions." His voice went soft at the end.

I felt ill. I breathed deep and slow. "Sweet Jesus," I said.

"He had broken our prohibition against bringing over children, and when Belle Morte found out why he had done it . . . she slew him. With full permission of the council, she slew him. They destroyed most of the children he had made. They were vampires trapped in children's bodies, and they had been abused." He shook his head. "Their minds did not survive, not whole."

"So how did Valentina escape?" I asked.

"She was his newest and had yet to be touched. She was a child and a vampire but she was not mad. Belle took her in and found her people to care for her. She had human nannies for many years. She had human playmates. I must say that Belle did her best for Valentina. I think she blamed herself for not realizing what a true monster Sebastian was."

85

"Why do I think this ideal picture doesn't stay ideal?"

"You know us too well, *ma petite*. Valentina tried to turn some of her playmates into vampires, so she would not be the only one. When her nanny discovered her, Valentina slit her throat. That was the end of human nannies and human playmates."

"That's why the vampire nanny," I said.

He nodded. "She does not truly need one in the traditional sense of a child's need, but she is forever eight years old, and even today she cannot catch a taxi by herself, register in a hotel, without people wondering. Some well-meaning human will call the police to report the poor abandoned child that's staying in their hotel."

"She must hate it."

"It?"

"Her existence," I said.

He gave half a shrug. "I do not know. I do not speak to Valentina."

"You're afraid of her."

"*Non, ma petite*, but I am unnerved by her. The few children that survive for centuries are twisted things. It cannot be otherwise."

"How did she end up with Musette's entourage?"

"Valentina was taken before her body grew large enough for much physical pleasure. She has turned such energies into other," he licked his lips, "avenues of interest."

I sighed. "Musette is Belle's torturer, which means that Valentina is what, her little assistant in the torture?"

He nodded, head resting against the chair back, eyes closed. "Valentina has been a very apt pupil."

"She's tortured you?"

He nodded, eyes still closed. "I told you that the price for Belle saving Asher's life was my servitude for a century among them. But Belle wished to punish me for leaving her, and for a long time she gave me to pain rather than pleasure."

I went to him, crawling on the floor by his chair, smoothing my skirts down automatically, though there was no one there to see. "So Valentina won't be asking for a lover."

"*Non*."

"Will she try for a . . . what? Submissive?"

"*Oui*."

86

"Can we just refuse?"

"*Oui*."

"Can we make the 'no' stick?"

He opened his eyes and looked down at me. "I believe so, but to say absolutely would be too close to a lie."

I shook my head. "If Musette left tonight, and returned in three months, would we have less ground to stand on?"

"She will not leave, *ma petite*."

"No, that's not what I mean. What I mean is, if she had come in three months after good faith negotiations had gone through, would I still have been allowed to get away with what I did tonight? Or would we have faced the council's wrath?"

"We would have chosen a victim for Musette, or chosen a lover for her, or both before she arrived. It would have been settled and not a surprise."

"You know most human guests don't expect their hosts to supply them with sex partners."

"Nor do most of the bloodlines that descend from the council, but Belle's line is built upon sex, and it has become custom to offer any of Belle's line sex when they visit you. It is assumed that we all carry a touch of her succubus within us."

"That's not true," I said.

"*Non*, but no one of her line has ever wished to dissuade others of the lie."

I smiled, thought about laughing, and was too tired. "We can keep Willie and Hannah safe because they've got to be in charge of the two clubs. We've already negotiated that our businesses are not to be disrupted by the visit," I said.

"Belle was always one to keep her mind on where the money was coming from, so yes, Willie is my manager for The Laughing Corpse, and Hannah is temporary manager of Danse Macabre. The two weakest of my flock are safe away."

"Damian is my vampire servant, I'm your human servant, you're Master of the City, Jason is your *pomme de sang*, Nathaniel is my *pomme de sang*, Micah is my lover and my Nimir-Raj, Richard is Ulfric, and the bodyguards can't guard our bodies if they're screwing other people."

"We have made everyone as safe as we can, *ma petite*."

"There's one name that's conspicuously absent from that list, Jean-Claude."

"Three actually, *ma petite*, four if you count Gretchen."

"Gretchen is crazy, Jean-Claude. You got a special pass for her from Belle because she's still ill, right?" Gretchen had tried to kill me once; as punishment, she got locked up in a coffin for a while. The isolation had driven her even crazier.

"*Oui*, Gretchen will keep to her room for Musette's visit, but that does not protect Meng Die or Faust."

"Faust likes men, and to my knowledge nobody in Musette's party is gay, right?"

"*Oui*, but that is not always a barrier."

"We laid down the law tonight, that no one was to be hurt again. Forcing someone to have sex with a partner they find repugnant is a form of rape, and thus it's harm."

He looked at me, surprised. "*Ma petite*, you are becoming devious."

I shook my head. "Nope, just practical. So Faust is safe, because he only likes men and none of Musette's men likes men. Torture is out, because that's just harm."

"Meng Die will fascinate Bartolomé."

"But again, Meng Die doesn't like children, so Bartolomé would have to rape her to get his way with her, thus . . ."

"She is safe from his advances." He seemed to think about that for a second or two. "But what of Angelito?"

"Isn't he a couple with Musette? Aren't they doing each other?"

"When they wish to, yes."

I frowned at him. "Not a hot pair?"

"Musette's true love is not sex, which is why she and Valentina have been so close for so long."

"Not our problem. If everyone has access to someone they can fuck, or we have no suitable partners for them outside of rape, then everyone's covered. Or have I missed something?"

He thought about it quietly for a few minutes. "*Non, ma petite*. Your machinations are worthy of Belle herself, if her intention were to keep her people safe." Then he looked at me. "Except for one problem. Musette has had sex with Asher in the past, so you cannot make a charge of rape."

"Having sex in the past doesn't mean it can't be rape in the present," I said.

He waved that away with his hand. "I know that you believe that, *ma petite*, I will not even disagree, but Musette will not be dissuaded by the argument. Asher likes both men and women, he has had sex with her and enjoyed it in the past. You have made sure she cannot physically harm him, so it would be merely sex, merely fucking. He would not be harmed by that."

I raised eyebrows at him. "You believe that, that there'd be no harm to it?"

"*Non*, nor does Musette in truth. Musette knows, Belle knows, that to have sex with Musette again after all these years will be painful for Asher. It will harm him, but not in a way that Belle will let us negotiate around. To Belle Morte, if a man has an orgasm, then he must have enjoyed himself. It is her reasoning."

"She really doesn't understand that there's a difference between lust and love, does she?"

"*Non, ma petite, très non.*"

"Why is it always Asher that we can't protect? Asher that we can't save?"

He shook his head. "I have asked that for a very, very long time, *ma petite*. I have yet to find an answer."

I laid my cheek against his knee. "This is the longest I've ever been able to go between feedings." I glanced a my watch. "It's almost two."

"Dawn will come in three, almost four hours. I must rescind the control I have lent you for the *ardeur* before then. You must feed it."

"It's not only your control, is it?"

"No, it is fear and exhaustion, and thinking too hard, and your own growing abilities. In a few more months you will be down to one feeding a day, or a night. You will be able to store up the feedings and go longer."

"My head is practically in your lap, and I don't feel the least stirrings."

He stroked my hair, and it was a comforting touch. I wanted to be held more than I wanted sex. I wanted him to hold me while I drifted off to sleep. That sounded better than anything else I could think of right now.

"Once dawn comes my tie with you will weaken, and you will not be able to keep the *ardeur* at bay. I am sorry, *ma petite*, but we must feed it."

"You're as tired as I am," I said.

"I want nothing more than to climb between the silk sheets and wrap our nude bodies around one another. I want to hold and be held. Sex is a wondrous thing, but tonight I wish to be comforted more than pleasured. I feel like a child in the dark who knows the monsters are under the bed. I want to be told it will be alright, but I am far too old to believe such comforting lies."

Maybe it was because I was tired. Maybe it was because Jean-Claude had just said out loud almost exactly how I felt. I remembered other nights when we'd all been this tired, this frightened, this unsure of what the next nightfall would bring. I remembered Asher and Julianna, and I, we, Jean-Claude holding each other. Simply holding each other, the feel of bare skin and warmth, like a grown-up version of a teddy bear. *Hold me tonight*, Julianna used to say, and unspoken between the two men had been how often her fears allowed them to be as close and frightened as they truly were.

Julianna had been the bridge between the two men. They would never have been able to be so close for so long without her. I had the memories, I knew how many times her needs had brought them together, her love for each of them had bound them close. Jean-Claude had been the brains, Asher the charm, though both were charming and both intelligent, but Julianna had been their heart. One living, beating heart for all three of them.

I could never be Julianna. I didn't have her kindness, her gentleness, her patience. We were so unalike, but here I was centuries later with the same two men. I let out a long breath, took in another, let it out, listened to it shake.

"Is something wrong, *ma petite*, I mean more wrong than I know?"

I raised my face from his knee. "If Asher was truly a ménage à trois with us, then Musette would have to leave him alone, wouldn't she?"

Some expression passed over his face, quickly swallowed away, hidden behind that beautiful, polite mask he wore when he was not

90

sure what expression would help, and what would hurt. "If we had been able to answer truthfully tonight that Asher was in our bed, then Musette could not have asked for him. This is true."

"If he joined us tonight, then tomorrow he'd be safe." My voice sounded so matter of fact, as if I were proposing we go shopping, or get dinner.

His voice was even more careful than mine. "That would be true."

"If I had just let you and Asher be a couple when I wasn't around, then he would have been safe, but I can't." I shook my head. "In theory I don't have a problem with it. I like men. I see men as attractive, so I understand everyone seeing them as attractive. That men are attracted to men makes perfect sense to me. But in practice I can't bring myself to share my man with another man. I can't do it. If I found out you and Asher had been doing it behind my back, I'd dump your ass. I know it's amazingly unfair. I'm sleeping with Micah, and damn near sleeping with Nathaniel, and was having sex with Richard until a few months ago. Yet you have to be with just me. It's monstrously unfair, I know that."

"I am not alienated from your bed when the others are with you, except for Richard, who would never share."

"I know, you get blood from the men because I still won't donate blood to you, but it's not the same."

"I want no one but you, *ma petite*. I have made that clear."

I looked up at him then. "You've made it clear, but I know that you do want someone else besides me. I've felt what you feel when you look at Asher. I see the way you two look at each other. It hurts sometimes just to watch you be in a room together."

"I am sorry, *ma petite*."

I tucked my knees to my chest and hugged them there. "Let me finish this thought, Jean-Claude, please."

He motioned for me to go ahead.

"I can't let you take Asher to your bed, and I can't take Asher to mine. But I remember what it was like for the three of you. I remember how safe it felt. There are moments when I forget that these aren't my memories and I long for what the three of you had. It seems a hell of a lot more peaceful than what we're doing."

91

I hugged my legs so tight, my arms trembled with the force of it. "I don't know if I can go through with it, but I'd like to try."

"Try what, *ma petite*?" His voice was very careful.

"I want Asher safe."

Jean-Claude had gone very still. "I do not understand, *ma petite*."

"Yes, you do."

He shook his head. "*Non*, I will have no misunderstandings here. You must be precise in your meaning."

I couldn't look at him while I said it. "Bring Asher in here for the night. I don't promise, but I want him warm and nude beside us. I want to chase that hurt from his eyes. I want to show him with my hands and my body that I find him lovely." I looked up at him, then, and found his face unreadable. "I don't know at what point I'm going to scream foul and bail on you both. I'm sure there's going to come a point, there usually is, but if we bring him into our bed tonight, in whatever way, then he's safe for tomorrow, right?"

"What will your Nimir-Raj say?"

"He assumed that you and I were intimate with Asher when he got to town. A lot of people assume it."

"You have told him the truth?"

"Yes."

"And won't he be angry about sharing you with yet another man?"

I shook my head. "Micah is more practical than I am, Jean-Claude. It's not just love, or lust, that brings me back to Asher. Tonight it's securing our power base. If Asher is safe, then we're all safer. His pain can't be used against us."

"How very practical of you, *ma petite*."

"I've learned from the best."

He gave me a look, one eyebrow raised. "If I were truly practical in matters of the heart, things would have gone more quickly between us."

"Maybe, or maybe not, you knew if you pushed too hard, I'd have either run, or tried to kill you."

He gave that graceful shrug. "Perhaps, but I should ask, so there are no misunderstandings, do you mean to bring Asher to our bed only for tonight?"

"Would it make a difference?" I asked.

"It may to him."

I tried to wrap my head around it all, and failed. "I don't know. I know that I don't want to give up alone time with you, just you. I know that I don't want to always have company."

"Julianna and Asher managed alone time even though we were a threesome."

"For the first time in a long time my personal life is as close as it's ever been to working. I don't want to screw that up."

"I understand."

"I guess, I want Asher safe, I want to chase that flinching out of his eyes, but in the real world we are just running this up the flagpole. If it works, great, but if it doesn't work, then what? Will Asher have to leave? Will you lose your second? Will it hurt you and Asher more? Will . . ."

He touched fingertips to my lips. "Shhh, *ma petite*. I have called Asher. He comes even now."

I felt my eyes go big, my breath freeze in my throat, while my pulse beat like a crazed thing. What had I done? Nothing yet. The ten thousand dollar question was, what was I about to do, and could I live with it later?

# 11

ASHER CAME THROUGH the door, slowly, his face carefully hidden behind a fall of golden hair. He'd changed to a fresh, unbloodied shirt. It was white and the color did not suit him. "You called," he said. I froze, still hugging my knees, my pulse suddenly pounding in my throat. Yet my breath stopped for a second or two.

"We did," Jean-Claude said in that careful voice.

Asher looked up then, a glimpse of face through all that hair. I think it was the "we" that brought the reaction.

Jean-Claude had sat up very straight before Asher came to the door. He was elegant, poised, in his leather and silk.

I was still huddled on the rug at his feet, staring at Asher like he was the fox and I was the rabbit. Jean-Claude touched my shoulder, and I jumped.

I looked up at him, and he was staring down at me. "It must be your decision, *ma petite*."

"Why is everything always my decision?" I asked.

"Because you will not tolerate anything else."

Oh, I remembered now. "Great," I whispered.

He squeezed my shoulder gently. "Nothing has been said. We can go on as we are."

I shook my head. "No, I won't be the one responsible for tomorrow night if it goes all wrong. I won't risk him, because of my moral outrage."

"As you like, *ma petite*," he said, in that careful voice that said nothing.

"What has happened now?" Asher asked, and his voice wasn't quite empty, there was a thread of fear in it. With what was sleeping down the hall, I couldn't blame him.

I eased my arms from around my knees. They were stiff from holding on too tight. I tried to smooth my numb hands down my legs to touch my skirt and found only my hose. The navy skirt was too short for me to have been sitting the way I was. If there'd been anyone in the room to see, they'd have been able to tell my underwear matched it.

I got my knees under me, moving slowly, stiffly, my body tight with tension.

"What has happened?" Asher asked, and this time his voice was bland.

"Nothing, *mon ami*," Jean-Claude said, "or rather, nothing more."

"It's my fault," I said. I got to my feet, still moving slowly.

"What is your fault?" Asher was looking from one to the other of us, trying to read something from our faces.

I stepped off the fur, and my high heels made a sharp sound on the floor. "That you're in danger from Musette."

"You have done all you can to protect me, Anita, more than I had ever dreamt. No one challenges Musette for fear of Belle Morte. You have done what many council members would fear to do."

"Ignorance is bliss," I said.

He gave me a quick look through the shine of his hair. "What does that mean?"

I walked towards him, where he still stood just inside the door. "It means that maybe I can be brave because I don't know any better. I've never seen Belle in person. Don't get me wrong, she's impressive enough from a distance, but I've never met the real thing."

I was standing in front of him now. He had turned his face so that only the perfect half showed. He hadn't hidden himself from me this completely in months.

I reached up to touch the side of his face he'd turned away, and he flinched, jerking back hard enough to make the door rattle. "*Non, non.*"

"I've touched you before," I said, and my voice was low, soft, the voice you'd use to talk to a skittish animal or a man on a ledge.

He turned his whole face away from me. "You saw the paintings. You saw what I once was, and you have seen now what I looked like when the . . . wounds were fresh." He turned his back, hands on the door, shaking his head. "You have seen what Belle Morte saw."

I shook my head, realized he couldn't see it, and touched his shoulder.

He flinched.

I glanced back at Jean-Claude, and his face was empty, only his eyes showing the barest glimpse of a pain so deep it had nearly destroyed three people.

I pressed my body against Asher's back, moved my arms up his sides, hugging him from behind. He froze under my touch, so still, folding himself away, going deep inside where it wouldn't hurt. I pressed my cheek against his back and held him while his body went quiet under my touch.

I swallowed past tears that I would not shed. My voice was steady, though. "I have seen you through Jean-Claude's memories long before tonight. I remember the glory of you under my hands, against my body." I molded my body against his, clung to him. "I needed no painting to show me your beauty."

A shudder ran through his body, and he tried to turn, to throw me off, but I held on, and he couldn't move away without hurting me. "Let me go, Anita, let me go."

"No," I said, "no, not tonight."

He made small struggling motions trapped against the door, like a man trying to pace a room that was only an inch wider than his own body.

"What do you want from me?" There was something close to tears in his voice.

"Join us tonight, that's what I want, join us."

He stopped his restless movements and went still again, but not like before. I could feel his heart beating against my cheek. I'd have sworn it hadn't been beating a second before.

"Join you how?" his voice was a strangled whisper.

I grabbed his shirt and used it to turn him around. He moved slowly, like trying to turn the earth against its axis. He pressed his back to the door and showed me only what remained of that perfect profile.

I pulled on the shirt, trying to lead him into the room, but he would not be moved this far. He looked past me to Jean-Claude. "I cannot do this." His voice held such pain.

"What do you think she is asking?" Jean-Claude's voice was still so carefully empty.

"She will do anything to keep her people safe, even take a cripple to her bed for one night."

I wadded the shirt in my hands and was forced to go to him, because he would not come to me. "I do want to keep you safe from Musette, and this will do it, but that's not why, not really."

He looked down at me, and there was a world in his eyes, a world of pain and need and horror, so big, so lonely. The first hot tear grazed my cheek. I spoke softly to him in French, and I understood some of what I said.

Asher grabbed my wrists and forced me away from him. "*Non*, Jean-Claude, not like this. It is either her desire, or it is not to be. I will not divide you from what remains of your triumvirate. I would rather spend a night in Musette's bed than weaken your power so. You must be strong while they are here, or we will all perish."

I took a deep breath, and it was as if something had pulled back from me, like a veil being lifted. I turned and glanced at the vampire behind me. "Did you do that on purpose?"

He hid his face in his hands and said, spoke, voice no longer empty, "I cannot help wanting what I want, *ma petite*, forgive me."

I turned back to Asher. "It isn't my desire you want, Asher. You know I'm attracted to you."

He tried to look away, but I touched his face, and this time he didn't flinch away. He let me turn him to face me again, my fingers on the edge of his chin. The skin was still smooth there, even though it was on the right side where most was ruined. It was almost as if the people that had done this to him couldn't bring themselves to ruin the perfect curve of his lips.

"It's not lust you want from me."

His gaze dropped. He almost closed his eyes, the expression on his face like a man bracing for a blow. He whispered, "No."

I went up on tiptoe, put my hands on either side of his face, one so smooth like satin and silk, but softer, the other rough, pitted, hardly feeling like skin at all. "I do love you, Asher."

His eyes opened, and they were so raw, so full of so many things that could be used to hurt.

"I don't know how much was Jean-Claude's memories at first, but whatever it began as, I do love you. Me, no one else."

"Yet you have not taken me to your bed."

"I love a lot of people that I don't sleep with. Okay, that I don't have sex with."

The expression in his eyes began to die. I realized what I'd said, "I want you to come to bed tonight, please, Asher, and not just for sleeping."

He put his hands on either side of mine. "Only to keep me safe from Musette."

I couldn't argue that, but . . . "That's true, but does that matter so very much? Does it matter that that's why?"

He smiled gently and moved my hands away from his face. "Yes, Anita, it does matter why. You will take me to your bed tonight, but tomorrow you will feel guilty and you will run away again."

I frowned at him. "You talk like I've done this before with you, and I haven't."

He patted my hands between his. "You took four men into that bed over there, four of us, yet you have sex with only Jean-Claude. You feed the *ardeur* from Nathaniel, but you have not fucked him." He let go of my hands and shook his head, laughing. "Only you could have the strength of will to sleep night after night beside such beauty and not take all that Nathaniel had to offer. I have met saints and priests over the centuries that had not your will to resist temptation."

"I don't seem to be resisting all that much anymore," I said, hands on hips.

He laughed again, smile fading as he did it. "Jason you have put firmly back into the box, marked 'friend.' But what of me? I do not wish to join you in that bed again, if tomorrow I will be merely another friend. I cannot bear it."

I frowned up at him. I'd done my best to forget what happened when Belle Morte caused the *ardeur* to rise months ago. Thanks to her, I'd participated in the closest thing I hoped to ever get to an orgy. No intercourse, but a lot of hands and bodies touching where they shouldn't have been. Asher was right; I'd done my best to ignore the whole thing. Ignore it hard enough, and it never happened. But of course it had happened, and I'd not dealt with it.

"What do you want me to say? I'm sorry that I'm a little squeamish about having been in bed with four men at the same time. Yeah, it embarrassed me, so sue me."

"Tonight will embarrass you, too."

"A lot of things embarrass me, Asher, I can't help that."

"You cannot help but be who and what you are, Anita. I would not change you, but I also will not be just a night of charity in your bed. I tell you I could not bear being cast out again."

I knew in that instant that he didn't mean me casting him out from our bed after the *ardeur*. He meant what Belle had done to him all those centuries ago. She had thrown him away like a damaged toy. After all, you can always buy more toys.

I started to pace back and forth in front of him, not looking at either of them, but doing something, anything for the nervous energy that was building up. "What do you want from me, Asher? A guarantee?"

"Yes," he said, at last. "That is exactly what I want from you."

I stopped pacing and looked at him. "What kind of guarantee? That I won't freak out about this tomorrow?" I shook my head. "I'm sorry, I can't promise, because I don't know how I'll feel."

"What will Micah say, if he finds out you've been with me?"

"Micah is okay with it."

Asher looked at me.

"I know, I know, I keep waiting for him to pitch a fit about something. He's fine with sharing me with Jean-Claude, and Nathaniel, and, I quote, 'anyone else that you need to include,' unquote."

Asher widened eyes at me. "My, isn't he understanding."

"You have no idea," I said. "When he came into my life, he said he'd do anything to stay with me, anything to be my Nimir-Raj. So far he's meant it."

"He seems perfect for you," Asher said, voice full of a soft irony.

"I know, makes me wonder when the other shoe will drop and he'll turn on me."

Asher touched my face, which made me look at him. He was looking full at me now, those ice blue eyes so sincere. "I would

99

never want to do anything that would damage what you have built in your life. If we do this and you run away, then Jean-Claude will have damaged his relationship with you, and I will leave."

I felt my eyes go wide. "What do you mean, you'll leave?"

"I mean if you take me to your bed tonight and cast me out tomorrow, I will leave. I will no longer watch Jean-Claude be in love with others while I wait. It will take time to find another Master who will want me, and probably not as a second. I know that I am weak for a master. I have no animal to call," he shook his head, "so many of my powers are useless except in intimate situations, and once," he almost touched the scarred side of his face, but let his hand fall away, "once this happened, no one would let me get close enough to use my powers on them."

He licked his lips, sighing at the same time, and that one gesture made me catch my breath. I did want him, I'd wanted him the way a woman wants a man for a long time. But lust alone had never been enough for me.

"You're saying that if we take you to our bed tonight, but I freak tomorrow, and it's only this one time, that you'll leave us?" I asked.

He nodded. He didn't even need to think about it.

"You're giving me an ultimatum, Asher, I'm not good at ultimatums."

"I know that, but I have to protect myself, Anita. I cannot live this close to heaven and not be allowed inside. I think it will drive me mad in the end." He leaned back against the door and looked past me to Jean-Claude. "I have been thinking for some months now that I should go. It is too hard on all of us. Know that it has healed some of the wounds to be with you as a friend again, Jean-Claude." He turned and smiled at me. "And seeing the way you watch me has helped, more than it's hurt, Anita." He turned, put his hand on the doorknob.

I put my hand flat on the door, holding it.

Asher looked at me. "Let me go, Anita, you know you don't want this."

"What am I supposed to say to that, Asher? That you're right? That if Musette hadn't come today that I wouldn't be making this offer now? You're right, I wouldn't be." I pressed myself against the side of the door. "But the thought of you leaving, of never seeing you again . . ." I shook my head, and damn it if I was going to cry again. "Don't go, please, don't go."

"I have to go, Anita." He touched my shoulder, tried to move me out of the way so he could open the door.

I shook my head. "No."

He frowned at me. "*Ma cherie*, you do not love me, not truly. If you do not love me, and you do not want me, then you must let me go."

"I do love you, and I do want you."

"You love me as a friend, you want me, but you want many men, yet you do not give yourself to them. I have all eternity, but my patience is not good enough to out-wait you, *ma cherie*. You have defeated me. I would have tried to seduce you, but . . ." Again he almost touched the scarred side of his face, but his hand fell away, as if he could not bear to touch himself. "I have seen the men you have turned down. Such perfection, and you walk away without so much as a regret." He frowned as if he didn't understand it, but he knew it to be true. "What could I offer that they could not?"

He put his hands against my shoulder and gently tried to move me out of the way. I pressed my back into the doorframe, my hand on the doorknob. "No," was all I could think to say.

"Yes, *ma cherie*, yes. It is time."

I shook my head. "No." I pressed my back into the door so hard that I knew I'd be bruised in the morning. I couldn't let him go. I knew somehow that if he opened that door, we would never get another chance.

I prayed for words. I prayed to be able to speak my heart and not to be afraid. "I let Richard walk out on me. I think he'd have gone anyway, but I just sat on the floor and watched him go. I didn't stand in his way. I figured it was his choice, and you can't hold someone if they don't want to be held. If someone really wants to be free of you, you have to let them go. Well, fuck that, fuck that all to hell. Don't go, Asher, please, don't go. I love the way your hair shines in the light. I love the way you smile when you're not trying to hide or impress anyone. I love your laughter. I love the way your voice can hold sorrow like the taste of rain. I love the way you watch Jean-Claude when he moves through a room, when

101

you don't think anyone's watching, because it's exactly the way I watch him. I love your eyes. I love your pain. I love you."

I closed the distance between us, wrapped my arms around him, pressed my cheek to his chest, dried tears on the silk of his shirt, and was still whispering, "I love you, I do love you," when he raised my face and kissed me, really kissed me, for the very first time.

# 12

WE BROKE FROM that gentle kiss, and I led Asher to the bed by the hand. He pulled back, coming like a reluctant child.

Jean-Claude stood by the bed, his face as blank as he could make it. "There is one thing I must say before we begin. I am controlling *ma petite's* *ardeur*, but there will come a point in all this where I will lose control. I cannot guarantee what will happen when that control is lost."

Asher and I stood beside him, holding hands. He was clinging to my hand with a fierceness that was almost painful. His voice did not show the tension I felt in his body. "If I thought it was only the *ardeur* which made Anita want to take me to her bed, then I would say no, because when the *ardeur* had cooled, she would cast me aside as she did before." He raised my hand to his lips and laid the softest touch across my knuckles. "I believe Anita wishes me in her bed. The *ardeur* may rise, or fall, it is all the same to me now."

Jean-Claude looked at me. "*Ma petite.*"

"I would rather do as much of this as possible before the *ardeur*, but I understand that it's going to be . . . hard on you." I shrugged. "I don't know. I know I'm committed to this, so I guess it's okay."

He raised an eyebrow at me. "You are never convincing when you lie, *ma petite.*"

"Now that's just not true," I said, "I lie very well, thank you."

"Not to me."

I shrugged. "I'm doing the best I can here, Jean-Claude." I looked up at the ceiling as if I could see the sky through all the rock above us. "I know one thing, I want whatever we're doing done before dawn. I do not want you guys to fade in the middle."

"*Ma petite* still finds it unnerving that we die at dawn," Jean-Claude said.

"What time is it?" Asher asked.

103

I looked at my watch. "We're down to about two and a half hours."

"Barely enough time," Asher said. And something about what he said, or the way he said it, made Jean-Claude do that masculine chuckle that only men do, and only about women, or sex. I wasn't sure I'd ever heard that sound from Jean-Claude.

I was suddenly very aware that I was the only girl, and they were both men. I know that sounds silly. I mean, I knew that already, but . . . I suddenly felt it. It was like walking into a bar and feeling all those eyes follow you as you walk, like lions watching gazelles.

If either of the men had turned that same look to me, I think I would have bolted, but they didn't. Jean-Claude crawled onto the bed, still fully clothed, and held out his hand to me. I stared at that long-fingered, pale hand, graceful even in that small movement. Asher's hand squeezed, more gently, on my other hand.

I realized in that moment that if I chickened out, that would be the end of it. There would be no pressure from either of them. But Asher would be gone, not tonight, but soon. I didn't want him to be gone.

I took Jean-Claude's hand, and he pulled me gently onto the silk bedspread. Silk is slippery when you're wearing hose. Their hands on mine kept me from slipping off the edge of the bed. They half pulled me onto the bed.

"Why is it," I said, "that *you* never slide off the bed when you're wearing silk?"

"Centuries of practice," Jean-Claude said.

"I recall when you weren't so practiced. Remember the Duchess Vicante?" said Asher.

Jean-Claude blushed, a faint hint of pink. I hadn't even known he could blush. "What happened?" I asked.

"I fell," he said, trying for dignity and failing, because he smiled.

"What he will not say is that he cut his chin on a silver mirror that he broke when he fell off the Duchess and her silk sheets. Blood everywhere, and the cuckold husband on the stairs."

I looked at Jean-Claude. He nodded, shrugged.

"What happened?" I asked.

"The duchess cut herself on one of the shards of glass and told her husband it was her own blood. She was a very enterprising woman, was the Duchess Vicante."

"So you both knew each other when you weren't perfectly suave."

Jean-Claude said, "No, Asher watched me learn my lessons, but he had five years with Belle before I came to court. If he had rough edges they were worn away by the time I arrived."

"I had them, *mon ami*," Asher said, and he smiled. I was over-whelmed with a flood of images of that smile. That smile when his hair was in long locks and the hat on his head graceful with feathers, that smile by candlelight, that smile while we played chess and Julianna sewed by the fire, that smile in a spill of clean sheets and Julianna's laughter.

It had been a long time since we'd seen that smile. We drew him to the bed, and the smile vanished. Jean-Claude swept the bed-spread aside to reveal sheets a little bluer than Asher's eyes, blue as the daytime sky, cerulean blue. But Asher stayed on his knees, as if afraid to lay upon the bed. I could see his pulse thudding in his throat, and it had nothing to do with vampire or shape-shifter powers, only fear, I think.

Asher was afraid. I could taste his fear on the back of my tongue. I could swallow it, enjoy the bouquet of it, like a fine wine to whet the appetite.

The fear called to that piece of me that was Richard's beast. It roiled inside me like a cat stretching, exploring the space it was trapped in. A thin growl trickled from my lips.

"Control, *ma petite*, do not lose it so soon."

It was hard to think, let alone talk. I came to my knees and raised Asher's shirt, my fingers playing along his skin. I wanted to rip his shirt off and put my mouth to that tender skin. But it wasn't sex I was thinking of. Vampires may not feed off each other, but a werewolf will eat a vampire.

I closed my eyes, forced my hands away from his body. "I'm trying, but you know what happens if I push the *ardeur* off too long."

"The other hungers rise, *oui, ma petite*. I have not forgotten."

"You can't help control Richard's beast." My voice sounded hoarse.

*"Non."*

I looked into Asher's wide blue eyes, so afraid, so very afraid, and not of my beast. It helped steady me, but I knew it wouldn't last long, whatever we were going to do had to be done quickly.

"I want to see you nude for the first time without the *ardeur* riding me, Asher. But there isn't much time." I tried to draw him down onto the bed, but he wouldn't come.

Jean-Claude propped himself up on the pillows and held out his arms, almost the way you'd reach for a baby. He spoke softly in French, but I couldn't catch it all, most of it was a plea to hurry.

Asher crawled onto the bed completely, though every movement was slow, reluctant. He let himself be settled down against Jean-Claude's body, but they were both fully clothed, and the way they were sitting, they could have been in any club. It wasn't so much sexual as comforting.

I looked at the two of them and knew someone was going to have to take off some clothes. Fine. I stripped off my jacket and tossed it to the floor.

Jean-Claude raised eyebrows.

"If we keep going this carefully it'll be dawn and nothing will have changed." I had to slide off the bed to get the skirt off, and left it in a pile with my blouse. The panties and bra were a matched pair, a shiny navy satin. When I'd found them, they had reminded me of the color of Jean-Claude's eyes.

I expected to feel embarrassed standing there in my underwear, but I didn't. Maybe I'd spent too much time around the shape-shifters and their casual nudist policy. Or perhaps, it just didn't seem wrong to be undressed in front of Asher. I don't know, but I didn't question it. I climbed carefully back onto the cerulean silk, so that I didn't slide off again.

"You have truly decided to do this," Asher said, in a voice that was soft, uncertain.

I nodded, as I crawled in my thigh-high hose and high heels across the bed to them. I kept the heels because I knew Jean-Claude liked it, and he'd worn enough boots to bed for me. Turn about can be fair play.

I tapped Asher's ankles, and he opened his legs a little. I crawled between his legs, having to force my body up between his calves,

106

his knees. Jean-Claude's legs on either side of his seemed to hold him tight against me. I was left to worm my way between his thighs, using my hips, my legs, and finally impatient, my hands, to spread him wide before me. It left me, finally, kneeling between his legs, my knees pressed up against him, which was actually a lot less erotic than it sounds, because he was still wearing his pants, and the angle was odd.

I reached for the buttons on his shirt. Asher grabbed my hands. "Slowly, *ma cherie*."

I raised eyebrows at him. "We don't have time for slow."

He rolled his head back so he could see Jean-Claude. "Is she always this impatient?"

"She begins like an American man, but she does foreplay like she's French."

"What's that supposed to mean?" I asked.

"Let us help you undress, *mon ami*, and you will not need to ask questions, for you will know."

Asher's hands dropped away from mine, and I unbuttoned his shirt. I did do it quickly, because time was not on our side. I did not want to be in the bed with them when they died at dawn. I was still unnerved when Jean-Claude did it with me, I did not want to see it done in stereo.

Jean-Claude raised Asher up, and between the two of us we peeled the long-sleeved shirt off of his upper body. "I would love to linger on every piece of your body, Asher, but I want to see you nude before dawn. Next time, if we start earlier, we can take our time."

He smiled. "Next time, you have not seen all there is to see, do not promise until you have seen, as they say, the whole show."

I leaned into him, our faces only inches apart. "I don't believe there is anything you could show me that would make me not want you."

"I almost believe that, *ma cherie*, almost."

I leaned back enough on my knees to cradle his face between my hands. The difference in texture wasn't jarring, it was just part of touching Asher. I kissed him, long, slow, exploring him, softly with my lips. I drew back enough to see his face.

"Believe it." I drew my fingers down the edge of his jaw on

107

either side, tickling nails across the smooth line of his neck, one hand mirroring the other, until I came to his chest. It wasn't hands I wanted to use there.

I kissed along the scarred edge of his collarbone, but the scars made the skin too thick, I had to move to the other side to nibble along his collarbone, to give him that safe edge of teeth.

He shuddered for me.

I moved back to the right side and kissed down until I found his nipple, stranded in all that hardness. I wasn't sure if his nipple had the sensitivity it had had before. There was only one way to find out. I licked his nipple, a quick flick of tongue and felt the skin move, contract. I used my hands to help mound that side of his chest so that I could find a mouthful of him. The scars were harsh to my mouth, but his nipple drew tight under my tongue, my mouth, and lightly, teeth. Only when I'd thoroughly explored the right, did I turn to the left. His left nipple was easier to take into my mouth, easier to tease. I used more teeth, and he groaned as I marked him, lightly, nothing that wouldn't fade within moments.

I licked down the left side of his chest, his stomach, then moved back to the right and explored the scarred flesh as I had the other, because I knew now, that scarred or not, it worked. He could feel my mouth on his skin, my fingers trailing lower. If he could feel then I wanted to give him everything I could.

My mouth came to his waist, the belt, the top of his pants. I licked from one side of his waist to the other, then came back to the right side and licked along the front of his flat stomach, so the tip of my tongue eased inside the very top of his pants, even with the belt.

Asher's voice came breathy, harsh, "You have taught her well."

"I can take little credit for it, *mon ami*, she enjoys her work."

I rolled eyes up at them. "Please, stop talking about me like I can't understand you."

"Our most sincere apologies," Jean-Claude said.

"*Oui*," Asher said, "it was not an insult."

"No, but you assume that if I'm any good it has to be because a man taught me. That's so sexist."

"We can only apologize again, *ma petite*."

I undid the buckle on Asher's belt, and he didn't stop me this time. I got the top fastener undone, but I've never been good at unzipping a man when he's sitting down. I think I'm always a little afraid I'll get him caught in the zipper.

"Some help here," I said.

Jean-Claude lifted, Asher helped, and the zipper came down, revealing that he was wearing royal blue bikini's in silk, what else? There is no way to get real pants off of anyone gracefully. I peeled the pants down Asher's long legs, slipped off the shoes that he was still wearing, there were no socks to bother with. He lay back, cradled against Jean-Claude, wearing nothing but the tiny blue silk undies. I wanted to snatch them away from him. I wanted to see him completely nude, it seemed more important than anything else. To finally see if the scars went all the way across.

I crawled forward and licked the edge of his stomach, so that my tongue dipped just below the waistband of the silk, an echo of what I'd done to his pants. I could feel him pressed against the thin cloth, the hardness of him brushing against my chin as I moved around his waist.

I went back to the right side and the scars that dribbled down to mid-thigh. I licked, kissed, and bit along them until he cried out. Then I did the same to his other thigh, going lower until I licked the back of his knee, and he whimpered.

Jean-Claude's voice came almost strangled, "*Ma petite*, please."

I looked up, the tip of my tongue still playing lightly on the very edge of the bend of Asher's knee. Asher's eyes were rolled almost back into his head. I knew things through Jean-Claude's memories that only a lover would know, such as the fact that he loved having the backs of his knees licked.

"Please, what?" I asked.

"Please, finish it."

I knew what he meant. I crawled back up until I was kneeling between their legs again. The blue silk was stretched tight, and this time it was very erotic.

I slid my fingers in the top of the silk, and it was Asher's hands that spilled eager, helping slide the silk down his hips. I pulled the silk down his thighs, but was only half paying attention, because I was staring at what had been revealed.

Scars dribbled from his thigh towards the groin like white

109

worms frozen under the skin, but they stopped a few inches short of the groin, and he lay thick, and long, and straight, and perfect.

I had a confused image of him with the scars fresh, and he was misshapen, unable to become fully erect, twisted to one side, unable to perform.

I had to shake my head to clear the memory. I met Jean-Claude's gaze. I'd never seen him look so utterly lost, shocked, amazed. I had never seen so many different emotions flow across his face. He was finally caught between laughter and tears. "*Mon ami*, what . . ."

"There was a doctor only a few years ago, who thought that most of the scarring was in the foreskin, and it was."

Jean-Claude laid his head on Asher's shoulder, lost in that golden hair, and he wept, and cried. "All this time . . . all this time, and I thought it was my fault, you were ruined, and it was my fault."

Asher reached back and stroked Jean-Claude's hair. "It was never your fault, *mon ami*. If you had been with us when we were taken, they would have done to you what they did to me, and that I could not have borne. If you had not been free to save me, I would be dead now, along with our Julianna."

They held each other and cried, and laughed, and healed, and I was suddenly superfluous, kneeling on the bed in my lingerie. And for once, I didn't mind in the least.

# 13

JEAN-CLAUDE RELEASED THE *ardeur* with less than an hour to go, before they would die. I did not want to be trapped underneath anyone when that happened. But the *ardeur* had been denied longer than I'd ever denied it, and it was like a force of nature, a storm that broke over us, washed away Jean-Claude's clothes and what was left of mine.

I took Asher into my mouth and explored the perfection of him, found the one thin scar that trailed down his scrotum. I sucked the ridge of scar tissue into my mouth and made him cry out above me.

It was chance more than planning that put Jean-Claude underneath me, inside me, with Asher at my back, his weight beating into both of us, but without an opening to claim. Or without an opening I was willing to share. I could feel the length of Asher pressed along my back. Every time Jean-Claude pushed himself up inside me, Asher pushed himself against my back, wedged between the cheeks of my buttocks. They echoed each other perfectly. When one moved, the other moved. Until somewhere in the middle of it all, I begged Asher to enter me, take me.

Jean-Claude's voice came as if from a great distance, *"Non, mon chardonneret*, we have done no preparation. She has never had it done before."

Dimly I realized what I'd asked and was happy someone could think well enough to stop me from letting others hurt me. But part of me was angry, the *ardeur* wanted Asher inside, wanted to drink him in.

I rode Jean-Claude's body, while Asher's body rode mine. Jean-Claude's hands were on my waist, holding me in place, steadying me, directing me, the way you lead a dance partner. One of Asher's hands propped him up on the bed but the other had spilled up to cup my breast, his hand kneading, pulling, just this side of pain.

I felt the building pressure inside me, that feeling that preceded the explosion, and I didn't want it yet, not yet. I wanted Asher, the way I wanted Jean-Claude. I wanted, needed him to pierce my body. "Please, Asher, please, be inside me, please!"

He drew my hair to one side and bared my neck. The *ardeur* flared through me. "Yes, Asher, yes."

That warm deep well was filling up, up inside me, there were only seconds to have him join us. I wanted his release with ours. I wanted him with us.

There seemed like there was something else I should have been remembering but it was lost in the pounding of Jean-Claude's body, the rhythm of my hips, the feel of his hands on my waist, Asher's hand on my breast, tight enough for pain now, the feel of him so solid, so wet from his own body, so that he moved in a channel of his own moisture, yet I knew he had not come.

He raised the hand from the bed and cupped my head to one side, holding it, straining my neck in a long, clean line.

It was as if they knew, they both knew what my body was about to do, as if they could smell it, or hear it, or taste it. At the moment that that warmth spilled over the edge, as the first drop of it spilled over my skin, tightened my body; Asher struck. There was one moment of sharp pain, and the pain fed into the pleasure, and I remembered what I had forgotten. Asher's bite was pleasure.

I rode that pleasure over and over and over until I screamed out, wordless, soundless, skinless, boneless, I was nothing, but the warm spilling pleasure. There was nothing else.

Jean-Claude came screaming, his nails digging into my skin, and that brought me back, reminded me I had a body, that skin contained me, that bones and muscles rode the body underneath me. Asher came in a scalding wave against my back, as his mouth stayed locked on my throat. We fed on one another.

My *ardeur* drank Jean-Claude up through the warm moistness of my body, through the skin wherever it touched his. His *ardeur* drank me down, pulling down the long shaft of him like a hand inside my body taking things away. My *ardeur* drank Asher down, absorbed him where he lay on my skin, sucked him in as he pulled at me. The feel of his mouth locked on my neck was like a trap, the *ardeur* sucking him down through his mouth, and he, sucking my blood, feeding, swallowing, drinking me down. As long as he fed, he brought orgasm in one crashing wave after another, wave after wave of pleasure, and it wasn't until Jean-Claude cried out underneath me that I realized, through his own marks, he was able to feel what I was feeling.

Asher rode us both, rode us and brought us, rode us and brought us, until when he drew back there was blood pouring from his mouth and I knew he'd taken more than he needed merely to feed. It wouldn't kill me, but in that one shining moment I wasn't sure it mattered. It was the kind of pleasure you'd beg for, kill for, maybe, maybe even let yourself die for.

I collapsed on top of Jean-Claude, twitching, unable to control my body, unable to do more than shiver. Jean-Claude lay trembling underneath me. Asher collapsed on top of us. I felt him tremble against my back. We lay shaking, trembling, waiting for one of us to be able to move enough to walk, or scream, or anything. Then dawn came, and I felt their souls slip away, felt their bodies go slack and empty. I was pressed between the frantic pulse and warmth of their bodies, the fluids not even cooled on our skin, and suddenly, Asher was heavy, and Jean-Claude was totally limp under all the weight.

I struggled to get out from between them, but my arms and legs weren't working yet. I did not want to lie here while their bodies cooled. I couldn't get up. I couldn't get Asher off of me. I couldn't make my body work. How much blood had I lost? Too much? How much?

I was dizzy, light-headed, and I couldn't tell if it was from the sex, or if Asher had truly taken too much blood. I tried to push him off of me, I should have been able to do that, and I couldn't. The first edge of nausea hit me, and I knew it was blood loss. I touched my neck and found that blood was still seeping from the puncture wounds. That shouldn't have been happening. Should it? I never donated blood voluntarily. I didn't know how long the wounds should bleed.

I tried to lift with my arms, like doing a push-up, and the world swam in streams of colors, dizziness threatened to engulf the world. I did the only thing I could think of – I screamed.

# 14

THE DOOR OPENED and it was Jason. I don't think I'd ever been so happy to see him. I managed to say, "Help me." My voice sounded weak and scared, and I hated it, but I also was feeling nauseous and dizzy, and that wasn't post-coital languor, it was blood loss.

Now that I could see again, I realized I was drenched in blood – and other things – but it was mainly the blood that was worrying me, because it was all mine.

Jason rolled Asher off of me. He moved with that boneless ease that only a truly dead body has. I don't know what the difference between sleep and death is, but you know instantly when you move even an arm whether it's death, or whether it's sleep.

Asher lay there on his back, his hair spilled around his face like a halo, crimson blood glittered on his chin, his neck, his upper chest. The scars didn't take away from the beauty of him nude. They weren't the first thing you noticed, or even the third. He lay, drenched in my blood, like some fallen god, come down to death at last.

Even sick from loss of blood, I could not find him anything but beautiful. What the fuck was wrong with me?

Jason had to help me slide off of Jean-Claude, catching me in his arms, holding me like you'd hold a child. I was nude, he'd just dragged me from a bed where I'd obviously had sex with two men, yet Jason hadn't made a single quip, or joke. When Jason had this much ammunition but didn't tease, things were bad.

I laid my head against Jason's shoulder, and that helped the dizziness, made the world a little less shaky. He started to turn me away from the bed, but I said, "Wait, not yet."

He stopped moving. "What?"

"I want to remember this."

"What?" he asked again.

"The way they look together." They both lay on their backs, but

114

whereas Asher looked like some fallen death god, Jean-Claude looked like a god of a different kind. His thick black hair lay in a heavy mass around his head, carelessly arranged like a dark frame for that pale, pale face. His lips were half-parted, his lashes thick as lace upon his cheeks. He lay as if he had fallen asleep after some great passion, one hand across his stomach, the other at his side, one knee bent, so that he seemed almost displayed. Only Jean-Claude could die and look this pretty while he did it.

"Anita, Anita," I realized that Jason had been talking for a while. "How much blood did they take?"

My voice came out hoarse, my mouth was dry. "Not they, only Asher."

He settled me closer in his arms, almost like he was hugging me. His leather jacket creaked as he moved. His bare chest was very warm against my naked skin. "He didn't just feed." Jason sounded disapproving, which you didn't hear much.

"He got caught up in the moment, I think."

He shifted me so that he could free up a hand to touch my forehead, which seemed silly since I was nude, but we often fall into habit when we're stressed. You check someone's temperature on their foreheads, even if they're naked.

"You don't feel feverish. If anything you feel a little cool."

That made me remember something, and the fact that I'd forgotten said I was feeling worse than I knew. "Is my neck still bleeding?"

"A little."

"Should it be?"

He carried me towards the bathroom. "Have you never been bitten this badly before?" He opened the door with his knee and one hand, and carried me through.

"Not without passing out afterwards, *non*." I frowned. "Did I just say, *non*, instead of no?"

"Yep," he said.

"Shit," I said.

"Yeah," he said. He sat on the edge of the huge black marble tub, balancing me in his lap while he turned on the water. The water spilled out of a silver swan's mouth, which I'd always thought was ostentatious, but hey, it wasn't my bathroom.

115

The nausea had passed, the dizziness was waning. "Down, put me down."

"The marble is cold," he said.

I sighed. "I need to find out how well my body's working."

"Just try sitting up in my lap without me holding you. If you're okay, I'll fetch towels and you can sit on them, but trust me you don't want to sit naked on this marble."

"Practical," I said.

"Don't tell anyone I actually made sense, it'll ruin my image."

I smiled. "Secret's safe with me." I tried sitting up, while Jason fidgeted with the water, trying to get the right temperature. I could sit up. Great. I tried to stand, and only Jason's arm around my waist kept me from falling on the marble steps leading down from the tub.

He tucked me safely back in his lap. "Don't try and do so much so fast, Anita."

I leaned back against him, his arm like a safety belt around my waist. "Why I am so weak?"

"How can you have been around vampires this long and ask me that?"

"I don't let them feed," I said.

"I do, and trust me, when you've donated this much, it takes a little while to recover." He seemed satisfied with the water temperature at last. He turned the faucets on harder and had to talk louder over the sound of the water. "We'll get you cleaned up and see how you feel."

I could feel myself frowning, and I wasn't sure why. I felt like I should be angry. I should be something, and I wasn't. Now that I wasn't trapped between Jean-Claude and Asher anymore, I was strangely calm. No, not just calm, I felt good, and I shouldn't have.

I frowned harder, trying to chase this wonderful lassitude away. It was like trying to wake from a bad dream when it didn't want to let you go. Except instead of fighting to wake from a nightmare, I was fighting to destroy a good dream. That seemed wrong, too. Everything seemed wrong. I felt, vaguely, like I'd missed something important, but for the life of me, I couldn't place it.

I felt out of sorts and wonderful at the same time. It was as if my natural grumpiness was fighting some warm happy thought. The warm happy thought was winning, but I wasn't sure that that was necessarily a good thing.

116

"What's wrong with me?" I asked.

"What do you mean?" Jason asked.

"I feel good, and I shouldn't. I feel wonderful. A few minutes ago I was terrified, dizzy, sick, and scared. But once you got me out of the bed, it all seemed better."

"Just better?" he asked. He was slipping out of his leather jacket, one arm at a time, while he took turns holding me with the other arm.

"You're right, not just better. Once I wasn't scared, it was wonderful again." I frowned and tried to think, and was still having trouble doing it. "Why can't I think through this?"

He rearranged me in his lap so he could unzip his boots, and push them off with his feet. It finally hit me that he was undressing himself, while still holding me in his lap. Who says that the skills you learn at work don't come in useful in your everyday life?

"Why are you undressing?"

"You can't move around without falling down, I'd hate for you to drown in the tub."

I tried pushing this wonderful feeling farther away, but it was like trying to fight a warm, comforting mist. You could strike out, but there was nothing solid to hit. The mist just moved and reformed, and stayed.

"Stop," I said, the one word was firm enough, though I didn't feel very firm inside.

"What?" he asked, as he moved me enough forward so that he could unfasten the tops of his jeans.

"This should bother me, you trying to get naked, while I'm naked, in a tub, that should bother me, right?"

"But it doesn't, does it," he said. He was unbuttoning his button fly jeans with one hand. That took talent.

"No, it doesn't," I said, frowning again, "why doesn't it bother me?"

"You really don't know, do you?" he asked.

"No," I said, not even sure what I was saying no to.

He'd gotten his jeans unbuttoned. "I can either lay you down on the very cold tile, or I can throw you over my shoulder for a few seconds while I take the pants off, lady's choice."

The decision seemed too hard for me. "I don't know."

He didn't ask a second time, just tossed me, as gently as he

117

could over his shoulder, sort of half a fireman's carry. Being upside down made the world spin again, and I wondered if I was going to be sick all over his back. He balanced me there while he wormed out of his jeans.

I was now staring down his bare back as the jeans slid down the top of his butt. The nausea had passed, and I giggled – I never giggle – "Nice ass."

He choked, or laughed. "I never knew you noticed."

"Underwear," I said.

"What? "

"You had underwear, I caught a glimpse of it." I had this horrible urge to run my hands over his butt, just because it was there, and I could. It was like I was drunk or high.

"Yeah, I had underwear on, what about it?"

"Can you put it back on?"

"You don't really care if I have underwear on, or not, do you?" and there was something in his voice that was almost teasing.

"Nope." I shook my head, which made the world spin again. "Oh, God, I think I'm going to be sick."

"Stop moving, it'll pass. You wouldn't be sick at all if you hadn't fought to get out from between the two of them. Too much physical exertion right afterwards will make you sick as a dog. Sink into the feeling, just ride it, and it feels wonderful."

I felt a little silly talking to his ass, but it didn't seem nearly as silly as it should have. "What feels wonderful?"

"Guess," he said.

That made me frown. "Don't want to guess." God, what was wrong with me? "Tell me."

"Let's get you in the tub, a bath will help clear your head."

He moved me back to his arms, and stepped over the edge of the tub. "You're naked," I said.

"So are you," he said.

That had a certain logic to it that I couldn't quite argue with, though I felt I should have argued with it. "Weren't you going to put something back on?"

"The underwear is silk, I'm not going to ruin it by wearing it in the tub, because you think I should put it on. Besides, you don't really care if I'm naked or not. Remember?"

A headache was beginning just behind one eye. "No," I said, "but I should care, shouldn't I? I mean . . ."

Jason lowered us both into the water. It felt wonderful, so warm, so smooth, so good against my skin. Jason moved me gently in the water until I was sitting in front of him, cradled against his body.

The water was so warm, so warm, and I was so tired. It would feel so good to just sleep.

Jason's arm on my waist jerked me back. "Anita, you can't sleep in the bathtub, you'll drown."

"You won't let me drown," I said, and my voice was thick with warmth and sleep.

"No, I won't let you drown," he said.

I frowned, as I half-floated in the water. "What is wrong with me, Jason? I feel drunk."

"You have been well and truly rolled by a vampire, Anita."

"Jean-Claude can't, his own marks protect me," my voice seemed to be coming from a long way away.

"I never said it was Jean-Claude."

"Asher," I whispered the name.

"I've shared blood with him before, and it is the most amazing thing. Jean-Claude says he always holds back, because he knows I'm not his *pomme de sang*, I'm just a loaner."

"Loaner," I said.

"I don't think Asher held back with you tonight."

"The *ardeur*, we . . . were doing . . . the *ardeur*." Each word was thick with effort.

"The *ardeur* could have made him careless," Jason said. His hands were very solid on me, cradling me in the water more than against his body.

"Careless?" I said.

"Go ahead and pass out, Anita. When you wake up, we'll talk."

" 'bout what?"

"Things," he said, and his voice was sinking away into the candlelit dark. I didn't remember him lighting the candles that Jean-Claude usually kept around the tub.

I started to ask, *what things*? but the words never made it out loud. I fell into a warm, soft darkness, where there was no fear, no pain. So warm, so safe, so loved.

119

# 15

I WOKE TO the phone ringing. I huddled in the sheets, trying not to hear it. God, I was tired. The bed moved, someone else fumbling for it. It wasn't until Jason's voice said, "Hello," softly, as if he were afraid of waking me, that I woke completely. Why was Jason in my bedroom?

That question was answered as soon as I opened my eyes. I wasn't in my bedroom, in fact, I didn't know where the hell I was. The bed was a king-size, but it was only pillows and a bed, no headboard, no footboard, only a bed, very modern, very normal. The only light was from a small door directly across from the foot of the bed, I could catch a glimpse of a bathtub, or shower. I followed the dim light out and found bare stone walls and knew I was still inside the Circus of the Damned, somewhere.

"She's sick," Jason said. He was quiet for a second. "She's asleep. I'd rather not wake her."

I tried to remember why I was here and came up with nothing, just a blank. I started to roll over, I think to ask who it was, when I realized I was naked. I pulled the sheets up over my breasts and turned over to see Jason.

He was laying on his side, his back to me, the sheet pulled down enough that I could see the top of his buttocks. What the fuck was I doing naked in a bed with Jason? Where was Jean-Claude? Okay, probably in his coffin, or his bed. I never shared the bed when he was stone cold. But why hadn't I gone home?

"I don't think she's going to be well enough to come out today."

I tried to sit up and found that the world wasn't quite steady. Maybe sitting up wasn't such a good idea. I stayed on my back, sheet clutched to my chest, and had to try twice to say, "I'm awake." My mouth was incredibly dry.

Jason turned towards me. The movement pooled the sheet into

his lap and left the backside of his body bare. He covered the receiver with his hand. "How do you feel?"

"How did I get here? Why am I here?" I asked in a voice so hoarse it barely sounded like me.

"Do you remember anything?"

I frowned, and that hurt. My throat hurt. I raised a hand and found a large bandage on the right side of my neck. There was a vampire bite under the bandages, I knew that, and with that knowledge, I remembered.

I remembered everything, and it wasn't just my mind that remembered it. My body convulsed against the bed, my spine bowing, hands clawing at the sheets, a moan tore from my throat, before my body stole all the breath from me, and I bucked against the bed, caught in a sensory memory. It wasn't as good as the original, but damn it was close.

I dug my fists into the sheets, balling the cloth up, trying to find something to hold on to. Jason was suddenly beside me, he grabbed my upper arms, tried to hold me still. "Anita, what's wrong?"

My hands came up, automatically, grabbing his forearms, holding on. My eyes rolled back into my head, my body convulsed, and my hands tore down his forearms. I felt my nails sink into his flesh, felt his skin give under me.

Jason cried out, somewhere between a scream and a moan.

I lay back against the bed, panting, eyes unable to focus. I held onto Jason's arms, because it was the only solid thing I had.

"Anita," he said, his voice, strained, "are you alright?"

I tried to say yes, but finally was reduced to nodding. He pried my fingers from his arms, gently, folding my hands across the sheet and my stomach. I felt the bed move as he moved. I realized my eyes were shut. I didn't remember shutting them.

"What the hell was that?" he asked.

I started to say, I didn't know, but I did know. I remembered Asher sitting at a long banquet table with his hair in golden ringlets, dressed in gold and crimson. The wife of our host crushed her wine glass in her gloved hand, her mouth half-parted, her breath making the white mounds of her breasts rise and fall. A small sound escaped her, and when she could speak, she asked for

121

her maid and to be helped to her room, for she was ill. She wasn't ill. Asher had seduced her the night before, on Belle's orders. He had complained to Jean-Claude that the woman simply lay there, eyes rolled back in her head, true, but with almost no other reaction. It had been most disappointing.

She'd experienced a flashback of the orgasm the night before at the dinner table, but she was a quiet sex partner, which meant that her flashbacks could be explained away in public. Sort of.

I lay there staring up at Jason, seeing him now instead of candlelit rooms long deserted and people long gone to dust. I found my voice, and it was more hoarse than before, as if the screaming had taken the rest of my voice.

"It was a flashback." I coughed.

"To what?" he asked.

"Water, please?"

He hopped off the bed and knelt by a small refrigerator next to the bed. He got out a small bottle of some athletic juicer. "It helps replace the electrolytes better than water."

"I don't like this shit."

"Trust me, you'll feel better if you drink it than if you drink water. Water can make you nauseous."

Suddenly the neon blue drink looked a whole lot better. He opened it and handed it to me. Blood had filled the scratches on his forearms and was slowly seeping down his skin in red rivulets.

"Jesus, Jason, I'm sorry. I didn't mean to cut you up." I took a sip of the neon bright liquid. The taste was as bad as I remembered, but a few small sips, and I did feel a little better. When I talked, my voice didn't sound like I'd been in the desert for a month.

He held his arms up. "It's okay, though normally when I get this cut up it's because I did a wonderful job entertaining a friend." He smiled.

I shook my head, and I wasn't dizzy this time. Good.

"You said this was a flashback, a flashback to what?" he asked.

"To what happened with Jean-Claude and Asher."

He raised eyebrows at me. "You mean that was a flashback to what, the orgasm?"

I felt heat creep up my face. "Something like that," I muttered.

He laughed. "You're joking."

122

"I don't think so." I drank some more of the vile drink, and avoided looking at him.

"I've served as refreshment for Jean-Claude for years and I've never had any reaction like that."

"It's something Asher can do."

"What?" he asked.

"You're bleeding all over the place," I said.

"I'll doctor myself in a minute. First I want you to finish this explanation."

"You know, Asher's bite can be . . ."

"Orgasmic," he finished for me.

"Yeah," I said.

"I've experienced the mild version of it," Jason said. "So have you once in Tennessee when Asher was dying. He rolled your mind. If I remember right, you didn't like it much."

"It wasn't that I didn't like it, Jason, it was that I liked it maybe too much, so yeah, it scared me."

"Jean-Claude said that Asher always holds back unless he can keep the person, whatever that means."

I nodded, took a drink, nodded again. "I think, no, I know that Asher didn't hold back last night."

"How do you know?" he asked.

"I've got some of Jean-Claude's memories. I'm reacting like a woman that Belle had Asher seduce once."

"Acting how?" he asked. "Slicing people up?"

"I said I was sorry."

He sat down on the edge of the bed, one knee tucked up, the other down, so that he was pretty much flaunting himself at me. Generally I don't have trouble making eye contact with a man, but it was sort of eye catching.

"I'm just teasing, Anita." He seemed totally unaware of his nudity, like most of the shape-shifters I knew.

I handed him an edge of sheet. "Please cover up a little."

He grinned. "Why, we slept for," he glanced at the bedside clock, "four hours naked together. Why should I dress now?"

I frowned at him, and suddenly it was easy to have eye contact. It usually is when I glare.

"How are you acting like this other woman?" he asked.

123

"Echoes, flashbacks to the pleasure that happened when Asher took blood."

"Is that going to keep happening?" he asked.

I blushed again. "Off and on, fuck."

"What?" he asked.

"The woman I'm remembering was quiet in bed, she didn't jump around a lot, not according to Asher."

"So?"

"She could hide it better than I can."

He laughed out loud. "Are you telling me that all this jumping around is normal for you?"

I glared at him. "You should know, you've seen me in bed once, you helped bring me, remember." I was blushing so hard my head was beginning to hurt.

His smile faded. It had taken me months to be comfortable around Jason after that. "The *ardeur* was riding all of us," he said, "we were all a little jumpier than usual."

I shook my head, not looking at him, tucking my knees and the sheet to my chest. "Except for wanting to tear out your throat, that was about normal for me."

He coughed, laughed, and finally said, "No way."

I kept my eyes firmly on the sheets. "Fine, make fun."

He took the bottle from me. "I need a drink."

I hugged my knees to my chest, huddling in the sheet. "You are so not funny."

He slid to his knees beside the bed, so I'd see his face. "I'm sorry, really, but . . ." He gave a small shrug. "You can't blame me. You cannot tell me that you have these violent, amazing, orgasms, then expect me not to tease you. It's me, Anita, you know I can't really help it."

He looked so boyish, so innocent. It was all an act. By the time I'd met Jason he'd been ridden hard and put up wet, and his innocence had been long gone.

He handed the drink back to me. "Forgive me, okay, maybe it's just envy."

"Don't go there," I said.

"Not of you," he said, "but hell if Asher's bite is that good, why didn't I get the full treatment?"

124

I tried to frown at him, and only half-succeeded. "You said it yourself, you're not his *pomme de sang*, you're only a loaner."

"And you're Jean-Claude's human servant, not Asher's, so why do you rate the full orgasmic blowout?"

He had a point, a good point. I shrugged. "I think the *ardeur* overrode things. I don't know. I guess I'll have to ask them when they wake up." Why would Asher do this to me? Had it been on pur-pose? I knew only Asher could do with the mere taking of blood what most men couldn't do with their whole bodies. Asher had done something to me that Jean-Claude alone couldn't duplicate. The memory of it tightened my body, and I had just enough time to shove the bottle at Jason before I threw myself back on the bed.

It wasn't as violent as the last time, and Jason made no move to try and touch me. I guess he'd had enough scratches. When I was done, panting on the bed, with the sheet down around my stomach, and my vision clearing, Jason asked from the far side of the bed, "Is it safe now?"

"Shut up," I managed.

He laughed and bounced back on the bed. He raised me up with one hand and offered the bottle with the other. "Lean against the pillows, drink this slowly, I'm going to put some bandages on my arms."

"Antiseptic cream, too," I said.

"I'm a werewolf, Anita, I don't get infections."

Oh. "Fine, then why bother with bandages at all?"

"I don't want to bleed all over my clothes, and I can't let the police see me like this."

"Police, why police?"

"That was who was on the phone when you woke up. That is who's been calling for about the last hour. Lieutenant Storr and Detective Zerbrowski have both called, and have requested your presence. The lieutenant made noises about coming to find you and drag you out of my bed."

"How did he know I was in your bed?"

He grinned at me in the door of the bathroom, opening it wide so the light framed his body. "I don't know, maybe he guessed."

"Jason, you did not tease Dolph, please tell me you didn't."

He put a hand to his chest. "Me, tease someone?"

125

"Sweet Jesus, you did."

"I'd call him back ASAP, if I were you. I'd hate to have the SWAT team crash our little party."

"We are not having a party."

"I don't think your lieutenant friend will believe that if he finds us naked in the bedroom together." He held his arms up. "Especially if he sees this."

"He's not going to see your arms, or any other part of you. Just give me my clothes and I'll get out of your hair."

"And if you have another flashback while you're driving, what then? And let me just add that I've been donating blood to vampires a lot longer than you have. I know how hard it can be when you lose as much as you lost. You may feel fine, but if you overdo it, you'll get dizzy again, and nauseous. That wouldn't be good at a crime scene, would it?"

"Dolph does not let civilians at his crime scenes."

"I'll sit in the Jeep, but I can't let you drive yourself around today."

"Call Micah, or Nathaniel, they'll come pick me up."

He shook his head. "Nathaniel passed out at the club last night."

"What!"

"Micah thinks that feeding the *ardeur* at least once a day for three months has taken its toll on Nathaniel."

"Is he alright?"

"He just needs a day off. Jean-Claude only takes blood from me every other day, usually."

"I switch off with Micah and Jean-Claude for the *ardeur*," I said.

"Yeah, but Jean-Claude only needs to feed once a day, you need to feed twice a day. Let's face it, Anita, you need a larger stable of *pommes de sang.*"

"What, you volunteering?"

An expression of delight crossed his face. "Oh, hell yes, I'd love to be on the receiving end of one of those spine-cracking orgasms."

"Jason," I said, and the one word was warning enough.

"Fine, be that way, but who else are you going to put in Nathaniel's place while he recovers?"

126

I sighed. "Damn it."

"See, you don't know, do you?"

"I can feed on Asher now."

"Yes, but he's not going to wake up for hours and hours. You need some more day-walking donors, Anita. It doesn't have to be me, but it has to be somebody. Think about it. But today I am your escort, because you can't go out alone, not with the blood loss, and whatever the hell Asher did to you. You could call Micah, but by the time he drove out here, and the two of you drove out to wherever the police want to be, I think your police friends would be having fits."

"Fine, you've made your point."

"Have I? It's always so hard to tell with you. Sometimes I think I've won the argument, then you get a second wind and beat me all to hell with it."

"Just go, Jason, put some bandages on the scrapes."

"Scrapes hell, if I were human, you'd be taking me to the emergency room. Remember, Anita, you have some of the strength of both a vampire and a werewolf. We can punch our finger through someone's ribs."

"Are you really hurt?" I asked, all joking aside. I didn't want him hurt.

"Not permanently, but it'll heal almost human slow."

"I'm sorry, Jason." I remembered enough to say, "And thanks for taking care of me."

His grin faded, and something close to a serious look spilled through his eyes, then it was gone, hidden behind another smile. "All in a day's work, ma'am." He tipped an imaginary hat and started to shut the door. "I'd turn on the lamp before I close the door, it's damn dark without windows."

I reached over and switched on a small lamp beside the clock, on top of the little refrigerator. The glow seemed unnaturally bright.

"Your cell phone is on the floor on my side of the bed. I dropped it when you started convulsing."

"I was not convulsing," I said.

"Oh, sorry, I dropped it when you had your raging, overwhelming, screaming orgasm. Was that better? It sounded better, didn't it?"

"Go clean up," I said, sounding grumpy when I said it.

He was laughing as he closed the door.

I was left alone with the little lamp, the big bed, and no clothes in sight. I was about to debate on whether to try and find some clothes before hunting up my phone, when it rang again. I scrambled across the bed, jerking the sheets off so they wouldn't tangle me. I half slid, half fell to the floor and found my phone by sitting on it.

It was Dolph, and he wasn't happy. While he'd been waiting for me, there had been a second call, to a second crime scene. He was pissed with Jason's antics on the phone, with both crime scenes, and especially, it seemed, with me.

# 16

THE FIRST CRIME scene was in Wildwood, that new bastion of money and social climbing. The hot addresses used to be Ladue, Clayton, Creve Coeur, but they've all become passé. Nope, the hot new place to be is Wildwood. The fact that it's in the middle of freaking nowhere doesn't seem to dissuade the nouveau riche, or wanna-be rich. Personally, the only reason I lived in the middle of nowhere, at a much less fashionable address, was the fact that I didn't want to get my neighbors shot up.

By the time Jason had driven through all the windy roads that led to the murder scene, we'd found out several things. First, my eyes were light sensitive, so my sunglasses were my friends. Second, my stomach didn't like the twisting roads. We hadn't had to stop so I could throw up, which was good, since unless we pulled into someone's drive, there was no shoulder to the road. It was bordered by woods, hills, tame wilderness, where real wolves no longer roam and even the black bears have found deeper holes to hide in.

Normally I love a drive through the country. Today all the bright greens meant was that when my vision swirled, it did it in Technicolor green like a frog smeared across my vision, which actually made the nausea worse.

"How can you endure this?" I asked.

"If you'd slept the day away like a normal *pomme de sang* or human servant, you wouldn't be sick at all."

"Forgive me for having a day job."

"Also if Asher had taken enough for just a feeding, then you might be a bit sick," he negotiated a turn, "but I think that whatever Asher did to you along with taking blood made it worse." He paused. "Truthfully, you shouldn't be this sick, at all."

We crested the rise, and the soft hills stretched out for miles, shades of green with a hint of gold here and there.

"At least I'm not nauseous anymore when I look at the trees."

"That's good, but I mean it, Anita. After you'd slept, and then gotten up and around, you should have been fine." He took the next curve carefully, a lot slower than he'd taken the first one.

"So what went wrong?" I asked.

He shrugged, and slowed even further, trying to see the address on a cluster of mailboxes.

"Dolph said the crime scene was on the main road. You won't miss it, Jason."

"How can you be sure?"

"Trust me."

He flashed me another grin, his own blue eyes hidden behind mirrored sunglasses. "I do trust you."

"What went wrong?" I asked again.

"What were you doing when dawn broke?" he asked, speeding back up and taking the next curve a little faster than I would have liked.

"The *ardeur*, Asher was feeding, and . . ." I hesitated only for a second, "having sex."

"With both of them at once," he said, voice mock serious, "I am so disappointed in you, Anita."

"Disappointed why?"

"That I wasn't invited."

"You are so lucky you're driving right now."

He grinned, but didn't turn away from the road this time. "Why do you think I said it while I was driving?" He slowed. "I see what you meant about not missing it."

I turned my attention from Jason's face to the road. Police cars, marked and unmarked, were everywhere. Two emergency vehicles were parked on the edge of the road, which effectively blocked traffic. If we'd been planning to drive farther on, we'd have had to find another way around. But lucky us, we were stopping here.

Jason pulled the Jeep over, driving into the grass in a vain attempt to leave some space for anyone else that might be coming behind us.

A uniformed officer started walking towards us before Jason had turned off the engine. I got my badge out of my suit jacket pocket. I, Anita Blake, vampire executioner, was technically a federal marshal. All vampire hunters that were currently state licensed in the United States had been grandfathered in to federal status, if they could qualify on a shooting range. I'd qualified, and now I was a fed. They were still arguing in Washington, D.C., about whether they'd be able to give us anything more than the pittance that each state pays us per kill, which is not enough so you could afford to do it as a day job. But then, luckily the vampires haven't gotten so out of hand that any state needed a vampire hunter full time.

I wasn't getting any more money, so why had I wanted the badge? Because it meant I could chase the vampires, or other supernatural bad guys, across state lines, different law enforcement jurisdictions, and not have to ask anyone's permission. I also wouldn't be up on murder charges if I killed a vamp on the wrong side of a state line where I wasn't licensed.

But for me, more than most vampire hunters, there was an extra benefit to having a badge of my very own. I no longer had to rely on policemen friends to get me into crime scenes.

I didn't know the uniformed officer that was about to knock on our Jeep window, but it didn't matter. He couldn't keep me out of the crime scene. I was a federal marshal – I could stick my nose into any preternaturally related crime I wanted to. A real federal marshal could have intruded into any investigation, and technically my badge didn't specify that I was relegated to preternatural crime, but I know my limitations. I know monsters, and monster-related crime. A regular cop I am not. What I'm good at, I'm very good at, but what I don't know shit about, I don't know shit about. Take me away from the monsters and I wasn't sure how much use I'd be.

I was out of the Jeep and flashing my badge before the uniform got to us. He sized me up the way men will do from shoes to face – in that order. Any man who starts at my feet and then goes up has lost pretty much any chance he has to impress me.

I read his name tag, "Officer Jenkins, I'm Anita Blake. Lieutenant Storr is expecting me."

"Storr isn't here," he said, arms crossed over his chest.

Great, he didn't recognize my name – so much for being a celebrity – and he was going to play "don't want the feds pissing in my pond!"

131

Jason had gotten out on his side of the Jeep. Maybe I looked a little disreputable in my slightly wrinkled suit, with a run in my hose that went from toe to thigh, but Jason didn't look like a fed, or a cop. He was dressed in blue jeans that had faded through enough washings to be comfortable, a blue T-shirt that almost matched his eyes, still hidden behind the mirrored shades, and white jogging shoes. It had turned out to be one of those unusually warm fall days we get sometimes. Too warm for his leather jacket, so he hadn't bothered with anything else. The white gauze and tape on his forearms were very noticeable.

He leaned on the hood of the Jeep, smiling pleasantly and looking so not like a federal anything.

Officer Jenkins's eyes flicked to Jason, then back to me. "We didn't call the feds in."

Standing there in my three-inch heels on the slightly uneven road was making me feel light-headed again. I did not have the patience, or the strength, to debate.

"Officer Jenkins, I am a federal marshal, do you know what that means?"

"Nope," he said, making the word longer than it was.

"It means that I don't need your permission to enter this crime scene. I don't need anybody's permission. So it doesn't matter if the lieutenant is here or not. I told you who alerted me to this crime out of courtesy, but if you don't want to be courteous, officer, then we don't have to be."

I turned and looked at Jason. Normally, I would have left him at the car, but I wasn't a hundred percent sure I could make it up the rest of the hill without falling over. I genuinely didn't feel well enough to be here. But here I was, and I was going to see this crime scene.

I motioned Jason to me. He came around the Jeep, his smile fading around the edges. Maybe I looked as pale as I felt.

"Let's go."

"He's not a fed," Jenkins said.

I'd had enough of Jenkins. If I'd been feeling better I would have bullied our way through, but . . . there were other ways to bully.

I waited until Jason was there to steady me, then I moved my hair to one side showing the white gauze and tape on my own neck. I pulled on one side of the tape until it peeled down, and I could flash the bite at Jenkins. It wasn't a neat puncture wound. Asher had gotten carried away, because the edges of the wounds were torn.

"Shiiit," Jenkins said.

I let Jason tape the wound back up, while I talked to the other man. "I have had a hard night, Officer Jenkins, and I have the authority to go into any preternaturally related crime scene that I see fit to enter."

The tape was smoothed back into place, and Jason was standing very close to my left arm, as if he knew how unsteady I was feeling. Jenkins didn't seem to notice.

"It isn't a vampire attack," Jenkins said.

"Am I not speaking English here, Jenkins? Did I say it had anything to do with vampires?"

"No, sir, I mean . . no."

"Then either escort us to the crime scene, officer, or step aside and we'll find our own way."

Flashing the vampire bite had thrown him, but he still didn't want a fed messing with his crime. Probably his boss wouldn't like it, but that wasn't my problem. I had a federal badge. In theory, I had the right to the crime scene. In actuality, if the local police barred my way there wasn't much I could do. I could go get a court order and force the issue, but that would take time, and I didn't have that kind of time. Dolph was already pissed at me. I didn't want to keep him waiting that long.

Jenkins finally stepped aside. We started walking up the hill. I had to take Jason's arm about halfway up. My goal in life for that moment was not to fall down, throw up, or faint, while Jenkins was still puzzling over whether he'd done the right thing letting us get past him.

## 17

MY BADGE ON its little cord around my neck got us past most of the cops. The few that questioned us recognized my name, or had worked with me before. Always good to be known. They questioned Jason's presence. I finally told them that I'd deputized him.

A big statie, with shoulders wider than either of us was tall, said, "I've heard it called a lot of things, but deputy isn't one of 'em."

I turned on him, slowly, because I couldn't move fast, and the very slowness of the turn helped the menace. It's hard to be menacing to someone when you barely reach their waist, but I have had lots of practice.

Jason must have been afraid of what I'd say, because he said, "You're just jealous."

The big man shook his head in his Smokey the bear hat. "I like my women bigger."

"Funny," I said, "that's what your wife says."

It took him a minute to get it, then he unfolded those beefy arms and took a step towards us. "Why you . . ."

"Trooper Kennedy," a voice said from behind us, "don't you have some speeders to go catch?"

I turned to see Zerbrowski walking towards us. He was dressed in his usual – sloppy as hell, as if he'd slept in the brown suit, a yellow shirt with the collar on one side pointing up, and a tie at half-mast, already stained with something, even though he probably hadn't had breakfast. His wife, Katie, was always neat as a pin. I'd never figured out how she let him go out looking like that.

"I'm on my own time here, detective," Trooper Kennedy said.

"And this is my crime scene, trooper. I don't think we need you here."

"She says that she deputized him."

"She's a federal marshal, Kennedy, she can do that."

The big man looked perplexed. "I didn't mean anything by the comment, sir."

"I know you didn't, Kennedy, just as Marshal Blake here didn't mean anything by hers. Did you, Anita?"

"I don't know his wife, so no, just pulling your leg, Officer Kennedy, sorry about that."

Kennedy frowned, thinking harder than was good for him, I think. "No offense taken, and none meant, ma'am." He couldn't quite bring himself to call me officer, or marshal, which was fine with me. The federal status was so new that I didn't always look up when someone called marshal. I kept forgetting they meant me.

When the big trooper had wandered away to his car, Zerbrowski called over one of the other detectives on the Regional Preternatural Investigation Team, affectionately know as RPIT. If you wanted to piss them off, call them RIP.

"See if you can clear out some of the personnel we don't need."

"You got it, Sarge," and the man went to talk with all the nice policemen from all the many jurisdictions.

"Sarge," I said, "I knew Dolph made lieutenant finally, I didn't hear your news."

He shrugged, running a hand through his already messy curls. Katie would make him go in for a haircut soon. "When they moved Dolph up, he needed a second whip, I got tapped."

"They throw you a party yet?"

He adjusted his wire-rimmed glasses. They didn't need adjusting. "Yeah."

If I'd been a man, I'd have let it go, but I was a girl, and girls poke at things more than men. "I was invited to Dolph's party for making louie, but not yours?"

"I like Micah, Anita, but Dolph . . . didn't expect you to bring Micah. I don't think he could take seeing him at my shindig, too."

"He just can't handle the fact that my main squeeze is a shapeshifter."

Zerbrowski shrugged. "Katie gave me strict orders to invite you and Micah over for dinner the next time I saw you. So here it is, and when can you come over?"

There are points where you stop pushing. I didn't ask if Katie

135

had really told Zerbrowski that, she probably had, but, whatever, he was trying to offer a social peace pipe, and I was going to take it.

"I'll ask Micah what our schedule looks like."

His eyes flicked to Jason, and he grinned. The grin reminded me so much of Jason's grin, that it made me wonder what Zerbrowski had been like in college, when Katie and he met. "Unless you've changed guys again?"

"No," I said, "Jason's just a friend."

"The friend speech," Jason clutched his heart with his free hand, the other still wrapped around mine, "it cuts so deep."

"Yeah, I've been trying to get into her pants for years. She just won't come across."

"Tell me about it," Jason said.

"Both of you, stop it, right now," I said.

They both laughed, and the laughs were so similar that it was kind of unnerving. "I know you have the right to make him a deputy, but I know what Mr. Schulyer here is, and where his primary residence is." Zerbrowski leaned in close enough to us that no one else would hear. "Dolph would kill me if I let him into the crime scene."

"You catch me if I pass out, and he can stay out here."

"Pass out," Zerbrowski said, "you're joking, right?"

"I wish I was." I had both hands on Jason's arm now, fighting the urge to totter on my high heels.

"Dolph said that you'd said you were sick. Did he know how sick?"

"He didn't seem to care, just wanted me to get my ass out here."

Zerbrowski frowned. "If he'd known you were this shaky, he wouldn't have insisted."

"Pretty to think so," I said. I could feel the blood draining from my face. I needed to sit down, soon, just for a few minutes.

"I would ask if it's the flu, but I see the bandage on your neck. What did it?"

"Vampire," I said.

"You want to report a crime?"

"It's been taken care of."

"You kill his ass?"

I looked at him through the dark lenses of the glasses. "I really

136

need to sit down for a few minutes, Zerbrowski, and you know I wouldn't ask if I didn't need it."

He offered me his arm. "I'll escort you through, but Schulyer there can't come." He looked at Jason. "Sorry, man."

Jason shrugged. "It's okay, I'm really good at entertaining myself."

"Behave yourself," I said.

He grinned. "Don't I always?"

I would have stayed there and made sure he promised me how good he would be, but I had only about enough energy to walk into the house and sit down before my legs gave. I'd leave the police officers and emergency crews to Jason's mercy. He wouldn't do anything bad, just irritating.

I stumbled on the steps leading up to the small front porch. If Zerbrowski hadn't caught me, I'd have fallen.

"Jesus, Anita, you should be in bed."

"That's what I told Dolph."

He eased me through the door and found me a small straight-backed chair in the hallway. "I'll tell Dolph how sick you are and let the kid take you home."

"No," I said, though I did lay my forehead on my knees while the world steadied around me.

"Jesus, Anita, you're as stubborn as he is. Dolph won't take *no* for an answer, so you drag your ass out of a sickbed to come down here. I give you an out, where I'll take the heat from Dolph, but nooo, you're going to show Dolph that you're just as stubborn and bullheaded as he is. You planning to faint in his arms? That'll really show him."

"Shut up, Zerbrowski."

"Fine, you sit there for a few minutes. I'll come back and check on you, and I'll escort you through the crime scene. But you're being stupid."

I spoke with my face still in my lap. "If Dolph were sick, he'd still be here."

"That doesn't prove you're right, Anita, that just proves you're *both* stupid." With that he walked away, farther into the house. It was good that he left, because for the life of me, I couldn't have argued with him.

137

## 18

WHEN ZERBROWSKI FIRST led me into the room, I thought, *there's a man levitating against that wall*. He did look like he was floating. I knew that wasn't true, but for just a moment my eyes, my mind, tried to make that what I saw. Then I saw the dark lines where blood had dried on the body. It looked as if he'd been shot, a lot, and bled, but bullets wouldn't have kept him pinned to the wall.

Strangely, I wasn't faint, or nauseous, or anything. I felt light and distant, and more solid than I'd felt in hours. I kept walking towards the man on the wall. Zerbrowski's hand slipped away from mine, and I was steady on my high heels in the soft carpet.

I had to be almost underneath the body before my eyes could make sense of it, and even then, I was going to have to ask someone who was more tool-oriented if I was right.

It looked like someone had taken a nail gun, one of those industrial size nail guns, and nailed the man to the wall. His shoulders were about eight feet off the ground, so either they'd used a ladder, or they'd been close to seven feet tall.

The dark spots on the body were at both palms, both wrists, forearms just above the elbows, shoulders, collarbone, lower legs just below the knees, just above the ankles, then through each foot. The legs were apart, not pierced together. They hadn't tried to imitate the Crucifixion. If you went to this much trouble, it was almost odd to not echo that long-ago drama. The very fact that they hadn't tried seemed strange to me.

The man's head slumped forward. His neck showed pale and whole. There was a dark patch of blood on his nearly white hair just behind one ear. If the nails were as big as I thought they were, if that blood had been caused by a nail, the tip should have protruded from the face, but it didn't. I stood on tiptoe. I wanted to see the face.

The white hair and the face, slack with death, said he was older than the rest of him looked. The body was well cared for – exercise, probably weights, running – only the face and white hair said he was probably over fifty. All that work to maintain health and well-being, and some nutcase comes along and nails you to a wall. It seemed so unfair.

I leaned forward too far and had to put my fingertips out to catch myself. My fingers touched dried blood on the wall. Only then did I realize I'd forgotten my surgical gloves. Fuck.

Zerbrowski was there with a hand on my elbow to steady me, whether I needed it, or not.

"How could you let me come in here without gloves on?"

"I didn't expect you to touch the evidence," he said. He fished a bottle of hand sanitizer out of one of his pockets. "Katie makes me carry it."

I let him pour some into my hands, and I scrubbed them. It wasn't that I was really worried about catching anything from that one small touch, I did it more out of habit. You didn't take pieces of the crime scene home if you didn't have to.

The gel evaporated against my skin making my hands feel wet, though I knew they weren't. I looked around at the crime scene, taking in what else was there.

Colored chalk had been used on the off-white walls. There were pentagrams of varying sizes on either side of the body. Pink, blue, red, green; almost decorative. Any fool that's trying to fake a ritual murder knows enough to use a few pentagrams. But there were also Nordic runes drawn among the candy-colored pentagrams. Not every nutcase knows that Nordic runes can be used in ritual magic.

I'd had one semester of comparative religion with a professor who had really liked the Norse. It had left me with a better knowledge of runes than most Christians had. It had been years, but I still recognized enough to be confused.

"This makes no sense," I said.

"What?" Zerbrowski asked.

I pointed at the wall, while I spoke. "It's been a while since I studied runes in college, but the perps used all the runes in a pretty standard order. If you're really doing ritual, you have a specific

139

purpose. You don't use all the Norse runes, because some of them are contradictory. I mean, you don't want to use a rune for chaos and a rune for order. I can't think of a true ritual where you would use them all. Even if you were doing a working where you wanted to invoke polarity, healing, harming, chaos, order, god, goddess, you still wouldn't. Some of them aren't easily made to fit any true polarity/opposite sort of thing. And they're also in a pretty standard textbook order."

I backed up, taking him with me, because he was still holding on to my elbow. I pointed to the left side of the body as we looked at it. "It starts with Fehu here and descends straight through, ending with Dagaz at the other side. Someone just copied this, Zerbrowski."

"I know this sounds funky, but do you feel any magic?" he asked.

I thought about that. "Do you mean was this a spell?"

He nodded. "Yeah, can you feel a spell?"

"No, there's been nothing of power in this room."

"How can you be so sure?" he asked.

"Magic, power of any kind of a metaphysical nature, leaves a residue behind. Sometimes it's just a tingling at the back of your neck, goosebumps on your skin, but sometimes it's like a slap in the face, or even a wall that you run into. But this room is dead, Zerbrowski. I'm not psychically gifted enough to pick up emotions from what happened here, and I'm glad. But if this had been some big spell, there'd be something left of it, and the room is just a crime scene, nothing else."

"So if no spell, why all the symbols?" he asked.

"I haven't the faintest idea. From the looks of things he was shot behind the ear and nailed to the wall. The body isn't arranged to imitate any mystical or religious symbolism that I'm familiar with. Then they threw some pentagrams around and copied runes out of a book."

"Which book?"

"There are a lot of books on the runes, everything from college textbooks to the occult to New Age. You'd probably have to go to a college store or one of the New Age shops, or you could probably special order it through any bookstore."

"So this isn't a ritual murder," he said.

"There may be ritual to it from the killer's point of view, but was it done with magical purpose? No."

He let out a deep breath. "Good, that's what Reynolds told Dolph."

"Detective Tammy Reynolds, your one and only witch on staff?" I asked.

He nodded.

"Why didn't Dolph believe her?"

"He said he wanted confirmation."

I shook my head, and it didn't make me dizzy to do it. Great. "He doesn't trust her, does he?"

Zerbrowski shrugged. "Dolph's just careful."

"Bull-fucking-shit, Zerbrowski, he doesn't trust her because she's a witch. She's a Christian witch for heaven's sake, a Follower of the Way. You can't get more mainstream in your occult expert than a Christian witch."

"Hey, don't get mad at me, I didn't drag you out of bed to double-check Reynolds's work."

"And would he have dragged her down here to check my work, if I'd been first on the scene?"

"You'd have to ask Dolph about that."

"Maybe I will," I said.

Zerbrowski went a little pale. "Anita, please don't go after Dolph angry. He is in a bad, bad mood."

"Why?"

He shrugged again. "Dolph doesn't confide in me."

"Is he just in a bad mood today, or for the last few days, what?"

"The last few days have been worse, but two murders in one night have sort of given him a reason to be grumpy, and he's taking full advantage of it."

"Great, just great," I said. My anger helped me stomp off towards the bank of windows that took up most of the other wall. I stood there and stared off at the amazing view. Nothing but hills, trees, it did look as if the house sat in the middle of some vast wilderness.

Zerbrowski came to stand beside me. "Nice view, huh?"

"Whoever did this had to have scouted the house." I motioned at the windows. "They had to know for sure that there was no neighbor out there that could see what they were doing. Shooting him, you might take your chances, but putting him up on the wall, and all the symbols, no, they had to be sure they wouldn't be seen."

"That's pretty organized for a wacko," Zerbrowski said.

"Not if it's really someone wanting you to think they're a wacko."

"What do you mean?"

"Don't tell me that you and Dolph haven't thought of that."

"What?"

"That it's someone near and dear to the dead man, someone who stands to inherit all this." I looked around at the living room, which was as large as the entire downstairs of my house. "I was too sick to really notice when I came in, but if the rest of the house is as impressive as this, then there's money to be had."

"You haven't seen the pool yet, have ya?"

"Pool?"

"Indoors, with a Jacuzzi big enough for twelve."

I sighed. "Like I said, money. Follow the money, find out who stands to gain. The ritual is only window dressing, a smoke screen that the murderers hope will throw you off."

He stood staring off at the beautiful view, hands behind his back, sort of rocking on his heels. "You're right, that's exactly what Dolph thought once Reynolds said there was no magic to it."

"I'm not going over to the other scene just to check her work again, am I? Because if that's the case, I'm headed home. I may not always like Detective Tammy, but she's pretty good at what she does."

"You just don't like that she's dating Larry Kirkland, your animator in training."

"No, I don't like that she and Larry are dating. She's his first serious girlfriend, so forgive me, but I felt protective."

"Funny, I don't feel protective of Reynolds at all."

"That's because you're weird, Zerbrowski."

"No," he said, "it's because I see the way Reynolds and Kirkland look a each other. They are dead gone, Anita, in L-O-V-E."

I sighed. "Maybe."

142

"If you haven't noticed, it's because you didn't want to see it."

"Maybe I've been busy."

For once Zerbrowski stayed quiet.

I looked at him. "You never answered my first question, am I going to the next murder scene to check Tammy's work?"

He stopped rocking on his heels and stood quiet, face serious. "I don't know, probably some."

"I'm going home then."

He touched my arm. "Go to the second scene, Anita, please. Don't give Dolph any more reason to be more pissy."

"That is not my problem, Zerbrowski. Dolph is making his own life hard on this one."

"I know, but the couple officers that have been at both scenes say the second one is a bad one. More up your alley than Reynolds's."

"Up my alley, how?"

"Violent, real violent. Dolph doesn't want to know if it's magic, he wants to know if something that wasn't human did it."

"Dolph's a fanatic about not giving details away to his people before they've seen a crime scene, Zerbrowski. What you've just told me would piss him off mightily."

"I was afraid you wouldn't go, if I didn't . . . add a little."

"Why do you care if Dolph and I are feuding?"

"We're here to solve crimes, Anita, not fight each other. I don't know what's eating Dolph, but one of you has to be the grown-up." He smiled. "Yeah. I know things have come to a sorry state when you're the one, but there it is."

I shook my head and slapped his arm. "You are such a pain in the ass, Zerbrowski."

"It's good to be appreciated," he said.

The anger was fading, and with it the spurt of energy. I leaned my head against his shoulder. "Get me outside before I start feeling bad again. I'll go see the second crime scene."

He put his arm around my shoulders and gave me half a hug. "That's my little federal marshal."

I raised my head. "Don't push it, Zerbrowski."

"Can't help myself, sorry."

I sighed. "You're right, you can't help yourself. Forget I said

143

anything, keep saying witty irritating things as you walk me back to Jason."

He started me across the room, arm still across my shoulders. "How did you end up with a werewolf stripper as your driver for the day?"

"Just lucky I guess."

## 19

THE SECOND SCENE was in Chesterfield, which had been a hot address for the up-and-comers before most of the money moved even farther out to Wildwood and beyond. The neighborhood that Jason drove us through was a sharp contrast to the big isolated houses we'd just seen. This was middle-class, middle America, backbone of the nation kind of neighborhood. There are thousands of subdivisions exactly like it. Except in this one, not all the houses were identical. They were still too close together and had a sameness about them, as if a hive mind had designed them all, but some were two-story, some only one, some brick, some not. Only the garage seemed to be the same on all of them, as if the architect wasn't willing to compromise on that one feature.

There were medium-sized trees in the yards, which meant the area was over ten years old. It takes time to grow trees.

I saw the giant antenna of the news van before I saw the police cars. "Shit."

"What?"Jason asked.

"The reporters are already here."

He glanced up. "How do you know?"

"Have you never seen a news van with one of those big antennas?"

"I guess not."

"Lucky you," I said.

Probably because of the news van, the police had blocked the street. When someone had time, they'd probably bring up those official-looking sawhorses. Right now they had a police cruiser, a uniformed officer leaning against it, and yellow do-not-cross tape strung from mailbox to mailbox across the entire street.

There were two local news vans and a handful of print media. You can always tell print, because they have the still cameras and no microphones. Though they will shove tape recorders in your face.

We had to park about half a block away because of them. When the engine shut off, Jason asked, "How did they hear about it so quickly?"

"One of the neighbors called it in, or one of the news vans was close for something else. Once something hits the police scanners, the reporters know about it."

"Why weren't there reporters at the first scene?"

"The first one was more isolated, harder to get to, and still make your deadline. Or there could be a local celebrity involved here, or it's just better copy."

"Better copy?" he asked.

"More sensational." In my own head, I wondered how you could get much more sensational than having someone nailed to their living room wall, but of course, those kinds of details weren't released to the media, not if it could be kept under wraps.

I undid my seat belt and put a hand on the door handle. "Getting through the press is going to be the first hurdle here. I'm something of a local celebrity now, myself, whether I like it or not."

"The Master of the City's lady love," Jason said, smiling.

"I don't think anyone's been that polite," I said, "but, yeah. Though today they'll be more interested in the murder. They'll be asking me questions about that, not Jean-Claude."

"You seem to be feeling some better," Jason said.

"I am, not sure why."

"Maybe whatever caused the bad reaction is fading."

I nodded. "Maybe."

"Are we going to get out of the car, or are we going to watch from here?"

I sighed. "Getting out, getting out."

Jason opened his door and was around to my side before I could get more than one foot on the ground. Today I let him help me. I was feeling better, but I still wasn't at my best. I'd hate to refuse help and then fall flat on my face. I was really trying to tone down the machismo today. Mine, not Jason's.

I put my hand on Jason's arm, and we started down the sidewalk towards the crowd. There were lots of people, and most of them

146

weren't reporters. The first murder scene had been isolated, no neighbors close enough to walk out their doors and see the show. But this neighborhood was thick with houses, so we had a crowd.

I had my badge around my neck on its little cord, I hadn't taken it off from the last scene. Now that I was feeling better, it occurred to me that Jason's arm was in the way if I had to go for the gun under my left arm. I didn't want him on my right side, because that was my gun hand, but even on my left he was in the way, a little at least.

I was feeling better if I could be worrying this much over my gun. Good to know. Feeling bad sucks, and nausea is one of the great evils of the universe.

I think because I had Jason on my arm it took the reporters longer to realize who I was, and that we weren't just part of the growing crowd of gawkers. We were actually working our way through the crowd, almost to the yellow tape before one of the reporters spotted me.

The tape recorder was shoved at me, "Ms. Blake, why are you here, was the murdered woman a vampire victim?"

Fuck, if I just said, *no comment*, they'd be printing *possible vampire kill* all over this one. "I'm called in on a lot of preternaturally related crime, Mr. Miller, isn't it? Not just vampires."

He was happy I'd remembered his name. Most people love to have you remember their names. "So it wasn't a vampire kill."

Shit. "I haven't been up to the crime scene yet, Mr. Miller, I don't know anymore than you do."

The reporters closed like a fist around me. There was a big shoulder cam on us now. We'd make the noon news if nothing more exciting happened.

The questions came from all directions, "Is it a vampire kill? What kind of monster is it? Do you think there'll be more victims?" One woman got in so close that only a death grip on Jason's hand kept us from being separated. "Anita, is this your new boyfriend? Have you dumped Jean-Claude?"

That a reporter would ask that question with a fresh body only yards away said just how bad the media interest in Jean-Claude's personal life had gotten.

Once the question was raised, several more asked similar questions. I did not understand why my personal life was more

147

interesting, or even as interesting, as a murder. It made no sense to me.

If I said Jason was a friend, they'd misconstrue it. If I said he was a bodyguard, they'd plaster the fact that I needed a bodyguard all over the papers. I finally stopped trying to answer questions and held my badge up so the uniformed officer could see it.

He raised the tape to let us inside and then had to push back the press of bodies that tried to follow us through. We walked towards the house to a hail of questions that I ignored. God knew what they'd do with the few things I'd said. It could be anything from the Executioner says, *vampire attack*, to the Executioner says *not a vampire*, to my love life. I'd stopped reading the papers, or watching the news, if I thought I might be on. First I hate to watch myself on a moving camera. Second, it always pissed me off. I was not free to discuss an ongoing police investigation, no one was, so the press were left to speculate on what few facts they had. And if Jean-Claude and our love life was the topic of choice, I never wanted to see, or read the coverage.

For some reason being caught in the media feeding frenzy had made me feel shaky again. Not as bad as earlier, but not as good as I'd felt when I first got out of the Jeep. Great, just great.

There were fewer cops here, and most of them were faces I recognized, members of RPIT. No one questioned my right to be at the scene, or Jason's presence. They trusted me. The uniform on the door looked pale, his dark eyes flashing too much white. "Lieutenant Storr is expecting you, Ms. Blake." I didn't correct the title to marshal. Marshal Blake made me feel like I should have been guest-starring on *Gunsmoke*.

The uniform opened the door for us because he was wearing rubber gloves. I'd left my crime scene kit at home, because when I raised a zombie for the higher-end clients, Bert liked me to not be covered in a baggy overall. He said it didn't look professional. Once he'd agreed to reimburse me for all dry cleaning incurred from this little rule, I'd agreed.

I told Jason, "Don't touch anything until I get us some gloves."

"Gloves?"

"Surgical gloves, that way if they find a latent print, they won't get all excited and then find out it was yours, or mine."

148

We were standing in a narrow entryway with stairs leading straight up from the door, a living room to the left, and an opening to the right that led into what looked like a dining room. There was an opening beyond that where I caught a glimpse of countertop and sink.

I couldn't see the color scheme clearly because I was still wearing sunglasses. I debated whether taking them off would make the headache come back. I slipped them off, slowly. I was left blinking painfully, but after a few seconds, it was okay. If I could stay out of direct sunlight I'd probably be all right.

It was Detective Merlioni who walked into the living room and saw us first. "Blake, thought you'd chickened out."

I looked up at the tall man with his curling gray hair cut short. The neck of his white long-sleeved shirt was unbuttoned, his tie tugged down crooked, as if he'd loosened everything without caring what it looked like. Merlioni hated ties, but he usually tried to be neater than this.

"It must be a bad one," I said.

He frowned at me. "What makes you say that?"

"You've tugged your tie all crooked like you needed air, and you haven't called me girlie or chickie, yet."

He grinned flashing white teeth. "It's early days, chickie."

I shook my head. "Do you have some gloves we can borrow? I wasn't expecting to do a crime scene today."

He glanced at Jason then, as if seeing him for the first time, but I knew he'd seen him. Cops see almost everything around a crime scene. "Who's this?"

"My driver for the day."

He raised eyebrows at that. "Driver, woo-woo, coming up in the world."

I frowned at him. "Dolph knew I was too shaky to drive, so he gave me permission to bring a driver with me. If there weren't enough press outside to cover an entire city block I'd have had him leave me at the door, but I don't want him going back out in that. They'll never believe he's not involved in the investigation."

Merlioni stepped to the big picture window in the living room and lifted the edge of the drape enough to peek out. "They are damned persistent today."

149

"How'd they get here so quick?"

"Neighbor called them probably. Everyone wants to be on fucking television these days." He turned back to us. "What's your driver's name?"

"Jason Schulyer."

He shook his head. "Name doesn't mean anything to me."

"I don't know who you are either," Jason said, with a smile.

I frowned. "You know Merlioni, I don't know your first name. I can't introduce you."

He flashed those pearly whites at me. "Rob, Rob Merlioni."

"You don't look like a Rob."

"My mama doesn't think so either, she's always after me – Roberto, I give you such a nice name, you should use it."

"Roberto Merlioni, I like it." I introduced them more formally than I think I'd ever introduced anyone to anyone at a crime scene. Merlioni was stalling, he didn't want to go back inside.

"There's a box of gloves in the kitchen, on the counter, help yourself. I'm going outside for a smoke."

"I didn't know you smoked," I said.

"I just started." He looked at me, and his eyes were haunted. "I've seen worse, Blake, hell we've waded through worse together, you and me, but I'm tired today. Maybe I'm gettin' old."

"Not you, Merlioni, never you."

He smiled, but not like he meant it. "I'll be back in a few." Then the smile widened. "Don't let Dolph know I didn't make your driver wait outside."

"Mum's the word," I said.

He went out, closing the door softly behind him. The house was very quiet, only the rushing hush of the air conditioning. It was too quiet for a fresh murder scene, and too still. There should have been people all over the place. Instead we stood in the small entryway in a well of silence so thick you could almost hear the blood in your own ears, thrumming, filling the silence with something, anything.

The hair at the back of my neck stood at attention, and I turned to Jason. He was standing there in his baby blue T-shirt, his peaceful face behind the mirrored shades, but the energy trickled off of him, raised the skin along my arms in a nervous creep.

150

He looked so harmless, pleasant. But if you had the ability to sense what he was, he was suddenly not harmless, or pleasant.

"What's with you?" I whispered.

"Don't you smell it?" his voice was a hoarse whisper.

"Smell what?"

"Meat, blood."

Shit. "No," I said, but of course his creeping energy along my skin raised my own beast, like a ghost in my gut. That phantom shape stretched inside me like some great cat waking from a long nap, and I did smell it. Not just blood, Jason was right, meat. Blood smells sort of sweet and metallic like old pennies, or nickels, but a lot of blood smells like hamburger. You know it's going to be bad, really bad, when a human being is reduced to the smell of so much ground meat.

My head lifted, and I sniffed the air, drew in a great breath of air and tested it. My foot was on the bottom step of the stairs before I came to myself. "It's upstairs." I whispered it.

"Yes," Jason said, and there was the thinnest edge of growl to his voice. If someone didn't know what they were listening to, they'd have thought his voice was just deeper than normal. But I knew what I was hearing.

"What's happening?" I asked, and I was still whispering, I think because I didn't want to be overheard. Maybe that was why Jason was whispering, or maybe not. I didn't ask. If he was fighting the urge to run upstairs and roll around in the murder scene, I did not want to know.

I hugged my arms, trying to rub away the goosebumps. "Let's go get those gloves," I said.

He looked at me, and even through the glasses I could feel him struggling to remember what I was saying, or rather what the words meant.

"Don't go all preverbal on me, Jason, I need you here with me."

He took a deep breath that seemed to come from the soles of his feet and slide out the top of his head. His shoulders hunched then straightened like he was trying to shake something off.

"I'm okay."

"You sure?" I asked.

"I can do it, if you can."

I frowned at that. "Am I going to have more trouble?"

"I don't have to go up into that room, you do."

I sighed. "I am so tired of this shit."

"Which shit?" he asked.

"All of it."

He smiled. "Come on, marshal, let's go get those gloves."

I shook my head, but I led the way through the dining room towards the kitchen. I could see the box of gloves sitting beside an open, nearly full trash bag. There'd been a lot of personnel through here to fill up one of those large bags. So where was everyone, and where was Dolph?

# 20

DOLPH FOUND US in the kitchen while I was helping Jason with the gloves. There's an art to putting them on, and it was Jason's first time, so he was like a small child with his first set of gloves, too few fingers and too many holes.

Dolph came in through the dining room the same way we'd come, though he almost filled the doorway, whereas Jason and I had walked through together with plenty of room to spare. Dolph is built like a pro-wrestler, wide, and he's six eight. I'm sort of used to him by now, but Jason did what most people do. He looked up, and up. Other than that, he behaved himself, which for Jason was a minor miracle.

"What's he doing here?" Dolph asked.

"You said if I wasn't well enough to drive I could bring a civvie driver. Jason's my driver."

He shook his head, his dark hair so freshly cut that his ears looked pale and stranded. "Don't you have any human friends left?" he asked.

I concentrated on helping Jason into the gloves and counted to ten. "Yeah, but most of them are cops, and they don't like playing chauffeur."

"He doesn't need gloves, Anita, because he is not staying."

"We had to park too far back for me to walk without someone to catch me if I needed it. I can't send him back through that pack of reporters."

"Yeah, you can," Dolph said.

I finally got the last finger in place. Jason stood there flexing his hands inside the gloves. "How come it feels wet and powdery all at the same time?"

"I don't know, but it always does," I said.

"He is out of here, Anita, do you hear me?"

153

"If he sits on the front stoop, they're going to have pictures of him. What if someone recognizes him? Do you really want the headlines to read werewolves attack suburbia?" I slipped into my own pair of gloves with practiced ease.

"Gosh," Jason said, "that was nifty, you made that look easy."

"Anita!" It was almost a yell.

We both looked up at Dolph. "You don't have to shout, Dolph, I can hear you just fine."

"Then why is he still standing here?"

"I can't send him back to the car. He can't sit out front. Where would you like him to be while I check out the crime scene?"

He balled his big hands into even bigger fists. "I – want – him – out – of – here." Every word was squeezed out through gritted teeth. "I don't care where he fucking goes."

I ignored the anger, because it didn't get me anywhere to pay attention to it. He was in a bad mood, it was a bad scene, and Dolph wasn't too fond of the monsters lately.

Merlioni came into the kitchen. He stopped in the doorway between kitchen and dining room, as if he'd picked up on the tension. "What's going on?"

Dolph pointed a finger at Jason. "He is out of here."

Merlioni glanced at me.

"You do not fucking look at her, you look at me!" The anger was hot in his voice. He wasn't yelling, but he didn't really need to.

Merlioni walked around Dolph, carefully, and reached out to take Jason's arm. I stopped him with one gloved hand on his hand.

Merlioni glanced back at Dolph, then moved a little farther down the kitchen, out of the line of fire, I think.

"Is there a backyard?" I asked.

"Why?" Dolph asked, his voice gone low and growling, not with the edge of any beast, but with anger.

"Merlioni can take him out back. He'll be out of the house and still safe from the reporters."

"No," Dolph said, "he's out of here. Gone, completely gone."

My headache was coming back, a flutter of pain behind one eye, but it had the promise of great things to come. "Dolph, I do not feel well enough for this shit."

"What shit?"

154

"Your shit with anyone not lily-human," I said, and I sounded tired, not angry.

"Get out."

I looked up at him. "What did you say?"

"Get out, take your pet werewolf and go home."

"You bastard."

He gave me that look that had been making grown policemen cringe for years. I was too tired and too disgusted with it all to flinch.

"I told you I was too sick to drive when you woke me up. You agreed I could bring a driver, even a civilian. You didn't say he had to be human. Now after dragging my ass down here, you're going to send me home without having seen the crime scene?"

"Yes," Dolph said, that one word almost choking in its brevity.

"No," I said, "you're not."

"This is my murder, Anita, and I say who stays and who goes."

I was finally beginning to get angry. You can only cut even your friends so much slack. I stepped in front of Jason, closer to Dolph. "I'm not here on your sufferance, Dolph. I'm a federal marshal now, and I have the right to investigate any preternatural crime that I see fit."

"Are you refusing my direct order?" his voice was very quiet now. Not heated – empty – and that should have scared me more, but I wasn't scared of Dolph. I never had been.

"If I think your direct orders are jeopardizing this investigation, then, yes I am."

He took one step towards me. He loomed over me, but I was used to that, a lot of people loomed over me. "Never question my professionalism again, Anita, never."

"When you act like a professional, I won't."

His hands were clenching and unclenching at his sides. "You want to see why I don't want him at this scene? You want to see it?"

"Yeah," I said, "I want to see it."

He grabbed me by the upper arm. I don't know if Dolph had ever touched me before. It caught me off guard, and it wasn't until he'd half-marched, half-dragged me across the kitchen to the dining room door that I unfroze. I looked behind me and shook my head at Jason. He probably didn't like it, but he settled back against the cabinets. I caught a glimpse of Merlioni's shocked face before we were into the dining room.

He dragged me to the stairs, and when I stumbled, he didn't give me time to get to my feet, but literally dragged me up the stairs.

The door opened behind us, and I heard a man say, "Lieutenant!" I thought I recognized the voice, but I wasn't sure, and there wasn't time to look, I was too busy trying not to get rug burns from the stairs.

I couldn't get my feet under me long enough to stand in the heels. The headache burst full-blown behind my eye, and the world was a trembling thing.

I found my voice, "Dolph, Dolph, damn it!"

He opened a door and jerked me to my feet. I staggered while the world ran in streamers of dark color. He held me with one of his big hands on each of my arms, only his grip kept me on my feet.

My vision cleared in pieces, as if the scene were some sort of video puzzle. There was a bed against the far wall. I glimpsed white pillows against a lavender wall, then a woman's head, and some of her shoulders. It didn't look real, as if someone had propped a fake head against the pillows. From about collarbone down, there was only a red ruin. I don't mean a body. I mean it was as if the bed had been dipped in dark fluid. The blood wasn't red, it was black. A trick of the light, or the fact that it wasn't just blood.

The smell hit me then – meat. Everything smelled like hamburger. I saw the pile of bedclothes, black, and red, and sodden, soaked in gore. Gore, not just blood, gore. I looked back at the woman's head, I didn't want to, but I couldn't help it. I looked, and I finally could see. It was all that was left of her, all that was left of an adult woman. It was as if she'd exploded with her head on the pillows, and her body . . . everywhere.

I felt the scream building in my throat, and knew I couldn't do it. I had to be stronger than this, better than this. I swallowed the scream, and my stomach tried to come up my throat. I swallowed that, too, and tried to think.

"What do you think?" Dolph said, and he pushed me, trapped between his big hands, towards the bed. "Pretty enough for you?

156

Because one of your friends did this." He pressed me too close to the bed, and my legs squeezed against the gore-soaked bedclothes. The blood was cool to the touch, and it helped keep my beast from curling up my body. What good was blood if it wasn't hot and fresh?

"Dolph, stop this," I said, and my voice didn't sound like me.

"Lieutenant," a voice came from the open door.

Dolph turned with me still gripped between his hands. Detective Clive Perry stood in the doorway. He was a slender African American man, dressed conservatively, neatly, but well dressed. He was one of the most soft-spoken men I'd ever met, and *the* most soft-spoken policeman.

"What is it, Perry?"

Perry took a deep breath, that moved his shoulders and chest up and down. "Lieutenant, I think Ms. Blake has seen enough of the crime scene for now."

Dolph gave me a little shake that sent my head rattling and my stomach churning. "Not yet, she hasn't." He jerked me around to face back into the room. He dragged me towards the headboard, which was painted a lavender so close to the wall's color I hadn't seen it. He pushed me forward until my face was inches from it. There was a fresh claw mark like a pale scar in the wood and paint.

"What do you think did that, Anita?" He jerked me around until he was holding me facing him, his big hands still wrapped around my upper arms.

"Let go, Dolph." My voice still didn't sound like me. No one else could have done this to me. I'd have fought back by now, or been scared, or pissed. I still wasn't any of those things.

"What do you think did that?" And he gave me a little shake. It made my head rattle, my vision stream.

"Lieutenant Storr, I must insist that you let Ms. Blake go." Detective Perry was behind him, to one side, so I could see his face.

Dolph turned on him, and I think only the fact that his hands were already full kept him from grabbing Perry. "She knows. She knows what did this, because she knows every fucking monster in town."

157

"Let her go, Lieutenant, please."

I closed my eyes, which helped the dizziness. His hands on my arms let me know where his body was. I rammed the pointed heel of my shoe into his instep. He flinched, his hands loosened. I opened my eyes and did what I'd been trained to do. I brought my arms up between his and swept outward, downward. It broke his hold on me, and I drew my right arm back, and hit him a short upper cut into his gut. If he'd been shorter I'd have tried for the solar plexus, but the angle was bad, so I hit what I could get.

The air went out of him in a grunt, and he bent double, hands over his stomach. I still haven't quite come to terms with being more than human strong. I had a second where I hoped I hadn't hurt him more than I meant to, then I stepped back, away from him. The world was trembling, like I was looking at everything through wavy glass.

I kept backing up, and my heels hit something slick and thicker than just blood, and down I went. I landed hard on my ass, and blood spattered upwards. It soaked through my skirt and I struggled to my knees to keep it from soaking into my panties. The blood was cool to the touch, and then my knee smeared in something that wasn't blood.

I screamed and scrambled to my feet. If Perry hadn't caught me I'd have fallen again. But he was moving too slow for the door. I didn't want to throw up in here. I pushed away from him and half-staggered, half-ran through the doorway. When I hit the hallway I fell to all fours and threw up on the pale carpet. My head roared with pain, and my vision exploded with starbursts of white, white light.

I crawled towards the head of the stairs, not sure what I planned to do. The floor came up to smack into my body, and there was nothing but a soft, gray nothingness, then the world was black, and my head didn't hurt at all.

# 21

THE TILE FELT SO good against my cheek, so cool. Someone was moving around. I thought about opening my eyes, but it seemed like too much effort. Someone put a cool cloth against my neck. It made me shiver, and I opened my eyes. My vision took a second to focus, then I saw the knee beside my face was wearing hose, and a skirt.

I knew it wasn't one of the men, unless they had hobbies I didn't know about. "Anita, it's me, Tammy, how you feeling?"

I rolled my eyes, but some of my own hair was in the way, and I couldn't see up that far. I tried to say, *help me sit up*, but it didn't come out. I tried again, and she had to lean close to hear me. She pushed a piece of her straight brown hair behind her ear, as if that would help her hear better.

"Help me," I swallowed, "sit up."

She got an arm under my shoulders and lifted. Detective Tammy Reynolds was five ten, and she worked out at least enough to keep the other – read male – cops from giving her grief. She didn't have much trouble getting me up, my back against the bathtub.

Staying there was my job, and that was a little more trouble. I propped myself on one arm and leaned against the tub.

She picked the rag up from the edge of the sink where she'd laid it, and put it against my forehead. The rag was cold, and I jerked away from her. I felt cold, that was a new symptom. I thought of something.

"Have you been," I coughed to clear my throat, "putting cool rags on me?"

"Yes, it helps me when I'm sick."

"Cold rags don't seem to be helping me." I didn't tell her that it was probably one of the worst things she could have done for me. Ever since I had inherited Richard's beast, or whoever's beast, cold didn't seem to help me when I was sick. I healed like a lycanthrope now, and that meant that my temperature ran hot when I was sick, like my body was cooking itself. A well-meaning doctor had almost killed me with ice baths for what they thought was a dangerously high fever.

I started to shiver.

She got up, rinsing the washrag out, and spreading it out to dry on the edge of the sink. "I threw up in the yard," she said. She put her hands on the sink, head bowed.

I hugged myself, trying to stop the shivering, but it didn't really help. I was cold. I hadn't been cold earlier today. Was a new symptom good or bad?

"It's a bad scene," I said, "I'm sure you weren't the only cop who lost their breakfast."

Tammy looked at me through a trailing edge of her hair. She had to keep her hair above her collar, just like the male policemen, but she kept it as long as she could. "Maybe, but I'm the only one who passed out."

"Except for me," I said.

"Yeah, you and me, the only women at the scene." She sounded so tired.

Tammy and I weren't actually friends. She was a Follower of the Way, Christianity's version of witches. Most of the Followers of the Way were zealots, more Christian than the right-wingers, as if they had to prove they really were worthy of salvation. Tammy had mellowed since she'd been dating Larry Kirkland, my fellow animator. But this was the first time I'd realized how much of that bright and shiny exterior had been worn away. Police work will eat you up and spit you out.

As women we needed to be tougher just to be accepted. Today hadn't helped either of us.

"It's not your fault," I said. The shivering was beginning to get a little worse.

"No, it's my damn doctor's fault."

I looked up at her. "Excuse me?"

"He gives me a prescription for birth control pills then prescribes antibiotics, and doesn't warn me that while I'm taking the antibiotic, the pill won't work."

160

My eyes went wide. "I'm sorry, are you saying . . ."

"That I'm pregnant, yes."

I know the surprise showed on my face, I couldn't help it. "Does Larry know?"

She nodded. "Yes."

"What . . ." I tried to think of something good to say, and gave up. "What are you going to do?"

"Get married, damn it."

Something must have showed on my face, because she knelt by me. "I love Larry, but I didn't plan on marrying now, and I certainly didn't plan on having a baby. Do you know how hard it is to get ahead in this job as a woman? Of course, you do. Sorry."

"No," I said, "it's not the same for me. Police work isn't my entire career." The shivering had started up again; no amount of astonishment could keep me warm.

She took her own jacket off, showing her gun in its front holster. She wrapped the jacket around me. I didn't argue, but clutched it closed with my hands.

"Is the shivering from the pregnancy?" she asked. "Someone said you said you were sick, are you?"

It took me a second or two, blinking at her sort of stupidly to understand what she'd said. "Did you just say 'pregnancy'?"

She made a face at me. "Anita, please, I haven't told anyone either, but they're going to guess. I threw up at the murder scene, I've never done that. I didn't pass out cold like you did, but I came close. Perry had to help me out into the yard so I could be sick. It won't take them long to figure it out."

"This is not the first scene I've thrown up at, not even the fourth," I said. I haven't done it in a while, but I've certainly done it before. Surely they've told you the story about me throwing up on the body. Zerbrowski loves that one."

"Sure, but I thought he was exaggerating. You know how Zerbrowski is."

"He wasn't exaggerating."

"You can lie to me if you want to, but unless you're planning to abort, they'll all figure it out sooner or later."

"I am not pregnant," I said, though I had a little trouble saying

161

it, because I was shivering so badly it was hard to talk. "I'm just sick."

"You're freezing, Anita, you don't have a fever."

How could I explain to her that I was having a bad reaction to a vampire bite and the fact that I shared Richard's beast. Odd metaphysics weren't easy to explain. Pregnancy was nice and simple, compared to that.

She grabbed my arms, a lot like Dolph had. "I am three months pregnant. How far along are you? Please tell me, tell me I haven't been a fool. Tell me I haven't ruined my life by not reading the fine print on a bottle of medicine."

I was shivering so hard, it was hard to talk, but I managed to get out, "I – am – not pregnant."

She stood and turned her back on me. "Damn you for not sharing."

I tried to say something, I wasn't even sure what, but she left, leaving the door open behind her. I wasn't sure being left alone was a good thing, the shivering was getting worse, like I was freezing to death from the inside. Larry Kirkland was off being trained to be a federal marshal. He didn't have four years as a vamp executioner yet, so he couldn't get grandfathered in. I wondered if the pregnancy was making it harder for him to be away from Tammy, or easier. Damn it, anyway.

Perry brought Jason up to me. He touched me. "God, you're cold." He picked me up in his arms like I weighed nothing. "I'm taking her home."

"We'll give you an escort through the press," Perry said.

Jason didn't argue. He carried me down the stairs. We waited for a few minutes, while Perry rounded up enough warm bodies to act as a sort of living gauntlet to try and keep the press at bay.

The door opened, the sunlight hit my eyes and the headache roared to life. I buried my face against Jason's chest. Jason seemed to know what was wrong, because he raised an edge of Tammy's jacket across my eyes.

"Are you ready?" Perry's voice.

"Let's do it," Jason said.

Normally, I'd have felt humiliated to be carried out of a murder scene like a wilting flower, but I was working too hard on keeping

162

the shivering under control. It took all my concentration not to let my body shake itself apart. What the hell was wrong with me?

We were outside, and moving at a good pace. I could judge how close we were to the press by how loud the yelling was getting. "What's wrong with Ms. Blake?" "What happened to her?" "Who are you?" "Where are you taking her?" There were more questions, lots more. They all melded into a noise like the ocean against the shore. The crowd surged around us. There was a moment when I felt them closing like a fist around us, but Merlioni's voice rose to a shout, "Back up, back up now, or we'll clear this area!"

Jason got me inside the Jeep, leaning his shoulder into me, so he could fasten the seat belt. The jacket was across my face now, and strangely it felt claustrophobic.

"Close your eyes," he said.

I was already doing what he'd asked, but I didn't say anything. The jacket moved away, and the sun was bright against my closed eyelids. I felt the sunglasses slip over my eyes, and I opened them cautiously. Better.

There was a line of detectives and uniforms in front of the Jeep, keeping the pack of reporters back, so we could make our getaway. Every camera they had was pointed our way. God knew what the captions would read once they were done with it.

Jason gunned the engine and backed up with a screech of tires. He was a ways down the street before I could chatter out, "You'll get a ticket."

"I've called Micah. He's waiting. You and Nathaniel can share the bathtub."

I managed to get out, "What?"

"I don't know exactly what's wrong, Anita, but you're acting like a shape-shifter that's been badly hurt. Like your body's trying to heal some deep wound. You need heat, and the touch of your group."

"I," teeth chattering so hard I couldn't finish, "haven't . . ." I stopped trying for a sentence and settled for, "Not hurt."

"I know that you're not hurt that badly. But even if it was the vampire bite, you'd be warm to the touch, hot, cooking to heal yourself. You shouldn't feel cold."

163

My ears started ringing. It sounded like someone was hitting a chime over and over. The ringing drowned out Jason's voice, the sound of the engine, and finally everything. I passed out for the second time in less than two hours. This was not turning out to be one of my better days.

# 22

I WAS FLOATING in water, warm, warm water. Arms held me in place, a man's body brushed against mine in the water. I opened my eyes to the flickering light of candles. Was I back at the Circus of the Damned? Two things happened to let me know exactly where I was: pale tile gleamed on the edge of the bathtub, and the arms around my shoulders tightened, drew me closer. The moment the back of my body settled firmly against the front of his, I knew it was Micah.

I knew the curve of his shoulder, the way my body seemed to slide into every line and hollow of his body. His tanned arms were delicate for a man's, but as he snuggled me against him, muscles moved under his skin. I knew how much strength there was in his slender body. He was like me, a lot more than met the eye.

"How are you feeling?" he asked, voice so close to my ear that a whisper seemed loud.

My voice came distant and hollow the way I'd been feeling all day. "Better."

"At least you're warmer," he said. "Jason said you were sick, dizzy. Has that passed?"

I thought about it, trying to feel my body, and not just the comforting warmth and closeness. "Yeah, I do feel better. What the hell was wrong with me?"

He turned me in his arms, so that he held me across him, and we could look at each other. He smiled down at me. The tan that he'd come with had started to fade a little, but he was still dark, and that darkness framed his most startling feature. His eyes were kitty-cat eyes. I'd originally thought they were yellow green, but they were yellow, or green, or any combination of either, depending on his mood, the light, the color of shirt he wore.

His pupils had spread like black pools, and the thin line of color

165

that chased round them was a pale true green. Human eyes weren't really green, not really. Grayish green, maybe, but a true clear green, rarely. But Micah's eyes were.

Those eyes sat in a face that was beautiful in the way a woman's face was beautiful. Delicate. There was a line to the jaw, a chin that was male, but gently so. His mouth was wide, with the bottom lip thicker than his upper, giving him a permanent pout.

I wanted to feel his lips on mine, feel the brush of his skin under my hands. He affected me as he'd affected me almost from the first moment I saw him – like he was a missing piece of myself that I had to bring as close to my body as I could, as if we'd meld together someday.

He didn't argue as I brought him down for the kiss. He didn't tell me that I was hurt and needed to rest. He just leaned in and pressed his mouth against mine.

Kissing him was like breathing, automatic, something your body did so that it wouldn't die. There was no thought to wanting to touch Micah, no waffling indecision like with every other man in my life. He was my Nimir-Raj, and from the moment we had been together it had been deeper than marriage, more permanent than anything words or paper could bind.

My arms slid over his back, his shoulders, the slick wetness of his skin, and our beasts rose. His energy was like a hot breath along my skin, shimmering everywhere we touched. My beast rose up through the depths of my body, and I felt Micah's beast echoing mine. They moved in our two separate bodies like two swimming shapes, up and up, each racing the other with only our skin to keep them apart. Then it was as if the skin was not enough to contain them, and our beasts swam through each of us. It bowed my back, brought Micah's voice in something near a scream. Our beasts writhed between our bodies, the energies intertwined more than our bodies ever could. They wove and danced like some invisible rope, knotting, tying, gliding in and out of us, until I raked my nails down Micah's body, and he set teeth into my shoulder.

I don't know if it was the pain, the pleasure, the beasts, or all of it together, but suddenly I could think again. Suddenly, I knew why I'd been sick all day.

I felt that long metaphysical cord that bound me to Jean-Claude, saw him in his bed at the Circus of the Damned with Asher still beside him. There was a shadow sitting on Jean-Claude's bare chest, a dark shape. The longer I looked at it, the more solid it became, until it turned a misshapen face to me, snarling, and showed me eyes burning with dark honey flame.

I looked at the hungry shadow of Belle Morte's power that had been trying to leech "life" from Jean-Claude all day. But the Master Vampire's fail-safe systems had kicked in – his human servant, and probably his animal to call. Richard had refused to help us directly, but he was probably paying the price for it today.

The thing hissed at me again, like some great demonic cat, and I decided to treat it like one. I threw my beast down the long line of metaphysical cord. What I hadn't planned for was that Micah's beast would follow mine, that when we attacked it would be together, ripping the thing to smoky tatters. It fled through the wall.

I wondered where it had gotten to, and the thought was enough. I saw it in the guest room we'd prepared for Musette. The shadow sat on her chest for a second, then seemed to melt into her body. There was a moment when that swimming thing moved underneath the vampire's dead skin, then all was quiet.

Angelito's voice, "Mistress are you there?"

Then I was back in the warm water, and Micah's arms. "What was that?" he asked, voice soft, strangled.

"The shadowy thing was a piece of Belle Morte's power that she gave to Musette."

"It was like it was trying to feed on Jean-Claude, but it couldn't."

"I'm his human servant, Micah. I think when Musette tried to steal Jean-Claude's strength, the attack deflected to me. She's been sucking on me all day."

"Did Jean-Claude do that on purpose?" he asked.

"No, he's truly dead to the world. It's just the way the system is set up. If she could have sucked Jean-Claude dry, then she could have taken the energy of all of his vamps, everyone that had a blood tie to him."

"Instead she's been feeding off of you."

167

"Yeah, and probably Richard. I bet he called in sick to school today."

Micah held me tight against him. "How do we keep it from happening again?"

I patted his arm. "You know that's one of the things I like most about you. Most people would spend time worrying about what could have happened, how bad it could have been, you go straight to the practical."

"We need to do something before it hops back through the wall."

"Is my cell phone in here anywhere?"

"In the pile with your clothes," he said.

"Can you reach it?"

He stretched out one long arm. His arms were longer than they looked. He used fingertips to move the phone close enough to pick up. He handed it to me without a single question. Micah didn't make me waste time explaining myself.

I called the Circus of the Damned, the special number that wasn't in the phone book. Ernie, who was Jean-Claude's human errand boy and sometimes appetizer, answered. I asked if Bobby Lee was still there. When I described him, Ernie said, "Yeah, can't get rid of him. Seems to think he's in charge."

Since I sort of thought he was in charge, too, that worked for me. Bobby Lee came on the line. "Anita, what's happening?"

"Ask Ernie to find you some crosses, and put them on the doors to the guest rooms."

"Can I ask why?"

"To keep the bad vampires from doing any more metaphysical tricks today."

"That explains absolutely nothing to me."

"Just do it."

"Don't you need to put crosses on the coffins to keep vampires from using their powers?"

"There's only one exit from each room, it's like a bigger coffin. Trust me, it'll work."

"You're the boss, at least until Rafael tells me otherwise." He asked Ernie for the crosses. I could hear Ernie's voice protesting in tone, though not the words.

Bobby Lee came back on line. "He's worried that the crosses being in plain sight on the doors will impede our vampires when they wake."

"Maybe, but I'm more worried about what our guests are doing right now. When night falls, we'll worry about it. Until then just do it."

"Are you ever going to explain to me why I'm doing it?"

"You want to know, fine, the new vamps are using vampire wiles to suck energy from Jean-Claude, and through him, me. I have felt like shit all day."

"You know, I like you, Anita, you explain things when I ask. I almost never understand what the hell you're talking about, but you talk to me like I'm bright enough to understand it, and know enough about magic to follow all the big words."

"I'm hanging up now, Bobby Lee."

"Yes, ma'am."

I handed the phone to Micah so he could put it close to the pile of clothes, which I had no chance of reaching without dribbling water all over the place.

I leaned back against Micah, and he sank deeper into the water, so that even the tip of my chin was submerged. I wanted to sink in against his body, be held, and drowse. Now that the shadow was off of Jean-Claude, I was tired. It was almost as if now I had permission to sleep.

But there was one other crisis to talk about. "Jason told me that Nathaniel collapsed at work last night."

"He's tucked into his room, sandwiched between Zane and Cherry. He's fine." Micah kissed the side of my head.

"Is it true that he collapsed because the two of you can't keep feeding my *ardeur* twice a day?"

Micah went very still around me, and his silence said it all.

"Did you know that the two of you couldn't sustain me?"

"You feed on Jean-Claude, too," he said.

"Fine, did you know that the three of you couldn't sustain me?"

"Jean-Claude keeps saying that your appetite should go down soon. The three of us could feed you if you only needed to be fed once a day. Twice a day is harder."

"Why didn't you tell me?" I asked.

169

He hugged me, and I let him, but I wasn't happy.

"Because I know how hard it is for you to take new people to your bed. I was hoping you wouldn't have to."

That reminded me. "I sort of did."

"Did what?" he asked.

"Took someone else to my bed." I felt like I should be squirming with embarrassment, but my ability to be embarrassed wasn't what it used to be.

"Who?" he asked, voice soft.

"Asher."

"You and Jean-Claude," he made it more statement than question.

"Yeah."

He cuddled me against him. "Why now?"

I told him my reasoning.

"You are going to make those vampires very unhappy tonight."

"I hope so." I turned in his arms enough to see his face. He looked peaceful enough by candlelight. "Does it bother you, about Asher?"

He seemed to think about it for a second or two. "Yes, and no."

"Explain the yes," I said.

"While you need the *ardeur* fed, there's plenty of your time to go around. I'm a little worried about what happens if you get a string of men now, with the *ardeur* rising, then the *ardeur* goes away. You're going to have some unhappy people, if you get too many of them."

I frowned. "I hadn't thought about that. I mean I haven't had intercourse with anyone but you and Jean-Claude."

"I'll say what Jean-Claude would say if he were here: *Ma petite*, you are splitting hairs."

"Fine, fine, I don't plan on kicking Nathaniel out of my bed just because the *ardeur* is quiet."

"No, but will you be willing to touch him the way he's come to expect?"

I turned so I wouldn't have to meet those honest eyes of his. "I don't know, that's the truth, I don't know."

"And Asher?"

"One step at a time with him, okay."

"And Richard?"

170

I shook my head against Micah's chest. "That's moot. Richard can barely stand to be within twenty feet of me."

"Are you seriously saying that if he showed up today and asked to come back, you'd say no?"

It was my turn to go quiet in his arms. I thought about it, tried to think about it, clearly, level-headed. The trouble was that Richard was never a topic I was logical on.

"I don't know, but I'm leaning towards no."

"Really?"

"Micah, I still have feelings for Richard, but he dumped me. He dumped me because I'm more comfortable with the monsters than he is. He dumped me because I'm too blood-thirsty for him. He dumped me because I'm not the person he wants me to be. I will never be the person he wants me to be."

"Richard will never be the person he wants himself to be," Micah said, softly.

I sighed. It was true. Richard wanted, more than anything else, to be human. He didn't want to be a monster. He wanted to be a junior high science teacher, marry a nice girl, settle down, have 2.5 children, and maybe a dog. He was a science teacher, but the rest . . . Richard was like me, he would never have a normal life. I had accepted that, but he was still fighting. Fighting to be human, fighting to be ordinary, fighting not to love me. He'd succeeded on that last.

"If Richard comes back to me, it won't be for good. He'll come back because he can't help himself, but he hates himself too much to love anyone else."

"That's harsh," he said.

"But true," I said.

Micah didn't argue with me. He didn't when he knew he was wrong, or knew I was right. Richard would have argued. Richard always argued. Richard seemed to believe that if he pretended the world was a nicer place than it really was, that that would change the world. It didn't. The world was what it was. And no amount of anger, or hatred, or self-loathing, or stubborn blindness would change it.

Maybe Richard would learn to accept himself, but I was beginning to believe that he would learn that lesson without me in his life.

I hugged Micah's arms around me like a warm coat, but I was tired now, achingly tired. If Richard knocked on the door today, and asked to come back, what would I do? Truthfully, I didn't know. But one thing I knew, Richard wouldn't let me feed the *ardeur* off of him. He thought it was monstrous. And he wouldn't share me physically with anyone but Jean-Claude. Even if he wanted to come back, unless he'd let me feed the *ardeur* off of others, it wouldn't work. Pure practicality. The *ardeur* had to be fed. Richard wouldn't feed it. Richard wouldn't let me feed it off of anyone but Jean-Claude. Jean-Claude alone couldn't sustain my appetite. Hell, Micah, Jean-Claude, and Nathaniel together weren't sustaining it. If Richard came back today, what would I do, offer him one-third of my bed, on the other side from Micah?

Richard had consented to dating me at the same time I dated Jean-Claude, but never to sharing a bed with him and me at the same time. Richard would try to go back to what we had. I couldn't do that.

What would I do if Richard knocked on the door right now? Offer to let him join us in the bathtub, watch his face show all the hurt and rage, watch him stomp out again. What would I do if Richard wanted to come back? The only thing I could do, say no. The question was, was I strong enough to say it? Probably not.

# 23

I DIDN'T SO much wake, as come to the surface of sleep, enough to hear voices. Micah's voice first, "What did Gregory say?"

"That his father tried to contact him," Cherry's voice.

"Why is that bad?"

"His father is the one that pimped him and Stephen out when they were children."

"Every time I think I've heard the worst of people, I'm wrong," Micah said.

I fought to open my eyes, and it was as if my eyelids weighed a hundred pounds apiece. I blinked and found Micah still curled against me, but propped up on one elbow. Cherry was standing beside the bed. She was tall, slender, long waisted, with blond hair cut boyishly short. She wasn't wearing any makeup which meant she was in a hurry, and she was actually wearing clothes which was unusual for one of the wereleopards. They usually only got dressed if I insisted. Either she was going out, or something was wrong. But of course, something was wrong.

I fought to wake up enough to say something, and it took more effort than was pretty. My voice came out thick, "What'd you say, 'bout Gregory?"

Cherry bent closer, and it took almost everything I had to keep her in focus as she moved in towards me. "You knew that Gregory and Stephen had been abused as children?" she made it half question.

I managed to say, "Yeah." I frowned up at her. "Did you say their father pimped them out as children?" Maybe I was dreaming? Either that, or I'd misunderstood.

"You didn't know," Cherry said. Her face was so serious.

I was suddenly more awake. "No."

Zane came through the bedroom door with Nathaniel in his

arms. Zane was six feet tall, stretched a little too thin for my tastes, but since he and Cherry were living together, it wasn't my tastes that counted. His very short hair was white-blond now. It was the first color occurring in nature that I'd ever seen him dye his hair. I had no idea what his true hair color was.

Zane carried Nathaniel tucked in against his chest, like he was a sleeping child. Nathaniel's nearly ankle-length auburn hair, in its heavy braid, was clutched in one of Zane's hands. If you tried carrying Nathaniel without controlling all that hair, you had a tendency to trip on it. On either side of the braid his body was bare.

"He's wearing underwear," Zane said, "we know the rules. No sleeping naked with you." He moved the hair enough to flash a pair of the satiny jogging shorts that Nathaniel was fond of wearing for jammies.

I tried to prop myself up on my elbows, but that seemed too hard. I settled for lying on my back with both eyes solidly open. "How's he doing?"

"He's fine," Micah said.

I looked at him. I tried to make the look skeptical, but I failed, so I had to say out loud, "He looks comatose."

"Say something to her, you lazy cat," Zane said.

Nathaniel turned his head slowly, almost painfully slow, as Zane carried him around to the other side of the bed. He blinked lavender eyes at me, and gave me a lazy smile. He looked almost as tired as I felt. And why not? Hadn't he collapsed for the same reason I had – because some vampire had been feeding off of him? The *ardeur* didn't take blood, but it was still a type of vampirism.

Micah crawled out from the covers, flashing the perfectly tanned line of his body. Mercifully, he kept most of his assets hidden from my view. I think I was too tired to be tempted, but I knew I was too tired to want to be tempted. He pulled clothes on with his back to me, but when he turned around, pants safely zipped, the look on his face said plainly that he knew I'd been watching him.

His dark, dark, brown hair curled around his shoulders. One movement of his head sent all that heavy hair sliding to one side of his face. The dark hair framed those extraordinary eyes, gleaming yellow and green at the same time now.

"If you don't move out of her line of sight, we'll be here all bloody day," Zane said.

"You sound jealous," Cherry chided him.

"Well," he said, "you don't watch me like that."

"I don't watch anybody like that," Cherry said.

Zane grinned at her. "I know."

They had one of those laughs that is a couple laugh, and you know that you are on the outside of an inside joke. Zane was right about one thing, I was delaying. It wasn't until I tried getting out of bed that I realized I was still naked. I'd sort of known that, but in a distant, floaty kind of way.

"I need clothes," I said.

Micah had pulled a polo shirt out of the communal drawer. It was one I'd bought with him in mind, a deep rich forest green. It brought out the green in his eyes. But the shirt fit both of us, as most of our shirts did. Our casual clothes had become common property – only the dress-up clothes were strictly his and hers.

Micah didn't so much make me lie back down, as touch my shoulder so I'd stop trying to sit up. I didn't seem to be coordinated enough to sit up in bed, keep the sheet over my breasts, and chew gum at the same time. It was as if my body just wasn't listening to me yet.

"Anita, if you don't rest you're not going to be any good to anyone."

"Gregory's my leopard, I'm his Nimir-Ra."

Micah smoothed his hand down the side of my face. "And I'm his Nimir-Raj. Go back to sleep. I'll take care of it, that's what you hired me for, right?"

I had to smile at him, but I didn't like not going to Gregory's rescue. It must have shown on my face, because he knelt beside the bed, taking my hand in his. "Gregory is having hysterics because his father's in town. I'm going to go and see how he's doing, maybe bring him back here so his father can't find him through the phone book."

I was having trouble focusing on Micah's face. I'd crawled out of sleep, but it was sucking at me again. "Yes," I said, voice starting to sound distant, even to me, "bring him back here."

He kissed me gently on the forehead, my hand still in his. "I

175

will. Now sleep, or you're going to make yourself sick. A sick Nimir-Ra can't protect anybody."

Since I couldn't keep my eyes from giving long blinks, it was hard to argue. Him kissing my hand was the first hint I had that he'd stood up. That had been a long blink.

The bed moved, and Nathaniel cuddled up against me. His arm across my stomach, one leg across my thigh. It was one of his favorite sleeping positions, but something wasn't right with it. "Clothes," I said, and I frowned harder. "Can't feed off Nathaniel again."

Micah reappeared in my line of sight. "You've only been asleep about two hours, that's why you're so tired. If you fed the *ardeur* at dawn, you've got at least six hours before you need to feed again. We're just putting him in here so he won't be alone."

The last few words floated out of the dark, and it wasn't until he'd been quiet for a long time that I opened my eyes to an empty room. Nathaniel was tucked in against me, his face hidden against my shoulder. He snuggled in tighter, leaving me with about an inch of bed to spare. I started to move him over and get out of bed to find the pajamas no one had given me, but I fell back to sleep. The wereleopards were having a bad influence on how comfortable I was being nude.

# 24

I DREAMED. BELLE Morte sat at her dressing table, her long black hair fell in waves, freshly brushed, gleaming in the candlelight. She wore a gown of deep yellow gold, and I knew before she turned those honey brown eyes to me that the color of the robe brought out the gold in them.

Her lips were red and moist, as if she'd just licked them. She held out her white hand towards me. "Come, *ma petite*, come, sit with me." She smiled with that red, red mouth, and I wanted nothing more than to go to her, to take that outstretched hand, and be held.

I actually started forward a step and found I was wearing a gown similar to hers. I could feel the layers of petticoats, the metal of the stays digging in, forcing my posture absolutely straight. The gown was a rich crimson, a color that made my own skin gleam white, my hair blacker for the contrast, my own lips redder than they truly were, my dark eyes nearly black.

I touched the unfamiliar clothes, and it helped me to think, helped me to hesitate. I shook my head. "No," and my whisper echoed oddly through the room.

She waved that pale hand at me. "As you like, *ma petite*, but come closer, so I may know you better."

I shook my head again, forcing my fingers to touch the heavy, unfamiliar fabric of the gown. "I am not your *ma petite*."

"Of course, you are, for everything that belongs to Jean-Claude is mine."

"No," I said. It seemed like I should have been saying more, but I couldn't think with her sitting there wrapped in candlelight, a bowl of old-fashioned roses on the table by her elbow. The roses were her rose, created and named for her centuries ago.

She stood in a swish of skirts, that rustling sound that made my

177

pulse beat faster, and my body tighten. *Run, run,* I screamed it in my head, but my body wasn't moving.

She walked slowly towards me, her breasts mounded by the tight clothing. I had a sudden flash of memory of what it was like to kiss along that gleaming skin.

I took two handfuls of the long skirt, turned on my high-heeled shoes, and ran. The room vanished, as I ran, and it was a long, endlessly long corridor that I ran down. It was dark, but it was the dark of dreams where even without light you could always see the monsters. Though what lurked in the alcoves along the hallway weren't exactly monsters.

Couples entwined on either side of me. Glimpses of flesh, pale and dark, images of carnal delights. I didn't see anything clearly, I didn't want to. I ran, and tried not to see, but of course, I couldn't not see everything. Breasts like ripe fruit spilling out of old-fashioned dresses. Full skirts lifted to prove that there was nothing underneath but flesh. A man with his pants around his thighs, and a woman bending over him. Blood gleamed down the pale flesh, vampires raised fangs to the light, and humans clung to them, begging for more.

I ran faster, and faster, struggling against the heavy skirts and the tight upright corset. It was hard to breathe, hard to move, and no matter how fast I ran, the door that I could see at the end of all these carnal nightmares never seemed to get closer.

There was nothing too terribly frightening happening in the alcoves. Nothing I hadn't either seen or participated in, in one form or another, but somehow I knew that if I stopped running they'd get me. And, more than anything else, I didn't want them to touch me.

The door was suddenly in front of me. I grabbed the handle, tugged on it, and it was locked. Of course it was locked. I screamed, and knew before I turned around that the things in the corridor weren't in the alcoves anymore.

Belle's voice, "Come to me willingly, *ma petite*."

I put my forehead against the door, eyes closed, as if, if I didn't turn around, didn't see them, they couldn't get me. "Stop calling me that."

She laughed, and it felt like sex sliding along my skin. Jean-

Claude's laugh was amazing, but this, this . . . the sound made me spasm against the hard wood and metal of the door.

"You will feed us, *ma petite*. It will happen, your choice is only in how."

I turned slowly, the way you do in nightmares. You turn, knowing that the hot breath on your skin really is the monster.

Belle Morte stood in the center of the vast echoing space of the corridor, and through Jean-Claude's memories I knew it was a real place, this corridor. The people from the alcoves crowded to either side of her and behind her, a huge, hungry-eyed, half-naked mob.

"I offer you my hand, come, take it, and it will be pleasure beyond your dreams. Refuse me . . ." she motioned, and that one small movement seemed to take in all the eager, leering faces. "It can be a dream, or a nightmare. The choice is yours."

I shook my head. "You don't give choices, Belle, you never did."

"Then your choice is . . . pain."

The mob at her back rushed me, and the dream shattered. I was left gasping in Nathaniel's worried face. "You cried out in your sleep. Were you having a nightmare?" he said.

My heart was beating so hard I could barely swallow past my pulse. I managed a breathy, "Oh, yeah."

Then I smelled roses, thick, cloying, old-fashioned, almost sickly sweet. Belle's voice echoed through my head, "You will feed us."

The *ardeur* poured through me, raising heat along my skin. Nathaniel jerked his hands back as if he'd been burned, but I knew it hadn't hurt. He knelt in the tangle of sheets, eyes wide, the little satin jogging shorts stretched tight over his thighs. They weren't stretched tight over the front of him yet, he wasn't excited yet, and I wanted him to be.

I rolled onto my side, reaching for him, one pale hand outstretched. "Come, take my hand." The moment the words left my mouth, I was back in my nightmare, except that I was playing Belle.

Nathaniel was reaching out towards me, to touch my hand, and I knew if he did, the *ardeur* would spread to him, and I would feed. Nathaniel had collapsed last night because I'd taken too much from him, what would happen if I fed again this soon?

179

"Stop," I said, and it was almost firm. If it had been almost anyone else, they wouldn't have stopped, but it was Nathaniel and he did what he was told.

He stayed on his knees, those tiny shorts stretched so tight across his body. He let his hand fall back into his lap. He was only inches away from me. All I had to do was close that small distance.

I needed to get out of the bed, to walk away, but that strong I was not. I couldn't seem to take my eyes away from him, so close, so eager, so young. That thought wasn't mine.

I frowned, and the confusion helped me push back the *ardeur* long enough to sit up, long enough to look at the mirror on the dresser against the far wall. I was trying to see if my eyes were shining with honey-brown fire, but they were my eyes. Belle hadn't possessed me like she had once upon a time. But she'd done something – awakened the *ardeur* hours ahead of time.

The bed moved, and my head swiveled back, like a predator hearing the mouse in the grass. Nathaniel was exactly where I'd left him, but he must have made some small movement, and that one small movement had been enough. My pulse was in my throat, my body tight and swollen with need. A need like nothing I'd ever experienced. I couldn't breathe past it, couldn't move around it. It was as if need had taken me over and there was nothing left of me.

This wasn't right. This wasn't me. I managed to shake my head, to let out the breath I'd been holding. I was being messed about with. I even knew who was doing it, but I didn't know how to stop it.

The door to the bedroom opened. It was Jason. He stood in the doorway rubbing his hands on his bare arms. He'd pulled on his jeans but hadn't bothered to zip or button them. I caught a flash of a new pair of silk undies, pale blue to match the shirt he wasn't wearing anymore.

"What are you doing in here, Anita? The power is crawling over my skin."

I tried to talk around the ripeness of my own pulse and failed twice, before I managed to say, "*Ardeur*."

He came farther into the room, still rubbing his arms trying to get rid of the goosebumps. "It's hours too early."

I wanted to tell him about the dream, about Belle, but all I could concentrate on was the glimpse of silk through his open jeans. I wanted to go to him, to pull his pants down around his ankles, to take him in my mouth . . .

The visual was so strong I had to close my eyes, had to hug myself tight to keep myself on the bed. There was another small movement from Nathaniel.

He had lain down on the bed, his braid trailing behind him like Rapunzel. His face was peaceful. He would let me do anything I wanted to him, even love him to death.

I drew my legs in against my body, wrapped my arms around myself so tight, and held on. "Get out, Nathaniel, get out."

I felt the bed move, but didn't dare look. I kept my eyes tight shut. "Get out!"

"You heard her, Nathaniel," Jason said, "leave now."

I heard small sounds as he crossed the room, then the door shut. "You can look now, Anita, he's gone."

I opened my eyes, and the room was empty, except for the play of sunlight, and Jason standing beside the bed. His hair was very yellow in the light, the color of butter, his eyes so blue. I followed the line of his body to the broad shoulders, the muscled edge of his arms, his chest with its pale nipples. There was no hair on his chest or stomach. A lot of strippers shaved their body hair. I'd seen Jason nude often enough to know that he was mostly shaved. I just hadn't really noticed how shaved. He was my friend, so even nude, he was still my friend. You don't stare at your friend's crotch to see how much body hair there is.

Now, sitting on the bed, holding myself tight, I didn't feel friendly, I felt crazed. I wanted to fling myself off the bed, onto him. I wanted him naked.

"What do you need?" Jason asked.

I looked up at him, and didn't know whether to cry or scream, but finally I found words, a hoarse voice squeezed past my pulse, "I have to feed."

"I know." He looked so solemn. "What do you need me to do?"

I wanted to tell him to leave, too, but I didn't. Micah wasn't here. The vampires were still dead to the world. Nathaniel was off-limits for today. There were others outside this room, but no one I wanted to touch. No one who was even my friend.

181

I looked up at Jason. A square of sunlight splashed across his chest, painting him gold and warm.

"What do you want me to do, Anita?"

My voice came out barely above a whisper, "Feed me."

"Blood, flesh, or sex?" his face was careful as he asked, solemn.

My *ardeur* was always mixed with other desires, but not today. Today there was only one need. "Sex." That one word, low, soft, while I kept myself from going to him.

His so-serious face split into a sudden grin. "I'll take one for the team."

I slid off the bed, to stand for a moment nude before him. I wanted to run to him, to jump on him, to fuck him. There was no other word for what my body was wanting. But I didn't want to do that. I wanted to avoid intercourse, if I could. I'd managed to avoid it with Nathaniel for months. Surely, just this once with Jason I could manage it.

I closed my eyes and took a few deep breaths, then I dropped to the floor on all fours. I crawled towards him, feeling like I had muscles in places that I shouldn't have. My beast curled through my body like a cat on its back, stretching in the sunlight. But the *ardeur* roared over my beast, as if the desire were some great hand, smashing down every other need.

"Aren't you going to complain about being naked in front of me?"

"No," I whispered it, not trusting anything louder. His feet were bare. I lowered my face to the smooth skin on top of his foot, licked along it.

His breath came out in a shiver. "God."

I used my hands to crawl up his legs, tugging on the jeans, until I knelt in front of him. I'd managed to pull the jeans lower on his hips without meaning to, exposing a wide triangle of the blue silk undies. My face was almost level with his groin. I could see him pressed tight and firm under the cloth, the tip of him straining against the elastic of the underwear, trapped. I wanted to lower that cloth, to help him.

I slid my hands around behind him, digging fingers into his jeans, gripping his butt. It drew a sound from low in his throat, but it kept me from ripping off his clothes.

182

I pressed my face against his thigh, turning it away from his groin. My control hung from a rapidly fraying thread. I'd learned through long practice with Nathaniel that the only way to keep from doing more was to do everything carefully, slowly. But I didn't want to be careful, and I felt anything but slow. I wanted to beg him to take me. Damn it, I could do better than this.

Jason stroked my hair, and that one gentle touch brought my face back up. I gazed up the line of his body to his face. There was that look that comes on a man's face when he's sure of you, sure of what will happen. I never thought to see that look on Jason's face, not for me. That look in his spring blue eyes brought a sound low in my throat. He touched my cheek. "Don't stop," he said, voice soft, "don't stop."

I lowered my face towards him, still gazing up. I licked him through the silk, and watched his face while I did it. I licked along the length of him until he threw his head back, his eyes closed. He was so hard, so firm against my mouth, under the cloth. I wrapped my mouth around the head of him through the silk, bringing one hand round to hold him, solid and thick.

He made a noise halfway between a word and a shout, as if I'd surprised him. He looked down at me, and his eyes were wild.

I drew back from him and the silk had turned dark blue where my mouth had touched him.

His hands went to the back of his pants and it was Jason that slid the silk and the jeans down his hips. Him that revealed himself to me while I knelt in front of him.

He was smooth, the head wide and rounded, graceful, straight and fine, running slightly to the side, so that he nestled in the hollow of his own hip.

I took him in my hand, and his breath quickened. I lifted him away from his body just enough so that I could spill my mouth over the head of him, rolling my tongue along that graceful curve.

He shuddered under my touch.

I drew more of him into my mouth, sliding my hand down to cup lower things. He was smooth to the touch, everywhere I could touch with hand or mouth, there was nothing but the smooth perfection of him. He was shaved smooth.

I'd been with men who trimmed, and shaved some, but never

183

one that was perfectly smooth. I liked it. It made so many things easier to take into my mouth, to roll and explore.

Every touch, every caress, every lick, seemed to bring some new noise from him – whimpers, soft cries, breathless words. It became a game to see how many sounds I could draw from him.

I drew his pants down farther, so that I could spread his legs, lick between them, along that thin line of skin between testicles and anus.

He cried out, and I moved up his body, one lick, one nibble at a time. I took him into my mouth again, as much as I could from this angle, wrapping my fingers in a ring around the rest of him, my other hand cupping his testicles, playing along that line that ran between his legs. His breath was coming quick and quicker. His body quivered against me.

He grabbed a handful of my hair, drew me back from him. He looked down at me like a drowning man. "Up," he said.

I frowned at him. "What?"

He bent down, grabbed my upper arms, drew me to my feet. He kissed me, and it was like he was trying to crawl inside me through my mouth, lips, tongue, teeth – something between a kiss and eating me.

His hands slid down my back, following the curve of my spine, then lower over the swell of my hips, until his fingers found my thighs. He lifted me, with just his hands on my thighs, our mouths still locked together. The movement of his hands spread my legs, pressed me against him. The feel of him so hard, so ready pressed against my body, drew small sounds from me, and he ate those sounds straight from my mouth, as if he were tasting my screams.

He used his hands to draw my lower body away from his, my arms still locked around his shoulders, one hand sliding through the baby silkiness of his hair. He moved one hand to my butt, supporting all my weight on one hand, while he moved the other hand between us. I had a second to realize what he was going to do. I fought the *ardeur*, I fought the feel of his mouth on mine, the feel of him in my arms, to rear back enough to try and say something, I managed to say, "Jason," and he drove his hips forward, upward. But the feel of him inside me was exactly what the *ardeur* wanted. Exactly what I wanted.

He entered me, and it wasn't hesitant, or gentle. He fought against the wet tightness of my body, both hands on the backs of my thighs, pulling me to him, as he pushed himself inside me. It drew small screams out of my throat, one after the other.

He walked us backward until he collapsed me on the edge of the bed, most of my lower body still held in his hands, trapped against him. He stayed standing, his body pinning me to the edge of the bed, his hands holding me as if I weighed nothing.

He stared down at me with eyes that were no longer human, but wolf. He drew himself out of my body, slowly, an inch at a time until I was almost free, then he shoved himself back, and made me scream again. It wasn't a scream of pain.

He found a rhythm that was fast, and deep, and hard, as if he were trying to shove himself out the other side of me. He beat his body into mine with a thick, meaty sound.

The orgasm caught me unprepared. One moment I was caught in the rhythm of his body in mine, and the next I was screaming, writhing underneath him. I raked nails down his body, anywhere I could touch him, and when that wasn't enough I clawed my own body.

Jason's screams echoed mine, and his body tightened against me, spine bowing, head thrown back, and a howl spilled from his lips. The *ardeur* drank him down, his skin, his sweat, his seed.

He collapsed on top of me. His breath came in a painful struggle, and his heart pounded like a trapped thing against my skin. He scooted us more solidly onto the bed, his body still deep within mine. When we were both lying on the bed, breathing hard, pulses quieting, he looked down at me, and there was something in his eyes, something serious, and very un-Jason.

His voice was still breathless, hoarse, when he said, "I know that this may be the only time I get to do this. When I move, let me hold you for just a little while."

My own voice wasn't much better than his, "Since I can't move from the waist down yet, sure."

He laughed then, and because he was still inside me and partially erect, the movement caused me to writhe underneath him, tightening, setting nails into his back.

He screamed, and his hips ground himself against me again.

185

When he could breathe again, he whispered, "Oh, God, don't do that again."

"Then get off me," I said, voice almost as breathless as his.

He raised up on his arms, almost like doing a push-up, and drew himself out of me. Feeling him pulling out made me writhe again. He collapsed beside me, half-laughing.

When I could talk again, I said, "What's funny?"

"God, you're amazing."

"Not bad yourself," I said.

"Not bad?" he said, and gave me wide eyes.

I had to smile. "Fine, you're amazing, too."

"Don't say it if you don't mean it," he said.

I finally managed to turn onto my side so I could see his face better. "I do mean it. You were amazing."

He turned on his side so we lay there facing each other, but not touching. "If I never get to do this again, I wanted it to be good."

I had to close my eyes, to fight off another urge to writhe on the bed. I let out a long, steadying breath, then opened my eyes again. "Oh, it was that. I had a really good time, but are you always this vigorous? Not every girl likes to be pounded into the mattress."

"I've seen the men you've been sleeping with, Anita, I knew I could be as hard and fast as I wanted to be, and not hurt you."

I frowned at him. "Are you implying that you're small?"

"No, I'm saying that I'm not huge. I'm good sized, but some of the men in your bed are more than good-sized."

I blushed. I hadn't blushed the entire time we'd been making love, and now I blushed. "I don't know what to say, Jason, I feel like I should defend your ego, but . . ."

"But inch for inch I know where I stand, Anita." He laughed, and slid an arm under my shoulders. I let him bring me into the curve of his shoulder. I slid my hand across his stomach, my other arm underneath the small of his back, my leg sliding over his thigh. We cuddled, almost as close now as we had been earlier.

"You were wonderful," I said.

"I noticed how wonderful you thought I was." He raised his free arm up so I could see the fresh bloody scratches I'd put down his arms.

I widened eyes at him. "Does your other arm look that bad?"

186

"Yes."

I frowned, and he touched my forehead. "Don't frown, Anita, I'm going to enjoy every mark. I'll miss them when they heal."

"But . . ."

He touched a fingertip to my lips, to keep me from finishing. "No buts, just amazing sex, and I for one want to feel the aches and pains of it as long as I can." He touched my arm where it lay across his stomach, raised it so I could look at it. There were nail marks, some of them seeping blood, some just red and raised. "These aren't my marks."

Of course, once I saw them, they started to hurt. Why is it that small wounds don't hurt until you see them? "Actually," I said, "they are your marks, or at least a sign of a job well done. I don't remember ever marking myself up this badly."

He gave that low masculine chuckle with an edge of laughter that was pure Jason. "Thanks for the compliment, but I know that whatever I did, it can't be half as wonderful as what Asher and Jean-Claude did a few hours ago. No amount of inches, or talent, will put a man in that league."

I shivered, hugging him. "That's not necessarily a bad thing."

"How can you say that? I've felt a fraction of what Asher did to you, and it's . . ." he seemed to be searching for just the right word, he finally said, "wondrous, mind-blowing."

"Yeah," I said, "the kind of pleasure you'd do almost anything to experience again." My voice sounded less than happy.

Jason touched my chin, raised me to look at him. "Are you thinking of not going back for more?"

I tucked my face against his shoulder. "Let's just say that I'm not completely happy about it."

"Why not?" he asked.

"I don't know exactly." I shook my head as much as I could pressed against him. "Truth, is that it scares me."

"What scares you?"

"Sex is great, Jason, but this . . . what Asher can do with his bite." I tried to put it into words, and knew that whatever I said would fail to describe it. "Asher feels like a Master Vampire in my head, his level of power, but he has no animal to call. He can do the voice trick like Jean-Claude, but that's a minor power. I was a

187

little puzzled, I mean, he feels like a master, but where's his power?" I shivered again. "I found out."

Jason rested his chin on the top of my head and said, "What do you mean?"

"I mean that his power lies in seduction, sex, intimate play. He can't feed off lust the way Jean-Claude can, and he doesn't cause lust in those around him the way Jean-Claude does, but damn, once the preliminaries are out of the way, he can cause such . . . pleasure. It really is something that people would kill for, sign their fortunes away for, do whatever Belle Morte wanted them to do, just as long as Asher would keep visiting their beds."

"So he's like this amazing lay," Jason said.

"No, you're an amazing lay, Micah is an amazing lay, I'm not a hundred percent sure that Jean-Claude is as good as I think he is, because I'm not sure anymore how much of it is true talent and how much is vampire powers. I did not have intercourse with Asher. We just shared blood."

Jason moved so he could frown down at me. "I'm sorry, but the wolf knows these things. It wasn't just Jean-Claude I smelled when I walked into the room."

I blushed again. "I didn't say Asher didn't have a good time, I just said we didn't have intercourse."

"And your point is what?" he asked.

"My point is that if that was only taking blood, I'm afraid to have real sex with him. I mean how much better could it be?"

He gave a laugh that held an edge of giggling, almost a giddy sound. "I'd love to find out."

I raised up on one elbow. "Are you telling me you'd do Asher?"

He frowned, the laughter still glinting in his eyes. "I was a little confused for awhile about exactly what my preferences were. I mean I've been Jean-Claude's *pomme de sang* for about two years now. It's amazing when he feeds, Anita, a-fucking-mazing. Enjoying being with him this much made me think I might be gay." He traced his hand down my shoulder. "But I like girls. I'm not saying that with the right person bisexual isn't a possibility, but not if it means never being able to do this again. I like girls." He drew "like" out into a multisyllabic word.

It made me laugh. "And I like men."

188

"I noticed," he said, still with a trace of laughter in his voice.

I sat up. "I think we've cuddled enough."

He touched my arm, face serious again. "Are you really not going to bed Asher?"

I sighed. "You know how you said Jean-Claude is so amazing when he takes blood."

"Yeah."

"Jean-Claude says that Asher's bite is orgasmic, literally. So that means that Asher's bite is more pleasurable than even Jean-Claude's."

"Okay," he said. He propped himself up on pillows, hands folded across his stomach as he listened to me.

I was sitting Indian fashion, still nude, and it didn't seem to matter. It wasn't sexual now, just comfortable.

"I've had sex with Jean-Claude, but never allowed him to take blood with it."

"Never?" he said.

"Never."

He shook his head. "You are the strongest willed person I've ever met. No one else would have refused the double pleasure, not this long."

"You haven't done both with him," I said.

He grinned. "It's considered bad form to fuck your *pomme de sang*, unless they initiate it. If they initiate it, then it's an extra treat, and only if they've been good."

"You sound like you asked him about this."

"I did."

I raised eyebrows at that.

"Oh, come on, Anita, I've slept with him longer than you have. You'd have to be more of a flaming heterosexual than I am to not wonder."

"He turned you down?"

"Very politely, but yeah."

I was frowning. "Did he say why?"

Jason nodded. "You."

I couldn't frown any harder, so I tried to stop, but I was puzzled. "Why me? You've been his *pomme* longer than I've been his girl-friend, and a hell of a lot longer than I've been his lover."

189

"By the time I asked, you were dating. He seemed to think that you would dump his ass if you found out he was doing another man."

"You're making my head hurt," I said.

"Sorry, but if you don't want the truth, don't ask." He settled the pillows more comfortably at his back. "But you've managed to avoid answering my original question."

"What was it?" I asked.

He looked at me. "Don't try to be coy, Anita, you're so bad at it."

"Fine, Asher, what to do about Asher. I made sort of promises to them both that we'd find a way to be a ménage à trois, or would that be a ménage *à quatre*."

"Who's your fourth?"

"Micah," I said.

"Darn," he said.

I frowned at him.

"Couldn't help myself, sorry."

"If I go back on that promise we'll lose Asher."

"What do you mean, lose?"

I explained about Asher's plans to leave.

"So if you don't come across, he's gone."

"Yeah."

He frowned, laughed, then shook his head. "Let me think this through. His bite is overwhelmingly orgasmic, mind-blowing pleasure. You think that if you fuck him while he takes blood that it will be even more amazing."

"Yes," I said.

"Why is this a problem?" Jason asked.

I hugged myself. "I'm afraid, Jason."

He sat up beside me. "Afraid of what?"

"Afraid of being . . ." I hesitated, tried to find the words, and finally, "I'm afraid of being consumed."

He frowned. "Consumed, I know what the word means, but I don't understand what you mean by it."

"Aren't you afraid of wanting one of them so badly that you'd do anything to have him with you?"

"Do you just mean vampires, or people in general?"

190

I rested my chin on my knees. "Vampires, of course."

"No, you don't mean just vampires, you're afraid of wanting *anybody* completely, aren't you?"

I wouldn't look at him. "I don't know what you mean."

He pushed my hair back behind my ear, but it was too thick to stay. "Don't lie to Uncle Jason, you didn't mean just vampires."

I looked at him, hugging my legs to me. "Maybe not, but the point is the same. I don't want to want anyone so much that if they aren't with me, I die."

A look passed through his eyes that I couldn't read. "You mean you're afraid of loving anyone more than life itself?"

"Yes."

He smiled, and it was gentle, and a little sad. "I would give one of my less favorite body parts for a woman to care for me as deeply as you do for Nathaniel."

I started to protest that I didn't love Nathaniel.

Jason touched a finger to my lips. "Stop. I know you haven't given yourself over heart and soul to Nathaniel, but then you haven't given yourself over heart and soul to anybody, have you?"

I looked away, because watching that patient, grown-up look in his eyes was uncomfortable to say the least. "One of my goals in life is, just once to have a woman look at me the way you watch Jean-Claude. The way you and Jean-Claude watch Asher. The way you watch Nathaniel. The way Nathaniel looks at you."

"You left Micah off the list."

"You and he have this comfort level that you don't have with any of the others, but it's almost as if the comfort comes at the expense of something else."

"What?" I asked.

"I don't know, I've never been in love, how should I know."

"So, what, I'm not in love with Micah?"

"That is not my question to answer."

"I cannot be in love with four men at once."

"Why not?"

I looked at him.

"It's not a rule," he said.

"It would be ridiculous," I said.

"You fought Jean-Claude, because you were afraid of him. Then

191

Richard came along, and I think you loved him, really loved him, and that scared you, so you backed off. I think you dated them both to keep from falling in love with either of them."

"That's not true."

"Isn't it?"

"Originally, Jean-Claude said he'd kill Richard if he didn't get a chance to woo me too."

"And why didn't you just kill Jean-Claude then? You don't tolerate ultimatums, Anita, so why tolerate that one?"

I didn't have an answer for that, or at least not a good one.

"Richard grows more distant, more caught up in his own personal angst, which leaves the field open for Jean-Claude. So suddenly you have Nathaniel bunking with you. I know, I know, he's your *pomme de sang*, your house leopard, but it was still interesting timing."

I wanted to tell him to stop, to not say anymore, but he didn't, he kept on. I'd never thought of Jason as relentless before.

"Somewhere in all this, Asher comes up on the radar, maybe it's Jean-Claude's old memories, maybe not. But whatever caused it, you're drawn to him, but he's so full of anger that it's not a threat. He's almost as full of self-loathing as Richard is. Then suddenly Richard walks away for real this time. You're left with just Jean-Claude, and Nathaniel, but Nathaniel isn't enough of a romantic threat to keep Jean-Claude at bay, and suddenly there's Micah. Out of the blue, instant lust, instant housekeeping. You have Micah, and now Jean-Claude is back to sharing you with someone else, and you're safe again. You can't fall madly in love with Jean-Claude, or anyone else, because you've divided your world up into different parts with each of them. Because no one man has your whole world, no one man can rock your whole world."

I got out of the bed, tugging the sheet around me like a robe. I suddenly didn't want to be naked in front of Jason anymore.

"I thought it was all accidental, and it was, and it wasn't. You're terrified of belonging to just one person, aren't you?"

I shook my head. "Not of belonging to just one person, Jason, of wanting to belong to just one person."

"Why, why is that so frightening to you? Most people spend their lives wanting exactly that, I know I do."

192

"I loved someone once with my whole heart, and he stomped on it."

"Please, not the fiancé in college. Anita, that was years ago, and he was an asshole. You can't spend the rest of your life nursing one bad experience."

I was at the foot of the bed now, wrapped shoulders to feet in the sheet. I was cold, and it had nothing to do with the temperature. "It's not only that," I said, voice soft.

"What is it then?"

I took a deep breath in, let it out slow. "I loved my mother with my whole heart and whole soul, she was my world. She died, and it nearly destroyed me." I thought about everything he'd said, and I couldn't argue with it, and I couldn't pretend it didn't make sense. "I never want to put my whole world in any one person's hands again, Jason. If they die, I won't die with them."

"So you'll hold a little of yourself back from everybody."

"No," I said, "I'll hold back a piece of myself for myself. No one gets all of me, Jason, no one, except me."

He shook his head. "So Jean-Claude gets sex, but no blood. Nathaniel gets intimacy, but not intercourse. Asher gets blood but not intercourse. Micah's getting intimacy and intercourse, what are you holding back from him?"

"I don't love him yet."

"Liar."

"I lust after him, but I don't love him yet."

"And Richard, what did you hold back from Richard?"

I stood there wrapped in the damned sheet, feeling the world sinking away to a small screaming thing. "Nothing," I said, "I held back nothing, and he dumped my ass."

Jason just sat there for a second or two, then he got off the bed. I think he meant to hold me, comfort me.

I put out a hand to stop him. "If you hug me, I'm going to cry, and Richard has gotten the last tear out of me that he's going to get."

"I'm sorry, Anita."

"Not your fault."

"No, but it wasn't any of my business either. I don't have the right to psychoanalyze you."

193

"You're just jealous," I said, and I tried to make it light, joking, and failed.

"About what?" he asked.

"That I have so many people that I could be in love with, if I'd only give that one last inch."

He sat back down on the edge of the bed. "You're right, damn it, but you're right. I am jealous, but I didn't mean to hurt you. I didn't understand until the moment you said how afraid you were of being consumed. I want to be consumed, Anita. I want someone to come along and burn me up."

"You're a romantic," I said.

"You make that sound like a dirty word."

"Not dirty, Jason, just useless." I started for the door. "I'm going to get cleaned up, help yourself to the upstairs shower if you want." Jason called to me, but I kept walking. I'd had all the pillow talk I wanted for one day.

# 25

I LOVED THE new shower that I'd had installed in the downstairs master bathroom. One of the bear lycanthropes in town turned out to be a plumber. I'd still paid full price, but at least I knew he wouldn't be asking stupid questions about my living arrangements. I liked a good long bath when the occasion called for it, but at heart I was a shower girl.

I set the showerhead on hard, so that the water beat against my neck, head, shoulders. I hadn't been embarrassed about having sex with Jason, and maybe that was wrong, but it hadn't felt sinful. Maybe because it was just another way for him to take care of me. But the little talk afterwards, that had bothered me. That hard emotional truths bothered me more than having intercourse with someone I wasn't in love with probably said something about how far down the well of moral decay I had fallen.

I stood in the hot, hot water, steam foaming against the glass doors of the stall, and was happy that I didn't owe my heart to anyone. It was mine damn it, and I was keeping it in one piece if I could. Richard had broken some part of me, some last bit that had been trying to hang onto a softer more romanticized view of love. He had left, dumped me because I wasn't human enough for him. My fiancé in college had dumped me because I wasn't white bread enough for his mother. My stepmother, Judith, had never let me forget that I was small and dark, and she and her children and my father were tall and blond, and blue-eyed. People had spent my lifetime rejecting me for things I could not change about myself. So fuck them, fuck them all.

I was sitting on the bottom of the shower. I hadn't meant to. I hadn't meant to huddle in the water, hiding. Why was I always chasing after the love of people who I could never be enough for? There were plenty of others who wanted me exactly as I was, small, dark, hard, bloody, thick with metaphysical shit. People who loved me just as I was. Unfortunately, none of them were me.

There was a knock on the door, and I realized that someone had been knocking for a while. I always locked the door when I went in, out of habit.

I turned the water down, so I could hear better. "What is it?"

"Anita, it's Jamil, I need to come in."

"Why?" That one word held a universe of suspicion. If his reason had been something I wouldn't hate he'd have already said why he needed to come in.

I actually heard him sigh through the door. "It's Richard, he's hurt, and we need to use the big bathtub."

"No," I said. I turned off the water and reached for the oversized towel.

"Anita, since the pack sold Raina's house we don't have any body of water big enough to soak him and other pack members in. I found him unconscious on his bedroom floor, he's ice cold."

I wound a smaller towel around my wet hair. "You are not bringing him in here, Jamil. There's got to be some place else to take him. Jean-Claude would let you use the tub at his place."

"Anita, he's icy, if we don't get him warm soon, I don't know what'll happen."

I leaned my head against the door. "Are you telling me that he's going to die?"

"I'm telling you, I don't know. I've never seen another werewolf this bad without some kind of wound to show for it. I don't know what's wrong with him."

I did, unfortunately. Belle hadn't only fed her people off of me, she'd been feeding off of Richard, too. I'd thought about that earlier in the day, but I hadn't dreamed that he wouldn't call his pack and have some of them near him, to strengthen himself on their collected energy. I hadn't known that he would just let himself die. Because long before he got that bad he'd have known something was very wrong.

"Did he call you for help?" I asked, still leaning against the door.

"No, I needed to ask him about pack business, and I tried him at

196

the school, but he'd called in sick. Then I called his house and got no answer. Anita, please, let us in."

Mother fucking son of a bitch. I could not believe that I was having to do this. The man that had broken my heart, called me a monster was about to get soaked in my bathtub for God knew how long.

I unlocked the door and opened it with me behind, hiding, so I couldn't be seen, or see.

Jamil eased through the door with Richard in his arms. It wasn't weight that made it hard – Jamil could have bench-pressed the entire bathroom – it was that Richard was broad-shouldered, and Jamil wasn't small himself.

I tried not to look at either of them, getting only a brief glimpse of Jamil's cornrowed hair, bright red beads intertwined. His shirt was a red to match the beads, his suit jacket black. I didn't take the time to see if his pants matched the jacket. I just started for the door, towels clutched to me.

"Can you turn on the water for me, Anita?" Jamil asked.

"No," I said, and I fled.

## 26

I GOT DRESSED. I couldn't remember if I'd gotten around to using shampoo on my hair, or only gotten it wet, and I didn't care. I had an image of Richard's face burned in my mind. Eyes closed, that perfectly square jaw with its dimple. But there had been no spill of that glorious hair around his shoulders. That wonderful hair that was brown shot with gold and copper, so that it almost glowed in the sunlight. He'd cut his hair. He'd cut his hair.

I remembered the feel of it in my hands, the silken slide of it over my body, the spill of it around his face when he rose over me. Richard lying underneath my body, his hair like a rich cloud on the pillow, as his eyes lost focus and his body thrust into mine.

I was sitting on the bed, crying, when there was a knock at the door. I had jeans on, but had only gotten to my bra. "Just a minute." My voice was only a little thick.

I slipped the red T-shirt on over the black jeans. I started to say *come in*, then realized it could be Richard. Unlikely since he was unconscious minutes ago, but I couldn't take the chance. "Who is it?"

"Nathaniel."

"Come in." I scrubbed at my eyes and had my back to the door, while I looked at my shoulder holster and tried to figure out what I'd done with my belt. I needed the belt to slide through the shoulder holster. Where the hell was my belt?

"The police are on the phone," he said, voice quiet.

I just shook my head. "I can't find my belt."

"I'll find it for you," he said. I knew from his voice that he was farther into the room now. I hadn't heard him move. It was like I wasn't hearing everything, like I was losing pieces of things.

"What's wrong with me?" I hadn't actually meant to say it out loud.

"Richard's here," Nathaniel said, as if that explained it all.

I kept shaking my head, trying to run my hands through my wet hair. It was tangled. I hadn't used shampoo, let alone conditioner. It was going to be a mess when it dried. "Fuck!"

He touched my shoulder, and I jerked away. "No, no, don't be nice to me. If you're nice I'll cry."

"Do you want me to be cruel, would that make you feel better?"

It was such an odd question that it made me look at him. He was still wearing the jogging shorts he'd left the room in, but he'd unbraided his hair and brushed it into a shining auburn curtain. A stray bit of sunlight gleamed in his hair. I knew what all that hair felt like rushing over my body. It was so thick, so heavy, that it made a sound like dry water when it cascaded around me. I'd always denied myself everything that Nathaniel could offer. I'd always backed off from enjoying every part of him. Jason's words came back to haunt me. That I hadn't really given myself completely to anyone. That I held back something from everyone. I'd held back huge chunks of myself from Nathaniel. More than any of the other men in my life, he was the one that I'd held back from the most, because I didn't believe I was keeping him. Once I had the *ardeur* under control I wouldn't need a *pomme de sang* every day. Once I could feed the *ardeur* from a distance like Jean-Claude could, I'd stop using a *pomme de sang*. Wouldn't I?

He looked worried. "What's wrong, Anita?"

I shook my head.

He took a step towards me, and that small movement sent his hair swirling over one shoulder. He gave a negligible flip of his head, sending it sliding back behind him.

I had to close my eyes, and breathe, in and out, concentrate on just breathing. I would not cry. I would not fucking cry again. Every time I thought Richard had gotten the last tears he'd ever get from me, I always seemed to be wrong. Every time I thought there was no other way he could tear me up, he found a new way. Nothing turns to hate so bitter as what once was love.

I opened my eyes and found Nathaniel close enough to touch. I stared into those compassionate lilac eyes, that soft, caring face, and I hated him. I don't know why. But I hated him just a little. I hated him for not being someone else. I hated him for the hair that

199

fell to his knees. I hated him because I didn't love him. Or maybe I hated him because I did. But it wasn't what I felt for Richard. I hated him, and I hated me. In that one instant I hated everyone in my life, everyone and everything, and me most of all.

"We are out of here," I said.

He frowned. "What?"

"You, me, Jason, we're out of here. I need to take Jason back to the Circus before Jean-Claude wakes up anyway. We'll pack a bag, and we'll give the house over to Richard."

Nathaniel widened his eyes. "You mean to leave this house until Richard is gone?"

I nodded, maybe a little too fast, maybe a little too often, but I had a plan, and I was sticking to it.

"What will Micah say?"

I shook my head. "He can join us at the Circus."

Nathaniel looked at me for a second, then he shrugged. "How long will we be there?"

"I don't know," I said, and looked away from him. He hadn't protested, hadn't accused me of cowardice. He just stuck to the facts. We were going. How long would we be gone?

"I'll pack for a couple of days, if we need other things, I'll come back for them."

"You do that," I said.

He moved towards the door, leaving me to stare around the room. "Your belt is at the foot of the bed."

That made me look at him. There was something in his eyes, something older than he was, something that made me want to squirm and look away, but I was already running from Richard, I couldn't run away from anything else. One act of extreme cowardice per day was about all my ego could handle.

"Thanks," I said, and my voice sounded too soft, too hoarse, too something.

"Do you want me to pack a bag for you, too?" His face had fallen back into neutral lines, as if he'd realized the look in his eyes was too raw for me, right now.

"I can pack," I said.

"I can pack for both of us, Anita, it's not a problem."

I started to argue, then stopped. I'd spent the last twenty minutes

200

trying to find a belt that I'd probably walked over twice. If I packed in the state I was in, I'd probably forget to bring underwear. "Fine."

"What do you want me to tell Sergeant Zerbrowski?" he asked.

"I'll talk to him while you pack."

Nathaniel nodded. "Okay."

I took the time to tuck my shirt in, put my belt on, and thread my shoulder holster. I checked that the clip in my gun was full, automatically. I started to say something to Nathaniel and those old eyes in that young face, but I didn't have anything worth saying. We were fleeing the house until Richard was gone. With that decision, I didn't know what to say.

I left Nathaniel and went into the kitchen to get the phone, wondering if Zerbrowski would still be on the other end, or if his patience would have faded before my confusion had.

## 27

I ENTERED THE kitchen and found the phone on the hook, and Caleb sitting at the kitchen table. Caleb was my least favorite of the new leopards who had come in when Micah and I merged our pards. He was cute enough in a young, boy-hooker, MTV sort of way. Curly brown hair with the lower part shaved short, and the top a crown of thick curls that flopped over his eyes artfully. His tanned skin was dark, not quite as dark as his hair. The tan had faded a little in the few months he'd been in town. His eyes were a nice solid brown with a silver hoop piercing one eyebrow. His smooth upper body was naked so I could see his belly button piercing. I also noted that he'd added two new piercings – both nipples were pierced with tiny silver dumbbells. He routinely went around with the top button of his jeans unfastened, his explanation was that the waistband irritated the belly piercing. I didn't believe him, but since I had never even pierced my ears, I couldn't really call him a liar.

He kept one hand on the coffee cup, but the other one traced over his chest and rolled one of the little silver dumbbells between his fingers. "I had them done a couple weeks ago. Like them?"

"What are you doing here?" I asked, and I didn't care that it sounded hostile. I was having a hard day and having Caleb in my kitchen wasn't going to improve it.

"Taking messages for you." He hadn't risen to my grumpy bait. It wasn't like Caleb to miss an opportunity to bitch.

"What messages?"

He held out a small sheet of paper to me. His face was as neutral as he could manage, only that faint gleam in his eyes that he never quite lost. That look that said, *I'm thinking wicked thoughts, about you.*

I took a breath, let it out slowly, and went over to him to get the paper. I recognized the notepaper; it was one of the sheets we kept near the phone. Caleb held on to it for a second too long, making me pull a little, but he let it go and didn't say anything irritating. That was almost a first.

I looked at the note. I didn't recognize the writing, which probably meant it was Caleb's. It was surprisingly neat, all block letters. "NO ONE'S DEAD. WHEN YOU HAVE TIME, CALL ME. DOLPH IS ON A TWO-WEEK LEAVE OF ABSENCE. LOVE ZERBROWSKI." I must have raised an eyebrow at the end part, because Caleb said, "I wrote down exactly what the policeman said. I didn't add anything."

"I believe you. Zerbrowski thinks he's a wit." I met Caleb's brown eyes. "Why are you here, Caleb?"

"Micah called me on his cell phone, told me to stay close to you today." He didn't look particularly happy about it.

"Did he mention why he wanted to stay close to me today?"

Caleb frowned. "No."

"And you dropped everything you had planned today to come baby-sit me, out of the goodness of your heart."

He tried to keep frowning, then gradually that smile of his that matched the wicked light in his eyes emerged. It was an unpleasant smile, as if he was thinking unkind thoughts, and those thoughts amused him very, very much.

"Merle told me he'd hurt me if I failed Micah on this."

Merle was Micah's chief bodyguard, six foot of muscle, and attitude that would make a Hell's Angel think twice. Caleb was about five six and soft in ways that said he had nothing to do with muscles.

I had to smile. "Merle's threatened you before, and it hasn't impressed you much."

"That was before Chimera died. He liked me better than he liked Merle or Micah. I knew he'd protect me, no matter what Merle said."

Chimera had been their old pard leader, in a way he'd been like the Godfather of lycanthrope groups. But he was dead now, and we'd divided his people up among ours. Most of them thought it was an improvement because Chimera had been a sexual sadist, a serial killer, and an all-round very bad man. But a few, who had enjoyed helping him mete out his little blood fantasies, seemed to miss Chimera. Since Chimera had been one of the scarier things I'd ever run into in a list that included would-be gods, and millennia-old vampires, I didn't trust any of his people that were nostalgic for the good ol' days. Caleb was one of those.

"Great, fine, glad you're beginning to take orders like a good soldier. Tell Micah when he comes back that I'll be at the Circus of the Damned."

"I'll go with you." He was already getting to his feet. He was barefoot. But of course, because it was Caleb, he was wearing a toe ring.

I shook my head. "No, you are staying here, give my message to Micah."

"Merle was pretty explicit. I am to stay near you today, all day."

I frowned. I had the beginnings of an awful idea. "You're positive that neither Micah nor Merle told you why they wanted you to be glued to my side today?"

He shook his head, but he looked worried. I wondered for the first time if Merle had done more than just "talk" to him.

"What did Merle say would happen if you didn't stay close to me?"

"He said he'd cut all my piercings with a knife, especially the newest one." His voice didn't sound the least bit like teasing. He sounded tired.

"Newest one? The nipples?" I said, and made it half question.

"No." He shook his head.

His hands went to the top of his jeans and the already partially unbuttoned line. He undid a second button.

I held up my hand. "Stop, that's plenty. I get the idea. You've pierced something . . . there."

"I thought, why not, I'll heal in a matter of days instead of weeks, or months for a human."

I wanted to ask, *Didn't it really hurt?* But since silver burned a lycanthrope's skin, you had to be masochistic to get anything pierced. I'd asked one of the other leopards that was pierced, why not use gold? Answer: their bodies grew over the gold, healing over the wound. But they didn't heal over silver.

"Thanks for over-sharing there, Caleb."

There was a shadow of his usual smile, but mostly his eyes

looked worried, almost scared. "I'm trying to do what I was told to do, that's all."

I sighed. One thing I hadn't expected was to feel sorry for Caleb. Damn it I didn't need another person to take care of right now. I was having enough trouble taking care of myself. "Fine, but Nathaniel and I are taking Jason back to the Circus so he'll be there in time for Jean-Claude to wake up."

"I'll go with you."

I just looked at him.

The worry bloomed to outright fear. "Anita, please, I know I've been a pain in the ass, but I'll be good. I won't cause any trouble."

Had Micah really sent Caleb here in case the *ardeur* rose early? I disliked Caleb, intensely; did Micah really think I'd use him like that? Of course, the first time I'd met Micah I'd fed off of him. It had also been the very first time the *ardeur* rose, and my control had been nonexistent. I was better now, but what I'd done with Jason proved not that much better.

I'd complain to Micah about his choice of baby-sitters later, and he'd probably argue, if not Caleb, then who? For that, I didn't have a good answer. Hell, I didn't even have a bad answer.

# 28

W‌HEN MORE WOLVES arrived from Richard's pack, and the screams started, I left. He had a half-dozen baby-sitters. He did not need me. Hell, he didn't even want me.

I didn't know what to do for Richard anymore. I could help the pack as a whole, but helping Richard seemed beyond me. He needed healing, and I didn't know how to do that. If you needed someone killed, or threatened, or even hurt, I was your girl. I did self-defense, murder wasn't beyond me in a good cause, but suicide, I did not do that. Richard had let himself grow cold, his energy sucked away, and he hadn't called for help. That was suicide, passive suicide maybe, but the intent was the same.

Jason drove. He pointed out that I'd had weird physical reactions all day, and it would be bad to have one of the fainting spells behind the wheel of the car. I replied that I'd fixed the reason for the fainting spells by putting crosses at the Circus. He'd countered with the fact that we weren't one hundred percent sure that was the only reason I'd been fainting. Wouldn't caution be better? With that, I couldn't argue. My pride was not worth crashing the Jeep with three other people in it. If it had only been my skin at stake I'd have probably taken my chances. I was usually more cautious of other people's safety than my own.

The fact that all three were lycanthropes and would probably survive a wreck better than I would had nothing to do with it. If you throw the furry through a windshield, do they not still bleed?

We were on Highway 21 turning onto 270, when I smelled roses. "Do you smell that?" I asked.

Jason glanced at me, his hair still damp from the shower, his white T-shirt dark in spots from water as if he'd dried in a hurry and missed places. "What did you say?"

"Roses, I smell roses."

He glanced behind us at Nathaniel and Caleb. Nathaniel I'd invited. Caleb had nearly cried when I didn't want to bring him. Whatever Merle had said to him had well and truly scared him.

I could taste the sweet, cloying perfume on the back of my tongue. And no one could smell it but me. Shit.

Belle Morte's voice whispered through my head, "Did you truly believe you could escape me?"

"I did escape you."

"What?" Jason asked.

I shook my head, concentrating on the voice in my head, and the thickening scent of roses.

"You did not escape, you fed me, and you will feed me again, and again, until I am sated."

"Jean-Claude says you're never sated."

She laughed in my head, and it was like having the inside of my skull rubbed with fur, as if she could touch things with her voice that no one should have touched with their hands. That purring, contralto laugh rolled through my body, raising goosebumps along my skin.

I had an image, a memory in my head. There was a huge bed, and a mass of bodies on it. It was a jumble of arms, legs, chests, groins, all male. Then one man raised up, only his upper body, and I glimpsed Belle underneath him. He lowered his body and she vanished from view. It was like watching a nest of snakes, so much movement, disconnected in the candlelit dark, as if each limb were something separate and alive without the body. Belle's arm rose above the mass of bodies, then she swam her way to the top, peeled the men from her naked body, until she stood in the midst of them, their hands reaching up to her, pleading with her. She had released the *ardeur* upon them, and fed, and fed, and fed, until she rose from the mass of flesh glowing with power, her eyes so bright with dark flames that they cast shadows as she half stepped, half floated from the bed. One man's body had fallen to the floor, forgotten. He lay very still as she stalked nude and ripe with curves, glowing with power. She walked over the body of the man who had given everything to satisfy her needs, while the other men reached for her, begged for her not to stop. The men began to rise to their knees, or fall off the bed in an effort to follow. At least two other bodies lay on the bed forever still, forever gone. Three of them dead, loved to death, and still the others begged her for more, still they tried to stand and follow her.

I knew it was Jean-Claude that she had tied to a chair and made watch. I knew it was him, and not me, that watched her with fearful, hungry eyes. But when she walked past him, without so much as a caress, I choked on his despair. Part of his punishment for daring to leave her.

"Anita, Anita," the voice seemed distant. Someone touched my shoulder, I gasped, and was brought back blinking, breath harsh in my throat. I was still seat-belted into the Jeep. We were still on 270, about to turn onto 44. I wasn't tied to a chair, I wasn't in Belle's lair, I was safe. But the sweet scent of roses clung to me like some kind of evil perfume.

Jason had been calling my name, but it was Nathaniel's hand on my shoulder. "Are you alright?" Jason asked.

I nodded, then shook my head. "Belle's messing with me."

Nathaniel squeezed my shoulder. I had opened my mouth to say, *maybe you shouldn't be touching me right now,* when the *ardeur* roared through me. The heat rushed over my skin in beads of sweat, brought my pulse pounding, rising like some ripe fruit to fill my throat, stop my breath, so for a moment I was drowning in the beat and pulse of my own body. I could hear my blood like a roaring flood. I could feel every pulse, every drop to the tingling tips of my fingers and toes. I had never been so aware of how very much blood was coursing through my veins as in that one heart-stopping moment.

I put my hand over Nathaniel's where it still gripped my shoulder. His skin was so warm, almost hot. I turned towards him. I looked into those lavender eyes, and just the intensity of my gaze, drew him closer, close enough to rest his cheek against my seat. I had enough left of me inside my head to think, dimly, he must have undone his seat belt, but there wasn't enough left of me to care for his safety. All I could think was that it brought him closer to me, and I wanted him closer.

"Anita," Jason's voice, "Anita, what the hell is happening? My skin is crawling with whatever it is, it feels like the *ardeur.* But it's not."

I never took my gaze from Nathaniel's face. Jason's voice was like a buzzing insect noise, something I heard, but didn't really listen to.

I lifted Nathaniel's hand from my shoulder and pulled it gently against my lips. His hand cupped the lower part of my face, my breath was warm against him, and the heat of it brought the scent of him to me. His hands smelled not only of warmth, and blood, but of everything he'd touched that day. Faint traces that soap could not erase completely. His hands smelled of life, and I wanted it.

"Anita, talk to me," Jason said.

"What's happening?" Caleb asked, "why is it hard to breathe in the car?"

"Power," Jason said, "I don't know what kind yet."

I pulled Nathaniel's hand past my face, until my lips glided over his wrist, and there, there, just under the skin was a new warmth.

I flicked my tongue across the skin of his wrist, and he shuddered.

"Anita!" Jason said.

I could hear him, but it was utterly unimportant. The only thing that was important was the warmth of skin, and that faint pulse just below. I opened my mouth wide, lips pulled back to taste that pulse.

The Jeep swerved violently, throwing Nathaniel backwards and to one side, tearing his hand from me. He landed in Caleb's lap.

I looked at Jason then, really looked at him. In the back of my mind I knew it was Jason, but in the front of my mind, all I could really see was the pulse in the side of his neck. It beat against his skin like a trapped thing. I knew I could free it, make it rush red and hot into my mouth.

I unbuckled my seat belt. That froze me for a second, because I was fanatic about seat belt safety. My mother would be alive today if she'd used hers. I never rode in a moving car without one. Never. So deep rooted was that fear, it pushed Belle back, pushed back the blood lust she'd raised in me.

I found my voice, hoarse and strange, but mine, "I thought it was the *ardeur* she raised, but it's not."

209

"Blood lust," Jason said.

I nodded, my hands still frozen on the unbuckled seat belt.

"Blood lust feels like the *ardeur*, but not. Sometimes you don't know which lust it is until you find out if he's going for your neck, or your groin."

I blinked at Jason. "What did you just say?" I never heard the answer, if there was one, Belle roared back through me, and I was suddenly more concerned with the beating of his pulse in his neck, than the fact that his mouth was moving. I heard no sound except that overwhelming thunder of my own blood, my own heart, my own throbbing, pulsing body.

I was sliding over the front seat towards him, and hadn't remembered moving, or wanting to. He hit the wheel again, sending me back across the car against the far door. The moment my back hit the door I could hear the angry honking of horns, as the Jeep slid through traffic, sideways. Then it evened out, going straight again. Jason was giving me wide eyes.

"I can't drive with you feeding on me."

My voice was thick, "I don't think I care." I sat up, my hands on the seat to keep him from throwing me against the door again.

"Nathaniel, Caleb, keep her away from me until I can find a safe place to pull over."

I was awkwardly straddling the gearshift when Nathaniel put his arm in front of my face. He didn't try and touch me, but held his wrist close enough for me to smell the warmth of his skin, then he slowly drew his arm back into the backseat, and I followed, sliding between the seats, following the pull of his flesh, like there was a line tied from him to me.

I spilled into the backseat. Nathaniel was sitting on his side of the seat now. I knelt over his body, straddling him. I could feel him stretched tight inside his shorts even through my jeans, but today that wasn't nearly as important as the smooth line of his throat. He'd braided his hair before we left, so that his neck was bare.

The Jeep swerved again, and I fell onto the floorboard, at Caleb's feet. We'd been lucky so far to avoid an accident or the concrete median on the road. Our luck would run out, and I wasn't sure I cared.

"If you can't take sex from Nathaniel yet, I don't think you

210

should take blood. He's still weak." I heard Jason's voice, as though it were coming from far away.

I stared up at what sat above me, his jean-clad legs brushing my body. For sex, Caleb wasn't desirable, but for blood . . . I came to my knees between his legs, and began to pull myself up Caleb's body, fingers digging into the jeans, feeling the flesh underneath.

My hands slid under his untucked, button-up shirt with its loud comic book pictures. His skin was so warm. My fingers slid upward, touching the ring in his belly button. I hesitated there, tracing the edge of the metal ring, pulling on it gently, feeling the skin stretch, until he made a small sound of protest. I stared up into his face, and whatever he saw there widened his eyes, made his lips part in a small ooh of surprise.

I traced my fingers up his stomach, his chest, my arms lost under the oversized shirt, until when my hands slid over his shoulders, the shirt began to rise exposing his stomach. The sight of that bare skin began to raise other hungers, for flesh instead of merely blood. But Belle roared down that metaphysical leash she'd attached to me, and the beast receded before it had truly risen. She wanted me to want what she wanted, and in that moment I knew that though she had animals to call, she did not share their beast, their craving of flesh. The thought was too rational, and the leash loosened and I could think for myself.

"Why do you care if I take blood or flesh, you can feed off both energies? You've been feeding on Richard all day," I asked.

"Perhaps I am tired of flesh."

I had a flash, as if I read her thought. "You couldn't make Richard feed. He fought you all day, let you suck him dry, but you couldn't make him attack anyone else."

Her anger was like hot metal shoved against my skin. It bowed my back, brought a gasp from my throat. Caleb grabbed my arms, or I would have collapsed.

Belle's voice purred through my head, "The loup was surprisingly strong, but he is not my animal to call, nor is he attracted to the dead, but you are, *ma petite*, oh, yes, you are." Her power poured over me, but it wasn't the heat of blood lust, it was cold, the coldness of the grave. The moment the energy touched me, my own power flared to life, that part of me that raised the dead. It

211

flared inside me as if Belle's cold energy was some sort of fuel for my own cool fire. "You are mine, *ma petite*, mine in ways that the loup cannot imagine. His connection to the dead is accidental, yours was fated from the moment you were born."

Her power was the power of the grave, of death itself, but so was mine. She meant to prove a point, but she'd wakened my necromancy, and she was just another kind of dead. I knew how to handle the dead.

I drew a breath, drawing in my own magic, getting ready to cast her out. I'd done it before. But her chill changed to heat before I could finish that breath. The blood lust washed my magic away, drowned it in a flood of need.

Her voice dripped across my skin like warm honey, as if the dark-power of her eyes had melted across my skin. "The power of the grave is yours to control, but not the power of desire. Desire, in all its forms, is mine to control."

If I'd had air to breathe, I would have screamed; but there was no air, and no sight for a swimming, dizzying moment. But I was drowning in sounds, blood rushing through my body, my heart wet and thudding, my pulse like a second heartbeat in a thousand places under my skin. I could hear, and I could feel.

I could feel Caleb's chest under my hands, feel the roughness of the hair that traced the edge of his nipples, and finally the nipples themselves, growing hard and firm under my fingers. The tiny metal barbells that pierced them were a distraction. I wanted to roll his nipples between my fingertips, and the metal interfered. Like a toothpick in your sandwich, they got in the way. I had a moment where Belle thought about ripping them out, and that was so not my thought that it helped me crawl back into my own head, at least a little.

When my vision cleared, Caleb's eyes were unfocused, his lips half-parted. Through me, it was almost as if Belle herself touched him, and her touch spread lust, lust of every kind.

I was in my own head, my own skin, but Belle's hunger was inside me, too, and I couldn't push it out. She was right; the blood hunger was not death.

I tore my arms through Caleb's shirt, popping the buttons loose, baring his upper body. When I channeled Jean-Claude's blood lust,

I was always attracted to neck, wrist, bend of the arm, sometimes the inside of the groin, all nice major arteries or veins, but Belle didn't look high, or low. She gazed at Caleb's chest like it was a prime piece of steak, cooked just right.

My own logic tried to argue. There were other places where there was more blood, much closer to the surface. The sheer surprise of not going for someplace more usual helped me push her back.

Caleb's voice came heavy, "Why did you stop?"

"I don't think it's sex she's wanting," Nathaniel said, voice quiet.

His voice turned my gaze to him. If what was driving me had been the *ardeur*, it might have been enough to have me crawl to him. But Nathaniel was right, this wasn't about sex, this was about food, and Nathaniel wasn't food. Did that mean that Caleb was food? Not a pretty thought.

"What do you mean?" Caleb asked.

I gazed up at Caleb's bare chest, that young, half-finished face. He looked so puzzled. I said it out loud, though I wasn't talking to anyone in the car. "He doesn't understand."

Belle's whisper, "He will soon enough."

"It looks like it's your turn to take one for the team," Jason's voice from the front.

"What?"

"You're going to get munched on," Jason said.

The combination of my own moral dilemma with the fact that Belle had picked an odd spot for taking blood, one that just didn't make sense to me, was helping me swim to the surface. I knelt back on the floorboard, pulling a little free of Caleb's body.

"No," I said out loud, and none of the men answered me, as if they'd all caught up to the fact that I wasn't really talking to any of them.

Belle's voice in my head. "I have been gentle until now, *ma petite*."

"I am not your *ma petite*, so stop fucking calling me that."

"If you will not take kindness from me, then I will cease to offer it."

"If this is your idea of kindness, then I'd hate to see . . ." I never

213

finished the thought, because Belle showed me that indeed she had been kind.

She didn't roll over me, she crashed into me, in a mind-numbing, breath-stealing, heart-stopping, swat of power. For an instant, or for an eternity, I hung suspended. The Jeep was gone, Caleb was gone, I couldn't see, or feel, or be. It was neither light, nor dark, nor up, nor down. I'd had near-death experiences, I'd fainted before, passed out, but that moment when Belle's power fell through me, that was the closest to true nothingness that I'd ever experienced.

Into that nothingness, that void, Belle's voice fell, "Jean-Claude has begun the dance, but he has left it unfinished between you, the wolf, and himself. He has allowed sentiment to cloud his judgment. It makes me question how well I taught him."

I tried to speak but couldn't remember where my mouth was, or how to draw a breath. I couldn't remember how to answer her.

"I discovered this with the wolf, but could not mend it, for he is not my animal to call. I do not understand dogs, and a wolf is very much a dog." Her voice whispered through me, low and lower, trembling through my body, but for her voice to dance through my body, I had to have a body for her to use. I fell back into my body as if falling from a great height. I was left gasping on the floor-boards, eyes staring up at Caleb's startled face and Nathaniel's worried one.

Belle's voice glided through my body like a knowledgeable hand. I suddenly knew who had trained Jean-Claude to use his voice as a tool of seduction. "But you, *ma petite*, I understand you."

I drew a deep, quaking breath and it hurt all the way to my chest, as if I'd gone a long time without breathing. My voice came hoarse, "What are you talking about?"

"The fourth mark, *ma petite*, without the fourth mark, you are not truly Jean-Claude's. It is like the difference between engagement and marriage; one is permanent, the other not necessarily so."

I understood what she meant a second before I saw two dancing honey-colored flames appear in the air over me. I knew it was the second mark because I'd had the second mark three times before; twice from Jean-Claude, and once from a vampire I'd killed. I'd

214

never been able to protect myself from it before. I knew from experience that nothing physical would save me. It wasn't something you could hit, or shoot. I hated things you couldn't hit or shoot. But I had other skills now that weren't exactly physical.

I reached down that long metaphysical cord to Jean-Claude. Belle's voice floated over me, she was delaying her moment, drawing out her pleasure and my fear. "Jean-Claude is hours dead, he cannot help you."

The dark flames of her eyes began to descend, like some evil angel coming to eat my soul. I did the only thing I could think to do. I reached down the other half of our metaphysical cord. I reached out to a place that hadn't helped me for months. I reached out to Richard.

I had an image of Richard in the hot bath water, cradled in Jamil's arms. Richard looked up as if he could see me. He whispered my name, but either he was too weak to push me away, or he didn't try. For a moment, it was as if it was meant to be, then I was yanked back, shoved into my own head, my own body again. Richard hadn't cast me out this time. Dark honey flames hovered over my face, and there was a vague outline, a ghost of long dark hair, the mist of a face.

Caleb was yelling, "What's in the car with us? I can't see anything, but I can feel it. What the fuck is it?"

Nathaniel's voice came hushed, and strangely loud, "Belle Morte."

I had no time to look up, to see the others, because those phantom lips were speaking. "I will not allow you to gain strength from your wolf. I have given you the first mark and you did not even know it. I will give you the second mark here and now, and tonight with Musette as my proxy I will give you the third. When Jean-Claude and I are equal within you, three for three, then you will come to me, *ma petite*. You will travel the world if I ask it, do anything, simply to taste my sweet blood."

That phantom mouth lowered towards mine. I knew somehow that if she laid a ghostly kiss on me that I would be hers. I did what I always did, I tried to hit at that face, and there was nothing to touch. I screamed wordlessly, and sent out a metaphysical cry, "Help me!"

215

Suddenly, I could smell forest, trees, fresh-turned earth, wet leaves underfoot, and the sweet musk of wolf.

Belle could stop me from reaching out to Richard, but she couldn't keep him from reaching out to me.

Richard's power rose like a sweet-scented cloud above me, pushing back those glowing eyes, that phantom mouth.

She laughed, and it slid over my body, made me shudder, my breath catch in my throat. It felt so good, so good, even while my head screamed that it was bad.

"Did you hear someone laugh?" Caleb asked it.

Jason said no. Nathaniel said yes.

Belle whispered along my skin, and even Richard's power breathing against my body couldn't keep her voice out. "With the touch of your wolf's flesh, you might keep me at bay, but not from a distance. The closer the flesh, the closer the ties, and the more powerful. You are already mine, *ma petite*, you cannot win free of me." Those eyes began to float lower again. Richard's power rose above me like a soft shield. Belle's power floated on the surface of that energy like a leaf on a pond, then she began to push into it, through it.

"Help me!" I screamed it out loud to everyone, anyone, and no one. I felt Nathaniel's hand on mine, and that phantom kiss did hesitate, did turn and look at Nathaniel. I felt her call him, like a deep thrumming down my bones. Leopard had been her first animal to call. If she owned me, she'd own my pard.

Nathaniel reached out his free hand as if he could see her.

"No!" I jerked free of him and the moment I broke physical contact it was as if Nathaniel was less real to her. She turned those dark-honey eyes back to me.

"I will have them all, *ma petite*, eventually."

"No," I said it, but my voice was soft, because I believed she was right.

"You will give them to me, all of them."

Fear poured through me as if I'd been plunged into ice water. The thought of what Belle would do to my pard, my friends. No, I could not let this happen.

"Fuck you, fuck you, Belle, and the horse you rode in on." My anger, my fear, seemed to feed Richard's power. The sweet, nose-

216

wrinkling musk of wolf was so thick it was like being wrapped in invisible fur.

The Jeep slewed to one side. The angry honking of horns and squealing brakes followed it. Jason had given up on finding a safe place and just stopped against the concrete median. Nathaniel and Caleb were thrown across the seat and into the passenger side doors. I didn't have time to worry about the fact that no one seemed to be wearing their damn seat belts.

Belle's eyes pushed through Richard's power. It wasn't effortless. He made her work for every inch, but those burning eyes, that ghostly outline got closer, closer . . . until I held my breath as if afraid, if I breathed in too hard it would bring her against my mouth.

I caught movement from the corner of my eye. Jason was between the seats. He'd stopped the Jeep, thrown off his seat belt. He shoved his hand through the ghost thing above me, as if he couldn't see it. He grabbed my shoulder and the moment he touched me, Richard's beast welled up inside me. I'd always thought it was my beast that moved through me, but this, whatever this was, was Richard, not me.

His wolf poured into me like scalding water rushing into a cup, filling me to the brim, emptying my skin of leopard or death, until my spine bowed, my hands flailed, my mouth opened in a soundless scream. I could feel fur rubbing inside my body, strong nails, digging. The wolf was struggling to find some way out of my body.

Belle hissed at me like some great ghostly cat. The eyes retreated, hovering in the air near the Jeep roof, as Jason pulled me into the front seat and cradled me against his body. His closeness seemed to quiet the wolf, so that I felt it sit, panting, eager-eyed, staring up at the shape by the ceiling with hungry, arrogant eyes. Jason's eyes were his wolf's eyes, and today they seemed perfect for his face. But it was Richard's power, the power of the Thronnos Rokke clan that wrapped around both of us. I had never felt Richard's beast so thick inside me. It was as if I was a purse, a bag, holding his beast, feeling it pace inside me as if my flesh were a cage it could not escape from.

Belle's voice floated down upon us, and this time it stung, hot

217

with her anger. "You can ride all day in the arms of your wolf, but there is still the banquet tonight. Musette will be there, and through her, *ma petite*, I will be there."

My voice came out with a low edge of growl, "I am not your *ma petite*."

"You will be," she said, and the eyes slowly faded, until only the lingering scent of roses remained to remind me that we'd won this round, but there would be others. Jean-Claude's memories knew Belle too well to think otherwise. She would never give up, not once she decided to own something, or someone. Belle Morte had decided that I would be hers. Jean-Claude had never known her to change her mind about something like that. That was so unfair, wasn't it a lady's prerogative to change her mind? Of course, Belle wasn't exactly a lady.

She was a two-thousand-year-old vampire, and they weren't known for changing their minds, their habits, or their goals. The last time a Master Vamp had come to town and tried to steal me from Jean-Claude, I'd ended up in a coma for a week. Richard had gotten his throat torn out, and Jean-Claude had nearly died for real. Vampires were always either trying to kill me, or own me. God I hated being popular.

# 29

NATHANIEL HAD GOTTEN one of the extra crosses out of the glove compartment. I always carried spare crosses, just like spare ammo; when you hunt vampires, running out of either one is really bad. It was sheer stupidity on my part to have put crosses around the Circus of the Damned, but not on me. Some days I'm just slow.

I was back in the front seat, but I was shaking. No, that didn't quite cover it. There was a fine tremble in my hands; small muscles in my body kept twitching at odd moments. I was cold, and it was one of those glorious end of summer days, sun-warmed, sparkling, bright, and soft at the same time. We drove through a wash of blue sky, and sunshine, and I was cold – a cold that no amount of blankets was really going to help.

Nathaniel was curled over my lower body like a living blanket, wedged between my legs and the floorboard. I'd bitched about how dangerous it was, but I hadn't complained too much. I didn't have any real blankets in the car. I was spending so much time in shock lately, I'd have to remedy that. The trees along 44 had given way to houses and an occasional old school being rehabbed into apartments, churches, buildings of no discernible use, but old, tired. Okay, maybe that last was just me.

I stroked my hand over Nathaniel's head, over and over, on the warm silk of his hair. His head in my lap, his arms wrapped around my waist, his body wedged between my legs. Sometimes Nathaniel made me think about sex, but sometimes, like now, it was just comfort. Just closeness. You can't have that with most people, because they're busy thinking about sex. I think that's why dogs are so damn popular. You can cuddle a dog as much as you like and the dog never thinks about sex, or pushing your social boundaries in any way, unless you happen to be eating. Dogs will invade your social boundaries for table scraps, unless trained to do otherwise.

But hey, it's a dog, not a person in a fur suit. Right now, what I needed was a pet, not a person. Nathaniel could be both. An uncomfortable, but truthful fact.

Jason drove. Caleb had the backseat to himself. No one spoke. I don't think anyone knew what to say. I wanted Jean-Claude awake. I wanted to tell him what Belle had done. I wanted him to tell me there was a way to keep her from doing anything else, short of giving me the fourth mark. The fourth mark would make me ageless and immortal as long as Jean-Claude didn't die. Theoretically, he could live forever, and with the fourth mark, so could I. So why had I refused it so far? One, it scared me. I wasn't sure as a Christian how I felt about living forever. I mean, what happened to heaven, and God, and the judgment thing? Theologically, what would it mean? On a more mundane level, how much closer would it bind me to Jean-Claude? He could already invade my dreams, what would it mean if I took that last step? Or was refusing the fourth mark just another way to not give myself completely to anyone? Maybe. But if the only way to keep Belle from taking me was to let Jean-Claude have me, I knew which choice I was making. I wondered, if I called my priest now, could he get back to me on the theological implications of the fourth mark before full dark tonight? Father Mike had answered questions equally as weird for me over the years.

"Anita," Jason said, and his voice held a note of anxiety.

I glanced at him and realized he'd probably been trying to get my attention for a while. "Sorry, thinking too hard."

"I think we're being followed."

That raised my eyebrows. "What do you mean?"

"When I nearly caused the four-car pileup so I could touch you, I caught a glimpse of a car in the rearview. It was close, like tailgating close. It was one of the cars that nearly hit us when I slammed on the brakes."

"So, we're in heavy traffic, a lot of people tailgate."

"Yeah, but everyone else that was close to us when I stopped got away from us as fast as they could. This car is still behind us."

I glanced in the side mirror, and saw a dark blue Jeep. "Are you sure it's the same car?"

"I didn't get a number, but it's the same make, same color, and there are two men in it, one dark-haired, one blond with glasses."

I studied the Jeep that seemed to be following our Jeep. Two men, one dark, one light; it could have been a coincidence. Of course, maybe it wasn't.

"Let's go on the theory that it is following us," I said.

"What?" Jason said, "I lose them?"

"No," I said, "cut across traffic and take the first exit as long as it doesn't take us to the Circus. I don't want to lead them to Jean-Claude."

"Almost every monster in St. Louis knows that the Master of the City's lair is under the Circus of the Damned," Jason said, but he changed lanes, moving us a little closer to the exit row.

"But the guys behind us don't know that that's where we're headed."

He shrugged and moved over two more lanes, setting up for the exit. The blue Jeep waited until we were actually exiting with two cars between us before it crossed over. If we hadn't been watching for it, or there had been a taller car between our Jeep and theirs, I wouldn't have seen them exit. But I was, and there wasn't, and I did.

"Shit," I said, but I was feeling warmer. Nothing like action to ground and center a person.

"Who are these guys?" Jason asked out loud what I was wondering.

Caleb glanced behind. "Why would someone be following us?"

"Reporters?" Jason made the word a question.

"I don't think so," I said. I'd lost sight of everything but the top of the Jeep floating above the car roofs behind us.

"Which way do I turn?" He'd come to the bottom of the exit ramp.

I shook my head. "I don't know, dealer's choice." Who were they? Why follow us? Usually when people start following me I know that I'm into something. Today, I had no clue. Neither of the current cases that I was helping RPIT with should have had people following me. I wished they were reporters, but the situation didn't have that feel to it.

Jason turned right. One car turned left, one turned right, and the Jeep pulled in behind it. There were little flags on the street signs,

Italian flags with the words, "The Hill," on them. People on The Hill always let you know you were there and they loved their Italian heritage. Even the fire hydrants were painted green, red, and white like the flags.

Nathaniel raised his head off my thigh enough to say, "Is it Belle?"

"What?" I asked, vision still glued to the side mirror.

"Are they daytime help for Belle?" he asked in his quiet voice.

I thought about that. I'd never run into a vamp that had more than one human servant, but I'd run into several that had more than one Renfield. Renfield is what most American vamps called humans that served them not through mystical connections, but because they acted as blood donors and wanted to be vampires themselves. Back when I hunted vampires and didn't sleep with them, I'd called all humans associated with vamps human servants, now I knew better.

"They could be Renfields, I guess."

"What's a Renfield?" Caleb asked. He was turned in the seat looking directly back at the car between us and the blue Jeep.

"Turn around, Caleb. When that car turns off I don't want the Jeep to know we've noticed them."

He turned around immediately without arguing, which was unusual for Caleb. I didn't approve of threatening people to gain their obedience, but there were some that nothing else seemed to work with. Maybe he was one of them.

I explained what a Renfield was.

"Like the guy in Dracula who ate insects," Caleb said.

"Exactly," I said.

"Cool," he said, and seemed to mean it.

I'd once asked Jean-Claude what they called Renfields before the release of the book *Dracula* in 1897. Jean-Claude had said, "Slaves." He'd probably been kidding, but I'd never had the heart to ask again.

The car behind us pulled into one of the narrow driveways. The blue Jeep was suddenly revealed. I forced myself to not look directly at it and only use the side mirror, but it was hard. I wanted to turn around and stare. Knowing that I shouldn't made it all the more tempting.

222

There was nothing ominous about the Jeep, or even the two men visible in it. They both had short hair, clean, well groomed; the Jeep was even shiny and clean. The only thing ominous was the fact that they were still behind us. Then . . . it turned into a narrow driveway. Just like that, not a threat.

"Shit," I said.

"Ditto," Jason said, but I saw his shoulder sag, as if tension drained away with that one word.

"Are we becoming too paranoid?" I asked.

"Maybe," Jason said, but he was still spending almost as much time staring back in the rearview mirror as straight ahead, as if he couldn't quite believe it. Neither could I, so I didn't tell him to watch the road. He was watching forward okay, and I, too, was expecting the blue Jeep to pull out and start after us again. Just a ruse, guys, not really harmless after all. But it didn't happen. We drove down the long car-crowded street, until the Jeep's driveway was hidden by trees and parked cars.

"Looks like it was just driving our way," Jason said.

"Looks like," I said.

Nathaniel rubbed his face against my leg. "You still smell scared, like you don't believe it."

"I don't believe it," I said.

"Why not?" Caleb asked, leaning in between the seats from the backseat.

I finally turned around in the seat, but I wasn't looking at Caleb, I was staring past him at the empty street. "Experience," I said.

I smelled roses, and a second later the cross around my neck began to glow, softly.

"Jesus," Jason whispered.

My heart was thumping painfully in my chest, but my voice came solid. "She can't roll me while I'm wearing a cross."

"You sure of that?" Caleb asked, as he moved back away from me into the far reaches of the seat.

"Yeah," I said, "I'm sure of that."

"Why?" he asked, eyes wide.

I blinked at him as the soft, white luminosity grew brighter in the tree shadows, almost invisible in full sunlight, over and over again. "Because I believe," I said, voice soft as the glow around my

223

neck, and as sure. I'd seen crosses burst into a white-hot light so bright it was blinding, but that was when I'd been face-to-face with a vamp that meant me harm. Belle was far away, and the glow showed that.

I kept waiting for the scent of roses to grow stronger again, but it never did. It stayed faint, definitely there, but didn't grow on the air.

I waited for Belle's voice in my head, but it didn't come. Every time she had spoken directly in my mind, the smell of roses had been thick. The sweet perfume stayed faint, and Belle's voice was gone from me. I squeezed the cross with my hand, feeling the heat, the power of it, skin prickling up my arm, thrumming like a continuous heartbeat against my hand. Caleb asked how could I believe. What I always wanted to ask, is, how can you *not* believe?

I felt Belle's anger like warmth on the air. Power filled the Jeep, in a neck-ruffling, breath-stealing tide, so much effort and all she could send was an image of herself sitting in front of her dressing table. Her long, black hair was unbound, like a cloak around a dressing gown of gold and black. She watched herself in the mirror with eyes full of honey-fire, like the eyes of the blind, empty except for the color of her power.

I whispered out loud, "You cannot touch me, not now."

She looked into the mirror as if I were standing behind her, and she could see me. Rage changed her beauty into something frightening, a mere mask of pale beauty that looked as false as any Halloween mask. Then she turned and looked past me, beyond me, and the look of fear on her face was so real, so unexpected that I turned, too, and I saw . . . something.

Darkness. Darkness like a wave, rising up, up over me, over us, like a liquid mountain towering to the impossibly tall sky. The room that Belle had constructed of dreams and power collapsed, shredded like the dream it was, and what ate at the corners of that bright candlelit room was darkness. Darkness absolute, darkness so black that it held shines of other colors, like an oil slick, or a trick of the eye. As if this blackness was a darkness made up of every color that had ever existed, every sight that had ever been seen, every sigh, every scream, since time began. I had heard the term *primordial darkness*, but until this moment I had never understood

224

what it meant. Now I understood, I truly understood, and I despaired.

I stared up, up at an ocean of darkness that rose above me as if the earth and sky had never existed. This was darkness before the light, before the word of God. It was like a breath of an older creation. But if this was creation, it was nothing I could understand, nothing I wanted to understand.

Belle screamed first. I think I was too awestruck to scream, or even to be afraid. I looked into the primordial abyss, the first darkness, and knew despair, but not fear.

My mind kept trying to find words to describe what it was. It did loom over me like a mountain, because it had weight and that claustrophobic feel of a mountain poised to come crashing down, but it was not a mountain. It was more like an ocean, if an ocean could have risen up taller than the tallest mountain and stood before you, waiting, defying gravity and every other known law of physics. Like with an ocean, I knew – could sense – that I only saw that wide glimpse from shore, that I could only begin to guess at the depth and width, the unthinkable fathoms of darkness that lay before me.

Did strange creatures swim inside it? Were there things within the dark that only nightmares or dreams could reveal? I watched the flickering, liquid dark and felt the numbness of despair begin to wear away. It was as if the despair had been a shield to protect me, to numb me, so that my mind wouldn't break. For a few moments I had been intellect, thinking, *What is it?* How can I make sense of it? The numbness began to recede as if that huge blackness sucked it away, fed on it. I was left standing before her, her . . . trembling, shaking, my skin running cold, and I felt that darkness sucking at me, feeding off my warmth. In that moment I knew what I faced. It was a vampire. Maybe the very first vampire, something so ancient, that to think of human bodies or flesh to contain this darkness was laughable. She was the primordial dark made real. She was why humans feared the dark, just the darkness, not what lies in the dark, not what hides there, but why we fear the darkness itself. There was a time when she walked among us, fed on us, and when darkness falls, somewhere in the back of our skulls, we remember the hungry dark.

225

That shining ocean of blackness reached out towards me, and I knew that if it touched me, I would die. I couldn't turn away, couldn't run, because you can't run from the dark, not really. The light does not last. That last thought wasn't mine. Wasn't Belle's.

I stared up at the darkness as it began to bend over me, and knew it lied. It's the dark that doesn't last. Dawn comes and slays the darkness, not the other way around. If I could have found enough air, I would have screamed, but I was left with only a whisper. The darkness bent towards me, and I couldn't shoot it, or hit it, and I didn't have enough personal psychic power to keep her at bay. I did the only thing I could think of, I prayed.

I whispered, "Hail Mary, full of Grace, the Lord is with thee . . ." the darkness hesitated, "Blessed are you among women, and Blessed is the fruit of thy womb," the faintest of shivers ran through the liquid dark, "Holy Mary, Mother of God, pray for us . . ." There was suddenly light in the darkness. My cross was around my neck in the dreamscape. The metal shone like a captive star, shining and white, and unlike in real life, I could see beyond the brilliance of it. I watched that pure, white light chase back the dark.

I was suddenly aware of the car seat, the seat belt across my chest, Nathaniel's body wrapped around my legs. The cross around my neck was glowing hot white even in sunlight, so that I had to look away from it, and still the white, white light blurred my vision. The cross wouldn't have still been burning if the danger had passed. I waited for the Mother of All Darkness to make her next move.

The air in the Jeep was suddenly soft, sweet, like the perfect summer night, when you can smell every blade of grass, every leaf, every flower, like a scented blanket that wraps you in air softer than cashmere, lighter than silk, a sweet blanket of air.

My throat suddenly felt cooler, as if I'd taken a sip of cold water. I could feel it coating my throat, and there was a faint under-taste, like jasmine.

Nathaniel buried his face in my lap to protect his eyes from the light. It was like wearing a white sun around my neck.

"Shit," Jason said, "I'm having trouble seeing the road. Can you tone it down?"

226

The world was full of white halos, and I didn't dare turn my head to look at him. The scent of night was all I could smell as if everything else had vanished. I could almost redrink the cool, perfumed water that coated my throat. So real, so overwhelmingly real. I managed to whisper, "No."

I kept waiting for words in my head, but there was nothing but silence, and the smell of a summer night, the taste of cool water, and the growing sense that something large was drawing nearer. It was like standing on the train tracks, when you feel that first vibration down the metal lines, and you know you should get off, but you can't see anything. As far as you can look, the tracks are clear, there's only that metallic vibration, like a pulse beat against your feet, to let you know that several tons of steel are hurtling towards you. People die every year on train tracks, and often their dying words are *I didn't see the train.* I've always thought that trains must be magical that way, or otherwise people would see them, and get the fuck off the tracks. I could feel the vibration of her rushing towards me, and I would gladly have gotten off the tracks, but the tracks were inside my head, nailed across my body, and I couldn't figure out how to run from that.

Something rubbed against my skin, like some large animal pressing its body along the length of mine. I felt Nathaniel draw back, but I couldn't see him through the white light. His voice came, breathless, frightened, "What is that?"

I opened my mouth, not even sure what I'd say, when that roll of invisible animal hit my chest, and the cross. The cross flared so bright that most of us screamed, cried out. Jason had to hit the brakes and stop the Jeep in the middle of the street, blinded by the light, unable to see to drive, I think.

The light began to dim. For a second I wondered if the brilliance had fried my retinas, then my vision began to clear through a veil of spots. I could still feel it, her, pressing against me, pinning me to the seat, pressing over the cross, as if she were eating the light.

Nathaniel stared up at me, his lavender eyes gone leopard, a deep, deep gray, that had a hint of blue in the sunlight. "She's a shifter," he whispered. And I knew why. Shape-shifters could not be vampires, or vice versa. The lycanthropy virus seemed to be proof against whatever made you a vampire. You could not be

227

both. It was a rule. But whatever pressed against me now was animal not human. I couldn't get a sense of what kind of animal, but animal it was.

How the Mother of all Darkness happened to be both a vampire and a shape-shifter at the same time was a problem for another day. Right then, I didn't care what she was, I just wanted her to leave me the fuck alone.

The cross was still glowing, but only the metal itself, as if it were hollow and candles burned inside it. The light was white and flickering now. I'd never seen a cross look so much like fire before. But it was a cold fire. The shape pushed and rolled like it was trying to climb inside me, but the cross kept glowing, acting as a metaphysical shield to keep her out of me.

"What can we do to help?" Jason asked. The Jeep was still stopped in the middle of the street. A car trapped behind us was honking its horn. There were cars parked on both sides of the residential street leaving the car with no way to get past us. The neighborhood was nothing but small neat houses, none with driveways. Jason hit the blinkers, and the car began to back away, trying to turn around.

I was almost afraid to open my links to Richard and Jean-Claude, what if the primordial dark could spill down the ties and take them, too? Jean-Claude had no faith to fall back on. Richard did, but whether he was actually wearing a cross or not was debatable. It had been a long time since I'd seen Richard wear a cross.

While I was still considering, Jason grabbed my hand. The scent of night didn't fade, it was added to, like a layer of color painted over another. The clean musk of wolves filled the night. The cool water that seemed to have passed down my throat now tasted more of loam and forest than perfume.

I had an image in my mind of a huge animal head with long teeth, like the largest fangs I'd ever seen. The fur on the head was gold and tawny, and reddish, shaded, rather than striped, more lion than tiger. Eyes like golden fire stared into mine, and that huge mouth opened wide, and screamed its frustration, in a sound like a panther's scream, but decibels lower. Pioneers were always mistaking panther screams for a woman's cries. No one would have

228

mistaken this for a woman – a man, maybe, a man being tortured and screaming for his soul.

I screamed back, as if that head were truly right in front of me and not thousands of miles across the world. My scream was echoed by two others. Nathaniel snarled up at me from the floor-board, his mouth showing teeth that were fast becoming fangs. Caleb had slid in between the seats, and his eyes were yellow cat eyes. He started to rub his cheek against my shoulder as if he was going to scent mark me, then stopped, snarling, as if he'd touched that other phantom cat.

Jason didn't scream, he growled, that low, fur-standing-on-end sound that has nothing to do with hunting and everything to do with fighting, not for food, but for survival. It was a sound for guarding territory, chasing out interlopers, getting rid of trouble-makers. The sound that says *get out or die*.

She screamed back, a sound that should have frozen the blood in my veins, and reminded me that my ancestors had huddled around their small fires and watched in terror for the shine of eyes outside that flame. But I wasn't thinking like a person. I wasn't even sure *thinking* was the word for what was moving through my mind. It was more like I was in the moment, completely, utterly. I could feel the leather seat cupping my body, Nathaniel pressed against my legs, his hands tracing higher, Caleb at my shoulder, his cheek against my face, his jaw straining as he snarled, Jason's hand on my arm like it had taken root, become a part of me.

I could smell Caleb's skin, the soap he'd used that morning, and the fear like something bitter under that clean skin. Nathaniel moved up on his knees, higher, so that his face was superimposed behind the saber-tooth's head for a moment. But I could smell the vanilla scent of his hair, and there was nothing from the phantom cat.

Jason moved in closer, putting his face close to mine, sniffing the air. I smelled soap, shampoo, and the smell of Jason, a scent that had begun to mean home to me, the way the vanilla scent of Nathaniel's hair, or Jean-Claude's expensive cologne, or, once, the warm bend of Richard's neck affected me. I didn't mean in a sexual way, but the way fresh baked bread or your mother's favorite cookies make you feel safe and smell like home. I turned

229

my head to Caleb, so that my nose touched his skin, and under the fear, the soap, the soft skin, he smelled of leopard, faint in his human form, but there, a nose-wrinkling, skin-prickling smell. I turned to the weight pressing against the still-glowing cross. I looked into those yellow eyes, gazed upon those fangs that were like nothing that walked the earth today, and it had no scent.

Jason was snuffling the air in front of me. His pale wolf eyes met mine, and I knew that he'd figured it out, too.

As a vampire she smelled of cool evenings and sweet water, vaguely like jasmine. As a wereanimal she had no scent, because she wasn't here. It was a sending, a psychic sending. It had power, but it wasn't real, not really real, not physical. No matter how much power you put into it, a psychic sending has limits to what it can do physically. It can frighten you into running into traffic, but it can't push you. It can try to trick you into doing things, but it cannot hurt you without a physical agent. When she was a vampire, the cross and my faith kept her at bay. As a wereanimal, she wasn't real.

Nathaniel had literally crawled up through the image I could still see hovering over my chest. He was the one who said it out loud, "It has no scent."

"It's not real," I said.

Caleb's voice came with an edge of growl so deep that it was almost painful to hear, "I feel it, some great cat, like pard, but not."

"But do you smell anything?" Jason asked.

Caleb sniffed along my body. Any other time, I would have accused him of getting too close to my breasts, but not now. He was as serious as I'd ever seen him, as he sniffed along my chest, pushed his face almost into that evil face. He stopped, staring into those yellow eyes from inches away. He hissed like any startled cat. "I can't smell it, but I see it."

"Seeing isn't always believing," I said.

"What is it?" he asked.

"A psychic projection, a sending. The vampire couldn't get past the cross, so it tried another form, but the kitty-cat doesn't travel as well as the . . . whatever the hell she is." I looked into those yellow eyes and watched that massive mouth roar up at me. "You have no scent, you aren't real, only a bad dream, and dreams have no power unless you give it to them. I give you nothing. Go back to where you came from, go back to the dark."

I had a sudden image of a dark, dark room, not pitch black, but as if the only light were reflected from somewhere else. There was a bed with a black silk cover and a figure lying under that cover. The room was oddly shaped, not square, not circular, almost hexagonal. There were windows, but I knew somehow that they did not look out upon the world. Windows to gaze down upon the darkness that never lifted, never changed.

I was drawn towards the bed, drawn the way you're drawn in nightmares. I didn't want to look, but I had to look; didn't want to see, and had to see.

I reached out towards that shining black silk, I could tell it was silk because of the way it reflected the light from down below, far down below outside the windows. The light flickered, and I knew it was firelight. Nothing electric had ever touched the darkness of this place.

My fingertips brushed the silk, and the body under the sheet moved in its sleep, moved the way someone will when they dream, but are not yet awake. I knew in that instant that I was a dream to her, too, and I couldn't truly be standing in her inner sanctum, that no matter how real or exact it was, I could not send myself to her, and pull the sheet away. Dreams could not do that. But I also knew in that same moment that all she had done to me today had been done in a sleep that had lasted long and longer, so long that the others sometimes thought she was dead, hoped she was dead, feared she was dead, prayed she was dead, if they had the courage of prayer left in them. Who do the soulless dead pray to?

A sigh moved through that close, airless room, and on that first breath of air, came a whisper of sound, the first sound that that room had heard in centuries, "Me."

It took me a moment to realize that it was the answer to my question. Who do the soulless dead pray to? *Me*, the whisper said.

The figure under the sheet shifted in its sleep again. Not awake, not yet, but she was swimming upwards, filling in herself, coming closer to wakefulness.

I jerked my hand back from that sheet; I stepped back from that

231

bed. I did not want to touch her. More than anything else, I did not want to wake her. But since I didn't know how I'd gotten into her room, I couldn't figure out how to get out of it. I'd never been someone else's dream before, though people had accused me of being their nightmares. How do you stop being in someone else's dream?

That whisper echoed through the room again, "By waking them."

She'd answered my question again. Shit. I was beginning to have an awful idea. Could the darkness become lost in sleep? Could the dark become lost in the dark? Could the mother of all nightmares be trapped in the land of dreams?

"Not trapped," the whisper in the dark said.

"Then what?" I asked it out loud, and the body under the sheet rolled all the way over, feeling the silence with the hissing glide of silk over skin. My throat closed around the words, and I cursed myself for not thinking.

"Waiting," still the air breathing around me, not a voice, not really.

I thought really hard, *waiting for what?*

There was no answer from the dark room. But there was a new noise. Someone beside me was breathing, deep, even breathing, as if they slept. Though I would have sworn that the figure on the bed hadn't been breathing a second ago.

I did not want to be here when she sat up, I so did not want to be here for that. What had she been waiting for all this time?

This time the voice came from the bed, the same voice as the wind, faint, long unused, so hoarse and soft that I couldn't tell if it were male or female. "Something of interest."

With that last, I finally felt something from that body. I'd been prepared for malice, evil, anger, but was totally unprepared for curiosity. As if she wondered what I was, and she hadn't wondered about anything in a millennia, or two, or three.

I smelled wolf, musky, sweet, pungent, so real I could feel it gliding over my skin. I suddenly had a cross around my neck, and the white glow filled the room. I think I could have seen the figure on the bed clearly by the light of the cross, but either I closed my eyes without remembering, or some things you shouldn't see, even in dreams.

232

I woke in the Jeep with Nathaniel and Caleb's worried faces hovering over me. There was a huge wolf sitting in the driver's seat, its long snout snuffling against my face. I reached up to touch that soft, thick fur, then saw the shine of liquid all over the driver's seat, where Jason had shape-shifted on the leather.

"Jesus, Mary, and Joseph, you couldn't have shape-shifted in the back in the cargo area. You had to shape-shift on the leather seats. It'll never come clean."

Jason growled at me, low and rumbling, and I didn't have to speak wolf to know what he was saying. I was being an ungrateful wretch. But it was so much easier to concentrate on my ruined upholstery than to think about the fact that I'd been in the presence of the Mother of All Vampires, the Mother of All Darkness, the Primordial Abyss made flesh. I knew through Jean-Claude's memories that they called her Mother Gentle, Marme, a dozen different euphemisms to make her seem kind, and, well, motherly. But I'd felt her power, her darkness, and finally, at the end an intellect as cold and empty as any evil. She was curious about me the way some scientists are curious about a new species of insect. Find it, capture it, put it in a jar, whether it wants to go with you, or not. It's just an insect, after all.

They could call her Mother Gentle if they wanted to, but Mommy Dearest was a hell of a lot more accurate.

## 30

CALEB HAD CLIMBED into the back of the Jeep to get the plastic I'd started carrying, for when I transported something messier than chickens, and spread it on the seat so Nathaniel could drive. I'd tried to insist on driving but Jason had growled at me. He had a point, I wasn't feeling my steadiest. Nathaniel, his eyes bled back to their normal lilac, had told me, "You passed out. You stopped breathing. Jason shook you, and you did this sort of gasp." Nathaniel shook his head, face very serious. "We had to keep shaking you, Anita. You kept not breathing."

If they'd been human I might have argued with them, that they only thought I'd stopped breathing, but they weren't human. If a bunch of shape-shifters were unable to hear or see me breathe, I had to believe them.

Had Mommy Dearest tried to kill me? Or had it been accidental – or incidental? She wouldn't have meant to kill me, but she might have done it by accident. And I'd touched enough of her thinking to know it wouldn't bother her. She wouldn't be sorry, she would feel no guilt. She didn't think like a person, or rather she didn't think like a nice, normal, civilized human. She thought like a sociopath – no empathy, no sympathy, no guilt, no compassion. In a strange way, that must be a very peaceful existence. Did you need more emotions than she possessed to be lonely? I'd think so, but I really didn't know. *Lonely* was not a word I would have applied to her. If you didn't understand the need for friendship or love, could you be lonely? I shrugged and shook my head.

"What is it?" Nathaniel asked.

"If you don't feel love or friendship, can you be lonely?"

He raised eyebrows at me. "I don't know. Why do you ask?"

"We've all just brushed up against the Mother of all Vampires, and she's more like the Mother of All Sociopaths. Human beings are rarely pure sociopaths. It's more like they're missing a piece here and there. True, pure sociopathy is really pretty rare, but Mommy Dearest qualifies, I think."

"It doesn't matter if she's lonely," Caleb said.

I glanced back at him. His brown eyes were very large, and underneath his fading tan he was pale. I sniffed the air before I could think, and the car was a playground of scents; the sweet musk of wolf, the clean vanilla of Nathaniel, and Caleb. Caleb smelled . . . young. I wasn't sure how to explain it but it was as if I could smell how tender his meat would be, how fresh his blood. He smelled clean, the scent of some lightly perfumed soap coated his skin, but underneath was another scent. Bitter and sweet all at the same time, the way blood is salty and sweet at the same time.

I turned as far as the seat belt would allow and said, "You smell good, Caleb, all tender and scared."

He was the true predator, not me, but the look he flashed me was all prey – huge eyes, face soft, lips opened just a breath. I watched his pulse beat against the skin of his neck.

I had an urge to crawl into the backseat and run my tongue over that frantic pulse, set teeth into that tender flesh, and set that pulse point free.

I had this image of Caleb's pulse like a piece of hard candy that would come free all in one piece and be sucked and rolled around in my mouth. I knew it wasn't like that. I knew that if I bit down the pulse would be destroyed, that it would die in a spill of red blood, but the candy imagery stayed with me, and even the thought of blood spraying in my mouth didn't seem terrible.

I closed my eyes so I couldn't see Caleb's neck beating and concentrated on my own breathing. But with every breath I drew in more of that bitter sweetness, the taste of fear. I could almost taste his flesh in my mouth.

"What's wrong with me?" I asked that out loud. "I want to tear Caleb's pulse out of his throat. It's too early for Jean-Claude to be awake. Besides I don't usually want blood. Or not only blood."

"It's close to full moon," Nathaniel said. "It's one of the reasons Jason lost enough control to change all over your seats."

I opened my eyes, turned my face to look at him, and away from

235

Caleb's fear. "Belle tried to get me to feed off Caleb, but she couldn't. So why suddenly does he smell tasty?"

Nathaniel had finally found another exit back onto 44. He eased in behind a large yellow car that needed a major paint job, or maybe was in the middle of getting one, because half of it was covered in gray primer. I caught movement in the rearview mirror. It was the blue Jeep. It was at the end of the narrow street with cars on either side. It had just cleared the corner, and seen us, and now it was hanging back, hoping, I think, that we hadn't seen it.

"Shit," I said.

"What?" Nathaniel asked.

"That damned Jeep is at the end of the street. Nobody look back." Everyone stopped themselves in mid-motion except for Jason. He hadn't even tried to look back, maybe wolf necks didn't work that way, or maybe he was staring at other things. I realized that he was looking at Caleb.

I looked at that huge shaggy head. "Are you thinking about eating Caleb?"

He turned and gave me the full force of that pale green gaze. People say that dogs are descended from wolves, but there are moments when I doubt that. There was nothing friendly, or sympathetic, or even remotely tame in those eyes. He was thinking about food. He met my gaze because he knew I'd caught him thinking about eating someone that was under my protection, then he turned back to gaze at Caleb, and think of meat. Dogs never look at people and think, *food*, hell; they don't even look at other dogs and think that. Wolves do. The fact that there is no recorded account of a North American wolf attacking a human being for food has always amazed me. You look into their eyes, and you know that there is no one home that you can talk to.

I knew that lycanthropes want fresh meat when they first change shape. New lycanthropes are deadly, but Jason wasn't new anymore, and he could control himself. I knew that, but I still didn't like the way he was looking at Caleb, and I liked even less that he was projecting his need onto me.

"What do you want me to do about the Jeep?" Nathaniel asked.

I jerked my attention back to Nathaniel and away from the hunger. It was an effort to think past it, but if the Jeep was full of bad guys, then I needed to be concentrating on them, not some metaphysical craving.

"Hell, I don't know. I don't get followed that much. Usually people just try and kill me."

"I have to either pull out onto the highway, or turn the other way. Just sitting here, they're going to know we saw them."

He had a point, a good one. "Highway."

He moved us forward, angling for the ramp. "Once we're on it, where are we going?"

"The Circus, I think."

"Do we want to lead the bad guys there?" Nathaniel asked.

"Jason said it earlier, most people know where the Master of the City bunks during the day. Besides, the wererats are still there, and most of them are ex-mercenaries, or something in that ballpark. I think I'm going to call ahead and ask Bobby Lee's opinion."

"Opinion about what?" Caleb asked, from the backseat. His eyes were still too wide, and he still smelled of fear, but he wasn't looking at the wolf on the seat beside him. Whatever he was afraid of wasn't something that close.

"About whether we catch them, or turn around and try to follow them."

"Catch them?" Caleb said. "Catch them how?"

"Not sure, but I know that I know a lot more about catching bad guys than about following people to see where they lead me. I'm not a detective, Caleb, not really. I can spot a clue if it bites me on the ass, and give an opinion about monster-related crime, but at heart I'm in a more direct line of work than detective."

He looked puzzled.

"I'm an executioner, Caleb, I kill things."

"Sometimes you have to track things in order to kill them," Nathaniel said.

I looked at him, that serious profile, his eyes searching the traffic, his hands on the wheel at exactly two and ten. He hadn't had his license a year, yet. If I hadn't insisted, I'm not sure he'd have ever had one.

"True, but I don't want to kill them, I want to question them. I want to know why they're following us."

"I don't think they are," Nathaniel said.

237

"What?" I asked.

"The blue Jeep didn't follow us onto the highway."

"Knew we spotted them, maybe."

"Or like everyone else knows where the Master sleeps. So it's not hard to find his girlfriend," Nathaniel said, voice quiet, eyes on the road. But he knew I hated being the Master's girlfriend, or at least being called that. Truthfully, he had a point. If you knew who someone was dating and where they lived, eventually, you could locate them again. I hated being predictable.

Jason's great shaggy head came around my seat and rubbed against my shoulder, the ruff of his face tickling along my cheek. I reached up and petted that great head without thinking, the way I would have done if he'd been a dog. The moment I touched him, the hunger thrilled through me from the top of my head to the bottom of my feet. The hair on my body stood to attention, and it felt like something was trying to crawl up the back of my skull, because the nape of my neck was prickling so badly.

The wolf and I turned as one to stare at Caleb. If my eyes could have bled to wolf, they'd have done it then.

Caleb looked terrified. I think if he'd just stayed still we'd have been okay, but he didn't. He unfolded his arms from his nearly bare chest and eased across the seat.

Jason growled, and I was out of my seat, on the floorboards in the back, before I had a chance to think, unseatbelted in a speeding car, bad idea. I think that would have put me back in my own head space, but Caleb ran. He spilled over the backseat, and Jason and I spilled after him. It was like being water, following the natural course.

We didn't pin Caleb, so much as kneel and sit around him. Caleb was pressed tight in the corner of the cargo area, his hands tight against his chest. He tried to take up as little space as possible. I think Caleb knew that touching either of us would be bad. Jason sat on his haunches, flashing fangs and letting the trickle of growl slide out. You didn't need words to know what it meant, *don't move, don't fucking move.* Caleb didn't move.

I was on my knees in front of Caleb, and all I could see was the pulse in his neck, thudding, thudding, against the skin, trying to break free. I wanted to help it.

238

I could suddenly smell forest, trees, and the scent of wolf fur that wasn't Jason. Richard breathed through my mind like a sweet-scented cloud. I saw him in my bathtub all those miles away. An arm darker than the tan Richard carried most of the year was across his chest, propping him up in the water, holding him. Jamil being a good Hati, making sure his Ulfric didn't drown. It was what Jason had done for me earlier, minus the sex. Richard was a little homophobic. He didn't like men who reminded him they liked men, especially if that man was himself. I couldn't throw stones on that one; I was pretty much the same way around women. No matter how sophisticated I was supposed to be, I kept forgetting that another woman could find me attractive. Always caught me by surprise.

Jamil's face hovered on the edge of Richard's, but it was as if in this dream vision all that was truly clear was Richard. I caught glimpses of his body through the water and the faint candlelight. Lycanthropes sometimes had light sensitivity problems, so there were no bright overheads, but the candles made the water dark, and hid more of Richard from view than I wanted. I felt like a meta-physical Peeping Tom. But the hunger was so easily turned to a different kind of hunger, it always had been.

Richard looked up at me, and the sight of his face, shorn of hair, caught at my throat. I wanted to ask, *why?* but he spoke first. It was the first time we'd spoken mind-to-mind like this, and it startled me. I'd known Jean-Claude and I could do it, but not Richard and me.

"The hunger's mine, Anita, I'm sorry. Something that creature did to me stripped most of my control." For a second I thought he meant the Mother of All Darkness, then realized he meant Belle.

I gazed down at Caleb's frightened eyes, and my eyes were drawn again to his neck, then down the line of his chest to his stomach. He was breathing hard enough, scared enough that there was a pulse low in his belly, vibrating through that line of hair that led down into his pants. The stomach was soft and tender, lots of flesh there.

"Anita," Richard said, "Anita, hear me."

I had to blink the image of Caleb's quivering flesh away, and I was suddenly seeing Richard's image more clearly than what actually lay in front of me. "What?" I knew that one word wasn't said out loud, only in my head.

"You can turn the hunger to sex, Anita."

I shook my head. "I think I'd rather eat Caleb than fuck him."

"You've never eaten anyone, or you wouldn't say that," Richard said.

I couldn't really argue with that. "Are you seriously saying you'd be okay with me fucking Caleb?"

He hesitated, the water flickering in the flame light, as his body moved restlessly. I caught a glimpse of knee, and thigh. "If it's a choice between eating him, or screwing him, yes."

"You didn't even like sharing me with Jean-Claude."

"We're not dating, Anita."

Ouch. "Sorry, forgot that for a moment," I said. The momentary flare of pain like a half-healed wound helped me think a little more clearly. "Jason is in wolf form Richard. I don't do furry."

"That I can do something about." I saw his beast like some golden shadow leap out of him and into me. It was like being on the receiving end of a metaphysical knife, until that power stabbed through me and into Jason, and I was suddenly in the middle of all that power, all that pain, all that rage. The beast feeds on pain and rage, sort of the ultimate id. I was left kneeling, gasping, too breathless to scream.

Jason screamed for me, and I felt his beast slide away from him, no, into him, like stuffing something impossibly huge into a suitcase that was already full. But this suitcase was Jason's body, and it hurt. I felt the bones twist, the muscles pop and reattach. Fuck, it hurt. I caught a distant thought from Richard that it was hurting so much because it was forced. When you fight the change it hurts more.

It was as if the fur was absorbed back into the pale flesh that rose through it, like something caught in ice, melting back to the surface. Jason's body melted back, and the fur sank into him, the longer bones, the muscles. It just all sank into him until he lay pale and shivering on a bed of clear liquid. The fluid had soaked my jeans from the knees down. Jason had changed, but not fed, now he'd been forced to change again less than a half-hour later. Maybe if he'd been allowed to feed he'd have been alright, but now, he lay, shivering, curling into a ball to hold himself and to keep in what warmth he had left and to take up as little space as possible. I think Jason, like Caleb, knew touching me would be bad.

Jason wasn't a danger to Caleb anymore. Until he rested, he wasn't a danger to anyone. In fact . . . I stared down at the curve of his butt, so smooth, so firm, so tender. I gazed on him nude, and didn't think about sex at all. All Richard had done was give me a choice of meals.

I looked at Richard down that vision that held him crystalline, and everything else hazy. "All I can think about is sinking teeth into his flesh. You've made him helpless, and I still need to feed, because you still need to feed."

"I'll find something here to eat. I will feed, but you don't have anything safe to hunt, Anita. You don't want to hurt either of them."

I screamed, loud and long, letting the frustration fill the Jeep, pour out of my mouth, scald up my throat, ball my hands into fists, and lash out, smashing the side of the Jeep. I heard the metal groan, and that made me blink, look at what I'd done. I'd dented the metal. A rounded dimple the size of my fist. Fuck.

Caleb made a small sound, and I looked down at him, and all I could see was the soft flesh of his stomach, I could almost feel it under my teeth. I was crouched over Caleb, my face sniffing along his stomach. I didn't remember getting this close.

Richard called to me, "Anita!"

I looked up, as if he were really in front of me. He pushed Jamil's arm away and leaned back against the side of the tub. He ran his hands over his chest, fingers tracing his nipples, one hand trailing lower, as he pushed himself out of the water. It cascaded down his body in silver flame shot lines, and that hand traced lower, lower. Over his stomach, down the line of hair, and finally to cup himself, play with himself. I watched him grow larger, and the hunger changed like turning a switch. But the moment the hunger became sex, the *ardeur* flared to life. It came from the center of my being like a flame, spreading, spreading, and Richard's hand, Richard's body fanned the heat, brought it in a roaring sheet over my skin.

But Jean-Claude wasn't here to help us, this time, and Richard couldn't shield today. The *ardeur* ran down that metaphysical cord

241

and hit Richard like a truck at full speed. It bowed his back, convulsed his hand where it gripped his body, made him fall back on the edge of the tub, his legs trailing into the water.

I looked into those big brown eyes, that face so empty without its mane of hair, and watched terror fight with desire. I don't think he'd ever felt the full force of the *ardeur* before. It overwhelmed him, left him breathless, immobile, but that wouldn't last. I knew it wouldn't last.

I told him what he'd told me, "You can turn the *ardeur* to hunger, but we're going to have to feed on something, or someone, Richard. It's too late for anything else."

Even his voice in my head seemed strangled, "I feel better and worse. I think I can hunt now. I couldn't have moved that much before."

"Everything has its upside, Richard, and its down." I was angry with Richard, a fine hot rage that helped keep me treading the water of the *ardeur* that was trying so hard to engulf me, drown me in desire. But I held my anger to my chest and treaded water for all I was worth.

I felt his hunger change, felt his belly tighten with need for flesh and blood and tearing, and only distant, very distant was the thrill of sex. "I'll hunt an animal, and I'll be fine, I think."

"That won't help me much, Richard," and I let the anger trail down the binding between us.

"I am sorry, Anita, I didn't understand."

I knew in that moment that I could force his hunger back into the *ardeur.* That just as he forced Jason to change form, I could force Richard's hunger to be the form of my choosing. I knew I could run magic down his skin and force him to feed the way I was going to have to feed. But I didn't. He'd done what he'd done in innocence; I couldn't return the favor, not deliberately.

"Go hunt your animal, Richard."

"Anita . . . I am sorry."

"You're always sorry, Richard. Now get out of my head before I do something we'll both regret."

He pulled away, but it wasn't a clean break. Normally, his shields were solid like metal doors clanging down. Today, it was like taffy pulling apart, clinging to each other, huge tendrils of sticky, melting candy that even when pulled apart was still two halves of a whole. I wanted to pull us together, to melt into the heat until we were one big hot sticky mess, and today Richard couldn't stop me. He didn't have the control to keep me out of him.

Jean-Claude woke. I felt his eyes flash wide, felt him take that first gasping breath, felt life fill him. He was awake.

Jason was gazing at me with his sky blue eyes. "He's awake."

I nodded. "I know."

Nathaniel spoke as if he'd understood way more of the unheard conversation than he should have, "We're almost to the Circus, Anita."

"How long?"

"Five minutes, less."

"Make it less," I said.

The Jeep leapt forward, accelerating. I crawled into the backseat and fastened the seat belt tight across me. It wasn't to keep me safe in case we had an accident. It was to remind me not to let myself loose until we got to the Circus, and Jean-Claude.

# 31

I FOUGHT THE *ardeur* on the drive to the Circus. I fought the *ardeur* when I ran through the parking lot and banged on the door. I ran past Bobby Lee's surprised face and managed to say, "Ask Nathaniel about the Jeep." Then I was past him and running for the stairs that led down, down to the underground.

Richard was running, too. He was running through the trees, limbs and leaves slashing at him, but he was never quite there, dodging, moving, like water made flesh, flesh made speed. He ran through the trees, and I heard something large crashing ahead of him. His head came up, and the chase was on.

I hit Jean-Claude's bedroom door, as Richard was catching glimpses of the deer that darted just ahead of him, sprinting for its life. There were other wolves in the forest, most of them in true wolf form, but not all.

I flung the door open and the guards on the door closed it firmly behind me. I don't know what they sensed, or what they saw, and that was probably just as well.

There were still blue silk sheets on the bed, and Asher was still framed in them, motionless, dead. Only the Master of the City was awake, only he moved. I sent a questioning thought and felt all the vampires asnooze in their coffins, tucked in their beds. I touched Angelito for a moment, and found him restless and pacing, confused, wondering why his mistress hadn't succeeded in her diabolical plan.

He looked up as if he saw me, or felt something, then I was back at the bathroom door. Richard had his deer down and struggling. A hoof caught him across the stomach, tore the skin, but there were other wolves there now, and the doe had no chance. A black furred wolf tore into her throat, and I felt Richard riding the deer in human form, holding her as the struggles grew slower, spasmodic,

244

involuntary. The deer's fear faded, like champagne opened and left to go flat.

The bathroom door flung open, hitting the wall, and I didn't remember touching it. I was through the door before it slammed shut behind me, and again, I didn't remember touching it.

Jean-Claude was in the black marble tub. He was kneeling, his long black hair clinging to his shoulders. He'd cleaned up. Feeling me coming towards him like a storm of need, he'd run a bath. Of course, he'd felt me like a storm of desire before, it didn't always mean the storm would fall on him.

I could smell the fresh, hot blood, as Richard leaned down towards the deer's throat. The wolf that had actually made the kill had backed off, so the Ulfric could feed. The deer's skin smelled acrid, almost bitter, as if the fear had bled out of the skin. I did not want to be in Richard's head when he put his mouth to that flesh.

I climbed into the bathtub in my clothes, the hot water soaking my jeans almost to the tops of my thighs. "Help me," it came out in a whisper that I'd meant to be a scream.

Jean-Claude stood up, water streaming down the perfect whiteness of his skin, drawing my eyes down the length of his body, finding him soft and not ready for me. I screamed, and Richard sank teeth into skin that was covered in hair.

Jean-Claude caught me, or I would have fallen into the water. I suddenly couldn't feel Richard anymore. It was as if a door had slammed in my face and there was a second of blessed silence, a quietness that went all the way to my soul.

Jean-Claude spoke into that silence. "I can shield you from our Richard, *ma petite*, and he from you, but I cannot shield us both from the *ardeur*."

I stared up at him, where I'd half-swooned in his arms, his hands at my back, my body bowed down towards the water, my legs soaked with the hot liquid.

I opened my mouth to say something, then he was as good as his word, and the *ardeur* came roaring back. I convulsed in his arms, and he nearly dropped me, trailing my hair in the water, pulling me upwards, pressing our bodies against one another. My hands, my mouth, my body swarmed over him, traced that slick, perfect skin, caressed the faint tracery of whip scars on his back, which were just another part of his perfection.

He drew back from my mouth enough to gasp, "*Ma petite*, I have not fed, there is no blood to fill my body."

I gazed up at him and found his eyes as normal as they ever got, midnight blue, lashed with black lace. But there was no power in them. Usually, by the time we've gotten this much foreplay in, his eyes had bled to pure pupilless blue.

I had to swim up through the *ardeur*; through the need to finally understand what he meant. I pushed my hair to one side, and said, "Feed, feed, then fuck me."

"I cannot roll your mind, *ma petite*, it will only be pain."

I shook my head, eyes closed, my hands tracing over the skin of his shoulders and arms. "Please, Jean-Claude, please, feed, feed on me."

"If you were in your right mind, you would not offer this."

I pulled the red T-shirt out of my pants, but had trouble pushing the straps of my shoulder holster down, as if I couldn't remember how. I screamed my frustration, wordless. Maybe because of that, or because Jean-Claude was trying to fight off too many things at once, I suddenly felt Richard feeding, hot flesh going in great gulps down his throat.

I choked, stumbled, collapsed against the edge of the tub, letting the hot water come up to my waist. I was going to be sick.

Jean-Claude touched my back, and I couldn't sense Richard anymore. "I cannot shield us from our wolf, fight both your *ardeur* and mine, and fight my own bloodlust. It is too much."

I sat on the edge of the tub, hands flat, trying to keep myself steady on the marble. "Then don't fight it all. Pick your battles."

"What battle should I choose?" he asked, voice soft.

The *ardeur* rose like a gentle wave, chasing back the nausea, cleansing me of the sensation of meat and flesh going down my throat. I hadn't realized the *ardeur* had any gentleness to it.

As if he'd read my thoughts, Jean-Claude said, "If you do not struggle against the *ardeur*, it is not so terrible."

"Like the beast, if you accept it, it doesn't beat the hell out of you."

He gave a small smile. "*Oui, ma petite*."

246

The *ardeur* drew me to my feet, and I wasn't shaky anymore. I was steady in my desire. I moved through the hot, thigh-deep water, my jeans clinging to me like a second skin, my jogging shoes sliding through the thickness of the water. I stood touching him only with my gaze. The strength of his thighs, the loose swelling of his groin, skin there slightly darker in color than the rest of him, the line of black hair that traced upward, around his belly button, to the smooth lines of his chest with the pale circles of his nipples, and the flat whiteness of the cross-shaped burn scar. I came to the grace of his shoulders, the line of his neck, and finally the face. I was never sure how to look upon his face and not be overwhelmed. If it had just been the dark glory of his hair, I could have borne it, but his eyes, his eyes, the darkest blue they could be and not be black. They were the richest blue I'd ever seen. His eyelashes were so thick they were like black lace. The bones in his face were delicate, small and finely chiseled, as if whoever had made him had paid attention to every curve of his cheek, every turn of his chin, every sweep of brow, and finally the mouth. His mouth was simply beautiful. So red against the white-ness of his skin.

I touched his face, traced the edge of it from temple to chin, and my fingers clung to the beads of water on his skin, sticking, so that touching him wasn't smooth, or easy. The *ardeur* was still inside me like a great warm weight, but I'd welcomed it this time, wel-comed it chasing back Richard's beast, and I could think, though only about the man in front of me.

I stared up into that face and said what I was thinking, "Was this the face that launched a thousand ships?" I slipped my hand behind his neck and began gently to bring him closer as if for a kiss, "And burnt the topless towers of Ilium?" I turned my face and swept my hair aside, exposing my neck, "Sweet Helen, make me immortal with a kiss!"

He spoke, "Why, this is hell, nor am I out of it: Thinkest thou that I who saw the face of God, and tasted the eternal joys of heaven, am not tormented with ten thousand hells in being deprived of everlasting bliss!"

The quote made me turn and look at him. "That's from *Dr. Faustus*, too, isn't it?"

247

"*Oui.*"

"I only know the one quote," I said.

"Let me give you another. 'I kissed thee ere I killed thee, no way but this, killing myself to die upon a kiss.'"

"That's not Marlowe," I said.

"One of his contemporaries," Jean-Claude said.

"Shakespeare," I said.

"You surprise me, *ma petite.*"

"You gave me too big a clue," I said, "Marlowe and Shakespeare are about the only contemporaries that people still quote." I frowned up at him. "Why are you fighting me on this?"

"Today with the *ardeur* riding you, you say *feed*. When your mind has cleared, you will call foul, and I will be punished by your regret." A look of such longing and frustration crossed his face. "I want more than almost anything to share blood with you, *ma petite*, but if I take it now when you are intoxicated, you will refuse me later more adamantly than ever."

I would have liked to argue with him. I would have liked to find another quote from someone to help persuade him, but my control over the *ardeur* wasn't as good as his, yet. Just staring up at all that beauty was making me forget. Forget what little poetry I knew. Forget logic, reason, restraint. Forget everything but his beauty, forget everything but my own need.

I didn't so much kneel as fall down his body. The hot water soaked through my shirt, my bra, my body, holding me in the heat of it, as I gazed up the length of Jean-Claude. He looked down at me, and still his eyes were human, normal, lovely to look at, but I wanted more.

I leaned my face in towards him, slowly, for a kiss on the mouth.

"*Ma petite*, there is nothing you can do until I have fed."

I laid a gentle kiss on his groin.

He closed his eyes, and his breath came out in a careful sigh. "I am not saying it is not pleasurable, but I will be of no use to you."

I took him in my mouth, and he was small and soft, so I didn't have to fight to get all of him inside. I loved the sensation of him when he was small, not just because I wasn't fighting the erection to breathe and swallow, but the difference in texture. There was nothing on a woman's body that had this feel to it. I rolled him

248

gently around in my mouth, and he shuddered. I sucked gently, pulling with my lips, rolling my eyes upward to watch him throw back his head, his hands convulse, grabbing at empty air.

I pulled back enough to whisper so that my breath caressed the wet skin of his groin, "Feed, so we can both feed."

He shook his head and looked down at me, and there was a look I hadn't seen much on his face. Stubbornness. "Pleasure I will take from you, *ma petite*, but not blood, not while the *ardeur* rides you. If you still wish to be embraced after the *ardeur* is fed, then I will gladly, joyfully, comply, but not like this."

I slid my hands up the smooth wetness of his hips. "I need to feed now, Jean-Claude, please, please."

"*Non*," and he shook his head at me, again.

The *ardeur* had been ready to be gentle, as gentle as I'd ever felt it, but being denied didn't make it, or me feel gentle. Angry, stubborn, cheated. I tried to think past it, and couldn't. I'd been good, so good for so long. I hadn't fed on Caleb, and no one would have screamed at me for it. I hadn't fed on Nathaniel, and he was my *pomme de sang*. I wanted him to go another day before he got munched on. I didn't like that he'd passed out at the club.

I hadn't bothered Jason, who had been too weak to argue. Once I felt Jean-Claude wake, I knew what I wanted. I hadn't even seen the other men I passed to get to this room. They hadn't existed for me. Now he was denying me, refusing me, rejecting me. Some small distant part of me knew that wasn't true, it wasn't even fair, but that was a distant voice. The voices in the front of my head were screaming, fuck him, feed on him, take him.

I'd fought until there wasn't enough of me left to fight. There was nothing but the need, and the need had no mercy.

I covered him with my mouth again, and I did something that I could only do when he was at his smallest. I drew his balls, gently, into my mouth, so that I held all of him inside my mouth. It was the most amazing sensation to be able to hold him, to flick my tongue on the loose skin between his testes, to roll the delicate eggs of his body against my teeth and cheeks. He filled my mouth this way, so wide, impossibly wide, but because there was no length to match it, I wasn't choking or fighting to breathe. It was as if I could have held him inside me like this for days. I sucked on him, the shaft, the balls, all at once, fitting my mouth around the base of him, so that my lips formed a seal against his body, and I sucked him, licked him, rolled him, explored him. I looked up and found his eyes had bled to blue at last, but I didn't care anymore. I closed my eyes, wrapped my hands around the smooth tightness of his buttocks, and gave myself over to the joy of it.

I heard his cries, felt his body shudder and quiver under my touch, but it was distant. His flesh filled my mouth, rolled so easily under my tongue. I'd always enjoyed the sensation of him when he was loose, but I'd never been able to indulge myself, because after a few touches, like all men, he didn't stay small.

I wrapped my mouth close and closer to the base of him and grazed my teeth ever so lightly there. There, the base of all of him, so that to bite too hard would take it all. I knew what an act of trust this was for him. I bit just hard enough to make him cry out, then pulled gently against his body, using mostly lips for pressure.

I let his balls slip out and sucked the rest of him back in my mouth hard and fast, pulling harder than I should have, sucking him as hard and fast as I wanted, no control now, no waiting, just the feel of him rolling in and out of my mouth, as I pulled on him.

He screamed my name, half pleasure, half pain, and the *ardeur* burst over both of us. The heat spread upward through me, and I felt it spread, thrust itself into Jean-Claude. So hot, so hot, so very hot, as if the water around us should boil. I had enough left of me somewhere in all that to let go of him with my mouth, so I didn't get too carried away. I convulsed against his legs, my nails digging into his butt, hips, thighs, as he rocked above me, and fought to keep his feet.

He finally half-sat, half-collapsed to the edge of the tub and sat there, propped on his arms, breathing too hard, and that he was breathing at all meant he'd fed his *ardeur*, as I'd fed off of him. Sometimes it was just an exchange of energy, sometimes it was a true feeding.

I climbed out of the tub enough to sit beside him, but didn't touch him. Sometimes right after the *ardeur* had been fed, touching of any kind could reignite it, especially between people who *both* held the *ardeur*. So it had been between Jean-Claude and Belle, so it was sometimes between us.

His eyes were still solid blue, like midnight skies when the stars have drowned. His voice was breathy, when he said, "You are getting better at feeding the *ardeur* without true orgasm, *ma petite*."

"I have a good teacher."

He smiled the smile a man gives a woman when they've just finished such things, and it isn't the first time they've done them, and it won't be the last. "An apt pupil, as they say."

I looked at him, and he was pale alabaster with that black, black hair, those blue eyes. The folds and hollows of his body exposed to the overhead lights were as beautiful and familiar to me as a favorite path that I could walk forever and never tire of.

I stared at Jean-Claude, and it wasn't the beauty of him that made me love him, it was just – him. It was a love made up of a thousand touches, a million conversations, a trillion shared looks. A love made up of danger shared, enemies conquered, a determination to keep the people that depended on us safe at almost any cost, and a certain knowledge that neither of us would change the other, even if we could. I loved Jean-Claude, all of him, because if I took away the Machiavellian plottings, the labyrinth of his mind, it would lessen him, make him someone else.

I sat on the edge of the tub with my jeans and jogging shoes soaking in the water, looking at him laugh, watching his eyes bleed back to human, and I wanted him, not for sex, though that was in there, but for everything.

"You look serious, *ma petite*, what are you thinking about so solemn-faced?"

"You," I said, voice soft.

"Why should that make you look so solemn?" The humor began to leak away from his face, and I knew without being a hundred percent sure that he was thinking I was about to run away again. He'd probably been worried about that from the moment I shared a bed with him and Asher. I usually ran after I'd made some big breakthrough. Or would that be breakdown?

"A surprisingly wise friend told me that I hold back some part of myself from all the men in my life. He said that I do it to keep myself safe, to keep myself from being consumed by love."

Jean-Claude's face had gone very careful, as if he were afraid for me to read his expression.

"I wanted to argue, but I couldn't. He was right."

Jean-Claude looked at me, face still empty, but there was a tightness around his eyes, a wariness that he couldn't quite hide. He was waiting for the blow to fall, I'd taught him to expect it.

I took a deep breath, let it out slowly, and finished, "What I hold back from you is sharing blood. We fed the *ardeur* off each other now, but I still won't let you take blood."

Jean-Claude opened his mouth as if to say something, then closed it. He'd sat up straighter, hands clasped in his lap. It wasn't just his face he was fighting to keep neutral, even his body language was so very careful.

"I asked you to feed off me a few minutes ago, and you said not while the *ardeur* was riding me. Not while I was intoxicated." I had to smile at the choice of words, because *intoxicated* was a good description of the *ardeur*. Metaphysical liquor.

"I've fed the *ardeur*, we both have. I'm not intoxicated any more."

He'd gone very still, that utter stillness that the old vampires could do. It was like if I looked away, he wouldn't be there when I looked back. "We have both fed the *ardeur*, that much is true."

"Then I'm still offering blood."

He took a deep breath. "I want this, *ma petite*, *you* know that."

"I know."

"But why now?"

"I told you, I had a talk with a friend."

"I cannot give you what Asher gave you, gave us, yesterday. With my marks upon you, I may not be able to roll your mind at all. It will be only pain."

"Then do it in the middle of pleasure. We've proven more than once that my pain/pleasure sensors get a little confused when I'm excited enough."

That made him smile. "As do mine."

That made *me* smile. "Let's fool around."

"And then?" he asked, voice low.

"When it's time, take blood, and then let's fuck."

He gave a surprised burst of laughter. "*Ma petite*, you are such a sweet-talker, how can I refuse?"

I leaned into him, pressed a gentle kiss upon his lips, and said,

"Her lips suck forth my soul: see, where it flies! Come, Helen, come, give me my soul again. Here will I dwell, for heaven is in these lips, and all is dross that is not Helena."

He gazed into my face with such longing. "I thought you said you could not remember more of the play."

"I remembered more," I whispered, "do you?"

He shook his head, and we were so close that his hair brushed against mine so that you couldn't tell where one blackness left and the other began. "Not with you this close to me, no."

"Good," I smiled, "but promise some night we'll get the whole play and take turns reading it to each other."

He smiled, and it was the smile I'd come to value more than any other, it was real and vulnerable, and I think one of the few things left of the man he might have been if Belle Morte had not found him. "I swear it, and gladly."

"Then help me peel off these wet jeans and leave the poetry for another night."

He cupped my face in his hands. "It is always poetry between us, *ma petite*."

My mouth was suddenly dry, and it was hard to swallow past my pulse. My voice came breathy, "Yeah, but sometimes it's dirty limericks."

He laughed as he kissed me, then he helped me out of the wet jeans, and the wet socks, and the wet shoes, and the wet everything. When my cross spilled out of my shirt, it didn't glow. It just lay there glinting in the overhead lights. Jean-Claude averted his eyes, as he always did when he saw a holy object, but that was the only hint I had that the cross bothered him. I realized with a start that I'd never worn a cross around Jean-Claude and had it glow at him. What did that mean?

I'm usually pretty straightforward except in emotional areas, but I was trying to be different, change that, so I asked, "Does it really hurt you to look at my cross?"

He looked determinedly at the edge of the bathtub. "No."

"Then why look away?"

"Because it will start to glow, and I do not want that."

"How do you know that it'll start to glow?"

"Because I am a vampire, and you are a true believer." He was

253

still staring at the water, the marble of the tub, anywhere and everywhere except at my chest with the cross still hanging around it.

"I've never had a cross glow when you were the only vampire around."

He glanced up at that, then quickly down. "That cannot be true."

I thought about it some more. "I can't ever remember it happening. You look away, then I take the cross off, and we go on about our business, but it doesn't glow."

He shifted in the water enough to send little splashes against my legs. "Does it matter?" His voice held just how unhappy he was with the line of conversation.

"I don't know," I said.

"If you do not wish me to feed, then I will go."

"It's not that, Jean-Claude, honest."

He put a hand on the edge of the tub and stepped out.

"Jean-Claude," I said.

"*Non, ma petite*, you do not want this, or you would not cling to your holy object." He took a vibrant blue towel that matched the sheets on the bed and began to dry off.

"My point is . . . oh, hell, I don't know what my point is, just don't go." I put my hands back to unfasten the clasp of the chain, and the door opened. Asher stepped inside, coated in dried blood, all of it mine. That should have bothered me, but it didn't. His hair still fell around his shoulders like spun gold, and with Asher, it wasn't a euphemism for blond. His hair was like gold spun to thick, soft waves. His eyes a blue so pale it was like winter skies, but warmer, more . . . alive. He walked towards us, his long body nude and perfect. The scars didn't make him less perfect, they were simply a part of Asher, and nothing marred the godlike grace as he moved into the room. He was so beautiful it stopped my breath in my throat, made my chest ache to see him. I wanted to say, *come to us*, but my voice was gone in the sheer wonder as he glided towards us on narrow bare feet.

The cross flared to life, not the white-hot glow it had had in the Jeep, but bright enough. Bright enough to leave me blinking. Bright enough to help me think. Asher was still beautiful, nothing could change that, but now I could breathe, move, talk. Though I had no idea what to say. I'd never had a cross glow around him either, until now.

It was Jean-Claude who said it, "What have you done, *mon ami*, what have you done?" He had his back to the glow of the cross and was using the towel to help shield his eyes.

Asher had thrown up an arm to protect his own pale blue gaze. "I tried to roll her mind just enough for pleasure, but the *ardeur* was too much."

"What have you done?" Jean-Claude asked again.

I watched them both in the light of the cross, one hiding behind the blue towel, the other his own arm, and I answered for him, "He rolled me. He rolled my mind, completely and utterly." Even as I said it, I knew he'd done more than that. I'd been rolled before. I'd even been rolled once upon a time by Jean-Claude when first we met. But vampire powers to cloud the mind are a dime a dozen, most of them can do it. Most of the young ones have to capture you with their gaze, but the old ones can simply think at you. I was immune to most of it, partly natural ability as a necromancer, and part Jean-Claude's marks. But I wasn't immune to Asher. The cross kept glowing, the vampires kept shielding their eyes, and even with them hiding away from the white light, I still wanted them, both of them, but now I had to wonder how much of it was me, and how much of it was Asher's mind tricks. Damn it.

## 32

WE ENDED UP in the bedroom but not for anything fun. I'd dried off
and thrown on extra clothes that I kept at the Circus. I had to put
the wet shoes back on though. My cross was safely underneath my
shirt again. Once it went under the shirt, it stopped glowing, but
there was still a pulsing warmth to it.

Jean-Claude had knotted the blue towel around his waist, where
it draped nearly to his ankles. He'd put a smaller towel on his hair
and the blue of the cloth brought out the blue of his eyes. Seeing
his face free of all hair made him look more like a boy to me. It
was the bones of his cheeks that saved his face from being utterly
feminine. He was still beautiful, but an inch closer to handsome
without that black veil of hair.

Asher was still clothed in nothing but the dried blood and the
spill of all his own hair. He was pacing the room like some kind of
caged beast.

Jean-Claude had simply sat down on the edge of the bed with
the blue sheets still stained with blood and other fluids. He looked
discouraged.

I stood as far from them as I could, arms clasped across my
stomach. I'd left my shoulder holster off, so that I wouldn't stroke
my gun while I argued. I was hoping to tone the hostility down, not
ramp it up.

Jean-Claude laid his face in his hands, all pale skin and blue
cloth, towels and sheets surrounding him. "Why did you do it,
*mon ami*? If you had only behaved yourself we would even now be
together as we were meant to be."

I wasn't sure I liked how sure Jean-Claude was of me, but I
couldn't really argue without lying, so I let it go. Shutting the fuck
up is seldom a bad move on my part.

Asher stopped pacing and said, "Anita has felt me feed. She

knew that I could roll her mind completely. She did not say not to do it. She said for me to take her, to feed from her, so I did. I did what she told me to do, and she was aware of how I would do it, because she has fed me once before."

Jean-Claude raised his face from his hands like a drowning man, coming up for air. "I know that Anita fed you when you lay dying in Tennessee."

"She saved me," Asher said. He'd come to the end of the big four-poster bed.

I watched the two of them framed against the blue sheets, where so recently we'd had a very good time. I stood there wanting them both, and my arms clung to me, as if by holding on tight I could keep it from happening.

"*Oui*, she saved you, but you did not roll her mind completely then, because I would have felt your touch upon her mind and heart, and it was not there."

"I tried to roll her mind because it seems to me that every vampire that takes blood from her is in some way under her sway, her power. It is almost as if when a vampire feeds from her, it is she who controls them, not the other way around."

I stayed where I was, but this I couldn't let go. "Trust me, Asher, it doesn't work that way. I've had vamps bite me and have me under their sway before."

He looked at me, with those pale, pale eyes. "But how long ago was that? I think that your powers have grown since then."

My gaze kept sliding down his body, tracing the blood pattern on that pale, slightly golden tinged skin. I closed my eyes to say the next because I needed to stop watching them. "Do you feel like you have to do what I say?"

He hesitated, and I fought the urge to look at him, to watch him think. "No." His voice was soft.

I took a deep breath, let it out slowly, opened my eyes, and fought like hell to stare at Asher's face and nothing else. "See, you're not in my power or anything."

He did a small frown. "Are you in my power then?"

"I can't stop watching the two of you. I can't stop thinking about what we did, what we could still do."

He gave a harsh laugh, and it hurt to hear it, as if it had struck a blow along my skin. "How can you not think about us, while we stand here in front of you like this?"

"Oh, you're not arrogant," I said, arms clinging to myself like it was the last safe place for them to be.

"Anita, I am thinking of you, too. The pale spill of your back, the curve of your hip, the mound of your ass, underneath me. The feel of me rubbing along the soft warmth of your skin."

"Stop," I said, and had to turn away because I was blushing and it was suddenly hard to breathe.

"Why stop? It's what we're all thinking."

"*Ma petite* does not like to be reminded of pleasure."

"*Mon Dieu*, why not?"

I looked in time to see Jean-Claude give that all-purpose Gallic shrug, which meant everything and nothing. Usually he made it look graceful, today it looked tired.

"Anita," Asher said.

I looked at him, and this time I could make eye contact, except that staring into those amazing eyes wasn't much safer than looking at his amazing body.

"You told me you wanted me inside you, as I remember. And when I bared your neck you said, 'Yes, Asher, yes.'"

"I remember what I said."

"Then how can you be angry at me for doing what you asked?" He took three strides closer to me, and I backed up. The movement stopped him. "How can you blame me for this?"

"I don't know, but I do. How that's unfair, or maybe not unfair, I don't know, but I do."

Jean-Claude spoke then, his voice like the sigh of the wind outside a lonely door. "If you had but restrained yourself, *mon ami*, we might even now be together in the bath."

"I don't know about that," I said. My voice sounded angry, and I was glad.

Jean-Claude gazed at me with those blue black eyes. "Are you saying that you could refuse such bounty, once having tasted it?"

I didn't blush this time, I paled. "Well, it's moot now isn't it, because he cheated." I pointed at Asher for dramatic emphasis.

He stared at me openmouthed. "How did I cheat?"

Jean-Claude was back to holding his head in his hands. "*Ma petite* does not allow vampire trickery to be played upon her." His voice came muffled but strangely clear.

Asher looked from one to the other of us. "Ever?"

Jean-Claude answered without moving, head still in his hands. "For the most, *oui*."

"Then she has never tasted you as you are meant to be tasted," Asher said, and his voice held a soft astonishment.

"That is her choice," Jean-Claude said. He raised his face up slowly, so I could meet that blue gaze, and there was something of anger in his eyes.

I didn't understand all of this conversation, and I wasn't sure I wanted to, so I ignored it. I've always been damn good at ignoring what makes me uncomfortable. "The point is that Asher used vampire wiles on me. He's done something to cloud the way I think about him. Now I won't know, won't ever know, if what I'm feeling is real, or a trick." There, I felt sure of moral high ground on this one, at least.

Jean-Claude did a sort of voilà gesture with his hands, as if to say, see, I told you.

Asher's face began to lose its anger and work towards that blankness they both did so well. "So it was just a lie."

I looked at both of them. "What was a lie?"

"That you wanted me to be with you and Jean-Claude."

I frowned. "No, it wasn't a lie. I meant it."

"Then this faux pas changes nothing," he said.

"You've messed with my mind, I don't think that's just a faux pas. I think that's damn serious." My hands were on my hips, better than clinging to myself to keep from touching anybody. I embraced my anger, because it made them less beautiful. Of course, it made everything less beautiful.

"So you did lie," Asher said, his face almost empty of any expression.

I hated watching him shut himself away like this, but I didn't know what to do to stop it. "Damn it, no, I didn't lie. You're the one who changed the rules, Asher, not me."

"I changed nothing. You said we would be together. You offered me your bed. You begged me to be inside you. Jean-Claude said that your sweet ass was not to be touched, and the deep pleasure of your body was full, where was I supposed to go?"

I fought not to blush and failed. "It was the *ardeur* talking, and you knew it."

He backed up until he came to the edge of the bed, and he half-collapsed on the blue sheets, grabbing the post to keep from sliding off the silk. His face was blank, but the rest of him acted as if I'd struck him, and I knew I'd said the wrong thing.

"I said that once the *ardeur* was cooled you would find a way to reject me, to reject this," and he gestured at Jean-Claude at the far end of the bed, and the bed itself, "and you have done just as I said you would do." He pushed himself up from the bed, clinging to the wooden post for a moment, as if he wasn't sure his legs would hold him. He took a tentative step away from the bed, almost staggered, then another, and another. Each step was steadier than the last. He was going for the door.

"Wait a minute, you're not just going to walk out," I said.

He stopped walking, but didn't turn around as he answered, giving a clear view of the perfection of the back of his body. "I cannot leave until Musette is gone. I will give her no excuse to take me back to the courts with her. If I belong to no one, she will do it, and I will have no grounds to refuse." He rubbed his hands over his arms as if he were cold. "When Musette is gone, I will petition for another Master of the City. There are those who would take me in."

I walked towards him. "No, no, you have to give me some time to think about what you did. It's not fair to walk off like this." I was almost to him when he whirled around, and the rage on his face stopped me like I'd hit a wall.

"Fair! What is fair in being offered everything you ever wanted and thought never to have again, only to have it torn from your grasp? Torn from your grasp because you did exactly what you were told you could do, what was asked of you." He didn't yell, but his anger filled his voice, so every word was like a red-hot poker flung at my face.

I didn't know what to say in the face of that anger.

"I will not, cannot, stay and watch you and Jean-Claude. I would rather be without the sight of either of you than so very

260

close, but cast from your bed, your arms, your affections." He covered his face with his hands and gave a low scream. "To be with us as our lover is to be seduced by our powers." He tore his hands away from his face and let me see his eyes drowning blue, his anger making up for the lack of blood. "I had never dreamed that Jean-Claude had not done so." He looked at the other man, still sitting on the edge of the bed. "How could you be with her for so long and resist the temptation?"

"She is most adamantly against such things," Jean-Claude said. "At least you have had her willing blood, I have never been so blessed."

Asher frowned, and it sat badly on that lovely face, like an angel frowning. "That astounds me still, though I knew that. But she has bestowed her charms upon you, and now I will never know them."

This was all happening way too fast for me. "Jean-Claude understands the rules, and we both live by them." Of course, I'd been just about ready to change the rules, but I didn't think Asher needed to know right now.

Asher shook his head, sending that foam of gold hair gliding over his shoulders. "Even if I understood the rules, Anita, I could not abide by them."

That made me frown. "What do you mean?"

"Anita, we aren't human, no matter how much some of us pretend. But not all of what we are is bad. You have entered our world, but you deny yourself the best of us, while only seeing the worst. But most horrible of all, you deny Jean-Claude the best of his own world."

"What's that supposed to mean?"

"He is celibate save for you, but he does not pleasure himself fully with you, or anyone else." He made a gesture that I didn't understand. "I see that look upon your face, Anita, that American look. Sex is not just intercourse, or even just orgasm, and that is especially true for us."

"Why, because you're French?"

He gave me such a serious look that my attempt at humor died in my chest like a cold weight. "We are vampires, Anita. More than that, we are Master Vampires of Belle Morte's line. We can give

261

you pleasure that no other can give, and we can take pleasure as no other can experience it. By agreeing to limit himself, Jean-Claude has denied himself a great deal of what makes this existence bearable, even enjoyable."

I looked at Jean-Claude. "How much have you been holding back?"

He wouldn't meet my gaze.

"How much, Jean-Claude?"

"I cannot make my bite true pleasure as Asher can. I cannot roll your mind completely as he can." He still wouldn't look at me.

"That's not what I asked."

He sighed. "There are things that I can do that you have not seen. I have tried to abide by your wishes in all things."

"Well, I will not," Asher said.

We both looked at him.

"Anita will always find some reason to keep her from openly taking both of us. She cannot even allow her one vampire lover to truly be vampire. How could she possibly endure the full touch of two of them?"

"Asher," I said, but didn't know what else to say, all I knew was that my chest hurt, and it was hard to breathe.

"No, you will always find something in your men that is not good enough, not pure enough. You come to us out of need, even out of love, but it is never enough. You will not allow us to be enough even for ourselves." He shook his head again, in a flurry of brightness that shattered the lights like golden mirrors. "My heart is too fragile to play these games, Anita. I love you, but I cannot live, let alone love, like this."

"I don't even get an hour to digest that you used vampire wiles on me."

He put a hand on either of my shoulders, and the weight of his hands made my skin run warm. "If it's not this, it will be something else. I have watched you with Richard, Jean-Claude, and now Micah. Micah wins his way through your maze by simply agreeing to everything you ask. Jean-Claude wins his place on the edges of your labyrinth by cutting himself off from unbelievable pleasure. Richard will not walk your maze, because he has his own, and only one person can be this confusing in a relationship at one time. Someone has to be willing to compromise, and neither you nor Richard will compromise enough."

He let me go, and the absence of his hands almost staggered me, as if he'd taken away a shelter, and I was lost in the storm.

He began to walk backwards towards the door. "I thought I would do anything to be with Jean-Claude and his new servant. I thought I would do anything to be back in the safety of the arms of two people who loved me. But I understand now that your love will always come with conditions and that no matter how good your intentions, something holds you back, Anita. Something will not allow you to give yourself completely to the moment, to that shining thing called love. You hold yourself back, and you hold back those who love you. I cannot live being offered your love one moment and denied it the next. I cannot live being punished for what I cannot change."

"It's not punishment," I said, and my voice sounded strange, strangled.

He gave a sad smile and flung his hair over the scarred side of his face, so he stared at me with nothing but that perfect profile showing. "To quote you, *ma cherie*, the hell it is not." He turned and strode for the door.

I called after him. "Asher, please . . ." But he didn't stop. The door closed behind him, and the room filled with a profound silence.

Jean-Claude spoke into that silence, and his soft voice made me jump. "Gather your things, Anita, and go."

I looked at him, then, and my pulse was in my throat, and I was afraid, really afraid. "Are you kicking me out?" My voice didn't even sound like me.

"*Non*, but at this moment I need to be alone."

"You haven't fed, yet."

"Are you saying you would willingly feed me, now?" He didn't look at me as he asked it. He was staring at the floor.

"Actually, I'm sort of not in the mood anymore," I said, and my voice was fighting to get back to normal. Jean-Claude wasn't kicking me out of his life, but I didn't like that he wouldn't look at me.

"I will feed, but it will be only for food, and you are not food. So, please, go."

"Jean-Claude . . ."

"Just go, Anita, go. I need you not to be here right now. I need to not have to look at you, right now." The first stirrings of anger had trickled into his voice, like a fuse freshly lit and running with fire, but not truly burning up, not yet.

"Would saying I'm sorry help?" My voice was small when I asked.

"That you understand that you have something to apologize for is a beginning, but it is not enough, not today." He looked at me then, and his eyes glistened in the lights, not with power, but with unshed tears. "Besides, it is not me that you owe the apology to. Now go, before I say something that we will both regret."

I opened my mouth, drew a breath to reply, but he held up a hand and said, simply, "No."

I gathered my gun and shoulder holster from the bathroom. The wet clothes I left on the floor of the bathroom. I didn't look back, and I didn't try to kiss him good-bye. I think if I'd tried to touch him, he'd have hurt me. I don't mean struck me, but there are a thousand ways to hurt someone you love that have nothing to do with physical violence. There were words trapped in his eyes, a world of pain shining there. I didn't want to hear those words. I didn't want to feel that pain. I didn't want to see it, or touch it, or have it rubbed in the wounds in my own heart right that moment. I believed I was right, and a girl's got to have some standards. I don't let the vamps fuck with my mind, they just get my body. It had seemed a good rule an hour ago.

I shut the door behind me, leaned into it, and fought to take a breath that didn't shake. My world had been more solid an hour ago.

# 33

I WAS STILL leaning against the door, shaking, when Nathaniel came up to me. I didn't see him at first, even though he was standing right in front of me. I was staring at the floor, and I saw his jogging shoes, his legs, his shorts, before I looked slowly up and found his face. It felt like it took a long time to look up his body, and find that familiar face with those lilac eyes.

"Anita . . ." his voice was soft.

I held out a hand, because if anyone was nice to me, I was going to fall apart. I couldn't afford that right now. If Asher was up, then probably so was Musette. Normally, the thought would have been enough to let me check on a nearby vampire. Today, it was empty. I was empty. I was what Marianne, my psychic teacher, called head blind. It happens sometimes if you've had a shock; physical, emotional, whatever. I wouldn't be worth shit for metaphysical stuff until this wore off – if it wore off. Right that second it felt like the world should open up at my feet and swallow me down the great black hole that was eating through my heart.

"What is it, Nathaniel?" My voice was a bare whisper. I cleared my throat, sharply, to repeat it, but he'd heard.

"The two men that were following us in the blue Jeep are outside watching the back parking lot. They've got a different car, but it's still them."

I nodded, and the black hole at my feet began to close. I still hurt, and I was still head blind, but for this it didn't matter. Guns don't care if you're psychically gifted. Guns don't care about anything. They don't bitch at you about the rules in your personal life, either. Of course, neither does a dog, but I don't have to use a pooper-scooper after I'm through shooting my gun. Sometimes a body bag is needed, but that's not usually my job.

I was feeling better. Steadier. This I could do. "Find Bobby Lee, I want the best people he's got for car work."

"Car work?" Nathaniel made it a question.

"We're going to box them in and find out why they're following us."

"What if they don't want to tell us?" he asked.

I looked at him as I slipped into the shoulder holster and unthreaded my belt, so I could rethread the holster. I didn't say anything as I readied the gun, got it exactly where I wanted it. I had to carry the butt of the gun a little lower than I might have wanted for speed, but hitting your breast with the edge of the gun slows your fast draw even more. So a little lower angle, to avoid the chest. Legends say that the Amazons chopped off a breast to make them better at archery. I don't believe that. I think it's just another example of men thinking a woman can't be a great warrior without cutting away her womanhood, symbolically, or otherwise. We can be great warriors; we've just got to pack the equipment a little differently.

Nathaniel was looking very solemn. "I didn't bring a gun."

"That's great, because you're not coming."

"Anita . . ."

"No, Nathaniel. I taught you about guns so you wouldn't hurt yourself, and so in an emergency you could defend yourself. This isn't an emergency. I want you to stay inside out of the line of fire."

Something flitted over his face, something that might have been stubbornness. It faded, but stubborn wasn't something that I'd ever seen on Nathaniel. I wanted him more independent, but not stubborn. He was about the only person in my life that did what I asked, when I asked. Right that second, I valued that.

I hugged him, and I think it caught us both by surprise. I whispered in his ear, against the sweet vanilla scent of his cheek, "Please, just do what I say."

He was quiet for a heartbeat, then his arms wrapped around me, and he whispered, "Yes."

I drew back from him, slowly, searching his face, wanting to ask him if he found my "rules" a burden, if I'd taken half the pleasure out of his life, too? I didn't ask, because I didn't really want to know. It wasn't that my courage failed me, it was more that my

266

cowardice overwhelmed me. I'd had about all the truth I could stand for one day.

I kissed him on the cheek and left to find Bobby Lee. Him, I trusted to be in the line of fire. But it was more than that; I wasn't sleeping with Bobby Lee. I didn't love him. Sometimes love makes you selfish. Sometimes it makes you stupid. Sometimes it reminds you why you love your gun.

# 34

I WAS LOOKING through a pair of binoculars at a car parked at the far corner of the Circus of the Damned employee parking lot. Nathaniel was right, it was the same two men, but now they were in a large gold Impala dating to the 1960s, or some such. It was big, old, but in good shape. It was also very different from the shiny new blue Jeep that they'd been in before. They'd switched so the blond was driving. With the binocs I could see that he looked youngish, under forty, over twenty-five. He was clean shaven, wearing a black mock turtleneck and silver frame glasses. His eyes were pale, gray, or grayish blue.

The dark-haired man had put a billed cap on and changed to a larger pair of sunglasses. His face was thin, clean shaven, with a good-sized mole at one corner of his mouth. What they used to call a beauty mark.

I watched them sitting there and wondered why they weren't at least reading a newspaper, or drinking coffee, something, anything.

They'd done everything they were supposed to do, according to Kasey Krime Stoppers 101. They'd changed vehicles. They'd made small changes to their appearances. All this might have worked, if they weren't sitting outside Circus of the Damned, doing nothing. No matter how cleverly you disguise yourself, very few people sit in a car in the middle of the morning and do nothing. Also the employee parking lot was almost empty before noon. Once darkness fell, they could probably have parked and not been noticed so quickly, but this time of morning there was no hiding.

Bobby Lee was explaining all the Kasey Krime Stoppers tips and more to me. "If they hadn't changed cars, and they hadn't done anything to change their appearance, it might mean they didn't care if you spotted them. Or even that they wanted you to

268

spot them. But they've changed enough I think they really are trying to follow you."

I handed him back the binoculars. "Why are they following me?"

"Usually, when people start following you around, you know why."

"I thought they might be Renfields working for Musette and company, but I don't think Renfields would have taken the trouble to change their appearance like this. Most Renfields aren't the brightest of people."

Bobby Lee grinned at me. "How can you be friends with so many bloodsuckers, and still be so damn disdainful of them?"

I shrugged, and my shrug wasn't graceful. It never had been. "Just lucky, I guess."

The smile stayed, but the eyes began to go serious. "What do you want to do about these two?"

For a second, I thought he meant Asher and Jean-Claude, then I realized he meant the two yahoos in the Impala. The fact that even for a second I thought he meant something else said just how bad my concentration was. Concentration like that will get you killed in a fire fight.

I took a deep breath, another, let them out slowly, trying to clear my head. I needed to be here, now, not worrying about my increasingly complex personal life. Here and now with men and women with guns, about to risk their lives because I asked them to do it. Maybe the two men in the car weren't dangerous at all, but we couldn't count on that. We had to treat them like they were. If we were wrong, no harm done. If we were right, well, we'd be as prepared as we could be.

I couldn't shake the feeling of impending disaster. I looked up at Bobby Lee's tall frame. "I don't want to get any of you guys killed."

"We'd kind of like to avoid that ourselves."

I shook my head. "No, that's not what I mean."

He looked at me, face suddenly very serious. "What's wrong, Anita?"

I sighed. "I think I'm losing my nerve for this shit. Not for my own safety, but for everyone else's. The last time the wererats

269

helped me I got one of you killed, and another one cut up pretty badly."

"I healed up pretty good." Claudia walked towards us all six feet six and serious muscle. Her long black hair was pulled back in a tight ponytail leaving her face clean and unadorned. I'd never seen her wear makeup, and maybe because I'd never seen her in any, she didn't need it.

She wore a navy blue sports bra and a pair of dark blue jeans. She usually wore sports bras, I think because she had trouble finding shirts that fit over the spectacular spread of her shoulders and chest. She was a serious weightlifter, but not to that point where you'd ever mistake her for masculine. No, Claudia was definitely all girl.

The last time I'd seen her she'd had her arm damn near shot off. There was a faint tracery of scars on her right shoulder, pale pink and white. Silver shot will scar even a shape-shifter. There'd even been a faint possibility that the silver could have lost her the use of her arm. But the right arm looked as whole and muscular as the left.

"You look great, how's the arm?" I asked, smiling. One of my favorite things about hanging with the monsters is the healing. Straight humans seemed to get killed on me a lot, monsters survived. Let's hear it for the monsters.

Claudia flexed the arm, and muscles rippled under her skin. It was downright impressive. I lift weights, but not like that. "Not all the way back to full strength. I still can't curl more than one hundred and forty pounds with it."

I could bench-press my own body weight, plus a few pounds, and until now I'd been pretty impressed with doing reps with forty pounds for curls. Suddenly I felt inadequate.

I wanted to ask her if she was okay with putting her life, and that impressive body, on the line for me again, but I didn't. Some questions you just don't ask. Not out loud.

I stood there pressed against the black-mirrored glass that, from the outside, looked like part of the wall. I'd always wondered how someone was usually there to meet me at the back door. Now I knew – they had a lookout. We could have watched the bad guys all day, and they'd never have seen us.

It was part of a narrow loft area up above the main part of the Circus of the Damned, but this one small nook was equipped with binocs, comfortable chairs, and a little table. The rest of the loft area was mostly cables, wires, stored equipment, like the backstage areas at a theater. Most of the ceiling of the Circus was open to girders and beams like the warehouse it originally was, but now that I knew the loft was here, I realized that there was a narrow band of enclosed space that went around the entire top of the building. I'd asked if there were other hidden lookouts, and gotten the answer *of course*. Ask an obvious question, and you get the obvious answer.

"Claudia's going to drive one of the cars for our little plan," Bobby Lee said.

"I thought the plan was for someone who looked harmless and normal to drive both cars."

Claudia gave me a flat unfriendly look.

"No offense, but you look anything but ordinary."

"She'll throw a shirt on over the muscles, take out the ponytail, and look like a girl," Bobby Lee said.

I looked at him and her. She was taller than he was, hell she was as broad through the shoulders as he was, and she had more bulk. "You know Bobby-boy if I had to choose between arm-wrestling you, or Claudia, I'd pick you."

He blinked at me, totally not getting it.

Claudia got it. "You're wasting your breath, Anita. No matter how much I work out, I'm still a girl to even the best of them."

Bobby Lee was looking from one to the other of us. "What are you two talking about?"

I tried being very clear, using small words. "Claudia is more muscled and taller than most of the other wererats you have here today. Why are you putting her out in the first car to look normal and harmless? She looks anything but harmless."

He blinked at me, frowning. "You won't see the muscles under the shirt."

"She's six-freaking-feet and six-fucking-inches tall, with a pair of shoulders as broad as yours. You're not going to hide that under a shirt."

"I'm aware of that, Anita."

"Then why put her out in front to look harmless?"

Bobby Lee tried to wrap his mind around it, but in the end he was a man that had spent most of his life being muscle – smart muscle, but still muscle. "She's the only girl we have here today, except you, and they'd recognize you."

"Are you really telling me that the bad guys would feel less threatened by Claudia than by a short, less-powerfully built man?"

That was clear enough that Bobby Lee finally got it. He opened his mouth, closed it, opened it again, smiled, and gave a small laugh. "I see your point, but truthfully, yeah, they'll be less intimidated. Men just don't see women as a threat, no matter how big they are, and all men are suspect no matter how small."

I shook my head. "Why, because we have breasts and you don't?"

"Give it up, Anita," Claudia said, "just give it up. They're men, they can't help it."

Since I wasn't a man, I took Bobby Lee's word that the bad guys would panic less if one of the people involved in our mock accident was a woman. I had to admit that even I was less physically afraid of another woman, but it seemed wrong somehow. Claudia threw a man's pale blue shirt over her jeans and buttoned it up, even the sleeves. She left enough buttons undone in front to flash some cleavage, then she took the tie out of her hair. She shook her hair out, and it fell around her face, over her shoulders, in a slick, brunette flood. The hair softened the strong lines of her face, and I suddenly had a glimpse of what she might look like if she put any effort into being a traditional girl. *Spectacular* was the word that came to mind.

Bobby Lee watched the hair cascade with nearly openmouthed attention. I think I could have shot him twice before he reacted. Shit. I'd thought better of him than that.

Claudia met my eyes and crooked one shapely eyebrow. It said it all. We had one of those moments of perfect understanding between girls, and I think that for her, like for me, there weren't that many of them. We both spent far too much time hanging out with the men. But no matter how many times you saved their lives, and they saved yours, no matter how much you could bench-press, no matter how tall, or strong, or competent – you were still a girl.

And the fact that you were a girl overshadowed everything else for most men. It wasn't good or bad, it just was. A woman will forget that a man is male, if they are good enough friends, but men rarely forget that a woman is feminine. Most of the time it bugged the crap out of me, but today we'd use it against the bad guys, because they'd see all that hair, those breasts, and they'd underestimate her, because she was a girl.

# 35

THEY'D ONLY BEEN following me for one day, as far as I knew, so why such determination to find out why? One: It's usually better to know than not to know when people are following you, and two: I was in a truly foul mood.

I had no idea what to do about Asher. I didn't want to lose him, and now I didn't trust the feeling. In fact I was pretty certain it was really vampire mind tricks. Maybe I'd never really loved him. Maybe that had always been a lie. The logical part of me knew I was kidding myself on that one, but the scared part was happy with the theory. The thing that bothered me the most was I was no longer certain which was the brave thing to do. Was it brave and right to dump Asher for his treachery? Or was he right, and he'd just done what I asked him to do? Was I wrong? And, if I was wrong about this, how many other things had I been wrong about, unfair about? I was losing my sense of rightness about so many things. Without my sense of holier-than-thou anger, I felt shaky and unreal. I didn't feel like me anymore.

What if I got Claudia killed, the way I'd gotten her friend Igor killed a few months back? Hell, what if I got Bobby Lee killed like his friend, Cris? I'd killed nearly fifty percent of any wererats that Rafael, their king, had loaned me. No one complained about it, but today, the thought of more losses seemed completely unacceptable.

If I wasn't willing to let people risk their lives, then this plan wouldn't work. We needed four vehicles to block four roads, and make sure there was no place for the bad guys to go. We'd cut off all escape routes and reason with them. That meant a minimum of four people in danger. More, since Bobby Lee wanted shooters hidden among the few cars in the parking lot. The shooters would move out of the Circus when the bad guys were busy driving around trying to figure a way out of the parking lot. Or, that was the plan.

It was a good plan, unless the bad guys pulled out guns and started shooting. Then we'd have to shoot back, and they might get killed, and I'd be no better off. I still wouldn't know shit, and I might have gotten some more of Rafael's people dead.

"You alright, Anita?" Bobby Lee asked.

I was rubbing fingertips against my temples and shaking my head. "No, I'm not. I'm really not okay with this."

"With what?"

"This, all of it." Even as I said it, I saw Claudia driving down the back road, and Fredo coming up the other road. I'd made sure I knew his name. You shouldn't ask people to die for you if you don't at least know their name. He was a few inches under six feet, a slender dark man, with large graceful hands, wearing more knives than anyone I'd met in a long time. Bobby Lee said that both Fredo and Claudia could make the accident look real, they were both drivers. He said *drivers* like it should have been in capital letters. I'd asked to be one of the drivers, and I'd been informed that I didn't know how to DRIVE, and I couldn't argue with that. But right that moment, waiting and watching other people take the risks for me was harder than risking myself.

I trusted Bobby Lee's judgment. I really did. What I didn't trust was the bad guys. They were bad guys, so you couldn't trust them to be anything but unpredictable and dangerous.

I watched the two cars get closer, and I almost yelled, *don't, don't do it!* But I wanted to know who was following me, and more than that, if I said stop, if my nerve failed here on something so mundane, what good would I be? The trouble was, my nerve had failed. I kept my mouth shut, but I felt like the only thing keeping my pulse in my mouth was the tight line of my lips.

I prayed, *Dear God, don't let anyone get hurt.* Then a thought occurred to me, seconds before the fender bender. If Bobby Lee and company could stage this, they could probably have followed the men, trailed them back to wherever. Following just hadn't occurred to me, only confrontation. Shit.

The cars collided; it did look real, accidental. Claudia got out, all tall and feminine even from a distance. Fredo got out, yelling, waving his arms around.

The bad guys started their car and went for the far entrance of the parking lot, farther down the street that had just been blocked off. They must have smelled a . . . rat.

The Impala stopped before they'd turned completely onto the road, which meant they'd spotted the third car tucked in beside the Circus, blocking the alley between the Circus and the building next door.

Bobby Lee led the way to the stairs, and we clattered down, trusting that the fourth vehicle, a truck, had blocked the far alley where the loading dock was located. We'd both sacrificed being one of the first shooters into the parking lot so we could watch the plan unfold.

By the time we hit the lot, gunmen had sprung up among the few parked cars, like mushrooms after a rainstorm. I felt almost silly drawing my gun and joining the half circle. Claudia, Fredo, and the two other drivers were the other half of the circle, coming in from the other side.

It wasn't a perfect circle, a perfect circle would have meant we were firing at each other, so the circle was sort of metaphoric, but the effect was perfect.

The Impala sat there in our circle of guns, engine on, and no weapons in sight, yet. The blond had his hands very firmly on the top of the steering wheel. It was the dark-haired one in his billed cap who had his hands out of sight.

There was a lot of shouting on our side, about hands up, and don't you fucking move. They hadn't moved, but the engine was still running, and the one guy's hands were still out of sight. I kept my gun pointed one-handed, but raised a hand. I don't know if anyone else saw it, or understood what I wanted, but Bobby Lee did. He held up his hand in almost the same gesture, and the yelling quieted. It was suddenly silent, except for the thrum of the car engine.

I spoke into that silence, making sure my voice carried, "Turn off the car."

The one in the billed cap said something that I couldn't hear through the windows. The blond very slowly lowered one hand, and the engine died. The ticking of the engine was very loud in the stillness.

Billed-cap man was obviously unhappy. Even with sunglasses

276

covering his face, it showed in the line of his mouth. His hands were still hidden. The blond had put his hand back on the steering wheel.

"Hands where we can see them," I said. "Now."

The blond's hands seemed to vibrate on the steering wheel, as if he would have put his hands where I could see them if they weren't already there. He said something to his companion, and bill-cap shook his head.

I lowered my gun, took a deep breath, held it, aimed, let the breath out slow and careful as I squeezed the trigger. The gunshot was loud in the stillness, and it took a moment for me to be able to hear the air hissing out of the tire. I aimed my gun back up at the blond's window.

His eyes flashed wide. He was speaking fast and frantically to his friend.

"Bobby Lee," I said, "have someone on that side of the car press the barrel of their gun against the passenger side window."

"You want them to shoot?"

"Not yet, and if they do have to shoot I don't want to chance hitting the blond with the same bullet." I looked up at him. "Aim accordingly."

It was Claudia who stepped forward and put her gun against the window, she angled it slightly down so she'd miss the man on the other side. Bullets have a nasty tendency to travel farther than you want them to.

She asked, without looking at me, never taking her eyes from the man she was aiming at, "Do I get to kill him?"

"We only need one of them to question," I said.

She smiled, a flash of white teeth, and it was fierce and frightening framed by all that dark hair, that lovely face. "Great."

"I won't ask again, put your hands where we can see them, or else," I said.

He didn't put his hands up. He was either stupid or . . . "Bobby Lee, does anyone have our backs?"

"You mean backup?" he asked.

"Yeah, he's awful stubborn, unless he thinks help is coming."

He said something quick and harsh, it sounded German, but it wasn't, and his Southern accent vanished when he said it. Some of

277

the wererats turned outward, watching the perimeter. We were in the open, no one was going to sneak up on us. The only real danger would have been if someone had a rifle and scope. There was really nothing we could do about snipers, and because there was nothing we could do about it, we had to let it go, pretend it couldn't happen, and take care of what was happening. But a spot from between my shoulder blades to the top of my head ran with goose-bumps, as if I could feel the scope on me. I was pretty sure it was imagination, but my imagination's always been a problem when I got overly excited. I tried to think of something else, like why the man wouldn't put his fucking hands up.

I aimed one-handed so I could free up my left hand. I held a finger up, one, then another finger, two.

The blond was speaking frantically. I could hear snatches of his voice, *do it, God, do it*.

I actually started to put up that third finger, when the bill-cap man put his hands up, slowly. Empty hands, but I was betting any amount of money that he had some nasty piece of hardware in his lap. Oh, yeah.

Claudia kept her gun against his window. I think because she hadn't been told to move away. Frankly, I liked her there, close enough to fire if he went for whatever was in his lap.

I made the universal sign for roll the window down, rolling my hand in the air. They were in an old enough car that they actually had to crank it down. The blond unwound the window, slowly, carefully, and kept his other hand glued to the steering wheel. He was a cautious man. I liked that.

He rolled the window down, put his hands back on the steering wheel, and said nothing. He didn't try to plead innocence, or con-fess guilt. He just sat there. Fine.

I was short enough that with a little stooping I could see into the other man's lap. It was empty, which meant whatever he'd been cradling was on the floorboard. He'd dropped it so we wouldn't see it. What the hell was it?

I raised my voice a little. "You in the cap, put your hands slowly on the dashboard, flat, and if they move from there, you will be shot. Is that clear?"

He wouldn't look at me.

"Is that clear?"

He began to move his hands towards the dashboard. "It's clear."

"Why were you following me?" I asked, mostly to the blond, because I was beginning to realize the other man wasn't going to volunteer much.

"I do not know what you are talking about." He had a faint German accent, and I had too many relatives with the same accent not to recognize it. Of course, they were all over sixty, and hadn't seen the old country for a few decades. I was betting Blondie was a more recent import.

"Where'd the pretty blue Jeep go?" I asked.

His face went very still.

"I told you," the bill-cap said.

"Yeah, we spotted you," I said. "It wasn't all that hard."

"You would not have seen us if you had not been swerving all over the road," Blondie said.

"Sorry about that, but we had some technical difficulties."

"Yeah, like one of you turned furry," the guy in the cap said. He definitely was middle American, middle of nowhere, no accent.

"So you wondered what was wrong, and got close enough to see," I said.

Neither of them said anything to that.

"You are both going to get, very slowly, out of this car. If either of you goes for a weapon, you may both die. I only need one of you for questioning, the other is just gravy. I'll do my best to see that one of you lives, but I won't break a sweat to save you both, because I don't need you both. Is that clear?"

The blond said, "Yes," the other one said, "Crystal fucking clear." Oh, yeah, he was American, only we have that poetic turn of phrase.

Then I heard the sirens. They were close, very close, like in front of the building close. I'd have liked to think they were just passing through, but when you're holding this many guns out in the open, you can't count on that.

"Never a cop when you need one," Bobby Lee said, "try to do anything illegal, and they're all over ya."

The billed-cap man said, "If you put all your guns away before the cops get in sight, we'll just pretend this didn't happen." He was

279

smiling as he leaned across, so I'd be sure and see the smug expression.

I smiled back, and his smile wilted because I looked too damned pleased. I wasn't smooth at digging my badge out of my pocket yet, not one-handed anyway, but I managed. I flashed the metallic star in its little case. "Federal marshal, asshole. Keep your hands where we can see them until the nice policemen arrive."

"What are you arresting us for?" the blond asked in his German accent. "We have done nothing."

"Oh, I don't know. We'll start with carrying concealed weapons without a permit, then suspicion of grand theft auto." I patted the side of the Impala. "This ain't your car, and whatever your friend over there dropped on the floorboard is going to be illegal. Just call it a hunch."

"Bobby Lee, we don't need this big a crowd."

He grasped my meaning and barked another order in that odd guttural almost-German.

The wererats melted away in that too-quick-to-follow-with-the-eye blur of speed I'd seen them use once or twice.

Claudia stayed at her post, and Bobby Lee refused to leave, but it was just the three of us when the first policeman saw us. Well, five if you count the bad guys.

Two uniformed officers came up the alley, walking, because the truck that was blocking the road hadn't moved, but the wererat that had been driving it was walking just ahead of them with his hands laced on the top of his head. With his hands up, it flashed that his shoulder holster was empty. They'd taken his gun.

I made sure my badge was held up as high as I could manage. I was yelling "federal marshal" as they came around the corner.

The cops used the few cars on that side of the lot for cover, and yelled, "Guns down!"

I yelled, "Federal Marshal Anita Blake, the rest of these people are federal deputies."

Bobby Lee whispered, "Deputies?"

I spoke out of the corner of my mouth, "Just agree with me."

"Yes, ma'am."

I stepped back from the car enough to flash my badge better and yell, "Federal Marshal Blake, glad to see you officers."

The officers stayed behind the engine blocks of the cars, but had stopped yelling at us. They were trying to figure out how much trouble they'd be in if we really were federal and they messed up what we were doing, but they weren't worrying about politics so hard as to risk getting themselves shot. I approved.

I lowered my voice and spoke to the men in the car, before I walked towards the policemen. "Carrying concealed without a permit, weapons on you that are illegal no matter what, a stolen car, and I'm betting when your prints hit the system it lights up like a Christmas tree." I was smiling and nodding at the two policemen hiding behind the cars. The badge had calmed them, but they still had their guns out, and I heard other sirens in the distance. They'd called for backup, I couldn't blame them. They had no way of knowing any of us qualified as a cop.

I glanced at the blond. "Besides, the police around here take a dim view of criminals following federal marshals around."

"We did not know you were police," the blond said.

"Your intel sucks," I said.

He nodded, his hands still on the steering wheel. "Yes."

I put my gun up and held my badge up very high, put both hands up to show I was currently unarmed, and walked carefully towards the two uniforms, and the others that were creeping, cautiously, guns drawn, out of the alley. There were days when I truly loved having a badge. This was sooo one of those days.

281

# 36

THREE HOURS LATER I was sitting in the outer office of the police station, sipping really bitter coffee, and waiting for someone to let me talk to my prisoners. I had a badge, and I had the right to deputize anyone I saw fit in an emergency. The police had taken Bobby Lee, Claudia, and the one driver in for questioning. They'd been sent home an hour ago. Bobby Lee had tried to insist he stay with me, but his lawyer had told him going home after only two hours was a gift and he should take it. He took it after I insisted. It helped that there had been an MP5 Heckler and Koch submachine gun on the floorboard, not to mention about half a dozen more smaller weapons, four knives, one of those collapsible clubs, an ASP. Oh, and that the car they were driving wasn't theirs.

The dark-haired guy who'd been so sullen turned out to be ex-army, so his prints came up. Strangely, he had no criminal record. I would have bet almost anything that he was a bad guy. But if he was a bad guy, he was good enough at it to have never been caught.

The blond didn't exist, his prints weren't in our system. Because of the German accent and my insistence, they'd forwarded both sets of prints to Interpol to see if our boys were wanted outside the country, but that would take time.

So I had been left to cool my heels in a very uncomfortable desk chair beside the desk of a detective that never seemed to be there. The nameplate read, "P. O'Brien," but as far as I'd seen in over three hours, he was a myth. There was no Detective O'Brien, they just sat people by his desk and assured them that he'd be coming to talk to them soon.

I wasn't under arrest, in fact, I wasn't in trouble at all. I was free to go, but I was not free to speak with the prisoners without someone present. Fine by me, I talked to them with the nice policemen present. None of us learned anything, but that they both knew that

282

they wanted their lawyers. Once they got read their rights that was all either of them would say.

There was enough to hold them for at least seventy-two hours, but after that we were up shit creek, unless their prints came back with an active criminal warrant.

I took another sip of the coffee, made a face, and set it carefully on the desk of the invisible detective. I thought I'd never meet coffee I couldn't drink. I was wrong. It tasted like old gym socks and was nearly as solid. I sat up straight and wondered about simply leaving. My badge kept me and the wererats out of jail, and made sure the two bad guys didn't get to go free, but that was about all. The local police weren't happy with anyone with "federal" as part of their title messing in local crime.

A woman came to stand in front of me. She was about five eight, wearing a black skirt that was longer than was stylish, but then, her comfortable black shoes weren't exactly cutting edge either. Her blouse was a dark gold that looked like silk but was probably something easier to clean. Her hair had been dark brunette, but was so streaked with gray and silver and white that it looked like she'd streaked it on purpose. Natural punk.

Deep smile lines showcased a truly nice smile. She held her hand out to me. I stood up to shake hands, and her handshake was firm, strong. I glanced at the black suit jacket on the back of Detective O'Brien's chair and knew who I was talking to even before she introduced herself.

"Sorry it's taken me so long to get back to you. We've had a busy day." She motioned me to sit back down.

I sat. "Understandable."

She smiled, but her eyes didn't match the smile now, as if she didn't believe me. "I'm going to be in charge of this case, so I just want to get a few things clear." She laid the folder she'd been carrying on her desk, opened it, and seemed to be reading some notes.

"Sure," I said.

"You don't know why these two men were following you, correct?"

"No, I don't."

She gave me a very direct look out of her dark gray eyes. "Yet,

283

you felt the matter was so urgent that you deputized," she checked her notes, "ten civilians to help you capture these two men."

I shrugged and gave her pleasant, empty eyes. "I don't like being followed by people I don't know."

"You told the officers on sight that you suspected the men of carrying illegal weapons. That was before anyone had searched them, or the car. How did you know they were carrying illegal weapons," there was the slightest hesitation before she said, "Marshal Blake?"

"Gut instinct, I guess."

Those warm gray eyes suddenly went as cold as a winter sky. "Cut the bullshit, and just tell me what you know."

I widened eyes at that. "I've told your fellow officers everything I know, Detective O'Brien, honest."

She gave me a look of such withering scorn that I should have wilted in my seat and confessed all. The trouble was, I had nothing to confess. I didn't know shit.

I tried for honesty. "Detective O'Brien, I swear to you that I just noticed that I had a tail today on the highway. Then I saw that the same two men were outside where I was in a different car. Until I saw them the second time, I was willing to believe I was being paranoid. But once I knew they were following me, I wanted them to stop doing that, and I wanted to know why they were following me in the first place." I shrugged. "That is the absolute truth. I wish I knew something to conceal from you, but I am as much in the dark on this one as you are."

She closed the file with a snap and hit it sharply on the desk as if to settle the papers inside it, but it looked like an automatic gesture, or an angry one. "Don't try batting those big brown eyes at me, Ms. Blake, I'm not buying."

Batting my big brown eyes? Me? "Are you accusing me of trying to use feminine wiles on you, Detective?"

That made her almost smile, but she fought off the urge. "Not exactly, but I've seen women like you before, so cute, so petite, you give that innocent face and the men just fall all over themselves to believe you."

I looked at her for a second, to see if she was kidding, but she seemed serious. "Whatever axe you're grinding, find someone else's forehead to sink it into. I have come in here and told nothing but the truth. I helped get two men off the streets that were carrying firepower with armor-piercing, cop-killing ammo. You don't seem very damned grateful."

She gave me very cold eyes. "You're free to leave anytime, Ms. Blake."

I stood, then smiled down at her, and knew my eyes were as cold and unfriendly as hers. "Thanks so much, Ms. O'Brien." I emphasized the *Ms*.

"That's Detective O'Brien," she said, as I'd almost been sure she would.

"Then it's *Marshal* Blake to you, Detective O'Brien."

"I earned the right to be called detective, Blake; I didn't get grandfathered in on some technicality. You may have a badge, but it doesn't make you a cop."

Jesus, she was jealous. I took a deep breath and let it out slowly. I would get nowhere rising to the bait and fighting with her. So I didn't. Bully for me.

"I may not be your kind of cop, but I am a duly appointed federal marshal."

"You can interfere on any case involving the preternatural. Well, this one doesn't involve the preternatural." She gazed up at me, face calm, but still showing signs of anger. "So have a nice day."

I blinked at her, and counted, slowly, to ten.

Another detective came striding up. He had short curly blond hair, freckles, and a big grin. If he'd been any newer to plain-clothes, he'd have squeaked when he walked. "James said we caught some sort of international super spy, is that true?"

A look passed over O'Brien's face, a look of near pain. You could almost hear her thinking, *shit*.

I grinned at the other detective. "Interpol came back with a hit, huh?"

He nodded eagerly. "The German guy is wanted all over the place, industrial espionage, suspected terrorism . . ."

O'Brien cut him off, "Go away, Detective Webster, go the fuck away from me."

His smile faltered. "Did I say something wrong? I mean the marshal here brought them in, I thought she . . ."

"Get away from me, now," O'Brien said, and the growl of warning in her voice would have done a werewolf proud.

Detective Webster walked away, without saying another word. He looked worried, and he should have. I was betting O'Brien carried grudges to the grave, and made sure everyone paid up.

She looked at me, and the anger in her eyes wasn't just for me. Maybe it was for the years of being the only woman on a detail, maybe the job had made her bitter, or maybe she'd always been a grumpy-grumpy girl. I didn't know, and I didn't really care.

"Catching an international terrorist in these days and times could make a person's career," I said, sort of conversationally, not really looking at her.

The look of hatred in her eyes made me want to flinch. "You know it will."

I shook my head. "O'Brien, I don't have a career in the police department. I don't even have a career with the Feds. I am a vampire executioner, and I help out on cases where the monsters are involved. Me having a badge is so new and so unprecedented that they're still arguing on whether we'll have rank as federal marshals, or be able to move up in rank at all. I'm not a threat to your promotion. Me taking credit won't help my career a damn bit. So help yourself."

Her eyes toned down from hatred to distrust. "What's in it for you?"

I shook my head. "Don't you get it yet, O'Brien? What did Webster say, international spy, industrial espionage, suspected terrorism, and that's just the top of the list."

"What of it?" she said, hands clasped over the file folder on her desk like she was shielding it from me, as if I'd snatch it and run with it.

"He was following me, O'Brien, why? I've never been out of the country. What does an international bad ass like this want with me?"

She gave a small frown. "You really don't know why they were following you, do you?"

I shook my head. "No, and would you want someone like that following you around?"

"No," she said, and her voice had softened, was uncertain. "No,

I wouldn't." She looked up at me, eyes hard, but not as hard as they had been. She didn't apologize, but she did hand me the file folder. "If you really don't know why they're after you, then you need to know just how bad a man you've dug up . . . Marshal Blake."

I smiled. "Thank you, Detective O'Brien."

She didn't smile back, but she did send Detective Webster for fresh coffee for both of us. She also told him to make a fresh pot, before he poured our cups. I was liking Detective O'Brien more and more.

# 37

HIS NAME WAS Leopold Walther Heinrick. He was a German national. He was suspected of almost every large crime you could think of. And by large I mean not petty. He wasn't a purse-snatcher, or a con artist. He was suspected of working for terrorist groups worldwide, mostly those with a decided Aryan bias. It wasn't that he'd never taken money from people that weren't out to make the world safe for bigots, but he seemed to prefer to work with them. He'd been linked to espionage that specialized in help-ing paler people either stay in power or get power over people that were less pale.

The file contained a list of known associates, with pictures of some of them. A few of the pictures were the equivalent of mug shots, but most were grainy faxes of surveillance photos. Faces in profile, faces caught dashing to cars, into and out of buildings in distant countries. It was almost as if the men knew they were being photographed, or feared they would be. There were two faces that I kept coming back to – two men – one in profile wearing a hat, and the other a blur of face staring out at the camera.

O'Brien came over to stand beside me, looking down at the two pictures that I'd laid side by side on the edge of her desk. "Do you recognize them?"

"I'm not sure." I touched the edge of the pictures, as if that would make them more real, make them give up their secrets.

"You keep coming back to them," she said.

"I know, but it's not like I know them–know them. More like I've seen them somewhere. Somewhere recent. I can't place them, but I know I've seen them, or two people very similar." I peered down at the grainy images, gray and white and black, made up of little dots, as if the fax was a copy of a copy of a copy. Who knew where the original had come from?

288

O'Brien seemed to pick up what I was thinking, because she said, "You're working from faxes of bad surveillance photos. You'd be lucky to recognize your own mother in these."

I nodded, then picked up the one with the big dark-haired man in it. He was about to get into a car. There was a generic older building behind him, but I wasn't a student of architecture, it told me nothing. The man was looking down as if watching his step off a curb, so I didn't have a full front view even. "Maybe if I could see a front shot. Or did they send us all they had?"

"They sent me all they had, or that's what they said." The look on her face said she wasn't sure she believed that, but she had to act as if she did. "They're pretty worried that more of Heinrick's friends might be in the States. We're going to be giving a stack of these photos to the patrol cops, with orders to follow and report, but not to apprehend."

"You think they're that dangerous?" I asked.

She gave me a look. "You've read Heinrick's résumé, what do you think?"

I shrugged. "Yeah, he sounds dangerous." I went over the list of known associates again. "None of these rings a bell." I closed the folder and laid it behind the two pictures. I picked up the second photo this time, the one of the pale-haired man. His hair looked white in the photo. White or a very, very pale blond. There wasn't much background to help me judge his size. It was a full-face shot, up close, only his upper body showing. He was leaning over a table, talking. This was a better photo, more detailed, but I still couldn't place him.

"Was this taken with one of those concealed spy cameras?"

"Why do you ask?"

I moved the photo so she could look straight down on it. "It's an odd angle for one thing, up, like the camera is low, about hip level. You don't usually take photos from the hip. Second, he's talking but not looking at the camera, and it's too natural. I'd bet good money he doesn't know he's being photographed."

"You could be right." She took the photo from me and looked at it, turning it a little to get a better angle on it. "Why does it matter how the photo was taken?" Her eyes had gone nice and cold, good cop eyes, suspicious, wanting to know what I knew.

"Look, I've watched you guys try to question Heinrick and his friend. They sound like a fucking broken record. You can hold them for seventy-two hours, but they can spend every hour of that time saying nothing."

"Yeah," she said.

"We could go fishing. Tell Heinrick that his friends really need to watch themselves better. You can't tell where these photos were taken. The blond is just in a room."

O'Brien shook her head. "No, we don't know enough to go fishing, not yet."

"If I remember where I've seen these guys, we might," I said.

She looked at me, as if I'd finally done something interesting. "We might," her voice was cautious.

"Even if I don't remember where I saw them, if it gets close to the seventy-two hours, can we try bluffing?"

"Why?" she asked.

I crossed my arms over my ribs, and fought the urge to hug myself. "Because I want to know why this bugger is following me. Frankly, if he wasn't following me specifically I'd be more worried about St. Louis in general."

She frowned. "Why?"

"If Heinrick and crew were in town in general, then I'd say we have terrorism to worry about. Probably something with a racial bent." I touched the folder without opening it. "Though he's worked a few times for people of color, as the saying goes. Wonder how he justified that to his white supremacist friends?"

"Maybe he's just a mercenary," O'Brien said. "Maybe the fact that he's worked for the white supremacist is coincidental. They were the people who had the money at the time he needed it."

I looked up at her. "You believe that?"

"No," she said, and smiled. "You think more like a cop than I thought you would, Blake, I'll give you that."

"Thanks." I took it as high praise, which it was.

"No, if it walks like a duck, and quacks like a duck, it's a duck, and his dossier reads like he's a white supremacist that isn't above taking money from the very people he wants to destroy. He's a racist, not a zealot."

I nodded. "I think you're right."

She looked down at me for a second or two, then nodded, as if she'd made up her mind. "If the seventy-two hours gets close, you can come and we'll play go fish, but I think we're going to need better bait than a couple of grainy photos."

I nodded. "I agree. I'll do my best to come up with more before we have to beard the lion in its den."

"Beard the lion in its den?" she shook her head. "What have you been reading?"

I shook my head. "I have friends that read to me, if there aren't pictures, I'm pretty much lost."

She gave me another of those looks, half disgust, half trying not to smile. "I doubt that, Blake, I doubt that very much."

Actually, Micah, Nathaniel, and I were taking turns reading aloud to each other at night. Micah had been shocked that neither Nathaniel nor I had ever read the original *Peter Pan*, so we'd started with that. I'd then discovered that Micah had never read *Charlotte's Web*. Nathaniel had read the book to himself as a child, but no one had ever read it to him. In fact, he didn't ever remember being read to as a child. That was all he said, just that he'd never had anyone ever read aloud to him when he was small, but that one bit of knowledge seemed to speak volumes. So we were taking turns reading aloud to each other, a bedtime ritual that was more homey, and strangely more intimate than sex, or feeding the *ardeur*. You didn't read your favorite childhood stories aloud to people you fucked, you read them to people you loved. There was that word again, *love*. I was beginning to think I didn't know what it meant.

"Blake, Blake, you in there?"

I blinked up at O'Brien and realized she'd been talking to me, and I hadn't heard her. "Sorry, really, I guess I'm thinking too hard."

"Whatever you were thinking about didn't look too happy."

What was I supposed to say, some of it was, some of it wasn't, like most of my personal life? What I said out loud was, "Sorry, it's unnerved me a little to have someone like Heinrick after my ass."

"You didn't look scared, Blake, you looked like you were thinking too damned hard."

"I've had hit men after me before, but not terrorists who specialize in politics. There is nothing political about what I do."

The moment I heard it leave my mouth, I realized I was wrong. There were two types of politics that I was deeply involved in, furry, and vampire. Shit, had Belle hired him? No, it didn't feel right. I'd touched her mind too intimately; she still thought she could own me. She wouldn't destroy what she believed she could control, or use.

Richard was still digging out of the political mess he'd made of his pack when he tried to make them a true democracy. You know – one vote per person. It so hadn't worked, because he'd forgotten to keep that presidential veto power. He was Ulfric, wolf king, but he'd gutted the office of Ulfric and still hadn't built back up the respect and power base he needed. I was helping him rebuild, but some of the pack saw my involvement as another sign of weakness. Hell, so did Richard.

But to my knowledge no one was trying to move in on Richard's pack. Neighboring packs were giving us a wide berth until the dust settled. There wasn't anyone worthy of challenging him for pack leader except Sylvie, and she had held off, because she liked Richard, and didn't want to have to kill him. If Richard hadn't been afraid of what Sylvie would do as Ulfric he might have just stepped down for her, but he knew, and Sylvie had admitted, that her first order of business would be to kill anyone she suspected of disloyalty. That could be a dozen, or two. Richard wasn't willing for that to happen. But Sylvie would have come directly to my face if she had a problem. So . . .

I looked up at O'Brien. She was watching me, trying to read me. I had no idea what she'd seen as the different thoughts played over my face. I was definitely not on top of my game today.

"Talk to me, Blake," she said.

I decided for half-truth, better than nothing. "I was thinking that there's one type of politics I do participate in."

"And that is?"

"Vampires. I've got close ties to the Master of the City of St. Louis. I don't think Heinrick would knowingly work for a vampire, but he might not know. Most people like this work through intermediaries, so no one ever sees faces."

"Why would some vampire want to kill you just because you're dating the Master of the City?"

292

I shrugged. "The last time someone tried to kill me, it was for pretty much that reason. They thought it would weaken . . . the Master, make his concentration bad."

She leaned on the edge of her desk, arms crossed on her stomach. "You really think that's it?"

I frowned and shook my head. "I don't know. I don't think so, but it's the only politics I could think of."

"I'll put a note in the file, pass it up the line," she said. "We could offer you some police protection."

"You got the extra budget for that?"

She smiled, but not like she was happy. "Heinrick has terrorist in his dossier. Trust me, right now, with the T-word in the picture, I could swing the man power."

"Wouldn't that be person power?" I said, straight faced, looking her dead in the eye.

She snorted. "Oh, please, I'm not that P.C., and I don't think you are either."

"Sorry, couldn't resist."

"Besides you've worked with the police long enough to know that it usually is man power."

"Too true," I said.

"How about the police escort, or some surveillance?"

"Let me think about it," I said.

She pushed away from her desk. She didn't exactly tower over me, but she was tall. "Why won't you let us help protect you, Ms. Blake?"

"Could I have a copy of the report?"

She smiled, but it wasn't a pleasant smile. "Apply through channels, I'm sure you'll have one in a day or two."

"Can't I just use the Xerox machine?"

"No," she said.

"Why not?"

"Because you wouldn't take police protection, which means you are hiding something."

"Maybe, but if you give me copies of the photos I might be able to I.D. them."

"How?"

I shrugged. "I've got a few connections."

293

"You think your connections give better intelligence than the government?"

"Let's just say that I know the motives and priorities of my connections. I can't say the same for every branch of my government."

We looked at each other for a few heartbeats. "I won't try and debate this with you."

"Good, now can I have a copy of at least the photos?"

"No." And it had that ring to it of finality.

"You're being childish," I said.

She smiled, but it was more a baring of teeth, a friendly snarl. "And you're hiding something. If it comes back and bites this investigation on the ass, I'll have your badge for it."

I thought about saying *try and see how far you get*, but I didn't. I was new enough to the badge that I wasn't really sure what I could lose it over, and what I couldn't. I probably should look into those kinds of details.

"I don't know enough about why Heinrick was trailing me to hide anything, O'Brien."

"So you say."

I sighed and stood up. "Fine."

"Have a nice day, Blake. Go talk to your connections and see where it gets you. I'll stick with the government and Interpol." She gave an exaggerated shrug. "Call me old-fashioned."

"Suit yourself," I said.

"Just go," she said.

I went.

# 38

I OPENED THE Jeep and heard my cell phone ringing. I kept leaving it in the car, forgetting I had it. I slid onto the warm leather of the seats, fumbling for the phone from under the seat, even as I closed the door behind me. Yeah, it would have been cooler with the door open, but I didn't want my legs hanging out the open door while I lay across the seat. Not because bad guys were after me, just normal girl paranoia.

I finally dug the phone out on the fourth and last ring before it went over to message mode. "Yeah, it's me, what?" I sounded rude and out of breath, but at least I picked up.

"*Ma petite*?" Jean-Claude made the word almost a question as if he wasn't a hundred percent sure he'd gotten me.

With the gearshift digging into my side, and the overheated leather against my arm, I still felt better. Better to hear his voice, better to know he'd called me first. He couldn't be all that mad at me if he called first.

"It's me, Jean-Claude, I forgot the phone in the Jeep again, sorry." I wanted to say other things, but I couldn't figure out how to get the right words out of my mouth. Part of the problem was I wasn't sure what the right words were.

"The police have taken Jason," he said.

"What did you say?"

"The police have come and taken Jason away." His voice was matter of fact, empty even. Which usually meant he was hiding a lot of emotions, none of which he wanted to share.

I moved over an inch so the gearshift wasn't stabbing me, and lay on the seats for a moment. The first hint of panic was fluttering around in my gut. "Why did they take him?" My voice sounded almost as normal and matter of fact as Jean-Claude's.

295

"For questioning about a murder." His empty, cultured voice said it, as if the M-word hadn't been there.

"What murder?" I asked, and my voice was getting emptier.

"Sergeant Zerbrowski said you'd figure it out. That bringing Jason to a crime scene was a bad idea. I was not aware you took anyone on your crime scene visits."

"You make it sound like I'm visiting friends."

"I meant no insult, but why was Jason with you?"

"I wasn't feeling well enough to drive, and the police didn't want to wait for me to feel better."

"Why were you unwell enough not to drive?"

"Well, it seemed to be because Asher took a hell of a lot of blood. And I was having a bad reaction to having my mind rolled. It left me feeling a bit sick."

"How sick?" he asked, and there was a note of something in his empty voice now, something I couldn't quite place.

"I fainted a couple of times, and threw up, okay? Now let's concentrate on the current crisis. Did they actually arrest Jason?"

"I could not get a good sense of that, but I think not. They did take him away in restraints, though."

"That's standard with any known, or suspected, lycanthropes," I said. I pushed myself up, so I could sit on the seat instead of lying across it. The front of a Jeep just wasn't made for lying across. "You do know that if they didn't arrest him then he's free to walk out of questioning at any time?"

"It is a pretty theory, *ma petite*," now he sounded tired.

"It's the law," I said.

"Perhaps for humans," he said, voice mild.

I couldn't keep the indignation out of my voice. "The law applies to everyone, Jean-Claude, that's the way the system works."

He gave a soft laugh, and for once it was just a laugh with nothing otherworldly about it. "You are not usually so naive, *ma petite*."

"If the law doesn't apply evenly to everybody, then it doesn't work at all."

"I will not argue this with you, *ma petite*."

"If Zerbrowski picked him up, I know where they took Jason. I'm not that far from RPIT headquarters."

"What are you going to do?" he asked, voice still holding the soft edge of his laughter.

"Get Jason out," I said, buckling on my seat belt, and trying to pin the phone against my shoulder enough to start the Jeep.

"Do you think that is possible?" he asked.

"Sure," I said, and nearly dropped the phone, but I got the Jeep started. I seemed to be having a little trouble coordinating everything today.

"You sound so confident, *ma petite*."

"I am confident." I was, the fluttering feeling in my stomach wasn't. "I've got to go."

"Good fortune, *ma petite*, I hope you rescue our wolf."

"I'll do my best."

"Of that, there is little doubt. *Je t'aime, ma petite*."

"I love you, too." We hung up, at least we'd ended with I love you. It was better than screaming at each other. I dropped the phone on the seat beside me and put the Jeep in gear.

One emergency at a time. Save Jason, contact some people I knew to see if they knew anything about Heinrick, then prepare for the big banquet with Musette and company. Oh, and figure out how to keep the mess with Asher from driving a permanent wedge between Jean-Claude and me. Just another day in my life. This was one of those days when I thought that maybe a new life, a different life, wouldn't be so bad. But where the hell had I put the receipt, and could you return something that was over twenty years old? Where do you go to get a new life when your old one has you so puzzled you don't know how to fix it? Wish I knew.

## 39

No ONE STOPPED me at the door. No one stopped me at the stairs. In fact, people kept saying, "Hi, Anita, how you doing?" I wasn't an official member of the Regional Preternatural Investigation Team, but I'd worked with them all for so long that I was like the office furniture, something that was there, accepted, even expected.

It was Detective Jessica Arnet that finally said something to me that wasn't just, hi. "Where's that cutie you always have in tow?"

"Which one?" I asked.

She laughed at that, and blushed a little. It was the blush that got my attention. She always flirted with Nathaniel, but I'd never thought much about it, until I saw her blush.

"You do seem to have more than your share of cuties, but I meant the one with violet eyes."

I'd have bet money that she knew exactly what Nathaniel's name was. "He stayed home today," I said.

She laid the stack of folders down on a desk, not her own, and pushed back her hair from her face. There wasn't enough of her dark hair to push back. It looked like an old gesture from when she'd had longer hair. The short, barely below-ear-level cut really didn't flatter her face. But the face was still good, triangular, with delicate bones that framed her smile nicely. I'd never really noticed, but she was pretty.

Did Nathaniel ever want to date, just date? Not the dominance and submission stuff, but like dinner and a movie. Someday I'd have the *ardeur* under control and wouldn't need a *pomme de sang*, right? That had been the plan. So Nathaniel should like – date. Shouldn't he? If I wasn't going to keep him, he should date.

I had a headache starting right between my eyes.

Detective Arnet almost touched my arm, but stopped in mid-gesture. "Are you alright?"

298

I forced a smile. "Looking for Zerbrowski."

She told me what room he was in, because she didn't know she wasn't supposed to. Hell, I wasn't even sure she wasn't supposed to. Technically, this was part of the investigation that Dolph had wanted my input on, so I had a right to be there when they questioned suspects. In my head it all sounded logical, but a little desperate, as if I were trying way too hard to convince myself.

I went up on tiptoe outside the door, so I could look in the little window. Television will make you think that all police interrogation rooms have huge one-way mirrors that take up almost an entire wall. Very few departments have either the budget or the space for that kind of thing. Television uses it because it's more dramatic and makes camera work easier. It seemed to me that real life is dramatic enough without big windows, and there are no good camera angles, only pain. Or maybe I was just in a rotten mood.

I wanted a quick peek into the room to make a hundred percent sure I had the right place. Jason was at the little table, Zerbrowski was sitting across from him, but what got me flat-footed, was that Dolph was leaning against the far wall. Zerbrowski had said he was on leave for a couple of weeks. Had Zerbrowski lied to me? That didn't feel right. But what was Dolph doing here?

I gave one sharp knock on the door. I waited, steeling myself to be calm, or at least to look calm. Zerbrowski opened the door a crack. His eyes looked surprised behind his glasses.

"This isn't a good time," he said. He tried to tell me with his eyes that Dolph was in the room.

"I know Dolph's here, Zerbrowski. I thought he was supposed to be on leave for a few weeks."

Zerbrowski sighed, but his eyes were angry. Angry at me, I think, for not slinking off and making things worse. Making things worse was one of my specialties; Zerbrowski should have known that by now.

"Lieutenant Storr is here because he is still head of the Regional Preternatural Investigation Team, and he brought this suspect to our attention."

"Suspect? Why is Jason a suspect?"

"You don't want to do this in the hallway, Anita."

"No, I don't, I want to come in the room, so we can all talk like

299

civilized human beings. You're the one keeping me out in the hall-way."

He licked his lips, and almost turned and looked at Dolph, but fought the urge. "Come in," he lowered his voice to a whisper, "but stay on this side of the room."

I followed Zerbrowski inside and went where he motioned so that I ended up with the table between me and Dolph. It was almost as if Zerbrowski didn't trust what Dolph would do.

"You are not letting her sit in," Dolph said.

Zerbrowski squared his shoulders and faced Dolph. "We asked her to help us on this crime scene, Dolph."

"I didn't," he said.

"Actually, yeah, you did," I said.

Dolph opened his mouth, then closed it in a tight thin line. He hugged his arms so tight, it looked like it hurt, as if he didn't trust what his hands would do if they weren't wrapped around some-thing. There was a look of such rage in his eyes. He usually had some of the best cop eyes I'd ever seen, empty, gave nothing away. Today his eyes gave everything away, but I didn't understand where the anger was coming from.

Jason was sitting at the end of the table, trying to seem as small and inoffensive as possible. Since he's not much taller than I am, he was doing a good job of it.

Zerbrowski shut the door and sat on the side of the table close to Dolph, leaving me the chair farther away.

I didn't sit. "Why did you pull Jason in?"

"He has defensive wounds on his body consistent with the crime."

"You don't actually believe that Jason was involved in that," I searched for a word, "*slaughter*, do you?"

"He's a werewolf and he's got defensive wounds," Dolph said, "if he didn't rape our vic, then he raped somebody."

"You're here to observe, Lieutenant," Zerbrowski said, but his face said plainly that he would have rather been anywhere than sit-ting here, telling Dolph to mind his own business.

Dolph started to say something, then stopped himself by force of will alone. "Fine, fine, Sergeant, carry on." Those last two words held more heat than a forest fire.

"Wait," I said, "did you say rape?"

"We found semen at the first murder site," Zerbrowski said.

"The crucifixion?" I asked.

"No," Dolph said harshly, "the woman who was ripped apart."

"Semen doesn't mean rape at a scene like that, just that he enjoyed himself. It's sick, but it doesn't necessarily mean true sexual contact. I saw the body, there wasn't enough left of her to know whether he touched her like that, or not." I had a thought, an awful thought. "Please tell me you don't mean the head."

Zerbrowski shook his head, "No. Scattered over the scene."

It was almost a relief. Almost. "So why did Dolph say rape?"

"There was a little more left of the second female vic," Zerbrowski said.

I looked at him. "I don't remember being notified about a second attack."

"You didn't need to know," Dolph said. "You were right, I called you in on the first one, but I didn't make the same mistake twice."

I ignored Dolph as best I could and looked at Zerbrowski. He mouthed, "Later."

Fine, Zerbrowski would fill me in when we had some non-Dolph time. Fine, great. I couldn't do anything about the psycho shape-shifter we had running around town, not right that second, but I might be able to do something about the current disaster.

"What did Jason say when you asked where he got scratched up?"

"Said a man doesn't kiss and tell," Zerbrowski said, "even I thought that one was lame."

I looked at Jason. He shrugged, as if to say, what was I supposed to say. He knew me well enough to know I wouldn't want him talking out of school. He was right on that. I so didn't want Zerbrowski and Dolph to know. Hell, I didn't want anyone to know. But my embarrassment wasn't worth Jason getting locked up.

I sighed, and spoke the truth. "The scratches aren't defensive wounds."

"He's cut up, Anita, and we got the Polaroids to prove it," Zerbrowski said. "Dolph noticed some scratches at the first scene. They're gone, but now he's got fresh wounds."

"I cut him up." My voice sounded bland, because I was fighting to sound bland.

Dolph gave a sound that was more snort than laugh. No words were needed to say he didn't believe me.

Zerbrowski said his out loud, "Shop it somewhere else, Anita, we're not buying."

I raised the sleeves on my shirt and showed my own healing scratches. "When I was afraid I'd hurt him more, I scratched myself."

Zerbrowski's eyes went wide. "Jesus, Blake, you always this rough?"

"You'll never find out, Zerbrowski."

"If that was a yes, then I'm okay with that." He almost touched some of the deeper scratches on my arm, then stopped and almost touched the scratches on Jason's arms. "I hope the sex was good."

Jason looked down at the tabletop, and did his best impression of an aw'shucks look. He managed to look coy and pleased with himself all at the same time.

"That's answer enough," I said.

Jason flashed me a grin that made his baby blues sparkle. "Whatever you say, mistress."

I gave him a very mean look, that didn't dim his enjoyment one bit.

Dolph pushed away from the wall to peer over the table at my arm. "I don't buy this, Anita. Maybe you scratched your own arms up on the way here to give him an alibi."

"The scratches aren't that fresh, Dolph."

He started to grab my arm, but I stepped out of reach. "I don't want to be manhandled again, thanks anyway."

He leaned across the table at me, and Jason began to ease his chair back, as if he didn't want to be in the middle.

"You're lying," Dolph said. "A shape-shifter heals anything but silver and wounds from another monster, real quick. You taught me that, Anita. He should be healed by now, if you really were the one who hurt him."

"Wouldn't that same logic dictate that if the scratches were from the female victim then they'd already have healed?"

"Not if they come from the second victim." Dolph slapped that bit of information down as if it were a blow, and in a way it was.

I looked at Zerbrowski. "I can't debate the healed scratches thing if I don't know the time line. I need a time."

He opened his mouth, but Dolph answered, "Why, so you can give the perfect alibi?"

"Gee, Zerbrowski, I don't see your hand up Dolph's ass, but it must be, because every time I ask you a question, the answer comes out his mouth." I was leaning across the table now, too.

"His scratches are older than yours, Anita," Dolph said, voice almost a growl of its own, "more healed. You'll never prove in court that they happened at the same time."

"He's a shape-shifter. He heals faster. I taught you that. Remember?"

"Are you really admitting that you fucked him?" Dolph said.

I was too angry to flinch at his choice of words. "I prefer the term *made love* to fucked, but yeah, we did the nasty."

"If that was true, the marks would have healed completely by now. If you're only human, like you keep telling me."

The headache between my eyes felt like something was trying to stab its way out of my skull. I really wasn't in any mood for this. "What I am, or what I am not, is none of your damn business. But I'm telling you that I marked him up in the heat of passion. More than that, chances are good he was with me when the second murder took place. We can give you times, if you want."

"Times would be good," Zerbrowski had scooted his chair a little farther down the table, but he hadn't deserted his post. He'd stayed closer to all that quivering rage than most people would have.

I had to think about it, but I managed to give him approximate times for the last two days. Truthfully, I wasn't much good on alibiing Jason for the first murder, but on the second, I was pretty sure I had him covered.

Zerbrowski was doing his best to give blank cop face while he wrote down what I said. The entire interview was being recorded, but Zerbrowski, like Dolph, liked to write things down. I hadn't really thought about it before, but Zerbrowski might have learned that habit from Dolph.

Dolph stayed standing near the table, looming over all of us, as I spoke. Zerbrowski asked small questions to nail the times as clearly as possible.

Jason stayed as quiet and still as he could through all of it. His hands clasped together on the table, head down, eyes taking small quick glances at all of us, without moving his head or body. He reminded me of a rabbit hiding in the long grass, hoping that if he just stayed quiet enough, still enough, that the dogs wouldn't find him. The analogy should have been laughable. I mean, he was a werewolf. But it wasn't funny, because it was accurate. Being a werewolf didn't protect you from the human laws, most of the time it hurt you. Sometimes it even got you killed. We weren't in that kind of danger, yet, but that could change.

A shape-shifter accused of murdering a human got a speedy trial and an execution. If a shape-shifter was declared rogue, one that was actively hunting humans, and the police couldn't capture it, then you could get a court order of execution, just like for a vampire. It worked almost the same way. A vampire that was suspected of murder but was still eluding capture and deemed a danger to the public could have an order of execution issued by a judge. Once you had the order of execution in hand you could kill it when you found it. Just insert shape-shifter for vampire into the formula and it worked the same way. There was no trial, no anything – just hunt it down and kill it. I'd done a few jobs like that. Not many, but a few.

There'd been a movement a few years ago to make a magic-using human subject to orders of execution, but too many human rights organizations had kicked a fit. As a magic-using human, I was happy. As someone who had executed people on orders of the court, I wasn't sure how I would have felt about hunting a human being down and killing them. I'd killed humans before when they threatened my life, or the lives of those I held dear. But self-defense, even proactive self-defense wasn't quite the same thing. A human witch or wizard got a trial, but if they were convicted of using magic for murder, it was an automatic death sentence. Ninety-nine percent of the time the witch or wizard was convicted. Jurors just didn't like the idea of people who could kill by magic walking around free. One of my goals in life was to stay the hell out of a courtroom.

I knew Jason hadn't done anything wrong, but I also knew enough about the way the system worked to know that for those of us who weren't exactly human, sometimes innocence didn't matter much.

"Can anyone else verify these times?" Zerbrowski asked.

"A few people, yeah," I said.

"A few people," Dolph said. He looked disgusted, and I didn't understand this emotion either. "You don't even know who the father is, do you?"

That made me give him a deer in headlights blink. "I don't know what you mean."

He gave me a look, as if I'd already lied to him. "Detective Reynolds told us her little secret."

I looked at him across the table. He was still leaning over, and I was still standing, so we were almost eye-to-eye. "So?"

He gave a sound between a snort and a cough. "She wasn't the only one who passed out at the murder scene, and she wasn't the only one who threw up." He looked as if he'd made a great point, driven it home with a surgeon's precision.

I frowned and blinked at him. "I'm sorry, what are you talking about?" I let myself look as confused as I felt.

"Don't be coy, Anita, you're not good at it."

"I'm not being coy, Dolph, you're making no fucking sense." Then an idea popped into my head, but that couldn't be it. Dolph wouldn't think . . .

I looked at him, and thought, maybe he would think that. "Are you implying that I'm pregnant?"

"Implying, no."

I relaxed a little. I shouldn't have.

"I'm asking, do you know who the father is, or have there been too many to guess?"

Zerbrowski stood, and he was close enough to Dolph that it forced him to move a little way from the table. "I think you should go now, Anita," Zerbrowski said.

Dolph was glaring at me. I should have been angry, but I was too surprised. "I've thrown up at murder scenes before."

Zerbrowski moved a little back from the table. He had a resigned look on his face, like someone who saw the train coming down the track and knew nobody was going to get off in time. I still didn't think things were that bad.

"You've never passed out before," Dolph said.

"I was sick, Dolph, too sick to drive myself."

"You seem fine now," he said, voice low and rumbling, filled with that anger that seemed always just below the surface lately.

I shrugged. "I guess it was just one of those viruses."

"It wouldn't have anything to do with the fang mark on your neck would it?"

My hand went up to it, then I forced myself not to touch it. Truthfully, I'd forgotten about it. "I was sick, Dolph, even I get sick."

"Have you been tested for Vlad's syndrome, yet?"

I took in a deep breath, let it out, then said, fuck it. Dolph wasn't going to let this one go. He wanted to fight. I could do that. Hell, a nice uncomplicated screaming match sounded almost appealing.

"I'll say this once, I'm not pregnant. I don't care if you believe me, because you're not my father, you're not my uncle, brother, or anything. You were my friend, but even that's up for grabs right now."

"You're either one of us, or you're one of them, Anita."

"One of what?" I asked. I was pretty sure of the answer, but I needed to hear it out loud.

"Monster," he said, and it was almost a whisper.

"Are you calling me a monster?" I wasn't whispering, but my voice was low and careful.

"I'm saying you're going to have to choose whether you're one of them, or one of us." He pointed to Jason when he said them.

"You join Humans against Vampires, or some other right-wing group, Dolph?"

"No, but I'm beginning to agree with them."

"The only good vampire is a dead one, is that it?"

"They are dead, Anita." He took that step closer, that Zerbrowski's moving had given him. "They are fucking corpses that don't have enough sense to stay in their godforsaken graves."

"According to the law, they're living beings with rights and protection under the law."

"Maybe the law was wrong on this one."

Part of me wanted to say, you know that this is being recorded?

part of me was glad he'd said it. If he came off sounding like a bigoted crazy then it would help keep Jason safe. The fact that it wouldn't help Dolph's career did bother me, but not enough to sacrifice Jason. I'd like to save all my friends, but if someone is bent on self-destruction, there is only so much you can do. You can't shovel other people's shit for them, not unless they're willing to pick up a shovel and help.

Dolph wasn't helping. He got down low, hands flat to the table and pushed his face into Jason's. Jason moved back as far as he could in the chair. Zerbrowski looked at me, and I gave wild eyes. We both knew that if Dolph touched a suspect the way he'd touched me earlier his career was well and truly over.

"It looks so human, but it's not," Dolph said.

I didn't like the use of the *it* for one of my friends.

"Did you really let him touch you?"

Him. See, even if you hate the monsters, it's hard to keep straight in your own head what's an it, and what's a him. "Yes," I said.

Zerbrowski was moving around Dolph, trying to get to Jason, to get between them, I think.

Dolph turned to look at me, still bent over low, way too close to Jason for anyone's comfort. "And the bite on your neck, was that the bloodsucker you're fucking?"

"No," I said, "that was a new one. I'm fucking two of them now."

He staggered almost as if he'd taken a blow. He leaned heavily on the table, and for just a second I thought he'd fall into Jason's lap, but he recovered himself with a visible effort. Zerbrowski touched the big man's arm. "Easy there, Lieutenant."

Dolph let Zerbrowski sit him down. He made no reaction when the sergeant eased Jason out of the chair and farther away from Dolph. Dolph wasn't looking at them. His pain-filled eyes were all for me. "I knew you were coffin bait, I didn't know you were a whore."

I felt my own face go hard and cold. Maybe if I hadn't been so tired, so stressed – but there was no real excuse for what I said next, except that Dolph had hurt me, and I wanted to hurt him. "How's that grandchildren problem coming, Dolph? You still got a vampire for a soon-to-be daughter-in-law?"

I felt Zerbrowski react to the news, and knew in that moment that only I had known. "You really shouldn't piss off people you've confided in, Dolph." The moment I said it, I wished I hadn't, but it was too late. Too fucking late.

He came up out of the chair, hands under the table, and upended it with a tremendous crash onto the floor. We all scattered. Zerbrowski stood in front of Jason against the far wall. I took a corner near the door.

Dolph trashed the room. There was no other word for it. The chairs hit the walls, and the table followed. He finally picked one chair up and seemed to take a special grievance against it. He smashed the metal chair against the floor, over and over.

The door to the interrogation room opened. Police filled the door, guns drawn. I think they expected to see a rampaging werewolf. The sight of a rampaging Dolph stopped them dead in the doorway. They'd have probably cheerfully shot the werewolf, but I don't think they wanted to shoot Dolph. Of course, no one volunteered to arm wrestle him either.

The metal chair folded in upon itself, and Dolph collapsed to his knees. His harsh breathing filled the room, as if the walls themselves were breathing in and out.

I went to the door and chased everyone back. I said things like, "It's okay. He'll be fine. Just go." I wasn't sure he'd be okay, or fine, but I really did want them to go. No one needs to see their Lieutenant lose it. It shakes their faith in him. Hell, my faith wasn't doing all that well.

I closed the door behind them and looked across the room at Zerbrowski. We just stared at each other. I don't think either of us knew what to say, or even what to do.

Dolph's voice came as if from deep inside him, as if he had to pull it up hand-over-hand like the bucket in a well. "My son's going to be a vampire." He looked at me with a mixture of such pain and anger, that I didn't know what to do with it.

"You happy now?" he said. I realized that there were tears drying on his face. He'd cried as he'd destroyed everything. But he wasn't crying as he said, "My daughter-in-law wanted to bring him over, so he'd be twenty-five forever." He made a sound that was halfway between a moan and a scream.

Saying I was sorry didn't seem to be enough. I couldn't think of anything that would be enough. But sorry was all I had to offer. "I'm sorry, Dolph."

"Why, why sorry, vampires are people, too." The tears started again, silent. You'd never have known he was crying if you hadn't been looking directly at him.

"Yeah, I'm dating a bloodsucker and some of my friends don't have a pulse, but I still don't approve of bringing humans over."

He looked up at me and the pain was flooding over the anger. It made his eyes harder and easier to meet all at the same time. "Why? Why?"

I didn't think he was really asking me why. I believed what I believed about vampires. I think it was the universal cry of why me? Why my son, my daughter, my mother, my country, my home? Why me? Why isn't the universe fair? Why doesn't everyone get a happy ending? I had no answer for that why. I wished to God I did.

I answered the implied why, because I couldn't answer the other more painful questions. "I don't know anymore, but I do know that it creeps me out every time I meet someone I knew first as a live human, then as a dead vampire." I shrugged. "It just seems, I don't know, unnerving."

He gave a big hiccuping sob. "Unnerving . . ." He half laughed and half cried, then he covered his face with his hands and he gave himself over to crying.

Zerbrowski and I just stood there. I don't know which of us felt more helpless. He walked carefully around the room, bringing Jason with him.

Dolph sensed the movement and said, "He goes nowhere."

"He had nothing to do with this," I said.

Dolph wiped at his face angrily. "You haven't alibied him for the first murder."

"You're looking for a serial killer. If a suspect is cleared of one of the crimes then he's usually innocent of all of them."

He shook his head stubbornly. "We can keep him seventy-two hours, and we're going to."

I looked around the destroyed room, met Zerbrowski's eyes, and wasn't sure Dolph had enough clout to make those kinds of pronouncements anymore.

309

"The full moon is in a few days," I said.

"We'll put him in a secured facility," Dolph said.

Secured facilities were run by the government. They were places where new lycanthropes could go and be sure of not accidentally hurting anyone. The idea was you'd stay until you got control of your beast, then they'd let you out to resume your life. That was the theory. The reality was that once you were signed in, voluntarily or otherwise, you almost never got out. The ACLU had started the years of court battles it would take to get them outlawed, or made unconstitutional.

I looked at Zerbrowski. He stared at me with a sort of growing horror and weariness. I wasn't sure he had the juice to keep Jason out of permanent lockup if Dolph pushed. This couldn't be happening. I couldn't let it happen.

I looked back at Dolph. "Jason has been a werewolf for years. He has perfect control over his beast. Why send him to a secured facility?"

"He belongs in one," Dolph said, and the hatred had chased back the pain.

"He doesn't belong in a lockup, and you know it."

Dolph just glared at me. "He's dangerous," Dolph said.

"Why?"

"He's a werewolf, Anita."

"So he needs to be locked up because he's a werewolf."

"Yes."

Zerbrowski looked ill.

"Locked up just because he's a werewolf," I said it. I wanted him to hear what he was saying, to disagree, to come to his senses, but he didn't.

"Yeah," he said. And he said it, on tape, evidenced, un-take-backable. It could and probably would be used against him. There was nothing I could do to help Dolph, but I knew in that moment that Jason wouldn't be going to a secured facility. Half of me was relieved, half of me was so scared for Dolph that I could taste metal on my tongue.

Zerbrowski went for the door, pushing Jason ahead of him. "We'll give you a few minutes alone, Lieutenant." He motioned at me with his head.

Dolph didn't try and stop us. He just knelt there, face shocked, as if he'd finally heard his words, finally realized what he might have done.

We all went out the door, and Zerbrowski closed it firmly behind us. Everyone in the squad room was looking at us. They tried not to be, but everyone had found something to do to keep them close at hand. I'd never seen so many detectives so eager to do paperwork at their desks, or even somebody else's, as long as the desk was close to the hallway.

Zerbrowski looked at the near wall of people and said, "Break it up, people, we don't need a crowd."

They all looked at each other, as if asking should we move, should we listen to him? They would have moved without question for Dolph. But finally, they did move, drifting off in ones and twos to other parts of the big room. The ones who were at their own desks close to the action seemed to remember phone calls they needed to make.

Zerbrowski bent close to me, and spoke low, "Take Mr. Schuyler with you and go."

"What'll Dolph say?" I asked.

He shook his head. "I don't know, but I know that Schuyler here doesn't deserve to go to one of those facilities."

"Thanks, Sarge," Jason said, and he smiled.

Zerbrowski didn't smile back, but he did say, "You're a pain in the ass sometimes, Schuyler, and you're a furball, but you aren't a monster."

They had one of those guy moments. Women would have hugged, but they were men, which meant that they didn't even share a handshake. "Thanks, Zerbrowski."

Zerbrowski gave a weak smile. "Good to know I'm making somebody happy today." He turned back to me. We looked at each other.

"What's going to happen to Dolph?" I asked.

He looked even more solemn, which considering he'd looked downright depressed before, said a lot. "I don't know."

Dolph had said enough on tape to lose him his job, if it got out. Hell, if the head of RPIT was this prejudiced it might bring all their cases under review, going back to the beginning.

311

"Make sure he takes the two weeks of personal time, Zerbrowski, keep him out of here."

"I know that," he said, "now."

I shook my head. "I'm sorry, of course you do."

"Just go for now, Anita, please, go."

I touched Zerbrowski's arm. "Don't go back in there without some backup, okay."

"Perry told me what Dolph did to you the other day. Don't worry, I'll be careful." He glanced back at the closed door. "Please, Anita, go before he comes out."

I wanted to say something. Something comforting, or helpful, but there wasn't anything. The only helpful thing I could do was leave. So we did.

Leaving felt cowardly. Staying would have been stupid. When it's a choice between being cowardly or stupid, I choose stupid every single time. Today I opted for the better part of valor. Besides, I wasn't sure that Dolph might come out of the room like some rampaging bull and try to attack Jason, or me. We might be able to hush it up in an interrogation room, but if he trashed the entire squad room, it would mean the end of his career. Right now, he maybe had shot his career in the foot. Even probably. But maybe and probably were better than certainly. I left Zerbrowski to pick up the pieces, because I didn't know how.

I was so much better at destroying things than fixing them.

# 40

JASON LEANED HIS head back against the passenger seat of the Jeep. His eyes were closed, and he looked weary. There were hollows under his eyes even with them closed. Jason was fair-skinned, not pale. He didn't tan dark, but nicely golden. Today he looked vampire pale, and his skin gave the illusion that it was too thin, as if some great hand had been rubbing around his eyes and across his face, rubbing him down like you'd worry a pebble in your hand.

"You look like shit," I said.

He smiled, without opening his eyes. "You sweet-talker."

"No, I mean it, you look terrible. Are you going to be okay about tonight, the banquet, and everything?"

He opened his eyes enough to slide his gaze towards me. "Do I have a choice? Do any of us really have a choice?"

Put that way . . . "No, I guess not." My voice suddenly sounded tired, too.

He smiled again, his head still back against the seat, eyes almost closed. "If the Lieutenant hadn't popped a major gasket, would I be on my way to a secured facility, right now?"

I buckled myself into the driver's seat and started the Jeep.

"You didn't answer me," he said, voice low but insistent.

I put the Jeep in gear. "Maybe, I don't know. If Dolph hadn't been popping a major gasket, as you put it, then he'd never have even thought of putting you in a facility." I eased out of the parking area. "But he might have called you in for questioning. You are pretty scratched up, and you are a werewolf." I shrugged.

He stretched his arms up over his head, arching his body against the seat, stretching all the way to his toes. It was an oddly graceful gesture. The movement flashed the cuts on his arms, making his T-shirt sleeves ride up, and he added a writhing movement, like a shudder, or a wave that flowed from the tip of his

313

fingers, down his arms, his chest, the arch of his neck, his waist, the ripeness of his hips, down the muscles of his thighs, to his calves, to his toes.

A loud honking and the screech of brakes brought me back to the road, and the fact that I was driving. I managed not to hit anyone, but it was close. I threaded my way through a forest of rude gestures and Jason's laughter.

"I feel better now," he said, laughter still thick in his voice.

I glanced at him, frowning. His blue eyes were sparkling, his face suddenly glowing with glee. I struggled, but finally had to smile back. Jason had always been able to do that to me, make me smile when I didn't want to.

"What is so damned funny?" I said, but there was an edge of laughter in my voice that I couldn't quite swallow.

"I was trying to flirt, and it worked. You've never reacted to my body before, not even when I was naked."

I concentrated on the road, really hard, while the blush burned my face.

He chortled. "You're blushing for me. Oh, God, yes!"

"Keep it up and you are going to piss me off." I turned onto Clark, and headed for the Circus.

"You don't get it, do you?" He looked at me, and I couldn't read the look on his face. Puzzlement, delight, and something else.

"Get what?" I asked.

"I'm not invisible on your guy-radar anymore."

"What?"

"You notice men, Anita, but you'd never noticed me. I was beginning to feel like the court eunuch."

I gave him a quick frown before turning back to the road. I did not want to risk another near miss. I'd had my adrenaline rush for the day.

"Come on, you know what I mean."

I sighed. "Maybe."

"Maybe it's because you don't do casual sex, but it means more to you than just fucking, even with the *ardeur* on."

If I'd been standing I would have shuffled my feet. I had to settle for concentrating really hard on my driving. "If you've got a point to make, Jason, make it."

314

"Don't get all grumpy, Anita. My point is that even if we never touch each other again, I'm on your radar screen now. You see me. You really see me." He looked deeply content.

I was confused. When I'm confused I usually try and concentrate on work.

"Do you think the lycanthrope that's raping and killing these women is local?"

"I know he's not," Jason said.

I looked at him, because he sounded so positive. "How can you be that sure?"

"It was a werewolf, it wasn't one of our pack. There are no werewolves in the St. Louis area that are not part of the Thronnos Rokke Clan."

"How do you know it was a werewolf? It could have been any of a dozen types of half-men predators."

"It smelled like wolf." He frowned at me. "Didn't you smell it in the house?"

"Mostly all I smelled was blood, Jason."

"Sometimes I forget you're not one of us, yet."

"Is that a compliment or a complaint?"

He grinned. "Neither."

"How can you be so sure it wasn't one of our werewolves?"

"It didn't smell like pack."

"Forget that I am human, and my nose isn't four hundred times more sensitive and scent discriminating, and explain it to me simply."

"My nose in human form isn't as good as my nose in wolf form. The world is so alive. Scenting is almost like sight. If you've never experienced it, it's hard to explain, but in human form touch is probably secondary to sight. In wolf form scent is secondary to sight, or in some cases, ahead of it."

"Okay, say that's so, what does that mean for this investigation?"

"It means that I know the killer is a werewolf, and I know he's not one of ours."

"Your opinion won't fly in court," I said.

"I didn't think it would. Honest, I would have mentioned what I'd smelled in the house sooner if I hadn't assumed you smelled it, too." He looked worried now, and suddenly younger because of it, all schoolboy charm.

What he'd said got me thinking.

"Most breeds of scent hounds won't track a werewolf, or any wereanimal for that matter. They go all shit-face, howling and whining and freaking out. They basically tell the hunters, you're on your own," I said.

"I knew dogs didn't like us, but I didn't know they didn't like us that much."

"Depends on the breed of dog, but most dogs don't want to mess with you guys. I can't say I blame them."

"So I guess going down to the pound and picking out a dog is out then."

"You'd set the place on its ear."

"Okay, did you have a point?" he asked, and grinned again.

"Yes, could a werewolf in wolf form track this killer?"

Jason thought about that, face all serious again. "Probably, but I don't think the police will go for it. They don't like us much, either."

"Probably they won't, but I'll float it by Zerbrowski when he calls."

"You're sure he's going to call?"

"Yes."

"Why?"

"Because we've got two dead women, and it's probably all over the media."

"If you watched television, read a newspaper occasionally, or even listened to the radio, you might know these things," Jason said.

"Probably true, but there's heat to solve this case, and more innocent lives at risk. Zerbrowski will call, because they're grasping at straws or they wouldn't have brought you in. If Dolph had a more promising lead, even out of his head like he is, he wouldn't have been busting your chops, or mine."

"You're sure of that?"

"He's a cop, above all else. If he had anything else to chase, he'd have been out chasing it, not wasting time with you."

"I don't know, Anita, I didn't see much of the cop left today. He

316

seems like a man who's let his personal problems eat everything else."

I would have argued if I could have, but I couldn't. "I'll mention the idea to Zerbrowski, if they get desperate enough they may go for it."

"How desperate would they have to be?"

I turned the Jeep into the parking lot of the Circus. "Maybe two more bodies, maybe three. Using a werewolf to track a werewolf might appeal to Zerbrowski's sense of humor, but getting the upper brass to agree would be the problem."

"Two more women, maybe three, Jesus, Anita, why not try the desperate measures before things get so damned bad?"

"The police are like most people, Jason, they don't like thinking outside the box. Using a werewolf in animal form as a sort of pre-ternatural scent hound is way outside the freaking box."

"Maybe," he said, "but I smelled what was upstairs, Anita. So much blood, so much meat. A human being shouldn't be reduced to meat and blood."

"Aren't we all just food on the hoof?" I tried to make a joke of it, but Jason looked offended.

"You of all people should know better than that."

"Maybe," I said, feeling my own smile slide away from my face. "Okay, I'm sorry, no offense meant, but I've had too many shape-shifters threaten me to have any illusions about where I am on the food chain. And there are an awful lot of shape-shifters that still believe they are at the top."

"I don't buy that radical crap about us being the top of the evo-lutionary ladder," Jason said, "if we were really the perfection of evolution, why have we been around for thousands of years, but yet, you poor humans outnumber us, and usually outkill us?"

I parked near the back door and turned off the engine. Jason opened his door, but said, over his shoulder as he was getting out, "Don't fool yourself, Anita, plain old humans kill more of us than we ever will of them." He smiled, but not like it was funny, "They even kill more of each other than we kill of them." Then he was striding across the parking lot. He never looked back.

I had offended Jason. Until that moment I hadn't been sure it was possible to offend him. Either he was growing up, or I was getting less diplomatic. Since I couldn't possibly get less diplomatic than usual, Jason must have been growing up. For the first time in a while, I wondered if he would always be content to be Jean-Claude's lap wolf and appetizer. And stripper, too. But you can't strip and feed the vampires forever, can you?

## 41

BOBBY LEE MET me at the door. Tall, light-haired, and almost shiny compared to the dim storeroom behind him. But his mood was not shiny. "The police should have let me stay with you."

"I don't think they believed my story about making you all deputies."

"You should have just said that we were your bodyguards."

"I'll do that next time, Bobby Lee." I filled him in on what I'd learned at the police department while we walked down the nearly endless steps that led from the storeroom to the lower parts of the Circus of the Damned. The stairs were wide enough for four people to walk abreast, but the steps themselves were oddly spaced, as if whatever they were originally carved for wasn't very human. They definitely had not been made for bipeds.

"I don't know the name Heinrick," he said.

I looked at him, so suddenly, that I stumbled, and he caught my arm. I realized in that moment that I didn't know that much about Bobby Lee, not really. "You work for Rafael, you can't be a white supremacist."

He let go of my arm when he was sure I was solidly on one of the odd wide steps. "Honey-child, I know white supremacists that specialize in hating people a little darker than Rafael."

"Real Southerners don't say honey-child."

He grinned at me. "They do if you Northern bastards expect it."

"We're in Missouri, that ain't exactly north."

"It is from where I came from."

"And that was?"

His smiled widened. "When we're not in the middle of an emergency we can sit down and share personal time over a beer, or coffee. Right now, concentrate, honey-child, 'cause we are neck-deep and sinkin'."

"If you don't know Heinrick, how do you know we're sinking?"

"I was a mercenary before Rafael's people recruited me. I know people *like* Heinrick."

"What would somebody like that want with me?"

"They were watching you for a reason, Anita, you probably know what that reason is, ya' just got to think of it."

I shook my head. "You sound like a friend of mine. He's always telling me that when the shit hits the fan that I should know why the bad guys are after me."

"He's right."

"Not always, Bobby Lee, not always." But the conversation did make me think of Edward. He'd started his professional life as a hit man, then killing humans became too easy, so he switched to monsters. Monsters covered a lot of ground for Edward. No, among the vampires and shape-shifters, he'd include serial killers, snuff film actors, anyone and anything that caught his fancy. Though the price had to be right. Edward didn't work for free. Well, not often. Sometimes he'd work simply for the thrill of chasing something that scared the rest of us mere mortals to death.

"Does anyone in Rafael's operation have contacts in nongovernmental channels? I don't want anyone owing anyone a favor for this. I don't want anyone getting in trouble. I just want to know what the regular government channels either don't know, or aren't sharing with the St. Louis police department."

"We have some ex-military, special forces, things like that. I'll ask around."

I nodded. "Good." And I'd call Edward, see if he knew Heinrick. I started walking down the steps again. Bobby Lee fell in beside me, though since he was six feet and I so wasn't, it was probably an awkward stride for him. He didn't complain, and I didn't offer to speed up. I wasn't exactly looking forward to seeing Jean-Claude or Asher again. I still didn't know what to say.

We were within sight of the big heavy door that led into the underground areas. It was partially ajar, waiting for us. "By the way, Jean-Claude and Asher request your presence in Jean-Claude's room."

I sighed, and my unhappiness must have shown on my face,

because he touched my arm. "Don't look so glum, honey, they said something about owing you an apology."

My eyebrows went up at that. An apology, them owing me. I liked the sound of that. I liked the sound of that a lot.

# 42

IT WASN'T THE apology I was expecting, but under the circumstances, any apology was better than none. Especially if I wasn't having to give it. Of course, it took them nearly five minutes to get me to hear the apology, because once I got a good look at the two of them in their banquet finery, I was rendered speechless, deaf, and damn near blind to anything else.

I don't think it was magic or vampire trickery. They just looked *fine*. Asher wore a jacket of pale gold with darker gold embroidery, and an edge of true metallic gold thread shot through the embroidery itself. There was a touch more gold at collar, lapels, wide cuffs. Just enough extra sparkle to mingle with the gold of his hair as it cascaded over his shoulders and add emphasis to the gestures of his hands. His shirt was a foam of white frills at chest and wrist, like a tamed cloud. I knew from rifling through Jean-Claude's closet that the shirt wasn't nearly as soft as it appeared. The pants were the same pale gold as the jacket with a line of embroidery down either side of his leg. Boots the color of oyster shells graced his legs, their tops folded down just above the knees, tied with pale brown leather belts and small gold buckles, which could be glimpsed as he moved.

I noticed Asher first, maybe because of his powers, or maybe because he was all shiny and gold and eye-catching. It was like noticing the sun. You couldn't help but see it, to turn to face the heat of it, to bask in the glory of it. But often when the sun is high in the sky, the moon is up there, too. A dim memory of what she will be in the night, but there, nonetheless, dim and misty, hard and white. At night, there is only the moon, the sun is nowhere to be seen. There are no distractions when the moon rules the night sky.

Jean-Claude's coat was a black velvet so soft and fine that it shown like fur. It was opera length, flowing down to his ankles.

322

There was embroidery on the lapels and wide cuffs, a deep royal blue. The embroidery on the coat matched that on the black vest, but the shirt that showed in all that black and royal was the same shade of blue of the silk sheets on the bed. Cerulean blue, a color caught between the skies of day and night. It brought out the blue of his eyes so that they were like living jewels set amid the black of his hair, the near pure whiteness of his skin.

The silk was mounded into soft ruffles at his chest, and tucked into the vest. A gold and sapphire stickpin pierced the ruffles at his chest. The stone was almost as large as one of his blue eyes. Cuff links winked as he gestured, gold, with sapphires almost as large as the one on his chest. The sapphires were that cornflower blue, like a drop of Caribbean Sea water made solid.

His hair was a mass of black curls. It was almost as if he'd done less to it than normal, letting it tousle around his face and shoulders. The black of his hair blended into the black of his coat, so that the hair was like a living accessory.

For a moment I thought he was wearing leather pants, until I realized the black boots ran up the entire length of his leg. He *was* wearing black pants but they were barely visible. I got just a flash of the back of the boots when he moved. The entire length of the boot from ankle to ass was tied with a blue cord that matched the startling blue of his shirt.

I was caught between going yippy-skippy I get to play with them both, and running like hell. I managed to simply stand there in the middle of the room and not run, or fall at their feet like a groupie. Though that last part took more determination than I'd ever admit out loud.

"*Ma petite*, have you heard a word that we have said?"

I remembered that their mouths had been moving while I gazed at all that masculine splendor, but for the life of me I couldn't repeat a word of it. I blushed as I admitted, "Not really."

He looked exasperated, hands on hips, spreading the coat backwards, flashing more of the blue cord as he paced towards me. "It is as I feared, Asher. She is besotted with you. If we cannot," he made a waffling motion with his hands and I saw the sapphire ring for the first time, winking at me in the candlelight, "tone this effect down, she will be useless tonight."

323

"If I had dreamt that she could be so totally affected I would have held back."

Jean-Claude turned and faced Asher. I could see that there was blue embroidery on the back of the coat. It made a pattern or picture, but I couldn't figure it out through the spill of hair. "Would you, *mon ami*, would you truly have withheld such pleasure? Could you have resisted?"

"If I had known this, *oui*. I would not have weakened us with Musette and her people here, not for any pleasure."

I frowned and shook my head. "Hold it, guys." They turned and looked at me. They both looked surprised, I think because I sounded so normal. "This can't be Asher's powers, not unless his fascination extends to Jean-Claude, because you both seem equally nifty. I feel like jumping up and down and saying yippee, I get to play with them both." I blinked and fought not to blush. "I'm sorry, did I just say that out loud?"

The two men exchanged glances, then Jean-Claude turned back to me, and Asher directed that pale blue gaze on me. "What are you saying, *ma petite*? I have never seen you stand so speechless and insensible before me."

I looked at the two of them and shook my head. "Fine, you need a reminder, I can do that." I walked past them to the full-length mirror that sat on the opposite side of the room. I motioned them both over. "Come on, come on, we don't have all night."

They finally drifted over to me, looking puzzled. I got a little distracted watching them glide towards me in all that silk and leather and sparkly stuff. But finally, I had them standing in front of the mirror, though they weren't looking at the mirror, they were looking at me, still puzzled.

I finally had to touch each of them lightly on the arm and maneuver them so that the golden cream of Asher's coat spilled against the black velvet of Jean-Claude's. So that black curls intermingled with golden waves. I pushed them together until the startling blue of Jean-Claude's shirt and the sapphire pin brought out the blue of both of their eyes.

"Look at yourselves, and tell me that any mere mortal isn't going to stand there and say wow, for a few minutes."

324

They looked into the mirror, they looked at each other, and finally Jean-Claude smiled. Asher didn't.

"If it were merely Asher's powers then, you are correct, *ma petite*, it would not extend to me." He turned to face me, still smiling. "But I have never seen you this besotted."

"You just haven't noticed."

He shook his head. "*Non, ma petite*, I would have noticed such a phenomenon before."

I shrugged. "Maybe I've never seen you both dressed to kill before. The double impact is a little overwhelming."

He moved away enough to turn in a graceful circle, arms out, showing off the outfit. "You think it is too much?"

I smiled, almost laughed. "No, not even close, but I'm allowed to stand dumbfounded in the presence of such beauty."

"*Très* poetic, *ma petite*."

"Looking at the two of you, I only wish I was a poet, because I can't do you justice. You look amazing, wondrous, spec-fucking-tacular."

Asher walked to stand at the far end of the room beside the false fireplace. It was hard to see in the dimness, but tonight someone had put two tapered candles on the mantelpiece, each encased in crystal, so they glimmered like jewels. Asher's hair sparkled in the uncertain light. He put one hand on the mantel, his head down to stare at the cold hearth, as if the new fire screen Jean-Claude had added was *très* fascinating. The fire screen was a huge antique fan encased in glass. The colors were vibrant reds, greens, a brilliant spray of flowers and delicate lace. It was pretty, but not that pretty.

I looked at Jean-Claude for some clue, and he merely motioned me to follow Asher across the room. When I just stood there, Jean-Claude took my hand and led me over to the other man.

Asher must have heard us coming, because he said, "I was very angry with you, Anita, very angry. So angry I did not think you might have just cause to be angry with me."

Jean-Claude squeezed my hand as if to tell me not to interrupt, but I seemed to be ahead on the discussion, so I hadn't planned to say a word. Never interrupt when you're winning.

"Jason told us how ill you were after I took blood from you. If you were as ill as he has reported then you would naturally fear my

325

embrace." He looked up, suddenly, eyes wide and almost wild, lost in the glow of his hair and the flickering candlelight. "I would not have hurt you. It has never been so . . ." he seemed to be searching for a word, "terrible for any of my other," again he hesitated, "victims."

I wasn't sure what to say to that, because I agreed with part of what he'd said. I felt that he'd made me a victim of his powers, by not asking first. But whether I'd been aware of it, or not, somewhere in the back of my mind I must have been thinking about the problem all damn day, because I knew one thing for certain. I wasn't completely in the right, either. Damn it.

I let go of Jean-Claude's hand, because the feel of his skin against mine made it harder to concentrate right now.

"I can see where you might have gotten the idea that I understood what sharing blood with you would mean. I did ask you to bite me, I did offer to feed you, and you were right, I did know that your bite could overwhelm my natural defenses." It was my turn to look down at the pretty fire screen that would never know the touch of flame. "I just was so out of my head with," I almost couldn't say it, "desire that I wasn't thinking clearly. But that wasn't your fault. You could only go with what I said out loud."

I looked up, met those eyes. "Oh, hell, Asher, even if you could have read my mind at that moment I wanted you to take me, whatever that meant. There were no rules or stop signs in my head." I let out a long breath, and it shivered, because I was afraid of this, afraid of admitting it out loud, afraid of it all. I was afraid of being consumed by desire or love or whatever the hell you want to call it. "I wanted you to take me while Jean-Claude made love to me. I wanted us all to be together as of old."

"It is not of old for you, Anita," Asher said. He looked past me at Jean-Claude. "See, it is as we feared, she is besotted with me through your memories. It is not real what she feels for me. With my powers of fascination or without them, it is not real."

"That sounds like what I've been saying, Asher," I said. "That because you mind-fucked me I'll never know if what I feel for you is real. But I can tell you this, what I felt for you before, that was real. It isn't you before the holy water that I think of, it's you now, just as you are."

He shook his head and looked away, making his hair a barrier between us, so I couldn't see his face. "But I did use my powers to fascinate you, as a snake fascinates a bird. I captured your mind, and I meant to do it."

I touched his hair, and he jerked away from me, moved down the mantel out of reach. I didn't try and follow. I took in a lot of air and blew it slowly out. I'd have rather faced a dozen bad guys than this next bit of conversation.

"In your defense, I think we were naked and doing the nasty before you rolled my mind."

He looked up, face barely clear enough through the shadows and uncertain light for me to see he was puzzled. "Nasty?"

"Having sex," Jean-Claude said. "It is a quaint American slang term for it, to do the nasty."

"Ah," Asher said, though he didn't look any less puzzled.

I plowed on. I'm nothing if not determined once I've made up my mind. "My point is this, we were already having sex. You hadn't rolled my mind when I agreed to everybody taking their clothes off. You hadn't rolled my mind when we had foreplay. You hadn't rolled my mind when I was licking the back of your knees, and other things." I forced myself to meet his slowly calming eyes. "I volunteered for all that. If I could have figured out a way for you to be inside me that didn't include fangs I would have, but I wanted you both inside me."

I had to close my eyes, because I suddenly had a visual so strong that it nearly made my knees buckle. With the visual came the wave of sensation. It didn't make me claw the air this time. But I was left with a death grip on the mantelpiece, and my breath coming in gasps.

"*Ma petite*, are you well?"

I shook my head. "Compared to the first time I flashed back on the orgasm, yeah, I'm peachy."

"*Quelle?*" Asher asked.

"She has experienced the pleasure of us earlier today."

Asher looked even less happy. "She has every symptom. I did not believe she would. I thought her necromancy would protect her."

"I should also tell you that I think Belle Morte had something to do with how sick I was. She was feeding on me and Richard through you two."

Jean-Claude leaned against the wall, arms crossed. "Jason had told us that, *ma petite*. But I still believe that your power has struggled with Asher's power all day. It is the old question of what would happen if an irresistible force met an immovable object."

"Asher being the irresistible force and me the immovable object," I said.

"*Oui.*"

I'd have liked to argue with the division of labor, but it was too damned appropriate. "So what does that mean for us being together as a ménage à trois again?"

Jean-Claude had a moment of something showing on his face, then he went to his blankest of blank faces. It was Asher who spoke, "You would be willing to do this again?"

I started to let go of the mantelpiece, decided not to, just in case, and said, "Maybe." I looked at Jean-Claude, his careful beautiful face. "I think Jean-Claude has finally found something that he won't compromise on."

"Whatever do you mean, *ma petite*?"

"I mean if I cost you Asher, it will drive a wedge between us."

"So I am something that you will take to your bed to be with Jean-Claude!" He was suddenly enraged, eyes full of liquid blue fire. His humanity folded away before my eyes to leave him pale and still beautiful, but it was the beauty of carved rock and jewels, a hard, bright beauty with no life to it, no softness, nothing human. He stood before me with his golden hair moving around his face like a halo, blown by the wind of his own power. He was wondrous and horrible, a terrible beauty, like the angel of death come to find you.

I wasn't afraid of him. I knew Asher wouldn't hurt me, on purpose. I knew more that Jean-Claude wouldn't allow it. But I'd had enough. Enough of Asher and of me. In some perverse way Asher and I were well matched in a bad need-therapy sort of way. We both had so many issues about personal intimacy and so many hoops that people had to jump through, that even I was tired of it.

I unbuckled my belt and started sliding it through the loops, when it was far enough back; I slid the belt out of the loop on my shoulder holster.

Asher asked in a voice that echoed through the room, crawled down my spine, "What are you doing?"

I finished taking my belt off, then shrugged out of my shoulder holster. "I'm getting undressed. I assume that Jean-Claude's got some clothes around here somewhere for me, too. Though I am so not wearing an outfit that matches yours if it has like petticoats and stays and stuff. You can't move in that shit."

"Have no fear, *ma petite*, I have held your preferences in the forefront of my thoughts, as I chose the clothing." He held his hands out to the side and struck a lovely, if overly dramatic poise. "Even our clothing is comfortable and easy to move about in."

We were both ignoring the vampire that was glowering at us. Nothing takes the wind out of your sails when you're trying to be scary like being ignored.

I started to take my shirt off, but stopped. I did not want to have to go through the glowing cross routine again. I did not want to mess with it. So I went for the bed, where I could take off my shoes in comfort.

"So Jason told you what else Belle did?"

"She has given you the first mark, *oui*."

"She knows, Jean-Claude, she knows that Richard and I don't have the fourth mark." I hopped up on the bed, laying my belt and shoulder holster beside me. I concentrated on untying my shoes, because I did not want to go where I feared the discussion would go.

"You will not look at me now, *ma petite*. Why, is it that you fear what I will say?"

"I know that if you gave me the fourth mark that she couldn't mark me again. I'd be safe from her."

"*Non, ma petite*, no lies between us. She could not mark you as hers, but you would not be safe. I could use this as an excuse to claim that last bit of you, but I will not, because I fear what Belle would do."

I looked up at him, one shoe in my hand. "What do you mean?"

"For now, she thinks she may be able to claim you as her human servant. She may be able to use you to increase her own power. If she finds you are beyond her reach in that way, she may decide that you are better off dead."

"If she can't have me, then nobody else gets me either, is that it?"

He gave a small nod, and an almost apologetic shrug. "She is a very practical woman."

"No, she's a very practical vampire. Trust me, Jean-Claude, that is a whole new level of practicality."

He nodded. "*Oui, oui,* I would argue if I could, but it would be lies."

Asher was walking towards us now. His eyes were still glowing that drowning blue as if a winter's sky had filled his skull, but for the rest, he looked as ordinary as he ever did. Which was extraordinary. But at least he wasn't raising a small wind of his own otherworldly power or levitating a few inches off the floor.

"You are both weakened by not sharing the fourth mark. Neither of you is as powerful without it. You know that, Jean-Claude."

"I do, but I also know Belle. She destroys that which she cannot use."

"Or casts it aside," Asher said, voice soft, holding sorrow enough to make my throat tight.

I had my shoes off, my jogging socks tucked into them on the floor. "Casting you aside did destroy you," I said. I meant it to be soft, but it came out pretty much like I usually sound.

He glared at me, his pupils swimming up through the blue fire like an island reborn from the sea.

"What I mean, Asher, is that she chose what would hurt you worse than death. To be cast out from her affections, from Jean-Claude's bed, since his bed was hers."

"She would not kill me because she promised Jean-Claude she would not."

I glanced at Jean-Claude.

"I came back to her for a hundred years, if she could save Asher's life. If he died, I was free of her."

"So she worked to keep me alive," Asher said, and his voice was bitter enough to choke on. "There were nights when I cursed you for my life, Jean-Claude."

"I know, *mon ami*. Belle Morte often pointed out that if only I would allow you to die, you could be spared such humiliation."

"I did not know that she gave you that choice."

330

Jean-Claude looked away, not meeting the other man's eyes. "It was selfish on my part. I would rather you alive and hating me, than dead and past all hope." He looked up then, and his face was raw with emotion, so unlike his usual polite blankness. "Was I wrong, Asher? Would you rather have died all those years ago?"

I sat on the bed, watching them, waiting for the answer. In a way I was an audience, in a way I wasn't there at all.

"There were moments when I longed for death."

Jean-Claude turned away. Asher touched his arm, fingertips on the velvet. That small touch seemed to freeze Jean-Claude. If he was breathing, I couldn't see it. "Last night was not one of those moments."

They stared at each other. Asher's fingertips barely touching Jean-Claude's arm. There was so much between them, centuries of pain and love and hate. It was as if all of it boiled in the air, almost visible in the flickering light. I wanted to say kiss and make up, but I knew they wouldn't. I don't know what issues they had about each other, but they seemed unable to do things like that without their Julianna. She'd been the bridge between them. The thing that allowed them to love each other. Without her, they stood on the brink of the abyss and gazed at each other, separated by a chasm that neither knew how to cross.

I could never be Julianna. I had too many memories of her. For God's sake she'd done embroidery. She'd been gentle and kind and everything I didn't think I was. But there was one thing I might be able to do.

I slid off the bed, and went first to Asher, because I didn't want to set him off again. I went on tiptoe, and he had to bend down a little for me to kiss him, but he didn't fight me. I held his face in my hands like it was a cup carved of some delicate stone, something that would shatter if you abused it. I kissed him softly, drinking from that cup as the sacred gift it was. I went to Jean-Claude with the taste of Asher still on my lips. I cupped his face as I had held Asher's, and I kissed him. He barely moved under my mouth.

I stood back from the two of them. "Now, we've kissed and made up. We need to get me dressed, and we need to talk before the banquet."

Jean-Claude's voice came out low and hoarse, as if he wasn't breathing well. "Talk of what, *ma petite*?"

"The Mother of All Darkness."

"Jason spoke of her, too, but I hoped he was misunderstanding."

"It cannot be the Sweet Mother," Asher said, "she has not woken in a millennium."

"She's not awake, Asher, but she's moving around like a restless sleeper."

The two men looked at each other. It was Asher who said, "I would put aside petty differences until we are at the bottom of this most grave mystery."

"What petty differences?" I asked.

"Whether we are to be a ménage à trois, or no."

I shook my head. "I adore you, Asher, but I don't have enough energy left to shovel this much emotional shit. Do you realize that you have more hang-ups about personal intimacy than I do?"

He opened his mouth, closed it, then gave that Gallic shrug.

"We're actually well-matched in a I-haven't-beaten-you-to-death-yet, sort of way. But for now, let's both try to put our personal mess aside. Okay, please."

He gave a graceful bow. "As my lady commands, so shall I obey."

"For as long as it suits you," I said.

He laughed then, and it was a good laugh, a sound that glided down my skin and jerked at things low in my body. It brought a sigh from my lips. "Now, where are my clothes for this little disaster tonight?"

332

# 43

I HAD, OF course, complained about my clothes. The black velvet and blue silk seemed to be offering my breasts up like pale ripe fruits. The colors emphasized the near translucence of my skin with the undertone of blue highlights. But I knew what the blue highlights really were – blood. Blue blood inside my veins that would burst red when oxygen hit it.

Stephen had done my hair and makeup. He'd done them before, for these little get-togethers. He regularly did it for the other strippers at Guilty Pleasures. I had let him put my hair in a pile of loose curls on top of my head, so that my neck looked white and bare. Asher's bite marks stood out starkly against all that flesh.

"My neck and breasts look like they should be on a plate with a sign saying 'come and get it.'"

Stephen stepped back from applying the last bit of eyeliner. "You look lovely, Anita." He probably meant it, but his blue eyes were all for the makeup, for his work. He saw me as a canvas. He frowned slightly, did some minute adjustment near my eyes that left me blinking. He dabbed with a Kleenex then stepped back again.

He looked me over from the top of my head to the end of my chin, then nodded. "It's good."

"It's positively appetizing," Micah's voice came from the door-way. He stepped into the room, closing the door behind him. The moment I saw him, I knew I'd lost all rights to bitch about what I was wearing.

The color was turquoise blue, with enough green to make his eyes blaze green. The shirt had holes at the top of his shoulder, in the middle of his upper arm, and two in the middle of his forearm. Black cord was threaded through the cloth and tied around his elbow, above and below the holes to keep the cloth from sliding around. The cuffs were wide and stiff, with shiny black buttons, with cutouts on the underside so the skin of his wrists was bare, just as the holes at his elbows left those spots bare. His skin looked very tanned, very smooth, very warm against the turquoise.

The pants matched the shirt – and not just in color. There were holes on the sides that flashed the perfect smoothness of his hip, down to glimpses of thigh. The holes probably went farther down, but black boots cut off the view just above his knee.

The pants were so tight that he really didn't need a belt, but there was a black cord threaded through the unnecessary belt loops that swung as Micah walked. He was actually almost to me when I realized there were holes on the inside of the pants legs, too.

I shook my head. "There's more holes than cloth."

He smiled at me. "I'm food, so you've got to be able to reach the blood. Jean-Claude didn't want anyone to have an excuse to undress anyone."

I glanced at Jean-Claude. "He's not feeding any of these people."

"*Non, ma petite*, he is ours, and ours alone, but we do not want to have to undress him either. If all of us keep our clothes firmly in place, then so will they. It would be a faux pas of gigantic proportions if they undress their food and we do not. It is our house, and our rules."

Put that way it was hard to argue, but I still wanted to. Then I looked at Micah's face more closely. "He's wearing eye makeup." I got off the chair that I'd sat in while Stephen fixed me and walked closer to Micah. He was wearing more than just eye makeup, but it was all so artfully done that you didn't see it at first.

"I could not resist those eyes," Jean-Claude said, "they deserved to be decorated."

Micah's hair was tied completely back from his face in a bun that was a graceful mix of French braid and sheer art. "Where did all the curl go?" I asked.

"It has been blow dried straight," Jean-Claude said. He came and almost touched Micah's hair, to show how lovely it was. "He did not protest anything that we did to make him so pretty." Jean-Claude gave me a look, out of his own black-lined eyes. "It was a refreshing change."

Micah blinked those amazing eyes that someone's art had made even more amazing. "You don't like it?"

I shook my head. "No, I like it. I mean, you're beautiful." I shrugged. "I don't know, it's just a very different look for you." I turned to Jean-Claude. "I've never seen you in this much makeup."

"Belle Morte broke me of wishing to see myself this way." He was shielding as he said it, as if whatever memory went with those words was nothing he wanted to share.

"So why pretty Micah up like this?"

"You don't like it," Micah repeated.

I frowned. "That's not it. Why do it now? What do we gain by having you look like this, because don't try and tell me there's no purpose to it." I turned to include Asher in his chair across the room in the look I gave Jean-Claude. "Neither of you would go to this much trouble tonight without a reason. I've heard nothing but both of you complaining that we don't have enough time to get everyone presentable for the banquet." I gestured at Micah. "This took a lot of time that could have been used elsewhere. So I'm asking, both of you, what gives?"

They exchanged a look, then Asher looked studiously at the floor. He pretended to be studying his perfectly manicured fingernails, but I wasn't fooled.

I turned back to Jean-Claude. "Out with it," I said.

He shrugged. It wasn't so much graceful as almost embarrassed. "Musette was finally forced to give us the complete guest list. She has withheld only three names, because they are part of the gift from Belle."

"So three mystery guests, what does that have to do with why you dolled Micah up?"

"One of the vampires coming tonight has an eye for a beautiful man. Both Asher and I fell afoul of him, more than once."

"And," I said.

"To flaunt such delectable meat in front of his table, yet not allow him a taste or a touch, pleases us."

"So you're being petty," I said.

Jean-Claude was suddenly angry, it showed in his face, filled his eyes with blue fire. "You do not understand, *ma petite*. Belle has sent Paolo to torment us. He is to remind us what we were, and

335

how helpless we were. We went to anyone that Belle gave us to, anyone. She did not do it casually, but if our bodies in another's bed would gain her something she wished, then she used us, and let others do the same."

He stalked in a tight circle, the black coat floating out around him like dark wings. "The thought of sitting at the same table with Paolo again sickens me, and Belle knew that it would. I loathe him in a way that I do not wish to describe. But we cannot harm him, *ma petite*. Belle has sent him to torment both of us by his mere presence. He will smirk and leer and remind us with every look, every touch of his hands on someone else, what he once was allowed to do to us."

Jean-Claude came to stand in front of me, his anger beating in the air like invisible flames. "But this we can do, *ma petite*, we can flaunt the bounty at hand. We can show Paolo what I am able to touch, and Asher is able to touch, but Paolo cannot have. Paolo is one of those men who always wants what others have. It eats at his soul if he cannot have, in every way, whomever he desires." He touched fingertips down my neck and left a trail of heat on my skin that made me gasp, almost pain, almost pleasure. "I want Paolo to suffer, if only a little, because I do not have it within my power to make him suffer a great deal."

I looked up into Jean-Claude's angry, angry face, and sighed. "It's going to be like this all night, isn't it? Belle's only sent people that make you uncomfortable, or that you hate, or hate you."

"*Non, ma petite*. We fear Musette, and Valentina. I believe Bartolomé came because he is bored. Paolo is the first name that truly incenses me."

I touched Jean-Claude's face, holding that anger against the palm of my hand. His eyes bled back to normal, or as normal as they ever get. I looked past him to Micah. "You okay with fang-teasing some male vampire?"

"As long as I don't have to come across, I'll play."

That made me smile. "If Micah's okay with it, so am I." I cradled Jean-Claude's face between my hands, but was trying for eye contact not a kiss. "But let's keep our eye on the ball, revenge is not why we're here tonight."

He put his hands over mine and held them both against his face.

"We are here tonight because Belle Morte is *le sourdre de sang* of our line, and we cannot refuse her right to send visitors our way. But make no mistake, *ma petite*, Musette and her company are here to have revenge upon us."

"Revenge for what?" I asked.

Asher answered from across the room, "Revenge for us leaving her, of course."

I looked at him. "Why of course?"

They exchanged another look, one that I couldn't read. It was Jean-Claude who said, "Because Belle Morte believes herself to be the most desirable woman in the world."

I gave him raised eyebrows. "She's beautiful, I'll grant you. But the most beautiful woman in the world, come on! I mean it depends on what you consider beautiful. Some people like brunettes, some people like blonds."

"I said the most desirable, *ma petite*, not beautiful."

"I don't get the difference."

He frowned at me. "Men have killed themselves when she exiled them from her bed. Wars have been fought between rulers who were driven mad at the thought of any other man sharing Belle Morte's favors."

It was my turn to frown. "Are you saying that once you've had Belle Morte that no one else will do?"

"That is her belief."

I looked at him. "You and Asher left, twice apiece."

"*Exactement, ma petite*, do you not see?"

"Not really."

"If we left her bed, if there is any touch that we prefer to hers, then perhaps she is not the most desirable woman in the world."

I thought about that for a second. "So, this entire expedition is to punish you two?"

"Not entirely. I believe Belle does want to test the ground, as it were, before she visits herself."

"Why does she want to visit at all?"

"It will be something political, of that you can be sure," Jean-Claude said.

"So punishing the two of you this time is what, an extra treat?"

They started to do another of those looks, but I touched Jean-

Claude's face, forced him to look at me. "No, no more mysterious looks, just say it."

"Belle is the most desirable woman in the world, her entire power base, her entire self-image is built on that. She must find a way to understand why we left, and why we prefer to stay away, even now."

"So," I said.

"You are being too subtle," Asher said, pushing himself to his feet and striding over to us.

"Fine, you tell me," I said.

"Just as Belle saw Julianna as a threat, so she will see you. But we hope to convince her that it is not another woman alone that keeps us entertained, but a man. Belle never did see men as competition, not as she did a woman."

"So that's why you've prettied Micah up."

"And others," Asher said.

I looked at Jean-Claude. "Others?"

He had the grace to look embarrassed, but it didn't work completely, his eyes looked pleased. "If Musette can report to Belle that I have a harem of men, then Belle will cease to be worried about you."

I shook my head. "I don't think so, Jean-Claude. I think she's got a taste of me now. She's either going to be afraid of me, or attracted to the power."

"I believe she marked you once to torment me, *ma petite*. She does not truly want you as her human servant, but she is angry with me, angry with you for having me." He shook his head. "She thinks like a woman, *ma petite*, and not a modern one. You think more like a man, so it is hard to explain to you."

"No, I think I've got an inkling. You're going to try and convince Belle's people that you didn't dump her for any woman, but for a lot of men."

"*Oui.*"

"And if the sight of a lot of gorgeous men torments Paolo, too, so much the better."

He smiled, but it left his eyes hard and unpleasant. "*Oui, ma petite.*"

I didn't say it out loud, but Belle Morte wasn't the only one who rarely did anything without having more than one motive.

## 44

THE BANQUET WAS in one of the inner rooms of the Circus. One I'd
never seen before. I knew that the place was huge and I'd seen only
a fraction of it, but I hadn't realized I'd missed a room this size. It
was literally cavernous, because it had originally been a cave, a
huge, towering, space that water had carved out of solid stone over
a few million years. There was no water now, only rock and the
cool air. It was the way the air tasted, the way it touched your skin
that let you know somehow that all this dark splendor was nature's
handiwork, not man's. I don't know what the difference between
natural caves and man-made ones is, but the air feels different, it
just does.

I expected torches for the night, but was surprised to find that
there was gas. Gas lamps placed around the room, chasing back the
dark. I asked Jean-Claude when he'd installed the gas, and he said
that some bootleggers had done it during prohibition, that the
cavern had been a speakeasy. Nikolaos, the Master of the City
before Jean-Claude, had let the bootleggers pay rent for the space.
Her vampires had also fed on the drunken revelers. It was a good
easy way to feed without getting caught. Since the prey was
already breaking the law, it wouldn't go to the police, to say where
the vampire attack had happened.

I'd never been in a room that was lit entirely by gas lamps. It
had that soft edge of firelight, but it was steadier and burned
cleaner. I'd half expected there to be an odor of gas, but there
wasn't. Jean-Claude informed me that if I smelled gas it would
mean there was a leak, and we should probably run like hell. Okay,
what he actually said was we should leave as quickly as possible,
but I knew what he meant.

The banquet table was both beautifully – and oddly – arranged.
It gleamed with golden flatware, and the gold picked up the

delicate gold pattern in the white fine-boned china. There were gold napkin rings around white linen napkins. The tablecloth was triple layered, one long and white that nearly dragged the floor, a gold edge of leaves and flowers embroidered around its hem. The middle layer was a delicate gold lace. The top was a different layer of gold – white and gold – as if someone had taken gold paint and dabbed it sponge-like on white linen.

The chairs had white and gold cushioned seats and richly carved backs in a dark, dark wood. The table sat like a gleaming island in the midst of the gaslit dark. But two things confused me. First, there were way more golden utensils at each place than I knew what to do with. What the hell do you use a tiny two-tined fork for anyway? It was set at the top of the plate, so it was either for seafood, salad, dessert, or something I hadn't thought of. I was hoping for seafood or dessert, since I thought I knew which fork was for salad. Having never been to a formal vampire banquet, I tried not to speculate on other possible uses for the two-tined fork.

Secondly, there were a number of complete place settings on the floor. Each setting had a white linen napkin spread under it, like miniature picnics. The place settings on the floor were spaced between the chair settings, so there was room to pull the chairs in and out. It was . . . odd.

I stood there in my black and royal blue gown with its faint sparkles of deep blue, tapping the toe of my black high heel, trying to figure out why there were plates on the floor.

Jean-Claude glided through the long black drapes that covered the entrance between this room and the smaller adjacent chamber. Everyone was mingling in the other room. I hated mingling under any circumstances, even at normal dinner parties. But tonight was like small talk, combat style. Everything had double or triple meanings. Everyone was trying to be subtly insulting. All so polite, so back-stabbing, so painful. My small talk skills were pretty limited, and among Musette and her crew, I was unarmed. I'd needed a break, before I started breaking things for real. At least Musette's underage *pomme de sang* was missing from tonight's festivities. We'd been told the girl had been sent back to Europe because her presence seemed to upset me so. My guess was Musette just didn't want to lose her toy, if things went badly.

Asher slipped through all that blackness like a golden vision, but he didn't glide after Jean-Claude, he hurried. Musette wasn't entirely ready to believe that Asher was truly ours. Since I wasn't a hundred percent sure he was either, it was hard for her not to smell a lie on me, even though it wasn't exactly a lie. I should never have left Asher on his own, but I was tired. Tired of vampire politics. Tired of digging out from problems that I didn't start, and didn't truly understand.

"*Ma petite*, our guests are asking after you."

"I'll just bet they are."

Jean-Claude did that long, slow, graceful blink that usually meant he was trying to figure out what I'd meant with a bit of slang or sarcasm. I used to think the blink was to show off his impossibly long eyelashes, but trust him to make something enticing out of what for anyone else would have been an irritating habit.

"Musette really is asking after you," Asher said, and he imitated her voice, "Where is your new beloved? Has she abandoned you so soon?" His pale blue eyes flashed white, showing that edge of panic that was just below the surface.

"It is not like you to wander off on such an important and potentially dangerous occasion. What is the matter, *ma petite*?"

"Oh, I don't know, an international terrorist following me around, the vampire council back in town, an evening of some of the most politely vicious small talk I've ever heard, Asher being his usual temperamental self, one of my friends and favorite policemen having a nervous breakdown, a serial killer werewolf on the loose in my town, oh, and the fact that Richard and his wolves haven't arrived yet, and no one's answering their phones. Pick one." I knew the smile on my face wasn't pleasant when I finished. It was a challenging smile. It said why wouldn't I be uptight?

"I do not believe anything has happened to Richard, *ma petite*."

"No, you're afraid he's going to take a pass on the whole evening. That would make us look damned weak."

"Damian flies almost as well as I do," Asher said, "he'll find them, if they are close."

"And if they're not? I mean, Richard is shielding so hard that neither Jean-Claude nor I can reach him. He doesn't usually do that without a reason, usually a pissy one."

341

Asher sighed. "I do not know what to say about your wolf king, but I know that he is not our only problem." He looked at me, and there was a stubborn set to that handsome face. "I am not being temperamental."

I didn't bother to debate him. Asher was temperamental, he just was. "Fine, but the problem is that Musette can smell this lie. She asks me if you're mine, I say, yes, she doesn't believe me. She doesn't believe me because I don't quite believe it. You aren't totally mine. It's too new to feel that real, and that's what she's picking up on. She's practically chased me around the room finding new ways to ask if I'm fucking you, and even that caught me." I shook my head, and missed the feel of my hair against my skin. I touched the back of my bare neck and it felt vulnerable.

"If it is only for their visit, I understand," Asher said.

"No, no, damn it, it's that we haven't had intercourse."

Asher looked at me, then raised his gaze to Jean-Claude. "In this she is very American. If you have not had intercourse, you have not had sex with *ma petite*. It is a very American mind-set."

"I covered her back in my seed, and that does not count?"

I blushed so suddenly that I felt dizzy. "Can we please change the subject?"

Jean-Claude touched my shoulder, and I jerked away. I desperately wanted comforting, and thus I couldn't let him do it. I know it made no sense, but it was still true. I'd stopped trying to talk myself out of myself and begun to try and work with what I had. I was a mess of contradictions. Wasn't everybody? Though admittedly, I might be a teensy bit more contradictory than most.

I walked away from him, from both of them, but that also took me away from the lights, closer to the waiting pools of darkness. I stopped. I didn't want to walk into the dark. I spoke half turned around, as if I didn't trust my back to the dark completely. "Why are there plates on the floor?"

Jean-Claude moved towards me, graceful in those amazing boots, the dark coat swirling around him, the embroidery catching the light here and there like faint blue stars. The blue shirt seemed to float from the darkness, bringing his face to my almost painful attention, emphasizing how truly lovely he was. Of course, he'd probably planned for exactly that effect.

His voice seemed to fill the cavern like a warm whisper, "Be at peace, *ma petite*."

"Stop that," I said, and realized I turned my back on the greater darkness, turned towards him like a flower turns to the sun, turned because I couldn't not look at him. This wasn't vampire powers, it was the effect he had on me, had almost always had on me.

"Stop what?" he asked, voice still warm and peaceful, like a comforting blanket.

"Trying to use your voice on me. I'm not some tourist to be soothed by pretty words and a good delivery."

He smiled, then gave a small bow. "*Non*, but you are as nervous as a tourist. It is not like you to be so . . . jumpy." The smile had vanished, replaced by a small frown.

I rubbed my hands up and down on my arms, wishing the silk and velvet wasn't there. I needed to touch my own skin, with my own hands. The cave was around fifty degrees, I needed the long sleeves, but I needed the skin contact more. I looked up to the towering ceiling above us, and the darkness that seemed to press down from it, hovering over the gaslight, pressing at the edges of the glow like a dark hand.

I sighed. "It's the dark," I said, at last.

Jean-Claude came to stand next to me; he made no immediate move to touch me, because I'd drawn away once. I'd taught him caution. He looked up briefly at the ceiling, then back to study my face. "What of it, *ma petite*?"

I shook my head and tried to put it into words, while I huddled into myself, as if I could hold in the warmth. I was wearing a cross. The silver chain traced down my neck into the generous cleavage revealed by the low-necked dress. There was a piece of black masking tape over the silver cross itself, so that it wouldn't spill out at the wrong moment. After the earlier visits from Belle and Mommy Dearest, I was not going anywhere without a holy item on me. I wasn't sure what that might mean to having sex with Jean-Claude, or any vampire, but for the short term, I wasn't sure that any sex was worth the risk.

Jean-Claude touched my hand gently. I jumped, but didn't move away. He took that as an invitation. He'd always taken anything that wasn't an outright rebuke as an invitation. He moved to stand behind me, putting his hands over mine where I still gripped myself. "Your hands are chilled." He pressed me in the circle of his body, arms sliding around me, pinning me gently against him.

He rested his cheek against the top of my head. "I ask again, *ma petite*, what is the matter?"

I settled into the circle of his arms, relaxing by inches against him, as if my very muscles couldn't stand the thought of giving in to anything soft, or comforting. I ignored the question and asked again, "Why are there plates on the floor?"

He sighed and held me close. "Do not be angry, because there is nothing I can do to change this. I knew you would not like it, but Belle is old-fashioned."

Asher came to join us. "Her original request was to put humans on large trays, like suckling pigs, bound and helpless. Then everyone could have picked a vein and enjoyed."

I turned my head against the velvet of Jean-Claude's coat, so I could stare at Asher's face. "You're joking, right?"

The look on his face was enough. "Shit, you aren't." I rolled my head up so I could look at Jean-Claude. He obligingly looked down at me. His face was more unreadable, but I was pretty sure Asher hadn't lied.

"*Oui, ma petite*, she suggested three humans would be enough for all of us."

"You can't feed this many vampires off of three people."

"Not true, *ma petite*," he said, softly.

I kept looking at him, until he looked away. "You mean drain them dry from multiple bites."

"Yes, yes, that is what I mean." He sounded tired.

I forced myself to settle back into his suddenly tense arms, and sighed. "Just tell me, Jean-Claude, I believe you that Belle insisted on it, whatever it is. I believe you that she wanted worse things done, just tell me."

He bent his head so that he whispered against my hair, his warm breath touching my ear. "When you have steak, do you invite the cow to sit at table with you?"

"No," I said, then turned my head to the side so I could see his face. The look in his eyes was enough. "You don't mean . . ." He did mean. "So who's sitting on the floor?"

"Anyone who is food," he said.

I gave him a look.

He spoke quickly to the look in my eyes. "You will be seated at table, *ma petite*, just as Angelito will sit at table."

"What about Jason?"

"*Pommes de sang* will eat from the floor."

"So Nathaniel, too," I said.

He gave a small nod and let me see how worried he was about how I'd take all this.

"If you were this worried about how I'd react, why didn't you warn me ahead of time?"

"In truth, there has been so much happening that I forgot. This was once very normal for me, *ma petite*, and Belle holds with the old ways. There are older still than she, who would not even allow the food to sit on the floor." He shook his head, hard enough that his hair touched my face, smelling of his cologne and that inde-finable something that was simply his scent. "There are banquets, *ma petite*, that you would not wish to see, or even know of. They are indeed horrible."

"Did you think they were horrible while you were participating in them?"

"Some, *oui*." His eyes filled with that wistful look, that lost innocence, centuries of pain. It didn't happen often, but some-times in his eyes I could glimpse what he'd lost.

"I won't argue if you tell me there's worse out there than this arrangement. I'll just believe you."

He gave me a look of disbelief. "No arguing?"

I shook my head and leaned back into his chest, held his arms around me like a coat. "Not tonight."

"I should leave this miracle alone, but I cannot. You have taught me bad habits, *ma petite*. I think I must ask, once more, what is wrong?"

"I told you, it's the dark."

"You have never been afraid of the dark before."

"I'd never met the Mother of All Darkness before." I said it softly, but her name seemed to echo into the darkness, as if the darkness itself were waiting for the words, as if the words could conjure her to us. I knew it wasn't true. All right, I was pretty sure it wasn't true, but it made me shiver just the same.

Jean-Claude tightened his grip around me, pulling me tight in against his body. "*Ma petite*, I do not understand."

"How could you?" came a voice behind us.

Jean-Claude turned me in his arms as he moved to face the voice, making it a dance-like movement, ending with my left hand in his right. His coat and my skirt swirled out and settled in a cloth whisper around us. Our outfits were designed to move and flow like some Goth version of Fred Astaire and Ginger Rogers.

Asher walked quickly to us, and even the way he moved was wrong. His posture was still perfect, but there was a hunching to it, like a dog that expects to be hit. He hurried in those white boots, hurried, and though still beautiful, there was little grace to his movement. There was too much fear in him to allow for grace.

Jean-Claude held out his hand, and Asher took it. We stood there, the three of us holding hands like children. It should have been absurd, considering the vampire we faced, but it wasn't Valentina that we wanted to huddle together against. I think for all three of us, it was the night in general. It was everything in the next room, and what it represented.

Valentina stood in front of the drapes. She looked like a tiny doll dressed all in white and gold so that she, like Asher, would match the table settings. Everyone in Musette's party matched the table, which meant that that, too, had been something they negotiated. Somehow clothes wouldn't have been high on my list, but then that was me.

Valentina's outfit was a miniature seventeenth-century dress with the skirt flared out to either side so that she was shaped like an oval. The skirt was very full and gave glimpses as she walked of tiny gold slippers and numerous petticoats. She even had a white wig that hid her brunette curls from view. The wig looked too heavy for that slender white throat, but she walked as if the jewels and feathers and powdered hair weighed nothing. She had absolutely perfect posture, but I knew that was from the corset that was under the dress. Those dresses don't fit right without the proper undergarments.

There had been no need for powder to make her skin white, rouge and red lipstick had been enough. Oh, and a black beauty mark in the shape of a tiny heart near that rosebud mouth. She should have looked ridiculous, but she didn't. She was like a sinister doll. When she flipped open her gold and lace fan with a sharp snap, I jumped.

She laughed, and only the laughter was childlike, a hint of how she might have sounded long ago.

"She has stood on the brink of the abyss and stared into it, and the abyss has looked back, has it not?"

I had to swallow hard to be able to answer, because my pulse was pounding, and I was suddenly shivering. "You talk like you know."

"I do." She walked towards us, gliding and graceful. She wore the body of a child, but she didn't move like one. I guess centuries of practice can teach anyone to glide.

She stopped farther back than an adult-sized person would, so she didn't have to strain to look up at me. I'd noticed she did that while everyone was mingling. "Once I was truly the child this body pretends to be. I wandered away from everyone, exploring as children do." She looked up at me with enormous brown eyes. "I found a door that was not locked. A room with many windows . . "

"And none of them looked outside," I finished for her.

She blinked up at me. "*Exactement*. What did the windows look out upon?"

"A room," I said, "a huge room." I looked up at the cavernous roof. "Like this one, but bigger, and the windowed room sits above it all."

"You have not been in our inner sanctum, of that I am sure, but you speak as if you stood where I stood."

"Not physically, but I have stood there," I said.

We looked at each other, and it was a look of shared knowledge, shared terror, shared fear.

"How close did you get to the bed?" she asked.

"Closer than I wanted to," I whispered.

"I touched the black sheets, because I thought she was only sleeping."

"She is sleeping," I said.

Valentina shook her head, solemnly. "*Non*, to say she sleeps is to say any vampire sleeps. It is not sleep."

"She's not dead, not dead the way the rest of you are when you sleep."

347

"True, but she is not asleep either."

I shrugged. "Whatever you call it, she's not awake."

"And for that we are truly grateful, are we not?" She spoke softly enough that I leaned in towards her to hear the words.

"Yes," I whispered back, "we are."

She reached up and touched my neck, and I flinched, not from the touch, but from the tension of our words. She didn't laugh this time. "Only you and I have been touched by that dark."

"Belle Morte, too," I said.

Valentina looked a question at me.

"Belle has called me into some kind of dream when the Darkness rose around us."

"Our mistress has not informed us of this," Valentina said.

"It only happened today, early today," I said.

"Hmm," Valentina said, folding her fan tight, running it through her tiny hands, each tiny nail done in gold. "Musette should know of this." She gazed up at me, and there was so much more of her than there should have been. She would always appear to be eight, a petite eight, but her eyes held an adult's awareness, and more.

"There are some unexpected guests that are about to make their appearance. I cannot spoil the surprise, for that would anger Musette, and through her, Belle, but I think that you and I will be equally unhappy with them. I think that you and I more than any will see it for the disaster it is."

"I don't understand," I said.

"Jean-Claude will explain their presence to you, when they appear, but only you and I will truly grasp why the mere fact that they are here is bad, very bad."

I frowned. "I'm sorry, but you've lost me."

She sighed and unfurled her fan with a practiced movement. "We will speak again after the surprise." She turned to walk back towards the curtain.

I called after her, "What saved you from the dark?"

She turned, the fan folding away again, as if playing with it had become habitual. "What saved you?"

"A cross, and friends."

She gave a small smile that left her eyes as empty and gray as a winter storm. "My human nurse."

348

"Did she see what was on the bed?"

"No, but it saw her. She began to shriek. She shrieked, and shrieked, and stood there, staring at nothing, until she fell down dead. Her body lay there for a very long time because no one wished to enter the room."

Valentina opened her fan with a snap. I managed not to jump this time. "The smell got to be quite atrocious." She smiled, and made a joke of it, a vicious joke, but she couldn't make her expression match the humor. Her eyes were haunted, no matter how cruel the smile. She left through a flick of black drapes.

All three of us visibly relaxed when the drapes swung shut, and we shared a glance. "Why do I think I'm not the only one too tense to pull this off tonight?" I said.

Asher kept Jean-Claude's hand, but moved around so he was facing both of us. "Musette smells a lie, and she will not let it rest."

"Valentina and I just finished talking about the mother of all bad vampires, and you're already back to harping on Musette."

Jean-Claude squeezed my hand, and sighed.

"The Sweet Dark will not take me tonight, Anita. It will not pin me to a table and unfasten my clothes and force itself upon me. Musette will."

"You're in our bed now, rules say she can't have you."

"But she smells that it is a lie."

"I can't help that the fact that we haven't had intercourse comes up on vampire radar as lying about fucking you."

"Musette wishes it to be untrue, *ma petite*. She is searching for anything that will allow her more room to play. Your doubts, Asher's doubts, give her that room."

I closed my eyes and counted slowly to ten. When I opened them, they were both giving me their best blank faces. It was like looking at two superb paintings, suddenly made three-dimensional, very lifelike, but not alive.

I squeezed Jean-Claude's hand, and he squeezed back. "Don't go all strange on me, guys. I'm having enough trouble tonight."

They both blinked, one long graceful blink, and they were "alive" again. I shivered and took my hand back from Jean-Claude. "That is so disturbing," I said.

"*Pourquoi, ma petite?*"

"Why. He has to ask, why." I shook my head, and crossed my arms. I had to cradle my breasts, because, thanks to the bra and the neckline, there was no way to cross my arms over my chest.

Damian came through the black drapes. His scarlet hair glowed against the cream and gold of his old-fashioned clothes. He could have stepped out of a seventeenth-century painting, complete with white hose below knee-length pants and those odd high-heeled buckle shoes the noblemen wore. Only his hair, loose and blazing, was untamed, and recognizably him. He had not volunteered to be one of Jean-Claude's pretty men. Damian was a touch homophobic. Boy, had he fallen in with the wrong bunch of vampires.

He strode across the carpet and went to one knee in front of me. For tonight we were being formal, so I didn't argue, and offered him my left hand. He took it, laying a kiss on my fingers. "The Ulfric and his party are almost here."

"Where have they been?" Jean-Claude asked.

Damian looked up, giving us the full force of his grass green eyes. He almost looked underdressed without eye makeup. I think almost every other person at this little party was wearing makeup. The corner of his mouth gave the smallest twitch, and I realized he was trying not to laugh. "They had to find someone to repair the Ulfric's hair. No one in their pack was a hairdresser."

"What does this mean, 'repair his hair'?" Jean-Claude asked.

I sighed. "You know how you forgot to tell me about the plates on the floor?"

"*Oui.*"

"I forgot to mention that Richard cut his hair off. I don't mean like go-to-the-beauty-parlor-and-get-it-styled. I mean hacked it off with scissors, himself."

Jean-Claude looked almost as horrified as I had. "His beautiful hair."

"Yeah," I said, "I know." I'd done my best not to think about it. I mean, Richard had said it, we weren't dating. It wasn't any of my business what length his hair was. My major concern was that sane happy people don't hack their hair off at home with scissors. Cutting your hair like that is usually a substitute for hurting yourself in other more permanent ways. Any counselor will tell you that.

350

Damian spoke, still on one knee, still holding my hand lightly. "They found someone to salvage what they could, but he is all but shorn."

Jean-Claude looked ill, which for a vampire is a neat trick. "Is he well enough for all this tonight?" I wasn't sure who he'd asked it of, maybe everyone, maybe no one. But Jean-Claude had grasped how bad a sign it was that Richard was "mutilating" himself.

"I'm not sure any of us are," I said.

He gave me an unfriendly look. "We are stronger than this, *ma petite.*"

"Strong, yes, but tired. I guess, I can only speak for myself, but if Musette comes up to me one more time and asks me about Asher, I'm going to smack her."

"That is against the rules, *ma petite.*"

"What would make her stop nagging us about Asher? Does she have to see us fucking in front of her to back off?"

Damian was stroking my hand in his. I jerked back from him. "I don't want to calm down. I'm pissed, and I have a right to be pissed."

"A right, *oui*, but not the luxury, *ma petite.*"

"What the hell does that mean?"

"Anger without purpose is luxury tonight, *ma petite*, and we cannot afford it. We do not wish to give Musette any reason to cross the boundaries that we have so carefully negotiated."

He was right, and I hated it. "Fine, fine, you're right, you're always fucking right about the political shit. But then what are we going to do to make Musette stop asking about Asher?"

"I have one possible solution," Jean-Claude said.

The solution had to wait, because Micah came through the curtain with Nathaniel and Merle in tow.

Nathaniel's outfit was mostly cream colored strips of leather that covered almost nothing. A white thong covered his front, but left his buttocks bare. He had cream colored boots that were over the knee but open in back, so you got glimpses of his legs to mid-calf when he walked away from you. There was a three-inch heel on the boots, and Nathaniel knew how to make the heel work for him. I knew he wore less than this almost every night at Guilty

Pleasures, but it bugged me, until Nathaniel assured me he was fine with it. Stephen had styled Nathaniel's auburn hair, looping it back and over itself, to form the largest French braid I'd ever seen. French braids just aren't meant to hit the knees. The delicate eye makeup was almost overwhelming to his violet eyes, making them almost painfully, shockingly beautiful. Lipstick had shaped his mouth and made it kissable, even from a distance. He would have looked like a girl, except that the outfit left no doubt that the body it was almost covering was very male.

Merle was wearing a variation of what all the bodyguards would be wearing: black leather. Black leather pants over black boots with silver points, a black T-shirt under a black leather jacket. Merle had had his own outfit. He was six feet plus with gray-streaked hair that fell to his shoulders and a mustache and partial beard that were both a darker gray than his hair. He looked like what he was – a longtime biker and hard case. At the moment he was livid, so angry that his beast was rolling in the air around him like an almost visible presence.

"What happened?" I asked.

Merle growled, "If that bastard touches my Nimir-Raj one more time, I'm going to tear off his arm and shove it up his ass."

Jean-Claude and Asher said in unison, "Paolo."

"Yes," Merle growled.

Micah looked amused. I don't think it bothered him, but not much bothered Micah. He was one of the most easygoing people I'd ever met. I guess he had to be to survive as my boyfriend.

"It isn't bothering me, Merle."

"That's not the point," the big man said. "It's insulting. It shows he has no respect for us."

"It's Paolo," Asher said, "he has no respect for anyone, except Belle."

"Let me guess," I said, "Paolo's pawing Nathaniel, too."

Merle gave a low, skin-crawling growl.

The curtains opened, and Bobby Lee stuck his head and shoulders in. "Unless we can just start tearing people up, you better get back in here."

We exchanged a look, sighed almost as a group, and we got back in there.

352

# 45

THERE WAS A wall of our black leather-clad bodyguards – wererats, werehyenas, wereleopards – so that we couldn't see who was making a high piteous noise.

"Make a hole," I said. I was ignored.

Merle yelled, "Make a hole, people," and the bodyguards parted like a black leather ocean.

It was Stephen making the noise. He had pressed himself up against the far wall, as if he were trying to shove himself into it and out the other side. Valentina was in front of him. She wasn't doing anything to him that I could see, or even feel. But she was standing very close, one tiny hand hovering in front of him.

Gregory was pressed into a different space. Bartolomé stood just in front of him, a look of near rapture on his young face. I concentrated on the vampire and I felt him feeding, feeding on Gregory's terror. I'd known a vampire or two that could cause fear in others, then feed. I hadn't known it was a power that Belle's line carried.

Stephen screamed, and the sound whipped me around to see that Valentina had laid a tiny hand on his bare stomach. She wasn't feeding on his fear. She wasn't hurting him in any way that I could see. Stephen hid his face, his long blond curls tangling across his made-up face, his naked upper body pressed into the stone, as if he thought he could make himself disappear.

Valentina slid her tiny hand down his waist, to the hips of his white leather pants, and that tore another scream from Stephen's throat. I suddenly had a clue why the twins were terrified of the children.

Bobby Lee pushed his way beside me. "Bodyguards are supposed to go first, Anita, not second."

I ignored the anger, because I knew it was frustration. We'd told the guards that we could not start violence under any circumstances, that Musette and her crew had to break truce first. As far as I was concerned this did break truce.

I started towards Stephen, and a strange vampire barred my way. I knew suddenly why our guards were simply standing there with their hands in their proverbial pockets. The vampire wasn't that tall, but he was bulky, and it wasn't just muscle. There was something to the hunch of his shoulders. The shape of his head was wrong, somehow. There was nothing specific I could put a finger on, except that he hit the radar as not human. Not human in ways different from other vampires.

He was also one of the few Black vampires I'd ever seen. Some people theorized that the same genetics that made many people of African descent immune to malaria also made them less likely to become vampires. He stood there looking at me, with his dark skin still somehow strangely pale, like chocolate ivory. His eyes were golden yellow, and the moment I looked into them, the words *not human* came to mind.

Another scream tore the air. It didn't matter what the thing in front of me was, or wasn't. I didn't care.

I tried sidestepping, and the vampire moved with me, not threatening, but not letting me through either. The room was suddenly quiet, so quiet. Gregory's voice came first, unnaturally loud in the tense silence. "Don't make me do this, oh, God, don't make me do this!"

Jean-Claude was murmuring to Musette, and I heard her voice, just a word or two in French. She was basically saying they hadn't broken truce, this was only entertainment.

I felt my shoulders relax, felt the decision settle into the center of my body. I stared up at the vampire. "You are a coward, an ugly, child-abusing coward."

The vampire didn't react, he ignored me, and I didn't think it was simply bodyguard cool. I tried a few more choice insults, concerning everything from his parentage to his physical appearance, and got glazed blinks. He didn't speak English. Good.

"Bobby Lee," I said.

He leaned in close to me, trying even now to insinuate his body between me and the big bad vampire. "Yes, ma'am."

354

"Overwhelm him with numbers."

"Can we cut him up?"

"No."

"Then we can't overwhelm him for long."

"I only need a minute."

He gave a small nod. "I might just squeeze a minute out of this mess."

I met his eyes. "Do it."

"Yes, ma'am."

He made a signal with his hand, and all the wererats moved at once. I sidestepped the mass of black leather, and went quickly to Valentina and Stephen.

I was talking before I'd really gotten to them. I wouldn't have much time. Micah appeared beside me. Merle and Noah, Micah's second bodyguard, were practically pressed to his back. I'd made sure all my bodyguards were busy with the vampire. If things went wrong, I wasn't sure either Merle or Noah would protect me if it meant endangering Micah. Oh, well.

"Stephen had been abused as a child. He was used for sex by his own father, and sold to other men," I said as I moved forward. I remembered what Jean-Claude had said, that Valentina hated child molesters because of her own past.

She turned that tiny heart-shaped face to me, her hand still caressing Stephen's shoulder. He had collapsed to the floor, huddled in an almost fetal position.

I was beside them now, and the noises behind me were escalating. There was going to be a fight soon, a bad one. "I swear to you that what I say is true. Look at him, look at the terror your touch inspires in him."

Stephen wasn't looking at either of us. His eyes were squeezed closed, and his tears had smeared the eye makeup to black tracks down his face. He hugged his body tight. He'd given himself up and over to what was happening, as if he were still a child.

Valentina looked down at him, and something like horror began to grow on her face. She stared at her tiny hand, as if it were something awful that had just appeared at the end of her arm.

She shook her head. "*Non, non,*" and more French that I couldn't follow.

"He's coming," Merle said, and I felt him and Noah brace themselves in front of Micah and me.

I touched Valentina's arm, and she raised eyes glassy with shock and turned towards me. "Call off Bartolomé, tell him why Gregory's afraid of him."

I felt the impact of the vampire slamming into Merle and Noah, and they pressed forward, taking the fight away from us by a few feet. Micah stood over me, ready. He could shape-shift and use claws, but he just didn't have enough body mass to stop the vampire.

Valentina's voice cut through the fighting, echoed through the room, and I realized she was using vampire powers to make herself heard, "We broke truce first, first blood is on our hands."

Musette screamed, "Valentina!"

Valentina repeated herself in French this time. The fighting slowed at Valentina's words, slowed, and began to die.

Valentina turned to face Musette, who was in a dress of all white, so that she looked like a bride. "It is truth, Musette. These two men have been abused enough by us. I will not let it continue."

"He was so afraid of me, Valentina, such fear to feed on," Bartolomé said, "now you've spoiled it." The slender boyish figure was dressed in nearly solid gold, old-fashioned, very seventeenth century, cloth, so that he sparkled as he moved.

Valentina spoke low and soft, in rapid French. Bartolomé's face didn't pale, but he looked back at Gregory. He turned to look at me. "Is this true? Their own father?"

I nodded.

Gregory's sobs were loud in the sudden stillness.

"To force yourself on children is an evil thing," Bartolomé said, "to use your own sons," he spat on the floor and said something in what I recognized was Spanish but couldn't follow.

"I brought them here tonight so they'd be under my protection, safe. Their father has returned recently, and is trying to meet with them again. They are here so he couldn't find them. I didn't think about the two of you."

"We would not have done this if we had been told," Bartolomé said.

"Musette was told," Jean-Claude's voice seemed to fill the tension like water in a cup.

We all turned to Jean-Claude, who was standing not too far off, near the mass of bodyguards that had taken on a second vampire like the one that had kept me from Stephen. "I told her of Gregory and Stephen's past, because the moment Stephen saw Valentina and Bartolomé, he said he could not feed them. That the memories it would waken would be too much for him to bear. I did tell Musette this. If I had not warned her, I would never have left Stephen and Gregory out here without Anita or myself to guard them."

All of us now turned to look at Musette. She was not wearing a wig, but had curled her hair into long banana curls so she looked like a porcelain doll, with her red lips, her carefully made up eyes, her pale skin, and the white seventeenth-century dress with its attached cape. Nothing would ever take her beauty from her, but physical beauty isn't enough to make up for sadism.

"Is this true?" Valentina asked.

"Now, *ma poulet*, would I do such a thing?"

"Yes," Valentina said, "yes, you would."

The two child vampires stared at Musette, stared at her wordlessly, until it was she who looked away, she who blinked big blue eyes. For a moment I saw what I thought I'd never see. Musette was embarrassed.

"Bobby Lee, capture her ass."

"*Ma petite*, what are you doing?"

"I know the rules, Jean-Claude, they've forfeited their safe conduct in our territory. That means that we are within our rights to put her under house arrest until her little company leaves."

"But we cannot harm her, she is too important to Belle," he said.

"Sure," I said. I glanced at Bobby Lee. "Escort her back to her room and put the cross back on the door."

He looked at me, then at Jean-Claude. "You mean, just like that, we can hurt them, jail them?"

I nodded.

He sighed. "Wish it worked that way with the shape-shifters."

"Occasionally, the vampires being so civilized comes in handy."

357

Bobby Lee grinned at me, and he and Claudia and about half a dozen others moved towards Musette. Angelito moved in front of her, blocking her from view. Her voice rang clear, though hidden, "Do not fear, Angelito, the wererats will not touch me."

Bobby Lee and Claudia were facing off with Angelito. He made them both look small. "We can do this easy, or hard." Bobby Lee said. "Move, and we all go quiet to the rooms. Stay put, and we'll hurt you, then drag your ass back to the rooms." There was an eagerness to his voice that said he was hoping for a fight. I think they all were. None of them had liked having to stand by and watch Gregory and Stephen be tormented.

"Move aside, Angelito," Musette said. "Now."

Angelito moved, his face showing how reluctant he was to do so. I was surprised that Musette was being so cooperative. She'd struck me as someone who'd have to be carried off kicking and screaming.

Bobby Lee reached out for Musette. She said, "Do not touch me." He stopped in mid-motion as if his hand had frozen in place.

"Take her, Bobby Lee," I said.

"I can't," he said, and there was something in his voice that I'd never heard before. Fear.

"What do you mean, you can't?" I asked.

He took his hand back, slowly, and cradled it against his chest, as if it had been hurt. "She told me not to touch her, and I can't."

"Claudia," I said.

The big woman shook her head. "I can't."

The first hint I had about how wrong things had gone was the real rat that waddled up to sniff at Musette's white skirts. It looked up at her with shiny black button eyes.

I looked at Musette, and her blue eyes had bled solid, so that she looked like a blind blond doll. Her face was exultant with triumph.

"Rats are your animal to call," I said.

"Didn't Jean-Claude tell you?" and the laughter in her voice said clearly, she knew he had not.

"He forgot to mention it."

"I did not know," Jean-Claude said. "Her only animal to call two centuries ago was the bat." His voice sounded empty, hiding whatever he was feeling.

"She gained the rat as her second animal about fifty years ago," Asher said.

I gave him a look. "It would have been nice to know that."

He shrugged. "It never occurred to me that anyone would actually try to put Musette under guard."

I turned back to the vampire in question. "Why didn't you use your new power to get rid of the wererat guards earlier?"

"I wanted it to be a surprise," she said, and smiled, smiled wide enough to flash fangs. She was so terribly pleased with herself.

"Fine," I said, "all shape-shifter bodyguards that don't happen to be rats, get her ass."

"Kill them," and I knew she was talking to Bobby Lee. That I hadn't foreseen. Shit.

But Bobby Lee and Claudia were both shaking their heads, and backing off from her. "You can order us not to harm you, but you can't make us hurt others. You ain't got that kind of power, girl."

The wererats were all backing away, looking confused and worried. More real rats had begun to scamper in from the far cavern. One of the problems with using a place that is naturally created is that you get nature. Nature isn't always pretty, or friendly.

It was mostly werehyenas that moved forward. Only two of the wereleopards qualified as bodyguards, and those two stayed close to Micah. The rest of our leopards had been brought along as food. Food doesn't fight, food just bleeds.

I realized something I hadn't before – there were no werewolves in the cave except for Stephen. Where had the werewolf guards gone?

Musette said something, and it wasn't in French. In fact it wasn't a language I could even guess at. The two vampires with their ivory gray skin and golden eyes moved in front of her.

Jean-Claude said, "Call them back, *ma petite*, I would not lose them over this."

"There's only two of them, Jean-Claude."

"But they are not what they seem."

I called everybody off and turned to Jean-Claude. "What?"

It was Valentina who came forward and answered my question. "There is a room where the servants of the Sweet Dark wait, asleep. The council members will go into that room from time to time and try to call them to their service."

I glanced at the two vampires, then back to Valentina. "These two woke," I said.

"More than these two," she said, "our mistress has called six of them awake. She believes it is a mark of her growing power."

Valentina and I looked at each other. "The Mother of All Darkness is waking, and her servants wake before her." I whispered it, but even whispered, it shivered and filled the room with dancing echoes.

"I believe so," Valentina said.

"Our mistress is more powerful than any other. The servants of our Sweet Mother wake to Belle Morte's command. It is a sign of our mistress's greatness," Musette declared it as truth, a ringing pride in her voice.

"You're a fool, Musette, the dark is waking. The fact that they are standing here is proof of that. They'll obey Belle Morte until their true mistress rises, then God help you all."

Musette literally stamped her foot at me. "You will not spoil our fun. You cannot touch me, they will not let you."

I looked at them, and frowned. "They're not just vampires, are they?"

"What do you mean, *ma petite*?"

I could feel them, feel a presence that shouldn't have been there. "They feel like shape-shifters. Vampires can't be shape-shifters." I realized even as I said it that that wasn't entirely true. The Mother of All Darkness was a shape-shifter and a vampire. I'd felt that.

"I thought Mommy Dearest was the first vampire, the one who made you all."

"*Oui, ma petite.*"

"Are there any vampires on the council that descend directly from her?"

Jean-Claude thought about that for a moment. "We all descend from her."

"That's not what I asked."

Asher answered, "There is no one that can claim direct descent from her line, but she founded the council of vampires. She began our civilization, gave us rules, so that we were no longer solitary beasts, killing each other on sight."

"So she's your cultural mother, not your line's originator."

"Who can tell for certain, *ma petite?* She is the beginning of what we are today. She is our Mother in all ways that are important."

I shook my head. "Not all ways." I stood out of reach and said, "Someone who speaks whatever they speak translate this for me."

Valentina stepped up. "They understand French now."

"Fine. Jean-Claude."

"I am here, *ma petite.*"

"Tell them that Musette has forfeited safe conduct, and we need to place her under arrest. She won't be harmed, but she won't be allowed to harm anyone else."

Jean-Claude spoke slow French, so I could understand a lot of it. I had picked up more and more over the years, but rapid speech still gave me problems. "I have told them."

"Then tell them this, too. If they don't move out of the way so we can arrest her, then we are within the rules that the Mother of All Darkness laid down – to kill them for disobeying the rules."

Jean-Claude looked doubtful.

"Just repeat it," I said. I walked away a little to find Bobby Lee. He was sweating and looked unwell.

"I am sorry, Anita. We failed you."

I shook my head. "Not yet you haven't."

He looked puzzled.

"Open your leather jacket, wide."

He did what I asked.

I took his gun out of its shoulder holster and got a glimpse of a second gun in his belt. Rules said only guards could be armed. I pointed the gun at the ground, and clicked off the safety.

His eyes were very wide. I wasn't actually sure if he could let me have the gun. But he did, and I threaded my way carefully back through the crowd to the front lines.

The gun was invisible, held in the folds of my full black skirt. "What did they say, Jean-Claude?"

"They don't believe anyone here can hurt them. They say that they are invincible."

"How long have they been asleep?"

Jean-Claude asked them. "They don't know for certain."

"How do they know they're invincible?" I asked.

361

He asked, and they drew swords from under their white coats. Short swords, forged of something darker and heavier than steel. Was it bronze? I wasn't sure. I just knew it wasn't steel.

We all stepped back from the drawn blades, whatever they were made of. "They say that no weapon born of man can harm them," Jean Claude said.

Musette laughed. "They are the finest warriors ever created. You will not touch me with them as my protectors."

I stepped back, put myself in as balanced a stance as I could get with the high heels, and raised the gun. I aimed for a headshot, and got it. The vampire's head exploded in a wash of blood and brains. The sound of the shot seemed to echo forever, and I couldn't hear the yell I saw on the lips of the second warrior as he charged me. His head exploded like the first one had. All the hand-to-hand combat training in the world is useless if your enemy doesn't let you get close enough to use it.

Musette stood blinking, too shocked to move, I think. She was covered in blood and gore. Her blond hair and pale face were a red mask, out of which her blue eyes blinked. Her white dress was half crimson.

I aimed the gun at her startled face. I thought about it, God knows, I thought about it. But I didn't need Jean-Claude's frightened, "*Ma petite*, please, for all our sakes, do not do this," to make me hesitate. I couldn't kill Musette, because of what Belle Morte might do in retaliation. But I let Musette see in my eyes, my face, my body, that I would kill her, that I wanted to kill her, and that, given the right excuse, I might forget Belle's vengeance for the second it would take me to pull a trigger.

Musette's eyes filled with glistening tears. She was a fool, but not so big a fool as all that. But I had to be certain, so we didn't have these misunderstandings again. "What do you see in my face, Musette?" My voice was low, almost a whisper, because I was afraid of what my hand would do if I yelled.

She swallowed and it was loud to my ringing ears. "I see my death upon your face."

"Yes," I said, "yes, you do. Never forget this moment, Musette, because if it happens again, it will be your last moment."

She let out a shaking breath. "I understand."

362

"I hope so, Musette, I really, truly, hope so." I lowered the gun, slowly. "Now, Merle can you oversee Musette and Angelito going to their rooms, right now."

Merle stepped forward, and a small army of werehyenas moved with him. "My Nimir-Ra speaks, and I obey." I'd heard him say things like that to Micah before, but never to me, or at least not like he meant it.

Merle stepped over the bodies of the dead vampires to take Musette's arm. The werehyenas looked pale, but happier. I'd just made all the muscle in the room happy, because things were simple now. We could kill them if they messed up again.

I caught Jean-Claude's expression. He was not happy. I'd made the soldiers' job easier, but not the politicians'. No, I think I'd just complicated the hell out of the political side of things.

Merle led Musette, none too gently, over the bodies. She stumbled, and only a mass of werehyenas kept Angelito from grabbing her. Musette regained her balance, and the room suddenly smelled like roses.

I thought I'd choke on my own pulse as Musette raised her head and showed eyes the color of dark honey.

## 46

BELLE MORTE LOOKED at me, out of Musette's face, and I think I stopped breathing. All I could hear for a moment was the hammering of my own heart in my head. Sound returned with a rush, and Belle Morte's voice slid out of Musette's mouth.

"I am vexed with you, Jean-Claude."

Merle kept trying to drag her across the room. Either he didn't know the shit had hit the fan, or one vampire was all the same to him. He was about to learn otherwise.

"Release me," she said in a calm voice.

Merle dropped her arm as if she'd burned him. He backed away from her the way that Bobby Lee had backed away from Musette, with a look of pain, holding his arm as if it hurt.

"The leopard is her animal to call," Jean-Claude said, and his voice carried into yet another heavy silence. But I didn't have time to think about silence, because Belle was talking, saying awful things.

"I have been gentle up 'til now." She turned and looked back at the two dead vampires. "Do you know how long the council has been trying to wake up the Mother's first children?"

I think we all thought it was a rhetorical question, one we were afraid to answer.

She turned back to face us, and something swam underneath Musette's face, like a fish pushing against water. "But I awakened them. I, Belle Morte, awakened the Mother's children."

"Not all of them," I said, and immediately wished I'd kept my mouth shut.

She gave me a look that was so angry it burned, and so cold, it made me shiver. It was as if all that had ever been of rage and hatred were in that one look. "No, not all of them, and now you have taken two away from me. Whatever shall I do to punish you?"

I tried to speak around the pulse in my throat, but Jean-Claude answered, "Musette broke the truce, and would not concede it. We have obeyed the law to the letter."

"It is true," Valentina said. The crowd of black leather-clad grown-ups moved so the child vampire could come and stand near Musette/Belle. Valentina kept out of reach, though. I noticed that.

"Speak, little one."

Valentina told the story of how Musette had withheld information about the child molestation and what had happened because of it. Musette's body turned to look at Stephen and Gregory. Gregory was holding his brother, rocking him. Stephen wasn't looking at anyone, or anything. Whatever his staring eyes saw, it was nothing in this room.

Belle turned back to us, and again there was that sense of another face swimming underneath, but this time I saw it like a ghost superimposed over Musette's face. Ghostly black hair bled over the blond, a face with more cheekbones, more strength to it, showed for a moment, before it sank back into the softer beauty of Musette.

"Musette did break truce first. I concede that."

Why was it that my heart rate didn't slow a single beat when she said that?

Her next words came out in a purring contralto, a voice like fur to caress the skin and ease across the mind. "You have acted within the law, and now so shall I. When Musette and the rest come back to me, Asher will come with them."

"Temporarily," Jean-Claude said, but his voice held doubt.

"Non, Jean-Claude, he will be mine as of old."

Jean-Claude took a deep breath and let it out slowly. "According to your own laws, you cannot take someone permanently away from those to whom he, or she, belongs."

"If he belonged to anyone, that would be true. But he is no one's *pomme de sang*, no one's servant, no one's lover."

"That is not true," Jean-Claude said, "he is our lover."

"Musette communicated with me, told me that she smelled your lies, your weak effort to keep Asher from her bed."

Belle was able to smell lies, too, if the lie was something she understood. No vampire could tell truth from falsehood if it was

365

about something they didn't understand. If a vampire had no loyalty, they couldn't discern it in others – that sort of thing. I was going to try and give her something she could understand.

"I didn't think it was a weak effort," I said.

Jean-Claude gave me a look, and I shook my head at him. He stepped gracefully aside, because he knew I had a plan, but his voice whispered through my head, "Be careful, *ma petite*."

Yeah, I'd be careful.

Belle turned her borrowed body to look at me. "So you admit it was an attempt to lie to Musette."

"No, I said it wasn't weak. I found the whole thing embarrassing, exciting, wonderful, and terrifying. Being in bed with Asher wasn't exactly what I thought it would be."

"You haven't lied, yet," she said, and her voice was so rich, it was as if I should have been able to get down on the ground and roll myself up in it like some soft, warm, suffocating carpet. Her voice was enticing like Jean-Claude's and Asher's could be, but also frightening.

"We took Asher to our bed, and by European standards we are lovers."

"By European standards," she looked confused, and her face pushed out against Musette's. This time it was like a mask. The sense of something larger, more dangerous pushing against Musette's face. I knew through Jean-Claude's memories that Belle wasn't physically much bigger than Musette, but physical size wasn't all there was to Belle Morte. "I do not understand what that means, 'European standards'."

Jean-Claude answered, "Americans have a most peculiar idea that only intercourse between a man and a woman constitutes true sex. Anything else does not truly count."

"I taste truth, but I find it most odd."

"As do I, but it is still true." He gave that Gallic shrug.

I added, "What Musette kept smelling wasn't a lie, it was my hang-up that Asher and I hadn't had true intercourse. Trust me, we were all naked and sweaty in the bed."

She turned that strange half-face to me. It would have looked more frightening if her face hadn't been surrounded by Musette's long blond banana curls. The Shirley Temple look was not meant for Belle. "I believe you, but by your own admission you are not lovers, not truly by your own standards. Thus, Asher is mine."

"You don't care about the truth, I forgot that," I said.

She narrowed those honey-gold eyes at me. "You have forgotten nothing, little one. You do not know me."

"I have Jean-Claude's memories, here and there. That's enough. They should have taught me better than to use truth."

She walked towards me, and as she did, her body seemed to fold over Musette's, so that she wasn't just a face, but a dress of dark gold, a longer arm, a pale hand with copper-colored nails. She moved like a ghost draped over Musette, so that you got glimpses of the other woman underneath. It wasn't perfect, Belle Morte wasn't really physically there, but it was close, and it was unnerving.

Jean-Claude had moved so that he touched me from behind by the time Belle came to stand in front of me. I leaned back against him, because she had marked me once, and that was without any physical touch. I leaned against Jean-Claude and fought the urge to draw his arms around me like a shield.

Belle stood so close that the edge of Musette's full skirt brushed my feet. Belle's ghostly dress seemed to bleed over my shoes, creep up my ankles. I couldn't breathe.

Jean-Claude moved us backwards, out of reach of that creeping power. I pulled his arms around me tight. Screw it, I was scared.

"If truth will not work with me, what will, *ma petite*?" Belle asked.

I found my voice, it was breathy, scared, but there was nothing I could do about it. "I am Jean-Claude's '*ma petite*,' no one else's."

"But whatever he has is mine, so you are my *ma petite*."

I decided to let that argument go, for now. There were other more important ones I needed to win. "You asked if truth doesn't work with you, then what does?"

"*Oui, ma petite*, I did ask."

"Sex or power," I said, "that's what works for you. You prefer both together, if you can get it."

"Are you offering me sex?" She purred at me, and the sound made me shudder and push myself harder against Jean-Claude. I didn't want to play with Belle, not in any way.

367

"No," I said, in almost a whisper.

She reached out towards me, that slender white hand with its dark copper nails, and that afterimage of Musette's hand underneath, as if Belle's graceful hand were a strange metaphysical glove.

Jean-Claude moved us back again, a fraction of a fraction of an inch, so that those long-nailed fingers missed my cheek by a breath.

Belle looked at him, her long black hair beginning to move around her body like there was a wind blowing around her. There was no wind, only Belle's power.

"Are you afraid that one touch and I will take her from you?"

"No," Jean-Claude said, "but I know more of what your touch can do, Belle Morte, and I am not sure that Anita would care for it."

He'd used my real name, he almost never did that. Perhaps because Belle was using my nickname, he didn't want to.

Her anger burned the air in front of us, like a real fire, stealing the oxygen from the lungs, making it impossible to breathe, unless you took that heat into your lungs. Then they would sear, and you would die.

The heat filled her words, so that I half expected them to be burned into the very air. "Did I ask if she would care to be touched?"

"No," Jean-Claude said; his voice was very still, and I felt him sinking away, even with his arms wrapped around me, he was sinking away, folding into that quietness that he went to when he hid from everything. I had a glimpse of that quiet place, and it was quieter than the place I went when I killed. There wasn't even static there, only complete silence.

The emptiness filled with the smell of roses, sweet, so sweet, cloying, choking. I gasped, and all I could taste was roses. Jean-Claude caught me, or I would have fallen. The perfume of roses filled my nose, my mouth, my throat. I couldn't swallow past it, couldn't breathe anything but perfume. I would have screamed, but I had no air.

I heard Jean-Claude yelling, "Stop this!"

Belle laughed, and even choking to death, the sound rode through my body like a knowledgeable hand.

A hand grabbed mine, and a breath of air clawed its way down my throat, fighting its way through Belle's power. Again if I'd had enough air, I'd have screamed. Micah's face hovered over mine. Micah's hand in mine.

*"Non, mon chat*, you are mine, as is she." Belle knelt beside us, reaching out to touch Micah's face.

Jean-Claude moved us all backwards, so that we collapsed on the floor at her knees, but we were out of reach again, barely. But barely was good right then.

Belle's eyes burned with honey fire, and the nails of her hand bled copper flames on the air, as she reached for Micah. Jean-Claude tried to help us crawl away, but we'd fallen in a heap of long skirts, long coats. Death by fashion.

Belle touched Micah's face, trailed those glowing claws down his cheek. The smell of roses closed over my head like sweet poisoned water, and I was drowning again.

Another hand on me, and this touch had nothing warm in it, it didn't call the *ardeur*, it didn't call my beast, it called something colder and more certain of itself. My necromancy came welling up and it burst over my skin, my body, and I stared up into Belle's burning eyes, and I could breathe. My throat was sore as hell, but I could breathe.

I moved my eyes enough to see Damian holding my other hand. His eyes were wide, and I could feel his fear, but he was there, kneeling beside me, facing the power that was Belle Morte.

Belle drew Micah's face towards hers. Her skin seemed to be made up of white light, black flame hair, the glittering molten metal of fingertips and eyes. Her lips glowed like a slash of fresh blood.

Micah's hand convulsed in mine, so strong it hurt, and the pain helped, made my thoughts clearer, harder-edged. He made a small sound in his throat as Belle pressed her mouth to his. I knew he didn't want to touch her, and I also knew he couldn't refuse her.

But he was mine. Micah was mine, not hers. Mine. I sat up with Micah on one hand and Damian on the other, the warm and the cold, the live and the dead, the passion and the logic. Jean-Claude's hands were still on my nearly bare shoulders. He

369

strengthened me, as I strengthened him, but this power was mine, not his. The leopards weren't his to call. They were mine.

I called that part of me that the leopards touched and realized for the first time that it wasn't tied to Richard, or even really Jean-Claude. The leopards were mine, and Belle's.

I sat up with my face so close to hers that the glow of her fire caressed my face, and the pleasure of that light touch sent a wave of shivers over my skin. It wasn't that I was immune to Belle's touch. It was that I had my own.

I usually fought my beast, whatever flavor it was, but not tonight. Tonight I welcomed it, embraced it, and maybe that was why it poured through me like a scalding flood of power. If I'd been a lycanthrope in truth, my beast would have burst from my skin in a flood of warm fluids, but I wasn't a lycanthrope. But the beast rode under my skin, screamed out of my mouth, and hit Micah's body like a train, a huge, liquid muscled train. It tore his mouth from Belle Morte's, and brought a scream to echo mine. My beast roared through his body, and his beast answered it. His beast rushed up from the depths to meet mine, like two leviathans racing for the surface.

We hit that metaphorical surface together, and our beasts wound in and out of our bodies, rolling like huge cats, luxuriating in the feel of fur and muscle. There was nothing to see with the eyes, but there were things to feel.

Belle brushed her glowing hands just above us, caressing that energy. *"Très de bon gout."* She touched Micah's skin, and that energy leaped to her, bringing a gasp from her throat. Micah turned, and I think would have gone to her again, but I caught his face in my hands. We kissed.

The kiss began as a brush of lips, an exploration of tongues, a nibbling of teeth, a pressing of mouths. Then our beasts rolled through our mouths, like two souls changing places. The rush of energy slammed our bodies together, sliced my nails through Damian's hand, convulsed Jean-Claude's hands on my shoulders. I felt both his body and Damian's bow backwards, a second before the power tore through them, and ripped sounds from both their throats that had more to do with pleasure than pain.

Micah and I rode each other, mouths locked in an endless kiss,

370

as if our beasts had merged into one. Then slowly, the entwined energies began to roll apart and slide into their separate houses of flesh.

I came completely to myself on the floor with Micah collapsed on top of me, Damian lying on the floor with only my hand holding him. Jean-Claude was still sitting upright, but he was swaying softly in place, almost like he was dancing to music I couldn't hear. I think he was simply fighting not to fall down, but even that he made seem graceful.

Belle was staring down at us with a look close to rapture on her face. "Oh, Jean-Claude, Jean-Claude, what toys you have wrought for yourself."

Jean-Claude found his voice while I was still fighting to breathe over my pulse, and Micah's heart was thudding so hard against my chest it felt like it would burst. The pulse in Damian's palm beat like a second heartbeat against my skin. None of the rest of us had found a voice that could override the pulse of our bodies.

"Not toys, Belle, never toys."

"They are all toys, Jean-Claude, some are merely harder to use than others. But they are all toys." She stroked her glowing hand down the back of Micah's carefully styled hair.

Her energy played along his body, brought a sigh from all of us, but it was faint, almost a knee-jerk reaction, that you couldn't quite prevent. We lay quiet under her touch.

Belle looked down at us, and it was hard to see through the glowing mask, but I think she frowned. She ran her fingertips down the side of Micah's face, and there was no reaction. She called to his beast, but his beast was well fed, sleepy, and content.

My voice came, hollow, as if I hadn't quite filled back up. "The leopards are mine, Belle."

"The leopard was my first animal to call Anita, and call them I shall."

I lay on the floor, feeling languorous, content. Micah rolled his face so his cheek rested on the soft pillow of my breasts. We watched her with lazy eyes, the way that only cats can. I should have been afraid, but I wasn't. The rush of power seemed to have taken all my fear along with it. I felt clear-headed and safe.

Belle poured that misty power on us, but though she raised

371

gooseflesh and brought sighs to our lips, there was no more. She could not call Micah as her beast, because he was mine. She could not call my beast, because I was Micah's. We truly were Nimir-Ra and Nimir-Raj, and together we were enough to keep her out of us.

She turned those gold-flame eyes to someone behind us, and I felt her reach out to one of the leopards. I'd known somehow it would be Nathaniel. If she'd tried it before Micah and I had merged, he would have come to her, but now it was too late. We'd shut that gate and barred it. Belle Morte could not touch our leopards, not tonight.

"This is not possible," she said, and her voice had lost some of its purring caress.

Jean-Claude answered her doubt. "You can call almost all the big cats, but you cannot call the cats that answer to the Master of Beasts."

"Padma sits upon the council, you are one of my children. That I cannot take what belongs to another council member is merely truth. That any of my children could keep me from possessing what is theirs is impossible."

"Perhaps," Jean-Claude said, and he got to his feet. He offered a hand to both Micah and me. Normally, I don't let people help me up, but tonight I was wearing a long skirt, high heels, and had just had what amounted to metaphysical sex in public. We took his hands together, and he pulled us to our feet. Damian still had a death grip on my other hand, but he stayed on his knees, eyes still only half-focused, as if the power rush had thrown him more than it had the rest of us. He was the only one of us who wasn't either a master or an alpha something. I drew him in to sit against my legs, but didn't try and make him stand; it didn't look like he was ready to yet.

"By American standards," Jean-Claude said, "this did not count as sex."

Belle laughed, and the sound still shivered across the skin, but it was distant. Either we were too numb, or too shielded for her to touch. "The Americans do not count this as sex, that is absurd!"

"Perhaps, but true nonetheless. You and I would consider it sex, would we not?"

"Oh, *oui*, sex enough for one of my entertainments."

I almost felt Jean-Claude smile. I didn't have to see it. "Do you truly believe we have not done this and more with Asher?"

She looked at him, and her anger lashed through the room again like a wind off the lakes of hell. "I will not be turned aside so easily." She gestured back at the two dead vampires. "You have no idea what your human servant has taken from me. They were not merely vampires."

"They were lycanthropes," I said.

She looked at me, and there was more interest than anger in her now. Belle had always been more interested in power than being petty, though if she could be both, well, that would be the best of all worlds.

"How do you know this?"

"I felt their beasts, and I felt the beast from Mommy Dearest earlier today."

"Mommy Dearest?" She managed to look puzzled underneath all that glittering power.

"The Sweet Dark," Jean-Claude said.

"I felt her stir in her sleep, Belle. The Mother of All Darkness is waking up, that's why her children, as you put it, finally came to someone's call."

"I called them," she said.

"You can call all of the great cats, and among other things, they are cats. I'll bet the Master of Beasts could call them, too, if he tried," I said.

I thought for a moment she was actually going to stamp her foot – or rather Musette's – at me. "They came to my call, no one else's."

"Doesn't it worry you that the children of the dark are rising? Doesn't that scare you?"

"I have worked long and hard to amass enough power to wake the children of the dark."

I shook my head. "You felt her today, Belle, how can you stand there and not understand that this isn't your power going to a new level, it's hers waking up."

Belle Morte shook her head. "*Non, ma petite*, you are seeking to deter me from my revenge. I never forget an insult, and I always make sure someone pays the price for it." She walked up to us, and that glowing edge of power swirled at my full skirts, but it didn't catch my breath this time. It was power, and it crawled across my skin like lines of insects marching, but it wasn't seductive, it wasn't special. We'd all had so much power poured through us that we just didn't have anything left for more fun and games tonight.

She ran her hand down Micah's chest, and I felt his body tighten, but it wasn't the effect she was used to. She touched Jean-Claude's face, and he let her.

"Marvelous, as always, Belle."

"No, not as always," she said. She turned to me, then.

I didn't want her to touch me, but I knew that I could let her do it now. She wasn't here in the flesh, not really, and it limited her power. Intellectually I knew that, the cold hard feeling in my stomach wasn't so certain. I made myself stand still while she put that glowing hand against my face. Her hand didn't exactly burn where it touched, but it was hot, and the power spread from it, marching down my body like hot water poured from my face down my skin. It made me shiver and want to pull away, but I could tolerate it. I didn't have to pull away. I didn't have to run.

She drew her hand back, and there was a lingering sense of power between her hand and my skin. She brushed it against her skirt, Musette's skirt. I wondered, was Musette still in there? Did she know what was happening? Or did she go away, only to come back when Belle was finished?

She turned last to Damian. He tucked himself in tight against me, like a dog that was afraid of being hurt, but he didn't run. Belle touched his face. He flinched, not wanting to meet her eyes, but as he knelt at my legs, and nothing worse happened to him than the feel of power over his skin, he looked up, slowly. There was something like wonderment in his eyes, and behind that, triumph.

Belle jerked her hand back as if it had been she who was burned. "Damian is of my line, but not of yours, Jean-Claude. It is not your power that he tastes of." She looked at me, and there was something on that beautiful, alien face that I couldn't understand. "Why does he taste of your power, Anita? Not you of his, but he of yours."

I wasn't sure truth would help here, but I knew a lie wouldn't. "Would you believe me if I said I'm not quite sure?"

374

"*Oui*, and *non*. You speak truth, but there is some evasion to it."

I swallowed and took a deep breath. I really didn't want Belle to know this part. I really didn't want it getting back to the council at large.

She looked at me, and her eyes went wide, and some of that glowing power began to seep away, sliding back into Musette's body, so that it was Musette with honey-brown eyes that met my gaze. "Somehow he is your servant. Our legends speak of this possibility. It is one of the reasons we once slew all necromancers on sight."

"Glad we've moved on from the good ol' days," I said.

"We have not, but when we thought you were Jean-Claude's human servant, then there was no harm, because your power was his." She shook her head and there was an afterimage of black hair over the blond, a dark ghost over all that bloodstained white. "Now I am not so certain. You taste of Jean-Claude's power, *oui*, but Damian tastes only of yours. And the leopards taste only of your power, also. No necromancer has ever had an animal to call." She shook her head. "Jean-Claude with his new human servant and her servants, has been able to keep me at bay. If I were here in flesh instead of spirit, this would not save you, I think."

"Of course, it would not," Jean-Claude said, "your beauty would overwhelm us."

"No false flattery, Jean-Claude, you know how much I hate it."

"I did not know it was false."

"I am not so certain that my beauty would overwhelm any of you. Somehow this one," and she motioned at me, "has cut me off from the leopards, and somehow, you have cut me off from the vampires that descend directly from you."

My pulse sped up a bit at that, because I hadn't even felt her trying to take over Meng Dei or Faust. They were standing as far from the show as they could, dressed in the bodyguard black leather. Though both were so small compared to the rest that they looked out of place. Meng Die looked scared, Faust didn't. Which could have meant anything and nothing.

"But not every vampire in this room is a direct descendant of yours, Jean-Claude. Because I am not here in flesh you may keep me from the flock that is yours, but not what was first mine."

375

I was afraid I knew what she meant, and hoped I didn't.

Belle Morte brushed past us, with a flare of power lost like a breeze against our skin. She was walking towards Asher. Because she had made him herself, and he was older than Jean-Claude. Asher owed nothing to Jean-Claude except the vows any vampire makes to his Master of the City, and love, perhaps love. I wasn't sure love was enough to save him from Belle Morte. I believed in love, but I believed in evil, too. Neither love nor evil conquers all, but evil cheats more.

# 47

THE WOLVES CHOSE that moment to come in through the far curtain. Their entrance stopped everything briefly because they doubled our bodyguards. I didn't need to see Belle's – or Musette's – face to know she didn't like it. It showed in the sudden stiffening of her shoulders, the slight clenching of her fists. I realized suddenly that I was seeing Musette begin to rise up through Belle like a fly caught in melting ice.

It was when I saw Jason in an outfit that was mostly dark blue straps, which covered about as much of his body as Nathaniel's outfit covered of his, that I realized that there had been no wolves present until now, except Stephen who had ridden with Micah from my house. I'd known that Richard was delayed, but I hadn't noticed that none of the wolves had been here. Usually, there were always some wolves here for Jean-Claude. Jason walked in smiling in his black over-the-knee boots, but there was something in his eyes, some small warning that I couldn't decipher. I'd expected to see him wearing makeup like Micah and Nathaniel, but he wasn't. None of the male wolves were.

Richard came into sight, easy to spot above the sea of black leather that was his pack. I knew that he had butchered his hair, but I hadn't really grasped how much until I saw him. I'm sure the hairstylist had done his or her best, but there was only so much they could do. They'd had to buzz his hair back to less than an inch of medium brown. It seemed darker this short, missing the gold and red highlights. He also looked remarkably like his older brother Aaron, and his father. The resemblance had always been strong, but now it was like they were clones.

He was wearing a black tux with a shirt of deep, rich blue and a matching bow tie. With the new haircut, and the more conservative clothes, he looked – out of place.

His eyes met mine, and the shock of how handsome he was still sent a thrill through me from head to toes. Without the hair to distract, you couldn't pretend that the cheekbones weren't knife-edge perfect, the dimple in his chin didn't soften the strong masculinity of his face. His shoulders were broad, his waist not slender, but small. Nothing about Richard was slender. He was built more like a football player than a dancer.

Jamil and Shang-Da, his Hati and Skoll, the Ulfric's personal bodyguards, flanked him. Jamil was wearing black leather straps for a shirt to complement almost ordinary leather pants and short boots. The bright red beads, worked into his cornrow braids, looked like drops of crimson blood against the darkness of his skin and the black of the leather. He met my eyes, and there was again that sense of warning that I'd gotten from Jason. Something was wrong, something beyond what was already happening, but what?

Shang-Da looked uncomfortable out of his usual suit, but black leather suited his tall frame the same way any kind of armor would have. Shang-Da was the tallest Chinese person I'd ever met. He was physically imposing by any standards. He was also a warrior, and protecting his Ulfric was all he did. He pretty much hated me, because so much of the pain I caused Richard was something he couldn't protect him against. Bodyguards can't do shit about emotional stress. He avoided my gaze.

Jason strutted towards me, making sure his body swayed seductively. He was by profession a stripper so he was pretty good at the seductive sway. His body language said sex, his eyes held a shadow of something else, and when he got to me, he slid an arm across my shoulders, pressing his body up against mine, but what he whispered in my ear wasn't sweet nothings, it was a warning.

"Richard has found his backbone, but he's decided to use it against Jean-Claude first." He smiled as he said it, his face full of the seductive promise that his walk had held. He ran his hands across the back of my neck, playing his fingertips in the hollow of my collarbone.

I whispered against the shell of his ear, "What does that mean?"

He turned my head towards his, so that my face was hidden from Richard and the pack. It looked like flirting. "Richard's going to try and take all his wolves away from Jean-Claude."

I was glad my face was facing only Jason, because I couldn't hide the shock. I fought to control my face, and Jason laughed at nothing that I'd said. He put a hand on either side of my face, giving me time to regain control of myself.

I whispered against his skin, "You too?"

He was still smiling, but he managed to let me see his eyes, his unhappy eyes. "Even me," he said, barely moving his lips and still smiling.

Shang-Da was suddenly beside us. He tried to grab Jason's arm, and Jason moved just out of reach. If you had been watching, you might not have realized what had happened at all.

A low growl trickled out of Shang-Da's human mouth, a sound that raised the hair on the back of my neck.

Jason growled back, and he was standing close enough that the growl whispered over my skin. It made me shudder, a shudder visible from a distance.

Richard said, "Shang-Da." One word, just his name, but the big man didn't try and grab Jason again. He lowered his head and spoke in a voice gone mostly to growl, "A man cannot serve two masters."

He was trying to be discreet, so he'd lowered his head over me, not Jason. I don't think he was worried that I'd take a chunk out of his face. I looked up into that face that was almost kissably close, and asked, "Your orders are to remind Jason who his pack leader is?"

His gaze slid from Jason, to me, and the look was equally unfriendly. "My Ulfric's orders are none of your business." He whispered it, because he was trying not to clue the bad guys into the division in the ranks. I realized in that moment that no matter how much Shang-Da hated me, he didn't entirely approve of what Richard was doing, not with enemies in town.

I caught movement out of the corner of my eye. Jean-Claude had gone to Richard, and they were speaking, low and earnest. Jean-Claude tried to get close enough to whisper as we were doing, but Richard moved back. He didn't want to be that close.

I glanced farther away to see Musette still standing close to Asher. But they were not alone; the wereleopards were ranged around him, not protecting him exactly, but making sure you had to

379

touch them before you touched Asher. Micah met my gaze, gave the tiniest nod. It said, clearly, I'll take care of it, 'til you're free. Micah didn't get distracted. Merle hovered over everything like an angry black leather mountain staring down at that petite figure in white. Musette stood there, looking very much herself, just herself.

Shang-Da was looking at Musette, too. It was almost as if he could smell where the danger lay. We turned back to meet each other's gaze at the same time. We were physically close enough to kiss, it should have been intimate, but it wasn't, it was almost frightening. Because we both understood each other, and that had never happened before.

I didn't argue that I was Bolverk for their clan, thus the Ulfric's orders *were* my business. Shang-Da disapproved that I was anything to them. I tried for logic. I leaned in close and whispered, "Whatever Richard is doing, tonight is not the night for it. We're in trouble here."

Something flicked through his eyes, and he dropped my gaze, but leaned in a fraction closer, so that his short black hair brushed the top of my curls. "I have spoken with him. He hears no one tonight." His eyes came up to meet mine, and there was something there I could read now. Pain. "Sylvie has already argued for this to wait until our enemies leave."

"I don't see her," I whispered, again leaning in closer, not thinking about it.

"She is not with us." He breathed it against my cheek.

I must have reacted, because he added, "She is not dead."

I moved back just enough to see his eyes, "He fought Sylvie."

"She fought him."

I widened eyes. "He won."

Shang-Da nodded.

"Is she hurt?"

He nodded again.

"Badly?"

"Bad enough," he said, and for the very first time I saw something that wasn't approval in his face. Tomorrow he would go back to hating me, but tonight was a dangerous night, and Shang-Da was too much the warrior not to see that, even if Richard couldn't.

"Jason must come with me," there was no outright pleading in

380

his voice, Shang-Da did not beg, but there was a softness there, room to compromise.

"For now," I said.

Jason had worked his way behind me, using me as shield against the bigger man. And being Jason, using the excuse to lean his nearly nude body against the back of my velvet and silk-clad one. He laid a gentle kiss on the back of my neck, and it made me shiver. "I can't go back to being just another pack member, I can't."

I knew what he meant, or thought I did. I answered without trying to make eye contact, as he kissed softly across the bare skin where neck met shoulders. Him playing with my neck was making it hard to concentrate. "only for tonight."

"What is it with you, Anita? Does everyone want to fuck you?" It was Richard. When he was really angry he could be more hateful than anyone I'd ever dated. The fact that he said the word *fuck* told me exactly how nasty he was going to be tonight. God, I didn't want to do this, shovel emotional shit while the big bad vampires munched on us.

I was close enough to see the look in Shang-Da's eyes; he didn't like what his Ulfric had said. I touched his face, which made him jump. I leaned in close enough that from Richard's point of view it probably looked like a kiss, but I whispered against Shang-Da's mouth, "Jason's yours tonight, but this can't be permanent."

Shang-Da stayed close, so that he breathed his answer on my lips, "We will discuss it."

He began to lean back and I caught the back of his head with my hand. "There will be no discussion."

His face went hard with his usual anger. He moved back forcefully enough that I either had to let him go, or take a handful of hair to keep him close to me. I let him go.

He held his hand out and said, "Your Ulfric wants you to stand with the wolves." His voice held only one emotion, and that dimly – anger.

Jason slid out from behind me, trailing his fingers across every piece of bare skin he could find, until he left me shuddering. Shang-Da led him away one hand on the smaller man's arm. Jason kept his gaze on me, like a child being carried away by scary strangers. But he wasn't really in immediate danger, and I couldn't say that about everybody in the room. Unfortunately.

"Maybe I should have made you Erato instead of Bolverk." Erato had been the muse of erotic poetry, among other duties. Now she was the title among most werewolves for the female that helps new little werewolves control their beast during sex. Eros, god of love and lust, was the male title. More first-time shape-shifters lost control and killed people during sex than during any other single event. The point of orgasm is to lose control, after all.

I looked across the room at Richard, met his angry brown eyes, and felt nothing. I wasn't angry. It was too ridiculous that he was fighting like this in front of Musette and her people. It was beyond ridiculous, it was foolish.

"We'll discuss this when our company goes back home, Richard," I said, and there was no anger in my voice. I sounded reasonable, ordinary.

Something crossed Richard's face, something that leaked through his tight shields. Rage. He was *so* angry. He'd turned that anger inward, and the depression had eaten him, to the point where he cut his hair. He'd pulled himself out of the depression, but he was still angry. If the anger couldn't go inward, then it had to go outward. Outward seemed to be directed at me. Great, just great.

"If you're Bolverk, then come and stand with your pack," his voice vibrated with the rage that he was having trouble containing.

I blinked at him for a second. "I'm sorry, what did you say?"

"If you are truly Bolverk for our clan, then you need to stand with us." He met my gaze, and there was no flinching in him now, no softness. I'd waited for him to stop flinching. I'd never dreamed it could mean this.

Jamil walked back across the room with Stephen held in his arms. Gregory was still clinging to Stephen's hand, so they moved as a unit. When Jamil was back with the wolves, Richard said, "Gregory is not one of us. He cannot stand with us."

I couldn't hear what Jamil said, but I think he was trying to persuade Richard that that wasn't necessary. Richard shook his head, then Jamil made a mistake. He looked back at me, and with his eyes alone asked for help. He'd done it before, many times, most of them had. Tonight, Richard saw it, understood it, and didn't tolerate it.

He grabbed Gregory's wrist and tried to jerk him away from Stephen. Stephen screamed and reared up in Jamil's arms, clinging with both hands to his brother's arm.

I'd had enough. I didn't care if Belle heard it all. I moved across the floor toward the pack. "Richard, you're being cruel."

He didn't stop trying to pull them apart. "I thought you wanted me cruel."

"I wanted you strong, not cruel." I was almost to them, and not sure what I was going to do when I got there.

"You're strong and you're cruel."

"Actually, I'm strong and pragmatic, not cruel." I was beside them now, and I knew I didn't dare touch anyone. If I touched Richard, or the twins, it would lead to more violence. I could feel it.

Stephen was making a high piteous noise like a baby rabbit being eaten alive. He was scrambling with his hands, trying to hold on to Gregory. Gregory was crying and trying to hold on to his brother.

"Pragmatic is saying that you're making us look weak in front of a council member. Cruel is saying that I'm Bolverk because you don't have the balls to be."

He stopped pulling on the twins, and Jamil took that one moment of hesitation to slide away. Of course, that left me facing Richard alone. And it was one of those moments when I realized how physically imposing he was. Richard was one of those big men who don't seem big, until suddenly, they do, and you go, oh, God, and it's usually too late.

We stood, glaring at each other. I hadn't been angry until he'd tried to hurt Stephen and Gregory. But once you get me angry I usually stay there. I enjoy my anger, it's the only hobby I have.

A dozen cruel remarks danced through my head, and I kept my mouth closed. I was afraid of what would fall out if I opened it. I walked forward, closing the remaining distance between us. I got to see something else in his eyes besides anger – panic. He didn't want me this close. Great.

I kept moving forward, and Richard actually moved back a step, then he seemed to realize what he'd done. When I took another step towards him, he stood his ground. I walked until the full skirt of my dress brushed his legs; the skirt swirled out and covered the toes of his polished shoes. I was close enough that it would have been more natural to touch each other than to simply stand there, as we did.

I looked up the length of his body and met his eyes with the knowledge in my eyes that I knew what was under that conservative suit, every inch of it.

Richard wasn't looking at my face when I looked up; he was staring at my décolletage. I took a deep breath, making the mounds of my breasts rise and fall as if a hand were pushing them from underneath.

He looked up from my chest, and met my eyes. The rage in his face was a nearly pure thing. An anger without purpose, without form. It was like one of those huge wildfires, that begins by eating the trees. Then somewhere along the way the fire takes on a life of its own, almost as if it doesn't need fuel anymore, it doesn't need anything to exist. It burns and grows and destroys, not because it needs fuel but because that's what it does, what it is.

I faced Richard's rage with my own. His was new and fresh, it hadn't had time to burn its way down to his soul, to hollow out a space that held nothing but the anger. Mine was old, almost as old as I could remember. If Richard wanted to fight, we could fight. If he wanted to fuck, we could fuck. At that moment either one would have been almost equally damaging. To both of us.

His beast rose to his anger like a dog to its owner's voice. Any strong emotion could bring on the change, and this was about as strong as emotions got for Richard.

The energy of his beast flared like heat off a road on a summer's day, a visible wave of power. It danced along the bare skin of my body. Once upon a time he'd brought me using nothing but his beast thrusting through my body. But tonight, we'd do other things. I doubted they'd be as fun.

Musette glided close to us in her blood-spattered white dress. Her eyes were blue again. She wove her hands through the energy of Richard's beast, playing between the two of us, not touching, literally playing with the energy. "Oh, you would be very good to eat, *très bon, très très bon*." She laughed, and it was the kind of laugh that would make you look twice in a bar, a laugh made to get attention. The sound didn't go with the blood drying like a mask on her face.

Richard let the rage fill his eyes and directed it at her. It was a look that I think would have backed up anyone else in the room. Musette laughed again.

Richard turned to face her. His anger really didn't care who the target was, anyone would do. "This is none of your concern. When we're done with pack business, then, and only then, we'll talk to the vampires."

Musette threw her head back and chortled, there was no other word for it. She laughed until tears leaked down her face, carving runnels in the drying blood. The laughter died slowly, and when she opened her eyes again, they were honey-brown.

Richard's breath caught in his throat. I was close enough to him to know that he stopped breathing, just for a moment.

The smell of roses was everywhere. "You remember me, wolf, I can feel it in your fear." That purring contralto shivered down my skin, and I saw Richard shudder, too. "I will play with you later, wolf, but for now," and she turned and looked at Asher, "for now I will play with him."

Asher was still pressed to the wall, doing that utter stillness that the old ones can do. He had sunk into the silence of eternity, trying to make this not happen, trying to hide in plain sight. It wasn't going to work.

As Musette's body glided towards him, Belle began to spill out of her. The dark gold gown overlaying the white like a ghost. The black hair spreading like phantom flames around her, moved by a wind that trickled through the room, the wind of Belle's power.

"What's happening?" Richard whispered, and I don't even know if he meant to have an answer, but I replied anyway.

"Musette is Belle Morte's surrogate."

His eyes were all for Belle's ghostly form overriding the other body, when he said, "What does that mean, exactly?"

"It means we are in a shit load of trouble."

He looked at me then. "I am Ulfric, Anita, that doesn't change just because some high-ranking vampire comes to town."

"Be Ulfric, Richard, great, knock yourself out, but don't destroy us all while you do it."

385

Some of the anger had leaked away on the tide of fear. It was impossible to be up close and personal with Belle's power and not fear it.

"I am either Ulfric, or I'm not, Anita. I am either master or slave, I can't be both."

I raised eyebrows at him. "Yeah, actually, you can." I held up a hand. "I don't have time for this tonight, Richard. Tomorrow if we're all still alive, then we can discuss it, okay?"

He frowned. "She's not here in flesh, Anita, it's only metaphysical games. How bad could it be?"

I realized in that moment that Richard was still living in that other world. The world where people played fair and horrible things never really happened. It must have been a peaceful place to live, the planet that people like Richard called home. I'd always admired the view, but I'd never lived there. The trouble was that Richard didn't live there either.

The first scream cut through the silence. The wereleopards had all backed away, crouching at Belle Morte's feet. Only Micah stayed standing. He'd put himself in front of Asher, but he was small like me, and he couldn't hide Asher completely.

I looked at Richard, and he had a look of such hurt in his eyes. He was never going to wake up and smell the blood. He wasn't going to truly change.

I turned away from him and started walking towards Asher and Micah. Jean-Claude moved up beside me, offered me his hand, and I took it. No one else moved with us. The wererats couldn't attack Musette. The wereleopards were doing their best, but it wasn't going to be enough. Only the wolves could have helped us, and Richard wouldn't let them.

In that moment I wondered how long it would be before I started hating Richard.

# 48

I COULDN'T FIGURE out why Asher was screaming. There was no blood, no rending of flesh, but he screamed all the same. Then as we got closer I watched the flesh of his face begin to seep away. It was as if his skin collapsed around the bones of his skull, as if Belle's touch were draining him dry, not of blood, but of *everything*.

I risked a glance at Jean-Claude, and he looked stricken, a second before his face showed nothing. I felt him pull away into that emptiness where he hid. "She could drain him to death this way." His voice was remarkably empty.

"But you're immune to it, right? She didn't make you."

"She is our *sourdre de sang*, none of us are immune to her touch."

I stopped and pushed him back. "Then you stay. I don't need two of you to worry about."

He didn't argue, but his gaze went past me to Asher. I wasn't sure he'd even heard me, and there wasn't time to check. I was half-running, when Micah pushed Belle back, pushed her back, using his whole body, broke her touch on Asher's face.

Asher collapsed slowly down the wall, and Belle's glowing face kissed Micah. The moment their lips touched, I felt the *ardeur* fill the room like hot water, spilled in stinging drops across my skin. It froze me in mid-step, made me stumble. I stood there, caught between Asher against the wall and Micah lost in that glowing embrace. I knew that I could have drained Micah to death with the *ardeur* over a matter of days, but part of me knew that Belle could do it faster.

Asher's hand reached out to me, skeletal thin, like sticks in paper. Micah was trying to push himself back from Musette/Belle's body, but she rode him, arms at his back, glowing crimson lips like

387

a red fog across his face. I had a moment of feeling Asher dying, fading, for lack of a better word. Jean-Claude went to him, but I knew that Jean-Claude had no life to share. Then the cross taped to my chest blazed to life.

It burned against my flesh as if the black tape held all the heat in. I half-screamed as I ripped the tape away and the cross spilled out into the light, white, hot, like a captive star on a chain.

Micah stumbled back from Belle Morte. Jean-Claude spilled the black velvet coat over himself and Asher. The other vampires hid their faces and hissed at the light. I saw movement from the corner of my eye, a second before Angelito slammed into me. There was no one to stop him now. The cross was a two-edged sword.

He grabbed me in one arm, completely off the ground, the other hand wrapping around the cross. I poked him in the throat with three fingers, stiffened to a spear point. He gagged and dropped me, but he held on to the cross, and as I fell, the chain broke, cutting into my neck as it came away. The moment the cross was his, the glow began to fade.

Musette's body turned to me, but her eyes were pools of dark gold fire, and it wasn't a ghostly image superimposed over her body this time, it was as if I were seeing double. My eyes saw Musette with the wrong color of eyes. But inside my head it was Belle. Belle in the flesh, a little taller than Musette, long black hair falling to her knees in waves, the dark gold of her dressing gown showing a triangle of white flesh, her face like something sculpted from a pearl, her lips a perfect red pout. She wrapped white hands around my arms, long dark nails, playing along the velvet of the sleeves. She pressed me against her body and leaned in to lay a kiss with that mouth upon mine.

A small voice in my head screamed, "Don't let her touch you." But I couldn't move, couldn't get away, wasn't sure I wanted to get away.

That red, red mouth hovered over mine. Her breath pushed against my lips. The world smelled of roses. Then, suddenly, I could taste Asher's kiss upon my lips. Tasted it as if I had kissed him but a second before. That one taste opened my eyes, helped me draw back from Belle's mouth. Helped me want to draw back.

Her eyes stared down at me, pools of golden fire like brown

water in sunlight. I realized that I had swooned, and she held me as if she'd dipped me in a dance. Her hand was behind my head, raising me up to meet her kiss.

I felt movement and rolled my eyes back to see Richard. Belle saw him, too. "Interfere, and I will raise the *ardeur* in you again, wolf. You brought no women with you. Did you think that would save you? It won't. The *ardeur* only wants to be fed, wolf, it doesn't care how."

Richard hesitated. I could taste his fear in my mouth, but underneath that was still the taste of Asher's kiss.

Jean-Claude was suddenly beside Belle. "It is me you want." He spread his arms in a wide dramatic gesture that spread the darkness of his coat, spilled his hair around him. "I am here."

I don't know what would have happened, or what she would have said, because the next thing that overwhelmed me was the memory of Asher's lovemaking. It came on me like it had once with Jason, but this was more, worse, better. It bowed my back, convulsed me in Belle's arms, surprised a scream from me, made my hands scratch at the air, and at Belle's face. She dropped me then, and I saw, dimly, as if through a white window, her hands grab Jean-Claude.

Richard caught me before I hit the ground, cradled me in his arms. He looked so worried. His hand touched my face. "Anita, are you hurt?"

I managed to shake my head, but even with Richard this close, his face soft and worried about me, I turned my head to look towards Asher. I couldn't help myself. Asher's hair was like golden Christmas tree tinsel, lifeless, hanging around a face that was more skull than flesh. His lips were a thin hard line around teeth that were mostly fangs. Only his eyes were still Asher, pools of pale blue fire, as if a winter sky could burn.

The moment I saw his eyes, I tried to crawl out of Richard's arms, tried to crawl to Asher.

"Anita, Anita, what's wrong?" He held me, turned me to look at him.

I found my voice, but all I could say was, "Asher."

He glanced at the fallen vampire, and the disgust was plain on his face. "I know, Anita, I'm sorry."

389

I wasn't sure what he was apologizing about, and I didn't care. There was something else I should have been more worried about, something I'd forgotten. But I couldn't think of anything except Asher's eyes and that I had to go to him. Had to.

Richard stood up, suddenly, with me still in his arms. I heard scrabbling as if of a thousand tiny claws. Rats, thousands of rats, flowed in a furry, squeaking wave across the floor of the cave.

Asher's power receded, and I knew it had cost him dear to let me go. Knew in that instant that I was the only one who could feed him enough energy to keep him alive.

Richard made a small sound of dismay and turned so that I could see what had paled him. The two vampires that had had the tops of their heads blown off were slowly rising to their feet. They were healed. Those strange cat-eyed faces were whole. There wasn't even a scar to mark where the bullets had struck.

"Fuck," I said.

One of the werehyena's nerve broke, and he fired into the squirming mass of rats. The next sound was a second gunshot, and he fell with a hole in his back, fell into the mob of rats. They boiled over him, and his body vanished from sight. The sounds, though, nothing masked the sounds. I hadn't been close enough to the gunshots to be deafened, and for the first time I was sorry about that. The sound of tiny teeth tearing flesh, squeaking voices squabbling over what used to be a man, seemed to drown us all.

One of the wererats was staring at the gun in his hand as if it had suddenly appeared. He turned a white face back towards us. I think he mouthed, "I'm sorry," before Bobby Lee's scream, "Guns down, guns fucking down, now. No one fire." He threw his own gun spinning across the room, and the other wererats followed suit.

Some of the werehyenas lowered their guns, but only one threw his away. Bobby Lee went to his knees and clasped his hands on top of his head. Claudia did it next, then one by one all the wererats followed. I knew why, they were afraid Musette/Belle would use them against us. But I wouldn't have wanted to be kneeling on the floor when the rats found me.

I finally could think enough to remember that Jean-Claude might be fighting for his life. But he wasn't. Belle held his beautiful face in her hands, but he was still standing. His own hands cupped hers, pressing her hands against his face. His face was still perfect, untouched. A soft smile played along his lips. It was Belle's eyes that were wide, her face that was unhappy. He couldn't eat her as she had Asher, but strangely, she seemed to be having trouble eating him.

I knew that Belle/Musette had called the rats. I didn't think she'd had a thing to do with the recuperative powers of the two children of the night. They were half crouched, one helping the other to stand, but they weren't looking at Belle, or anyone else. I had a moment to wonder if they were going to hold a grudge, when the wave of rats jumped on the first werehyena, tiny teeth trying to tear through the black leather. People were screaming, and the werehyenas began to fire into the small rats, blasting their bodies into red ruin. But there were so many of them.

The rats parted around the kneeling wererats like they were big rocks in a stream.

"Can you stand?" Richard asked.

"I think so."

He lowered me gently to the floor, then he glanced at the werewolves who were still standing in an unhappy group. Apparently Richard's point to Sylvie had been violent enough that none of them had disobeyed. Well, Jason was struggling in a joint lock that Shang-Da had on his arm, but no one else had tried to help. What the hell had Richard done to Sylvie?

The world suddenly smelled like the musk of wolf fur, the damp richness of leaf mold, the Christmas tree scent of evergreen, as if my furred shoulder had just brushed it with dew still on it, on a calm, still morning. I felt that piece of me that was Richard's beast pour up through my body and ease across my skin like wind.

Richard looked at me with amber wolf eyes. He'd opened the marks between us, opened them wide. He threw back his head and howled, and a dozen throats answered him, then the werewolves moved forward like a black wave of destruction.

Shang-Da and Jamil stayed at Richard's back, and they showed claws where fingernails should have been, the half-change of the very alpha. For the rest, I felt them slip their skin, felt the rush of energy like small tugging explosions in my gut.

391

I could feel now that Jean-Claude had shut his end of our triumvirate down as tight as he could. I could look at him, but for once I couldn't feel him at all. He'd expected to die, and he hadn't wanted to take us with him.

I found one of the guns that the wererats had discarded and felt instantly better. The weight of it in my hand was a very good thing.

Unfortunately, I wasn't the only human servant that had found a gun. Angelito fired at a werehyena, sending him spinning round, falling into the mass of biting rats. He screamed and writhed, trying to beat them off him.

I shot into the rats close to him, but there were too many. It was like trying to shoot water, you moved it, but didn't hurt it.

I knew one way to stop the rats. I sighted down the barrel at Musette/Belle's head. If I killed her, the rats would go back to wherever they came from.

I let out my breath, stilled myself for a shot that was far too close to Jean-Claude for my comfort. A rat jumped on my hand, dug its teeth into me. The wave of them began to jump on my dress, their claws catching in the heavy fabric. I screamed, and suddenly Micah was there, half-crouched, hissing at the rats. Those on the floor scattered, squealing in terror. The ones already on my body seemed immune to the fear. He helped me pick them off and threw them into the scurrying mass. The rats poured over their injured comrades and ate them, too.

The rats seemed more afraid of the wereleopards than of the wolves, and the wereleopards began to spread out from the wall, hissing, sending the small rodents back, gaining an ever-widening space.

The two vampires that I thought I'd killed had grown claws and fangs that no vampire ever had. They were wading through the werewolves in a spray of blood and white bone.

One great hand was raised at Shang-Da's back, and without thinking I fired, able to aim because I stood in the circle the leopards had made. The vampire's head exploded again. I knew now that if we wanted him to stay dead, we needed to take his heart and burn it all. Scattering the ashes over different bodies of running water wouldn't have hurt either.

Shang-Da had time for the barest of glances my way, then the

392

other vampire launched himself and sent all three of them to the floor for the rats to engulf.

Belle's voice rose over the noise like a storm, a thunderclap that froze all of us in mid-action. Even the furred sea of rats froze. "Enough!"

She stepped back from Jean-Claude, and he began to laugh. It wasn't his magical laugh that slithered across the skin and made you think of sex, it was just laughter, pure unadulterated joy.

"We will fight no more," Belle said, and though her voice was still deep, it had lost its sexy purr. She sounded not angry, but put out, as if she'd gotten badly surprised.

The rats pulled back like a furry ocean draining away. They squeaked and squealed, but they left. Most of the werewolves were covered in tiny crimson bite marks. The remains of the fallen were-hyena looked like it had been mauled by something much bigger.

Jean-Claude found his voice, and it was as joyous as his laughter had been. "You cannot feed from me. You cannot take back what you gave me, because I am no longer of your line. I am *sourdre de sang* of my own line now."

Belle stared at him, her face that blank emptiness that I knew so well. She was hiding how she really felt. "I know what it means, Jean-Claude."

"You can no longer treat me as a lesser member of your line, Belle. There are different niceties to be observed between two *sourdres de sang*."

She smoothed her hands down her full skirt, and I knew that gesture, it was one of Jean-Claude's. Nervous, Belle Morte was nervous. "I was within my rights to do as I have done, for I did not know, nor did you."

"True enough, but now that we do know, you must take all your people and go. Leave our lands tonight, for if you are found in our territory come tomorrow night, your lives will be forfeit."

"You would not truly kill my Musette?" But her voice held the lightest thread of uncertainty.

"To be able to kill Musette, legally, with no political repercussions." He made a small tut-tut sound. "That has been the fondest wish of many a Master Vampire, and I will do it, Belle. You can taste the truth of my words."

She stiffened, just a little. "I will retain control of Musette until we are out of your lands. She has an unfortunate temper at times."

"It would be a bad thing if she lost her temper here in St. Louis," Jean-Claude said, and his voice was empty, the joy seeping away.

Cherry appeared at my elbow. "Sorry to interrupt, I'm not an expert on vampires, but I think Asher's dying."

# 49

ASHER LAY AGAINST the far wall. He was a skeleton with dried parchment skin. He lay on a bed of golden Christmas tree tinsel, the glorious remnant of his hair. His clothes had collapsed around his sunken body, like a deflated balloon. His eyes were closed, and only the roundness of his eyes underneath that thin skin was flesh and solid. Everything else seemed to have withered away.

I fell to my knees beside him, because suddenly I couldn't stand.

"He's not dead," Valentina's child voice came, but she stayed out of reach. She offered comfort, but she wasn't stupid.

I looked down at what was left of all that beauty and didn't believe her.

"See with something other than your eyes, *ma petite*," Jean-Claude said. He didn't kneel, but stayed standing, facing Belle Morte, almost as if he didn't dare turn his back on her.

I did what Jean-Claude told me to do; I looked with power instead of my physical eyes. I could feel a spark inside Asher, some small part of him still burned. He wasn't dead, but he might as well have been. I looked up at Jean-Claude. "He's too weak to take blood."

"And he has no human servant," Belle Morte said, "no animal to call. He is without," and she paused, seemed to think upon her next word. Finally, she said, "Resources."

*Resources,* that was a nice word for it. But whatever word you used, she was right. Asher had nothing to feed on but blood, and if he was too weak to feed on that . . . I couldn't finish the thought even in my head.

"Belle Morte could save him," Jean-Claude's voice was neutral, empty. I looked up at him, then past him to her. "What do you mean?"

"She made him, and she is a *sourdre de sang*. She could simply give him back some of the energy that she stole from him."

"I stole nothing," Belle said, and her own neutral voice held a hint of anger. "You cannot steal what is yours by right, and Asher is mine, all of him, Jean-Claude, every piece of his skin, every drop of his blood. He lives only through my sufferance, and without that he dies."

Jean-Claude made a small gesture. "Perhaps *stole* is not the correct term, but you can restore some of his life energy. You could bring him back enough to be able to feed on blood."

"I could, but I will not." Her anger was like a scalding wind, biting along my skin where it touched.

"Why not?" I asked it, because no one else seemed willing to, and I had to know.

"I do not have to explain myself to you, Anita."

I still had the gun in my hand. Suddenly it was heavy, as if it had reminded me it was there, or maybe the shock of lifting it was enough for me to feel again. I stood up and aimed the gun at Musette's chest. "If Asher dies, so does Musette."

"You have not had much luck killing vampires with your little gun," Belle said, and she sounded confident. Of course it wasn't her body that I was about to riddle with bullets.

"I think the Mother's children are special cases. They probably can survive pretty much everything but fire. I don't think that's true of Musette." I had let out the breath in my body, so that I was as still as I could get. My free hand was resting at my lower back, half cradled on my buttocks. It was my favorite position for target shooting.

"Angelito will stop you," she said simply.

I looked back to find Angelito held on his knees by three werewolves, but hey . . . "If he makes a nuisance of himself he can die, too. He probably won't survive me killing Musette anyway."

Belle Morte's brown eyes widened just a bit. "You would not dare."

"Sure I would," and I smiled, but it didn't reach my eyes, because I had them on Musette's body. I was ignoring Belle's shape over Musette, concentrating on seeing that white dress with its dried blood. The more I concentrated, the more of Musette I could see, like a double image, Musette's chest in my physical eyes, and Belle's ghostly overlay in my head. It made me wonder how much of Belle everyone else had been seeing, or if I'd had a better show because of my necromancy. I'd ask someone later. Much later.

"Jean-Claude, you cannot allow this."

"*Ma petite* has her moments of rashness, but in this moment she has reminded me that the rules are not the same now. I am within my rights as *sourdre de sang* to punish one of your people for harming my second in command. It is perfectly within our laws."

"I did not know that Asher was the second in command to a *sourdre de sang* when I drank from him."

My arm was still steady, but it wouldn't last. You can't hold a one-armed shooting stance forever. Hell, you can't hold any shooting stance forever. "You know now," I said, "and he's not dead yet, so you're killing the second in command of another *sourdre de sang* with foreknowledge."

"We are within our rights to take Musette's life in payment for Asher's," Jean-Claude said. "You should be more careful, Belle. Sending people you value far away from you makes it so much harder to keep them safe."

I was fighting for my arm not to tremble. Eventually, I'd lose. "Let me make this easy for you, Belle, help Asher now, or I kill Musette."

The one thing that was the same in both the vision of my eyes and the vision of my head, was those honey-brown eyes. Those eyes looked at me, and I felt the draw in them. She wanted me to lower my gun, and my arm hurt, so why didn't I? My arm started to lower, and I caught myself a moment before Jean-Claude touched my shoulder.

I put the arm back where I'd had it. But just lowering and raising it had helped the lactic acid build up. I could hold the stance for much longer now.

"If you wish to play games with Musette's life, that is up to you," Jean-Claude said, and his voice danced over my skin, made my body shiver, made my hand convulse, and only practice kept my finger from squeezing the trigger. But I didn't tell him to stop, because Belle had used her mark on me to cloud my mind. It had been a long time since a vampire had gotten to me so casually.

Jean-Claude's sex ran over my skin while the fear ran like ice through the rest of me. Belle wasn't defeated, not even close. Arrogance would get more of us killed. So, no arrogance, just truth. "What you have to ask yourself, Belle," I said, in a voice that was very quiet because I was concentrating on my breathing, trying to be still, for when I fired, "is, is your love for Musette stronger than your hatred for Asher?"

"You do not hate lesser beings, Anita, you merely punish them." Her voice sounded so sure of itself.

Jean-Claude said one word, "Liar."

Those dark honey eyes flicked to him, and there was no love lost in that look. She hated Jean-Claude, too. She hated them both. They had told me why. They were the only two men who had ever left her bed voluntarily, as far as she saw it. They had deserted her, and no one leaves Belle Morte, because no one would want to. Strangely, their leaving had damaged her sense of self. But I didn't share this knowledge because hurting Belle Morte's pride wouldn't help us. To salvage her pride she'd let Asher and Musette die. I was almost sure of it. I swallowed the words, and fought to control my face, but I'd forgotten that she was a *sourdre de sang*, and she'd marked me once. It wasn't my face I had to worry about.

Her voice came in my head like a dream, riding on the scent of roses, "My pride is not so fragile a thing, Anita."

Jean-Claude's kiss on my cheek chased back the scent of roses, and that purring voice. "*Ma petite, ma petite*, are you well?"

I nodded. "Prove it," I said, "heal Asher."

Jean-Claude didn't ask to whom I was speaking. He'd heard through me, or he guessed, or he didn't bother to question, because we were running out of time.

"You will talk him to death," Valentina said.

Everyone but me looked at the child vampire. I was still fighting to keep a target on Musette's white-clad chest.

"If you do not give him the kiss of life soon, he will be beyond even your powers, Belle Morte," Valentina said.

Belle fought to keep her face calm, but the anger leaked through the room. Or maybe I was just more sensitive to it. "Have you changed sides, *petite morte*?"

"*Non*, but I do not wish to lose Musette by accident. If you choose Asher's death, that is one thing. To simply miss the chance to save him, another."

I wanted badly to turn and look at Valentina, but I kept my gaze on Musette, on Belle. Besides, Valentina's face would have been like all the old ones when they were hiding themselves, or risking themselves, blank, empty, a lovely mask.

Something passed between them. Something I could not read. Belle took a deep, impatient breath, smoothed her skirts, and began to walk forward. It wasn't quite the graceful glide that Musette's body normally had. I wondered if vampires had trouble gliding when they were nervous, because Belle was nervous. I could feel it.

I lowered the gun, as she moved, because if she was going to save Asher, Musette lived. That was the deal. Besides, my shoulder and hand were beginning to ache. If I'd known I was going to have to keep the stance so long, I'd have gone for a two-handed stance.

Belle Morte seemed to collect herself as she moved across the room, so that by the time she reached Asher she was gliding, and Musette's white dress was completely lost to Belle's dark gold, at least to my eyes.

She knelt by Asher's body. I couldn't think of it as anything else but a body. I was already distancing myself from him. I realized with something like shock that I didn't believe she'd save him. He felt so dead, so very dead.

Jean-Claude's hands squeezed my shoulders, and I realized that he was shielding from me, hard. He didn't want to share his feelings right now, and I didn't blame him. They were too personal for sharing, too frightening.

Richard was gone, too. I actually had to glance at him to make sure he was still in the room, that's how tight he was shielding. I wasn't sure when he went away behind his shields, which seemed strange. I should have noticed. He caught my look, and he couldn't keep the compassion, or the pain, off his face. I don't think it was pain for Asher.

Jean-Claude's hands tensed and the movement brought my attention back to Belle. Her hair fell out around her like a black

399

cloak, so that the gold dress showed only in hints through all that blackness.

I felt Jean-Claude gather himself, like it was a physical effort to gather his will, then he sighed, and he shook himself like a bird settling its feathers. He stepped out from behind me and offered me his arm, very formally. I hesitated for a heartbeat, then slid my arm through his. He was still shielding from me, still hiding his emotions, but I didn't need to be anything but his friend to know what he was thinking. It hurt his heart to see Asher reduced to this. It hurt me, and I didn't have centuries of history with the man.

He walked us forward, toward the kneeling vampire and what was left of the person that we both loved. I would never know if my love for Asher was because of Jean-Claude's feelings for him. It probably was, but I couldn't separate my feelings from Jean-Claude's. That should have panicked me, but it didn't. I was tired of being scared all the time. I was ready to try and be as brave with my heart as I usually was with the rest of me. Besides, I'd been careful with Richard, and in the end we'd broken each other's hearts. I glanced at him as I walked forward on Jean-Claude's arm. My heart still tugged at the sight of him. Earlier today I'd been ready for a reconciliation. I was always ready for a reconciliation with Richard, any time he gave an inch. The trouble was, he kept taking back that inch.

He caught me looking at him, and there was something in his eyes, a pain, a loss, as deep as the ocean, as wide as the sea. I loved him. I really loved him. Maybe I always would. I had this horrible urge to run to him, to let him sweep me up in his arms, to chase that hurt from his eyes. But he probably wouldn't sweep me up in his arms. He'd probably just look at me, uncomprehending. And that would make me hate him. I didn't want to hate Richard.

I turned away from him. I didn't want him to see the longing, the loss, or the first stirrings of hate on my face.

I felt Richard beside me, before he touched me. I had a moment of surprise while I gazed up into his face. His face was as close to unreadable as he could get. He didn't sweep me up into his arms, but he did offer me his arm. I hesitated, as I had with Jean-Claude, then slowly, I slid my arm through his. He pressed his hand over mine, so warm, so solid, pressing me against the solid weight of his muscular forearm.

I lowered my eyes so he wouldn't see how it affected me. We were all shielding like a son of a bitch, trying to stay safe in our own thoughts.

Richard and Jean-Claude exchanged a look over my head. I don't know what the look was supposed to mean. It should have seemed silly to be exchanging any looks when all we had to do was open the marks that made us a triumvirate. Then we could have nearly read each other's minds. But this was the first time in months that Richard was at our side. I think all three of us were being as careful as we knew how to be.

# 50

BELLE KNELT OVER Asher, her head lowered as if she were kissing him. But she held herself off his body, one hand on the floor, the other against the wall. The kiss looked so intimate, but she went to great pains to not touch him more than she had to. An intimate act ruined.

I should have been able to feel the power she was pushing into him, but I was shielding too tight. I wasn't good enough at shielding to filter out, and in, what I chose. When I shielded this hard, I shielded everything out. I wanted to feel what she was doing. I wanted to sense whether that faint spark inside Asher was growing.

I opened just a touch, like widening the shutter on a camera, only a little opening, only enough to reach out and touch that spark.

I tasted Asher's kiss upon my mouth, as if I had drunk a wine that tasted of him. The spark had become a flame, a cold flame that filled his body, and still Belle poured energy into him. Asher screamed through my mind, and that silent scream staggered me, would have knocked me to my knees if Richard and Jean-Claude hadn't caught me.

"Anita, what's wrong?" Richard asked.

"*Ma petite*, are you well?"

There was no time to explain. I pulled free of both of them, and they didn't fight me. I grabbed Belle by the shoulder and the hair, and it was almost shocking to feel Musette's careful curls crush under my hand as I jerked her back. I was expecting to feel Belle's waves under my hand, but Belle wasn't here, not really. She'd never been here. She was not illusion, but not exactly real either.

I flung her away from Asher, sending her sliding across the floor on the slick white cloth of Musette's dress. But it was Belle's

402

voice that thundered through the room, "How dare you lay hands on me."

"You're trying to bind him to you again, as of old. He doesn't want to be bound."

"He will fade and die without the power that I can breathe into him." She looked around as if she expected someone to help her to her feet. The only people who would have been willing to help were under guard, and no one else made a move. She finally stood on her own, but with nothing near to grab onto, and an old-fashioned corset on, graceful it was not. Good to know that some fashions even a vampire can't make work.

Belle turned eyes that glittered with brown fire to me. "Asher will die without me. Look at him, see what is left of him, it is not enough to survive."

Her power had poured some flesh in under that dry skin, but not much. It was as if I could see the individual muscles and ligaments under the skin, like a physiology diagram, to show where all the attachment points are. But it was not like a person. The hair was still a dry nest of golden tinsel, and the skin like faded parchment stretched over an obscenely thin frame. But the eyes, the eyes looked human, except for that extraordinary ice blue color. Even when he'd been human, his eyes could never have looked anything but extraordinary.

Asher was there in those eyes. He was trapped in that fragile, half-dead shell. He gazed up at me, and I felt the weight of everything he was in his eyes.

"Blood may save his life," Belle said, "but it will not give him back what he has lost. Only his maker, or the one who has taken his essence, can give it back." She stood there with her shining darkness coming out of the eyes in Musette's face. She didn't add that since she was both Asher's maker and the one who had stolen his essence, only she could return him to his former glory. Belle Morte had a little too much class to point out the obvious. But it hung unsaid in the air.

"He just needs power," I said, "it doesn't have to be yours."

"If he had a human servant, or an animal to call, but he has nothing," Belle said, and there was a tone of satisfaction in her voice that she couldn't, or didn't try to, hide. "He is alone, and binding

403

himself to me again is the only choice he has, unless you wish him to spend the rest of eternity as he is now." The note of satisfaction slid into cruelty without blinking an eye.

"You can't leave him like this," Richard said, and there was pity on his face, yes, but more, there was horror. "Being tied to Belle Morte isn't worse than this."

"If you had ever known her embrace," Jean-Claude said, "you might not be so quick to decide."

Richard looked at him, then back at Asher, then at Belle Morte. "I don't understand."

"No," I said, "you don't." Then I looked up at him, touched his arm, very lightly. "Think of yourself trapped forever with Raina."

A look of disgust and personal revulsion skipped across his face, before he could hide it. I still carried a piece of Raina's munin, her spirit memory, in me. She was a sexual sadist, but she'd also fiercely protected the very people she tortured. The woman had needed some serious therapy. In the end, the only therapy she'd gotten had been silver bullets. I never felt bad about killing Raina. Funny that.

Richard nodded. "I understand that, but . . ." he made a helpless gesture towards Asher, "this is not . . ." He seemed at a loss for words.

I couldn't blame him. I had no words at the thought of this being Asher's fate for the next few centuries. It wasn't bearable. It simply wasn't. But I couldn't make Belle give him the energy without strings attached. It was the nature of vampire energy that there was always strings attached. It was designed to bind a vampire to its maker, and through its maker, to the council, to the entire power structure of their world. Everything would fall apart if you didn't belong to somebody. There are masterless shape-shifters, but no masterless vampires. There are vampires who have lost their masters, but they are compelled to find a new master, to swear new blood oaths, to hunt someone else to rule them. A truly lesser vampire can even die without a master vampire to rule them. They go to sleep at dawn and never wake up again.

I knew all this. Knew all of it, and didn't care. I could feel Asher's – not thoughts – but will. He preferred a clean death to this. Or to being Belle's slave again.

I dropped to my knees beside him. I could give him a clean death. I knew all about death. I started to touch him, my hand hesitated. I didn't want to touch him. Didn't want to feel that once-living skin turned to this. Didn't want my last memory of him to be this. But I hate cowardice, almost worse than anything else, and if Asher could be trapped inside this body, then I could touch him one last time.

I laid my hand against his face, gently, oh, so gently. The skin felt thin as paper, dried, and brittle. I was afraid if I pushed, my fingers would go through his skin like the pages of an ancient book handled too roughly.

I'd forgotten that all vampire powers are stronger with touch. One second I was holding his face as delicately as I could, the next moment I had collapsed across his body, and was writhing with the memory of Asher's body on mine.

Hands grabbed me back, ripped me away from Asher, and I fought those hands, drove my elbow back into a groin. The hands didn't let go, but dimly I heard someone yelling my name, "Anita, Anita, Anita," over and over.

I blinked, and it was like waking, but I knew my eyes hadn't been closed. Richard's hands were still on me, but he was standing like something hurt.

I opened my mouth to apologize, but what came out wasn't an apology. "Why did you stop us?"

"I thought you were going to crush him."

Staring up into his so sincere face, I knew he meant it. Hadn't I just moments before been afraid I'd shove a finger through Asher's brittle skin? But somehow I knew that wasn't going to happen. Somehow I knew he was a lot more durable than he appeared.

Jean-Claude came to stand beside me, and the look on his face said that he'd figured out what Richard hadn't. But Richard wasn't good with the dead. It wasn't his area of specialty. Jean-Claude touched my face, gently, as if afraid I'd break. "He fed from you. From your memory of him."

I nodded. "Yes."

"How many vampires can you serve?" Belle asked. Apparently, Jean-Claude hadn't been the only one to notice.

I realized that she thought Asher had marked me, but that wasn't exactly it. "He hasn't marked me, Belle, if that's what you think."

"Then how can he feed from your strength?"

"Surprise," I said, "I don't think that Jean-Claude is the only vampire who's gained new power."

"This is not possible."

"But it's true," I said, and I didn't try and keep the triumph out of my voice. We didn't need her now. We didn't fucking need her now.

Richard was still holding my arms. I looked up at him. "Let me go, Richard."

He frowned down at me. He either didn't understand, or didn't want to.

I repeated myself, more gently. "Let go, Richard, please."

His eyes flicked to Asher lying against the wall, still looking mostly dead. "The last time we talked about this, you had the same rule I had. No one feeds off of you."

I searched his face, while he gazed at what was left of Asher's beauty. I tried to see something in that gaze that I could talk to, explain things to, but I wasn't sure there was anyone there that would understand.

"If I don't let him feed, Richard, he'll be trapped like he is right now. He won't die. He won't decay. He'll just exist, like that."

He tore his gaze away from Asher and looked at me. "He didn't take blood."

"It's more like an energy feed, like the *ardeur*." It suddenly occurred to me that Richard might not know that Asher really, truly was in my bed. I'd pretended in the past with more than one man that he was a boyfriend or lover to fool the bad guys. Richard might believe that it was just a game again. Now wasn't the time to explain all the gory details. There would be time later to find out if Richard had meant what he said in my mind in the Jeep, that he didn't care who I had sex with, because we weren't dating. If he meant it, it would upset me. If he hadn't meant it, then knowing about Asher would upset him. Either way, it could wait.

He still hadn't let go of my arms. "Have you let Asher feed on you before?"

I don't know what I would have answered because he let go of one of my arms. He reached up a slow hand to touch my chin. I knew what he was going to do, and I couldn't stop it. He turned my head to one side, and exposed the vampire bites on the side of my neck.

"When did you start sharing blood?"

"Last night."

He lowered his hand, and I turned to meet his eyes. One look was enough. He, like me, thought sex was the lesser evil. The problem with something being a lesser evil is that something else has to be the greater evil.

"Is it just Jean-Claude, or . . ." His gaze flicked to Asher.

"We'll talk about this tomorrow, Richard, I promise, but right now, I need to help Asher."

He shook his head. "Are those Jean-Claude's marks on your neck?"

I sighed and looked down at the floor. I made myself meet his eyes, but damn it, I didn't have time or energy for this, not right now. "No," I said.

Again his gaze flicked to Asher. "His?"

"Yes."

"How can you let them feed off of you?"

"If I hadn't let Asher feed last night, then tonight he'd be dead, or enthralled to Belle Morte for the rest of eternity. It's one of the reasons we did it."

"You knew he'd be able to feed?" He frowned at me.

I shook my head. "No, but Musette had claimed him for Belle, because he didn't belong to anyone. We made sure he belonged to us."

"Us?" he actually looked at Micah first.

Micah's face was as neutral as he could manage.

"Not Micah, Jean-Claude."

He looked at the vampire, then back to Micah. "How can you let her do this?"

"I'd feed him myself if it would help," Micah said.

Richard's eyes widened, and the look on his face was uncomprehending. "I don't understand that."

Micah just looked at him for a moment, then he looked at me, and there was something in his eyes that said he understood some of what all this cost me, cost us both, cost us all.

407

Richard had let go of my arm now. In fact he'd taken a step back from me, as if he didn't want to be that close. He acted as if I'd done something unclean. If he only knew. Or maybe the sex wouldn't bother him at all, maybe it was all about the feeding for him. My moral standards just weren't that finely cut anymore.

I sighed and turned to Jean-Claude. "Since you went along for the ride with Asher's feeding, he may be able to feed off of you through me."

Jean-Claude nodded. "Perhaps."

"If you touch me, while I touch Asher, and drop shields, we can try it. Between the two of us I think we can get him back to a place where one blood feeding should get him back to his normal glorious self."

"I am willing to try," he said.

I fought the urge to glance at Richard. "I know you are." I walked away from them both towards Asher. I wanted to feed Asher back to health, but truthfully, I'd had about enough of all the men in my life for one night.

# 51

JEAN-CLAUDE AND I knelt by Asher. He had gained enough from that first small taste to manage a smile. The smile was the barest phantom of what he had been, but I was so relieved to see it that it made me smile, too.

I gripped Jean-Claude's hand in my left hand, and laid my right on Asher's cheek. The moment I touched him, he was the most beautiful thing I'd ever seen. Nothing mattered but to touch him. Nothing mattered but to be with him. Nothing mattered but Asher. It was as if the world had narrowed down to his eyes, his body. The sun revolved around him, I just knew it.

In a dim part of my brain I realized that Asher hadn't been using vampire powers on me. That whatever I'd felt before this had been real. Because this was unreal. I'd never felt for anyone like this, because it wasn't love, or even lust, it was obsession. It was the sure knowledge that if I did not touch him I would die. Even as I thought it, I knew it wasn't true, but it felt true. God help me, it felt true.

I fought to free my left hand, something was holding it so I couldn't touch Asher with both hands. I needed to touch him with both my hands. I laid my body on top of Asher and caressed my hands down him.

His hands trapped my face between them, and in some part of me I knew they felt like old leather and sticks with things underneath them, but for the first time when dealing with vampire trickery, I didn't fight it. I let Asher's power turn what might have been horror into something erotic and beautiful.

I opened myself wide and let Asher roll through me like a stream, long dammed, flowing, flooding, filling up a land that has been too long without water. I did not ride his power, his power engulfed me, rolled me under with a weight of a thousand waves, pressed me to the bottom of the sand and held me at the bottom of the ocean. It wasn't that I didn't drown, it was that I didn't care that I drowned.

I woke, if *waking* was the term, with his body pressing me to the hard stone floor. I was staring up at a waving cloud of his hair, the lights sparkled through it like a golden veil. I ran my fingers through it, and it was soft, and alive again. The edge of his cheek was full and rough with scars again. I touched those familiar marks, and he turned to face me fully, and the sight of him caught my breath in my throat.

From the curve of his forehead, to the line of his cheek, the fullness of his lips, he was perfect once more. His eyes sat in that face like icy sapphires set among pearls and gold.

I laughed when I saw him, a joyous burst of sound. He cupped my face in his hand, and I turned to lay a kiss against his palm. The weight of his body against mine was one of the best feelings I'd ever had, because it was proof that he was back, that he was well, and that he was whole.

He half-rolled, and half-raised me to a sitting position in his lap, with his back to the wall. He turned with me held in his arms, to look across the room at Belle Morte. I didn't have to see the look on his face to know that it was not an entirely friendly one.

"Impressive, wouldn't you say?" Jean-Claude said.

"No, I would not. He can only feed on the energy of those whom he has taken blood from, and rolled their poor minds. You know as well as I do, Jean-Claude, that you can't allow Asher to roll the mind of every victim. It would be a parade of love-besotted fools following him everywhere."

I resented the love-besotted fool part, but I let it go. We were winning tonight. Never argue when you're winning.

"Be that as it may, Belle, Asher is restored to his glorious self. We have no more need of you tonight, so you, and yours, must be gone from our territory before tomorrow night."

"You would truly slay all of us?" She made it a question.

"*Oui.*"

"My vengeance would be terrible."

"*Non*, Belle, by council law you cannot chastise another *sourdre de sang* as you would a vampire of your line. Your hatred would be terrible, but your vengeance would have to wait."

"Not if the head of the council agrees with my vengeance," she said.

"I've touched her, Belle, she doesn't care about your vengeance. She doesn't even care about you, or me, or much of anybody," I said.

"The Mother has been asleep a very long time, Anita, when that sleep ends she may retire from the council."

I laughed, and it wasn't joyous now. "Retire! Vampires don't retire. They die, but they never retire."

It wasn't something that showed on her face, it was more a stillness to her shoulders, a movement in an arm. I don't know what made me see it. Asher's power, or something else. But I did see it, and I had a wonderful, terrible idea.

"You plan to kill her. You plan to kill the First Darkness and make yourself head of the council."

Her face was perfectly blank as she said, "Do not be absurd. No one attacks the Gentle Mother."

"Yeah, I know, and there's a very good reason for that. She'll fucking kill you, Belle. She will roll over you and destroy everything you are."

She fought, but she couldn't keep the arrogance off her face. I guess if you've been alive longer than Christ has been dead, you can't help but be arrogant.

"If you declare war on anyone now, Belle, as a *sourdre de sang* in my own right, neither I nor any of my people have to come when you call. You will find no aid here," Jean-Claude said.

"Aid from you, my two *petite catamites*? I have found other men to serve your purposes." She turned with a swish of Musette's skirts. "Come, my poppets, we will leave and shake the dirt of this provincial town from our shoes."

"A moment, my mistress." It was Valentina. She gave a very low curtsy in her stiff white and gold dress. "Bartolomé and I have had our honor besmirched by Musette's trick."

"What of it, poppet?"

Valentina stayed down in the low curtsy, as if she could have held the position forever. "We beg your indulgence to remain behind and make amends to the shape-shifters."

"*Non*," Belle said.

Valentina raised her gaze to the woman. "They were abused as I was abused, and we have made it worse. I beg permission to remain behind and make it better."

"Bartolomé," Belle said.

Bartolomé came forward and dropped to one knee, head bowed. "Yes, mistress."

"Is this what you wish?"

"*Non*, mistress, but honor demands that we remedy this error." He looked up then, and there was something on his face of the boy he might once have been. "They have grown into men, but the scars laid on the boys that they were are deep. Valentina and I have made them deeper. This I do regret, and you know, above all others, that I do not regret much."

I expected Belle to tell them, no, to gather her people up and leave, but she didn't. She said, "Stay until honor is satisfied, then return to me." She glanced at Jean-Claude. "If you will allow them to remain, that is?"

Jean-Claude nodded. "Until honor is satisfied, *oui*."

I didn't agree with this, but something in Belle's face, something in Jean-Claude's face, something in the tightness of Asher's body, let me know that things were happening that I probably didn't understand.

"If the wolves would be so kind as to escort our guests to their rooms to pack, then to the airport."

Richard seemed to startle awake, almost as if he, too, had been under some spell. I didn't think that was it. He was staring at me in Asher's lap, with Micah leaning against the wall beside us. Nathaniel had crawled towards us, and I raised a hand, let him lay his head and shoulders in my lap.

"We'll escort them out," he said, but his voice sounded empty. He opened his mouth as if to say more, then he turned, and his wolves moved with him. They gathered up Belle's people and began to escort them back towards the front and the main rooms.

Belle glanced back once at Valentina and Bartolomé as they stood in their shining white and gold clothes. That one glance back said worlds. I'd never be certain, but I think that Belle Morte felt guilty not just about Valentina, but about Bartolomé. Valentina I understood because a vampire of Belle's making had done the

412

unspeakable. But bringing Bartolomé over as a child had been simply good business. I hadn't thought Belle Morte lost any sleep over good business. But she'd still condemned him to an eternity in a child's body. A child's body with a man's appetite forever. Belle let them stay, though the excuse was weak. Belle let them stay because guilt is a wonderful motivator even among the dead.

## 52

I WOKE IN the dark with the comforting weight of bodies around me. I knew by the quality of darkness and the faint light from the nearby bathroom that I was in Jean-Claude's bed. I remembered Jean-Claude giving us the bed, because it was near dawn, and I don't think that either of us wanted a repeat of yesterday morning. Strangely, what had happened with Asher seemed to have sated my own *ardeur*. Or maybe I was just too tired. Once I would have assumed it meant I was gaining more control, but I'd stopped trying to second-guess the *ardeur*. I was wrong too often.

There really wasn't enough light to see clearly, but the tickle of curls along my cheek let me know it was Micah's face pressed into the hollow of my neck. His arm lay heavy and warm across my upper stomach, his leg entwined with my thigh. There was another arm across my hips, a second face pressed into my side, a second body curled into a tight ball against me. I didn't really need to touch the top of Nathaniel's head to know it was him.

The sliver of light from the bathroom showed a pale slender arm flung carelessly across Micah's one outstretched leg. The arm was all that was visible out of the covers. I knew the arm, and I knew somewhere under all the covers they'd stolen was Zane, and the rest of Cherry. I didn't mind sleeping in big warm piles, but I did mind sharing a large bed with such outrageous cover hogs. Cherry wasn't bad on her own, but put her with Zane, and you either fought for every inch of covers, which was not restful, or you gave up. I'd found that the silk sheets at Jean-Claude's were especially hard to keep track of in my sleep.

I wasn't sure what had awakened me, but I knew that the wereleopards had better hearing and better sense of smell than I did. If it hadn't alerted them, it was probably a dream.

Then I heard it, very, very faint. It was my phone, sounding like it was ringing from the bottom of a deep well. I tried to sit up, and couldn't. I was pinned by the two men.

There was a groan, and the slender arm across Micah's leg vanished under the dark bulk of sheet. The next moment there was a slithering sound, a thump, a curse, and the sound of clothes being pawed through. Cherry's voice was groggy as she said, "Yes."

Silence, then, "No, this isn't Anita, just a minute." Her other hand poked the dark bulk of the sheet at the foot of the bed. Zane's voice, "What!"

"Phone," she groaned.

His hand grabbed the phone, and before I could say anything, he said, "Hello."

Zane was quiet for a second, then, "Just a minute, she's here, hang on." A pale, more masculine hand appeared out of the welter of sheets and handed the phone vaguely in my direction, but I was still pinned. The phone dangled just out of reach.

I finally had to push Micah's arm off me, and try and sit up. "Micah, move, I have to reach the phone."

He made a small inarticulate noise and rolled off me, to give me the long line of his back. Nathaniel took the phone from Zane's hand, before I could take it.

His voice was the most awake, "Whom may I say is calling?"

I was finally sitting up. "Give me the phone," I said.

Nathaniel handed me the phone with a, "It's Zerbrowski."

I hung my head for a second, sighed, and put the phone to my ear. "Yeah, Zerbrowski, what's up?"

"How many people you got in bed with you, Blake?"

"None of your business."

"One of them sounded like a girl. Didn't know you swung that way."

I pressed the button on my watch, so I could see the time on the light-up dial. "Zerbrowski, we've had about two hours of sleep. If you just called to check up on my sex life, I'm going back to sleep."

"No, no, sorry. It just," he laughed softly, "just caught me off guard. I'll try to keep the teasing to a minimum, but, damn, you don't usually give me this much ammunition. Can't blame me for getting distracted."

"Did I mention the two hours of sleep?"

"You did," he said, sounding depressingly wide awake. I was betting he'd had coffee.

"I'm counting to three, if you haven't said something interesting by the time I'm finished, I'm hanging up, and I'm turning off my cell phone."

"We've got a fresh murder scene."

I scooted up so my back was against the headboard. "I'm listening." Micah stayed curled on his side, back to me, but Nathaniel cuddled up close so he was still pressed around me. Cherry and Zane were motionless under the pile of sheets. I think they'd gone back to sleep.

"It's the shape-shifter rapist again." The humor was leaking away from his voice, and he sounded tired. I wondered how much sleep he'd gotten last night.

I was wide awake now, my pulse fast in my throat. "When?"

"She was found just after dawn. We haven't been here long."

"I'll be there regardless, but is Dolph going to be there?"

"No," Zerbrowski said, "he's on leave." He lowered his voice, "Top brass told him he either takes voluntary leave with pay, or enforced leave without."

"Okay, where are you?"

It was Chesterfield again. "He's staying in a pretty small geographic area," I said.

"Yeah," Zerbrowski said, and that one word had so much tiredness.

I almost asked how he was holding up, but it's against the guy code. You're supposed to pretend you don't notice anything's wrong. Pretend, and it will go away. Sometimes, because I am a girl, I'll break the guy code, but today I let it stand. Zerbrowski had a long day ahead of him, and he was the man in charge. He couldn't afford to look at his feelings right now. It was more important that he held together than that he understood what he was feeling.

Zerbrowski started to give directions, and I had to tell him to wait until I had a pen and paper. There was no pen and paper anywhere in the room. I was finally reduced to writing directions in lipstick on the bathroom mirror. Zerbrowski was laughing his ass off by the time I found the lipstick and started drawing on the mirror.

He gasped a little, and finally managed to say, "Thanks, Blake, I so needed that."

"Glad I could brighten your day." I crawled back on the bed.

I thought about what Jason had said about a werewolf being able to follow the scent trail. I bounced the idea off of Zerbrowski.

He was dead silent for a minute. "There is no way I could get anyone to agree to letting another shape-shifter near this scene."

"You're the man in charge," I said.

"No, Anita, you bring another shifter around, and they're going to end up being questioned just like Schuyler did. Don't do it. This whole thing is going to turn into a witch hunt soon."

"What do you mean?"

"I mean they're starting to bring in all known shape-shifters for questioning."

"The ACLU is going to be up in arms," I said.

"Yeah, but not until they've held a few people over, and questioned them."

"It isn't one of the local lycanthropes, Zerbrowski."

"I can't tell the upper brass that our perp doesn't smell like the local werewolf pack, Anita. They'll say that of course the local wolves would say that, they don't want to be blamed for this shit."

"I believe Jason."

"Maybe I believe him, too, maybe I don't, but it doesn't matter, Anita. It really doesn't matter. People are fucking terrified. There's a rush bill in the state senate right now to declare varmint laws legal again in Missouri."

"Varmint laws, Jesus, Zerbrowski, you don't mean like some of the Western states still have on the books?"

"Yeah, kill it first, then if a blood test proves it's a lycanthrope, it's self-defense, not murder, and there's no trial."

"It'll never get into law," I said, and I was almost certain when I said it.

"Probably not right now, but Anita, we get a few more women torn up like this, and I don't know."

"I'd like to say people aren't that stupid," I said.

"But you know better," he said.

417

"Yeah."

He sighed. "There's something else." He sounded really unhappy.

I sat up a little straighter against the headboard, forcing Nathaniel to recuddle.

"You sound like you're about to give me really bad news, Zerbrowski."

"I just don't want to have to fight with you and Dolph and the top brass all at the same time."

"What's wrong, Zerbrowski? Why am I going to be mad at you?"

"Remember, Anita, Dolph was still in charge until now."

"Just tell me." My stomach was strangely tight like I was dreading whatever he'd say.

"There was a message at the first rape scene."

"I didn't see a message."

"It was by the back door, Dolph never gave you a chance to see it. I didn't know about it until later."

"What was the message, Zerbrowski?" A lot of thoughts went through my head. Was it a message for me, about me?

"First message read, 'We nailed this one, too.'"

It took me a few seconds to get it, or think I got it. The first murder, the man nailed to his living room wall. There had been nothing to connect that death with the shape-shifter killings. Except maybe for an odd message.

"You're thinking of the first man in Wildwood," I said. "The message could mean anything, Zerbrowski."

"That's what we thought until the second rape, the one Dolph wouldn't let us call you in on."

"There was another message," I said, voice soft.

"'Nailed another one,'" he said.

"It could still be a coincidence, *nailed* is a euphemism for sex."

"Today's message was, 'There wasn't enough left to crucify.'"

"The maniac that's slaughtering these women is not methodical enough, or neat enough, for that first murder."

"I know," he said. "But we didn't release the nails and the fact that our first vic was crucified. Nobody but the killer would know."

"One of the killers," I said. "The man's death was a group

effort." I thought of something. "Is there more than one type of sperm at the scenes?"

"Nope."

"So what, the rapist wants us to know the crimes are connected, why?"

"Why do any of these crazy buggers want us to know anything? It amuses him, Anita."

"What background did you dig up on the first vic?"

"He's ex-military."

"You don't get that house and the indoor pool on retired military benefits."

"He was an importer. Traveled around the world and brought back stuff."

"Drugs?"

"Not that we can find."

I had another thought, a record after only two hours sleep. "Name me the countries he frequented."

"Why?" he asked.

I filled him in on what he hadn't heard through the grapevine about Heinrick.

"If the dead man frequented the same countries, it might mean something."

"A clue," Zerbrowski said. "A real live clue, I don't think I'd know what to do with one."

"You've got lots of clues, they just aren't helping."

"You noticed that, too," he said.

"If Heinrick knew the dead man, I still don't know what it means."

"Me either. Just get here as soon as you can. And don't bring any shape-shifters with you."

"I understand," I said.

"I hope so." He spoke away from the phone for a second, "I'll be right there." Then he spoke directly to me. "Hurry," he said, and he hung up. I think Dolph had taught all of us not to say good-bye.

# 53

I'D EXPECTED THE scene to be bad, because the last scene had been bad. But I hadn't expected this. Either our rapist murderer had moved to the bathroom for his second kill, or we had a whole new killer. I'd smelled the same hamburger smell as I walked through the house. Zerbrowski had given me little plastic booties to put over my Nikes, and handed me the box of gloves. He'd said something about the floor being messy. I'd never thought of Zerbrowski as a master of understatement.

The room was red. Red, as if someone had painted all the walls crimson, but it wasn't an even job of painting. It wasn't just red, or crimson, but scarlet, ruby, brick red where it had begun to dry, a color so dark it was almost black, but it sparked red like a dark garnet. I tried to stay cold and intellectual and look at all the shades of red, until I saw a piece of something long and thin and meaty that had been glued to the wall with the blood, like a piece of offal tossed aside by a careless butcher.

The room was suddenly hot, and I had to look away from the walls, but the floor was worse. The floor was tile, and that didn't absorb liquid. It was covered in blood, blood deep enough that it sat liquid and shining on almost the entire floor. The floor space was small, admittedly, but it was still a lot of blood for one room.

I was hugging the doorframe that led into the room. My feet in the little booties were still on the relatively clean tile of the area where the stool sat, a tiny room, with a vanity area, complete with double sink beyond. The master bedroom was beyond even that, but the bed was carefully made, untouched.

There was a small lip of marble that held the shallow lake of blood inside the final room. A tiny ledge of stone to keep the rest of the rooms clean. I was grateful for that tiny ledge.

I looked at the walls again. There was a three-person, deep

shower in the far corner. The glass doors were splattered with blood, and it had dried to a nice candy red shell. The shower stall wasn't covered as completely as the other walls. I wasn't sure why yet.

Most of the rest of the space in the room was taken up by a bathtub. It wasn't as large as Jean-Claude's, but it was almost as large as the one I had at my house. I liked my bathtub, but I knew it would be days before I'd be able to use it again. This scene would ruin that particular pleasure for a while.

The tub was full of pale blood. Blood the color of dark red roses left too long in the sun, faded to a shade of pink that never looked quite pink, but always as if it had meant to be a darker color. Pink bloody water filled the tub almost to the brim, like it was a cup filled up with punch. Bad thought. Bad thought.

Thinking about food or drink of any kind was a bad thing right now, a truly bad thing. I had to look away, stare back into the smaller rooms, catch a glimpse of the bed and the police still milling around the far room. None of them had volunteered to accompany me on the tour. Couldn't blame them, but I suddenly felt isolated. They were only three small rooms away, but it felt as if it were a thousand miles. As if, if I screamed now, no one would hear me.

I used the farthest doorframe to get to the vanity sink area. I leaned on the cool tile sink and ran cold water over my hand. When it was cold enough I splashed it on my face. There was no hand towel, probably it had been bagged and sent to the lab, where it would be checked for hair and fiber and stuff. I untucked my T-shirt from my jeans and wiped my face dry. I came away with a few dark stains. The remnants of last night's makeup. I looked into the wide shining mirror, glaring bright in the overhead lights. I had dark smudges of mascara and eyeliner under my eyes. Waterproof really isn't. It's more like water tough, but not proof. I used the hem of my T-shirt to dab at the black marks, and got most of it. I also ended up with black stuff on my shirt, but it didn't seem to matter.

Zerbrowski looked in at me from the doorway. "How's it going?"

I nodded, because I didn't trust myself to speak.

421

He grinned suddenly, and if I'd felt better I would have dreaded his next comment, but today I was too numb. It didn't matter. Nothing mattered. Because for anything to matter I could not have gone back into that room, and I had to go into that room. So nothing mattered. I was empty, and quiet, and there was nothing.

"Who was the girl this morning? We've got a pool going. Some people think it's your best bud Ronnie Sims. Personally, I don't think so; she's still hot for that professor guy at Wash U. I'm betting on the blond wereleopard that's always at your house. Which is it?"

I think I just blinked at him.

He frowned then and stepped into the little room. "Anita, are you okay?"

I shook my head. "No, I am not okay."

His face was all concern, and he came close enough, almost took my arm, then stopped himself. "What's wrong?"

I stayed leaning on the sink, but pointed backwards with one hand, not looking where I was pointing, not wanting to look.

He glanced back where I was pointing, then his eyes flicked, very quickly, back to me. "What about it?"

I just looked at him.

He shrugged. "Yeah, it's bad. You've seen bad before."

I lowered my head so I was staring at the golden faucet. "I took a month off, Zerbrowski. Thought I needed a vacation, and I did, but maybe a month wasn't enough."

"What are you saying?"

I looked up into the mirror, and my face was almost ghost pale, my eyes standing out like black holes in my face, the remaining eyeliner making my eyes larger, more compelling, more lost than they should have been. What I wanted to say was I don't know if I want to do this anymore, but what I said out loud, was, "I thought the bedroom scene was bad, but this is worse."

He nodded.

I started to take a deep breath, but remembered in time about the smell, and took a shallow breath, which wasn't nearly as soothing to my psyche but better for my stomach. "I'll be okay."

He didn't argue with me, because Zerbrowski treated me by guy rules most of the time. If a guy says he'll be okay, you just

take him at his word, even if you don't believe it. The only exception is when lives are at stake, then the guy code can be broken,
but the man that you broke it with will probably never forgive
you.

I straightened up, hands still death-gripping the sink. I blinked
into the mirror a couple of times, then went back to the far room.
I could do this. I had to do this. I had to be able to see what was
there, and think about it logically. It was an awful thing to ask of
myself. I'd finally acknowledged that. Acknowledged that seeing
things like what lay in the next room were soul-destroying.
Acknowledged and moved on.

I was back in the bathroom door. Zerbrowski had come with me,
though, standing just behind me. There really wasn't room to stand
in the doorway together, not comfortably.

I looked at the room, at the walls with their coating of blood and
gore. "How many people were killed in here?"

"Why?" he asked.

"Don't be coy, Zerbrowski, I don't have the patience for it
today."

"Why?" he asked again, and this time there was a note of defen-
siveness in his voice.

I glanced back at him. "What is your problem?"

He didn't point at the carnage. In fact for a second, or two, I
thought he was going to tell me to mind my own business, but he
didn't. "If Dolph said why, you'd just answer him, not argue with
him."

I sighed. "Dolph's shoes hard to fill?" I asked.

"No, but I'm damned tired of repeating myself when I know that
nobody makes Dolph fucking repeat himself."

I looked up at him and felt a smile creep across my face. "Well,
actually, I make Dolph repeat himself, too."

He smiled. "Alright, alright, maybe you do, but you are such a
fucking pain in the ass, Anita."

"It's a talent," I said.

We stood in the doorway and smiled at each other. Nothing had
changed in that small horror chamber. There wasn't a drop less of
blood, or an inch less of gory bits plastered to the walls, but we
both felt better.

"Now," I said, still smiling, "how many people were killed in the bathroom?"

His smile slid into a full grin. "Why do you ask?"

"You bastard," I said.

He wiggled his eyebrows above the rims of his glasses. "Not what my mom says, though you're not the first to speculate."

I half laughed and knew that I'd lost. "Because, Zerbrowski, there are only two full walls in that room, both of them are so thick with blood and heavier bits that it's like two kills, one at one wall, one at the other."

"What about the bathtub?" he asked.

"The water's pale. I've never seen anyone bled out in a bathtub, so I don't know if the water would be this pale, or if it would be darker. But my gut tells me that no one was bled out in the tub. They may have been killed in the tub, but most of the blood is on the floor and walls."

"You sure about that?"

"No, like I said, I've never seen anyone bled out in a bathtub before, but I'm also wondering why the tub is so full, almost to the brim. You can't fill most tubs that full; they've got that little hole that stops it from overflowing. This one is so full that you couldn't even step into it without sloshing water all over the floor."

He watched my face while I talked, then his gaze slid away to look into the room beyond, then to the clean section of floor we were standing on.

"I'm right about at least two people being killed, aren't I?"

He had control of his expression now, and met my gaze. "Maybe."

I sighed, but it was more frustration now. "Look, I've worked with Dolph for years, and I like him. I respect his work methods, but damn it, Zerbrowski; you don't have to play it as close to the chest as he does. I've always hated playing twenty fucking questions. Let's try something new and different. I ask questions, you answer them."

He almost smiled. "Maybe."

I fought an urge to yell. I spoke very calmly, very quietly. "At least two people were killed, slaughtered against the walls." I forced myself to turn back and look at the two walls in question

424

again. Now that I had another human being to talk to, and he'd made me a little angry, I could think again. The walls weren't literally painted with blood. There were spots where the tile showed through, but the tile was a medium brown color, so that at first it looked worse than it was, and God knew, it was bad enough.

I turned back to Zerbrowski. "Okay, two kills one against each wall. Or at least they were sliced open, up, whatever, against each wall." I looked at the tub again. "Are there bits of bodies in the tub?"

"Dolph would make you go fish."

I stared up at him. "Maybe, probably. But you're not Dolph, and I'm not in the mood."

"We left the bits in there special for you, Anita. No joke." He held up his hands. "You're our monster expert, and if this isn't a monster, I don't know what is."

He had me there. "It's a monster, Zerbrowski, but is it a human monster, or something else? That's the sixty-four-billion-dollar question."

"I thought it was sixty-four-thousand-dollar question," he said.

"Inflation," I said. "Do you at least have any long gloves, or something?"

"No long gloves on me," he said.

"I fucking hate you," I said.

"Not the first to say it today," he said, and he seemed tired again.

"I am going to track blood all over hell and back."

He fished under the sink and retrieved a garbage bag. "Put the booties in here before you step out of the room."

"What can I possibly learn by fishing around in that mess?"

"Probably not a goddamned thing," he said.

I shook my head. "Then why should I do it?"

"Because we held the scene for you. We didn't drag that damn tub, just in case we spoiled some arcane piece of monster shit, that you would have noticed, and we would have thrown away."

"Arcane," I said, "what, Katie been reading the big grown-up books to you again?"

He smiled. "The faster you do this, the sooner we can all get the hell out of here."

"I'm not stalling," I said, even as I knew I was.

"Yeah, you are, and I don't blame you."

I looked into the next room, then back at Zerbrowski. "If I don't find some really nifty clue, I am so going to kick your ass."

He grinned. "Only if you can catch me."

I shook my head, took a shallow breath, and stepped over that last bit of doorway.

# 54

THE BLOOD CLOSED up around the plastic bootie, not quite to the top of it, not quite rolling over onto my shoe, but close. Even through the plastic, through my shoe, I could feel that the blood was cool. Not cold, but cool. I wasn't sure if it was my imagination or not. I didn't think I should have been able to feel the blood through the bootie and my shoe. But it felt like I could. Sometimes my imagination is not an asset at a crime scene.

I slid my foot forward, one hand still on the doorframe. I wasn't sure that the plastic booties would be slippery in this much liquid on a tile floor, but I so didn't want to find out the hard way. There were two things I didn't want to do in this room. One, was fall on my ass in the pool of blood, two, was put my hand in the bathtub. I had to do the second, but I would be damned if I did the first.

I eased my feet forward, slowly, cautiously, and kept my fingers on the doorjamb as long as possible. Actually the room wasn't that large, and it wasn't that big a reach between the door and the tub. I got a death grip on the edge of the tub with my glove-covered hands, and when I had both my feet planted as steady as I could get them, I looked down at the water.

It was like some kind of red soup. I knew it was mostly water, but the color . . . I kept thinking of the cups you use to dye Easter eggs. It looked like a great big cup for dyeing Easter eggs, and just like sometimes happened if you didn't get the mix right, it wasn't exactly red, or pink, but both. I concentrated on the thought of Easter eggs, the smell of vinegar, and better times than this.

The water seemed to swirl, heavier than it was. Probably illusion, but I suddenly had this image of something floating right below the surface. Something that would pop up and try to grab me. I knew it wasn't true. I knew it was just too many horror movies, but my pulse was in my throat, my heart thudding.

I glanced back at Zerbrowski. "You guys don't have any rook-ies to do this?"

"How do you think we got the first piece out?" he asked.

"That would explain the uniform that was throwing his guts up in the bushes as I came through."

"It's his first week on the job."

"You bastard."

"Maybe, but no one else wanted to put their hand in there. When you're finished looking, the techies are going to pump the water out and filter it for evidence. But you get to see it first. Tell me this wasn't a lycanthrope kill, Anita, tell me, and I'll tell the media. It'll quiet down the witch hunt."

"But not the hysteria, Zerbrowski. If this is a second killer, then we've got two of the worst psychos I've seen in St. Louis. I'd love to prove it's not a shape-shifter, but if it's not, then we've got other problems."

He blinked at me. "You'd really be happier if it's the same shape-shifter?"

"Traditionally two separate killers slaughter more people than just one."

"You still think more like a cop than a monster expert, Anita."

"Thanks." I turned back to the tub, and suddenly I knew I was going to do it. I wasn't fishing deeper than the gloves. Too fucking unhealthy, but if I could find a piece with the shorter gloves, I was going to do it.

The water was cold, even through the gloves. I reached down, the line of cold, bloody water creeping up my skin, and with my hand less than halfway in, I hit something solid.

I froze for a moment, took a shallow breath and ran my hand down along what I'd touched. It was soft and solid at the same time, meaty flesh. I came to bone, and it was enough to grip, and raise it free of the water. It was what was left of a woman's arm. The bone showed pinkish white as the water streamed away from it. The end that had attached to the shoulder was crushed. There were man-made tools that would do that kind of damage, but I doubted anyone would have gone to the trouble.

I set the arm aside and went back to where I'd found it. My hand sunk in a little farther this time, and I pulled out a nearly meatless bone. It didn't look like a piece of person, so I didn't think of it that way. I just looked at it as if I'd found an animal in the woods and was trying to figure out what had eaten it. Big teeth, lots of crushing strength. Very few real predators had this kind of bone-cracking strength, but most lycanthropes did. I doubted that some hyena had escaped from the zoo to rampage in a suburban bathroom.

I let the bone drift back into the water, slowly, easing it down, because for some reason I really didn't want it to splash on me.

I turned away from the bathtub, walked carefully to the doorway, stripped off the gloves, threw them in the sack that Zerbrowski held open for me, leaned against the doorjamb, removed the booties, threw them into the garbage sack, stepped out of that awful room, and kept walking until I hit the bedroom.

The air seemed cleaner, more breatheable here.

Zerbrowski followed me out, and it was Merlioni who said, "She did it, didn't she?"

"Yep."

Merlioni made a sort of crowing sound. "I knew it, I won."

I looked at him, then at Zerbrowski. "I'm sorry, what did you say?"

Zerbrowski didn't even look embarrassed when he said, "We had a bet going on whether you'd actually fish around in the tub."

I sighed and shook my head. "You are all such unmitigated bastards."

"Unmitigated, ooh," said Merlioni, "if you use big words to insult us, Blake, we'll never figure it out."

I looked back at Zerbrowski. "It's a shape-shifter. I don't know if it's the same one. The first vic was done in her bed. Was the second?" He nodded. "This was in the bath, and there's at least two bodies cut up in the bathtub."

"Why two?" Zerbrowski asked.

"Because the pile is too damn high to be only one woman's body, especially since he ate parts of it."

"You say 'he,' like you know."

I shook my head. "I don't know, but I'm assuming male, because you don't find many women willing to do this kind of shit. It happens, but it's rare."

"We actually got a witness that the woman who owns the house

429

and another girlfriend were seen entering the residence at about 2 A.M." Zerbrowski had his eyes closed, as if he were quoting. "They appeared drunk, and there was a man with him."

"You have a witness?" I asked.

"If the man who brought them home is the shape-shifter, and not part of what is in the bathtub, yeah."

I hadn't thought about that. "He could be in the tub. By the way, why is the water so deep, why isn't the overflow valve working?"

"Our rookie says a piece of body has been stuffed into the valve."

I shivered. "No wonder he freaking threw up."

"I lost on that one," Merlioni said.

"Lost on what?" I asked.

"Most of us bet you'd be sick."

"Who bet I wouldn't be?"

Zerbrowski cleared his throat. "Me."

"What did you win?"

"Dinner for two at Tony's."

"What did you win for me fishing in the tub?" I asked Merlioni.

"Money," he said.

I shook my head. "I hate you all." I started for the door.

"Wait, we got one more bet," Merlioni said, "who was the chickie on the phone when Zerbrowski woke you?"

I was about to let loose a scathing comment, when a voice from the door stopped me. "Haven't seen anything this bad since New Mexico?"

I turned to find my favorite FBI agent in the doorway. Special Agent Bradley Bradford smiled and offered me his hand.

# 55

BRADLEY WAS WITH the Special Research Section; it was a new division set up to handle preternatural crime. We'd last worked together on some very gruesome murders in New Mexico.

I took his firm handshake and gave one of my own. He smiled, and I think we were both actually glad to see each other. But his gaze swept the room until he found Zerbrowski. "Sergeant Zerbrowski, you must be living right."

Zerbrowski moved towards us. "What do you mean, Agent Bradford?"

He held up a slender manila folder. "There's a store across the street from the club where the two women went to last night. The store got robbed last year and put in a very nice surveillance system."

All the joking was gone; Zerbrowski was very serious all of a sudden. "And?"

"They caught a picture of a man matching the neighbor's description with the two women last night. They walked right past the store window." He opened the folder. "I took the liberty of getting a still made."

"And passed it to all of your men," Merlioni said.

"No, detective, this is the only copy, and I brought it here first."

Merlioni looked like he would have argued, but Zerbrowski cut him off. "I don't care who solves this, as long as we get this guy."

"I feel the same way," Bradley said.

I didn't exactly believe Bradley. Last time we'd talked, his little division had been in jeopardy of being disbanded, and their cases given back to the Investigative Support – read Serial Killer – Unit. Bradley was one of the good guys, he really did care more about solving crimes than career advancement, but he also cared about his new unit. He felt strongly that the feds needed one. I agreed

431

with him. So why was he handing over the only copy of the picture? Sharing made sense, simply giving it to us didn't.

"What do you think, Anita?" he asked me.

I glanced down at the photo. It was black and white, pretty good quality actually. Two women were laughing up at the tall man in between them. The brunette on the left matched some of the pictures downstairs. I hadn't asked the name of the woman who owned the house. I hadn't wanted to know. Not knowing had made it easier to go into that bathroom and paw through the remains.

The other woman looked vaguely familiar. "Wasn't the woman in a group picture downstairs? It looked like it was taken at a party."

"We'll check," Zerbrowski said.

"What about the man?" Bradley asked.

I looked at the man in the picture. The man that might be our killer or might be at the bottom of the pile of bones in the bathtub was tall, broad-shouldered. Straight brown hair was pulled back into a long ponytail that one of the women was tugging on, playing with. The face was high cheekboned, handsome. He wasn't like Richard handsome, but they reminded me oddly of each other, both tall, both broad-shouldered, both classically handsome. But there was something in this man's face even through the film that creeped me out.

It was probably knowing that the two women were only hours away from being butchered. It was probably my imagination, but I didn't like the look on the man's face when he glanced up and spotted the camera. I realized that that was what the look was, why it looked strange.

"He spotted the camera," I said.

"What do you mean?" Zerbrowski asked.

"Look at his face, he didn't like being on film."

"He probably knew what he was going to do to them," Merlioni said, "don't want to be seen with the vics before the murder."

"Maybe, probably." I kept looking at his face, and I thought it was familiar.

"Do you recognize him?" Bradley asked.

I stared up at him. His face was empty, guileless, but I didn't believe the innocent look. "Why would I?"

432

"Well, he is a shape-shifter, if he's our man, I thought you might have seen him around."

Bradley was lying, I could feel it. Even I wasn't tactless enough to accuse him of it to his face, but I was saved from having to come up with something to say by my cell phone ringing. I'd kept it with me today, hooked on the back of my belt, just in case Musette and company didn't go quietly out of town. Call me silly, but I just didn't trust them.

"Hello."

"Is this Anita Blake?" It was a woman. I didn't recognize the voice.

"Yeah."

"This is Detective O'Brien."

Strangely, with all the vampire politics and the new murder I hadn't given much thought to the internationally wanted terrorist Leopold Heinrick. "Detective O'Brien, good to hear from you, what's up?"

"We identified the two pictures you pulled."

"Really, I'm impressed, the photos weren't that good."

"Lieutenant Nicols, you met him once, he picked them out."

It took me a second to place the name. "The lieutenant that was in charge at Lindel Cemetery."

"Yeah, that's the one. He picked out the same two pictures that you did, and since the two of you have only met once . . ."

Before she could finish, I said, "The bodyguards, the freaking bodyguards. Canducci and . . ."

She said, "Balfour."

"Yeah, that's right. I can't believe I didn't remember them."

"You saw them once at night, Blake, and from what Nicols says, the widow was putting on quite a show."

"Yeah, but still. Did you bring them in for questioning?"

"No one knows where they are. They quit their job at the security agency the day after you saw them. They'd only worked there for about two weeks. All the references they gave are leading to dead ends."

"Shit," I said. I glanced down at the picture that Bradley was still holding down where I could see it. I suddenly knew why that picture looked vaguely familiar. He was another of Heinrick's known

433

associates. Or he looked amazingly like one of them. But I just didn't believe that coincidence would stretch that far.

I looked up at Bradley. He was still patiently holding the picture down where I could see it, lower than either of the other two men needed it. Maybe he was being polite, or maybe not. He met my gaze, and he gave me blank face. Cop face.

"What if I told you that I'm looking at a picture of one of the other known associates of Heinrick, and he's in town, too?"

Bradley's face never changed. Zerbrowski's and Merlioni's did. They looked surprised. Bradley didn't.

"How did you get the picture?"

"Long story, but he's wanted in connection with some murders here in town."

"Which man?"

"I think he was the only one with longer hair. I don't think it was back in a ponytail like it is here, but it was definitely shoulder length."

I heard papers rustling. "I've got it." I heard more papers rustling, then a soft whistle. "Roy Van Anders. He is a very bad man, Blake."

"How bad?"

"Strangely, we got files just today about Mr. Van Anders. Crime scene photos that would turn your stomach."

"A lot of blood, not a lot of body left?" I asked.

I could feel Zerbrowski tense beside me.

"Yeah, how did you know?"

"I think I'm at a crime scene right now that's Van Anders's work."

"You're on that lycanthrope murder, right?"

"Yeah."

"There's nothing in his record that says he's anything but human. He's just a sick son of a bitch, who likes to rape and kill women."

"Did anybody question how he dismembered the bodies, or where the rest of them went?"

"I haven't read through everything yet, but no. Most of his crimes were in countries where we're lucky to have gotten any pictures at all. Very low tech, very little money to do sophisticated crime work."

434

"How sophisticated do you have to be to figure out the difference between tools and teeth?"

"A lot of serial killers use teeth, Blake." She sounded like she felt she had to defend the honor of some far away police.

"I know that, O'Brien, but, oh, hell, it doesn't matter. What does matter is that he's here in our town, right now, and we aren't low tech, and we do have at least a little money to track down the bad guys."

"You're right, Blake. Concentrate on the here and now."

"Do we have enough to question Heinrick and his pal now?"

"I think we might. We can make a case that Heinrick knows about his pal's hobbies. That would make him an accessory before the fact, if not more."

"I'll be down there as soon as I can get out of here."

"Blake, this is not your case. You're one of the potential victims. I think that makes you too close to everything to be objective."

"Don't do this, O'Brien, I've played fair with you."

"This isn't a game, Blake, this is a job. Or do you want credit for everything?"

"I don't give a fuck about credit. I just want to be there when you question Heinrick."

"If you get here in time, but we ain't holding the party up for just you."

"Fine, O'Brien, fine, you're the detective in charge."

"Nice of you to remember that." She hung up on me.

I said a very heartfelt, "Bitch!"

Zerbrowski and Merlioni had eager expectant faces, but Bradley didn't. He could do cop face, but he wasn't an actor. I filled them in, and Zerbrowski was pissed at O'Brien, not for excluding me, but for not even bothering to consider contacting a member of RPIT.

"She's got them in lockup for what, following you around? We've got four murders, maybe more." He looked at me. "You want a ride in a car with sirens and lights, so that we can fucking get there before she does something to wreck our case?"

I liked the "our case," and I liked that he asked me along. Dolph probably wouldn't have, even if he hadn't been mad at me.

I nodded. "I'd love to go riding in and wave jurisdictional flags in her face."

He grinned. "Give me ten minutes to give everybody their marching orders, then meet me downstairs. We'll borrow a marked car. People always get out of the way faster for a marked car." He was out the door and down the stairs humming to himself.

Merlioni went after him, saying, "Who has to stay here with the tub o' death cleanup?" I don't think Merlioni wanted to be included in the cleanup, not even to supervise.

Bradley and I found ourselves alone. It was unheard of for a fed, two feds I guess, to be left alone at a murder scene like this. Most locals hated the feds, and the feds hated them right back.

I looked up at Bradley. "Now that I've made all the connections you wanted me to make, tell me why you really came down here."

He closed the manila envelope and handed it to me. "To solve a crime."

"Solving these crimes would add to your unit's clout. Last time we spoke you needed that clout."

He was looking at me carefully.

"Are you here officially, Bradley?"

"Yes."

I stared into his bland face. "Are you here officially just as an FBI agent?"

"Don't know what you mean."

"You told me once that I'd come to the attention of some of the less savory branches of our government, the spooks, I think you called them. Is Van Anders a spook?"

"No government in their right mind would want an animal like this in their country."

"Talk to me, Bradley, talk to me, or the next time we meet I'm not going to trust you like I do right this minute."

He sighed and suddeny looked tired. He rubbed at his eyes with his thumb and forefinger. "These murders were brought to our attention. But I'd seen crimes like this before. In a different country, in a place where the government was more worried about staying in power than protecting helpless women." There was a look in his eyes, something faraway, and pain-filled.

"You said you got out of that line of work."

"I did." He looked very steadily at me, no cop eyes now. "Men like Van Anders were one of the reasons I couldn't keep doing it.

436

But when certain people found out that Van Anders might actually have been let loose within the confines of the United States, they weren't happy. I have a one-time permission to help things along here."

"What's the price tag on this help?"

"Heinrick will be escorted out of the country. They'll never put a name to the second man he was taken in with. It will all disappear."

"Heinrick is a suspected terrorist. You think that they'll just let him walk?"

"He's wanted in five different countries that we have strong treaties with. Who do we give him to, Anita? Better to just let him go."

"Don't you want to know why he was in town? I know I want to know why he was following me."

"I told you why these kind of people would want you."

"So I can raise the dead for them. A political leader here, a few zombie bodyguards there," I tried to make a joke of it, but Bradley wasn't laughing.

"You know the man you found nailed to his living room wall?"

"Yeah."

"He knew Heinrick and Van Anders, and he felt that they were too extreme. He left and he hid, but not well enough."

"If it was an execution, why make it look like some sort of ritual murder?"

"So it wouldn't look like an execution."

"Why did they care?" I asked.

He shook his head. "It was a message, Anita. They wanted him dead, and they wanted him dead in such a way that it would be sensational enough to make headlines. They wanted his death out there for all the others like him, like me, that left."

"You don't know this for sure, Bradley."

"Not all of it, but I know that everyone involved wants Van Anders caught, and Heinrick gone."

"What about the others?"

"I don't know."

"Are they gone for good, or should I still be worried?"

"Be worried, Anita, I would be."

437

"Great." Something occurred to me. "I know this is all off the record for you. Well, I've got one thing off the record to ask you."

"I can't promise, but what is it?"

I gave him Leo Harlan's name, and a general description, because it's not that hard to change your name. "He says he's an assassin, and I believe him. He says he's here on a sort of vacation, and I believe that, too. But St. Louis is suddenly lousy with internationally wanted bad guys, and I'd be curious to know if my client is tied to them somehow."

"I'll check around."

"If he comes up on any of your hit parades, I'll avoid him, and refuse to raise his ancestor. If he doesn't, I'll do the job."

"Even though he's an assassin?"

I shrugged. "Who am I to throw stones, Bradley? I try not to judge people more than I have to."

"Or maybe you're getting more comfortable with murderers."

"Yeah, all my friends are either criminals, monsters, or cops."

That made him smile.

Zerbrowski yelled from downstairs. "Anita, yo, we're out of here."

I gave Bradley my cell phone number. He copied it down. I ran for the stairs.

# 56

O'BRIEN HAD STARTED the interrogation before we got there. People in St. Louis didn't seem to understand that sirens and lights on a police car meant get the fuck out of the way. It was almost as if the police car with all flags flying made a gawkers' block around us. The drivers were so busy trying to figure out why we were in such a rush that they forgot to get out of the way.

I had never seen Zerbrowski so angry. Hell, I wasn't sure I'd ever seen him angry. Not for real. He'd raised enough of a fuss to drag O'Brien out of the interrogation, but she kept saying, "You can have him when we're through with him, Sergeant."

Zerbrowski's voice had crawled down so low it was almost painful to listen to it. That dragging, careful voice held enough heat to make me nervous. O'Brien didn't seem impressed.

"Don't you think, detective, that questioning him about a serial killer that's already butchered three, maybe four people, takes precedent over questioning him about following a federal marshal?"

"I am questioning him about the serial killer." A small frown formed between her eyes. "What do you mean three, maybe four?"

"We haven't finished counting the pieces at the last crime scene. There may be two victims."

"You can't tell?" she asked.

He let out his breath in a loud humph of air. "You don't know anything about these crimes. You don't know enough to be questioning him without us." His voice shook with the effort not to start screaming at her.

"Maybe you can sit in, sergeant, but not her." She jerked a thumb in my direction.

"Actually, detective, technically, you can't exclude me from the interrogation now that Heinrick is a suspect in preternatural crimes."

439

O'Brien looked at me, a blank, unfriendly stare. "I excluded you just fine before, Blake."

"Ah," I said, and felt myself smiling, I couldn't help it. "But that was when Heinrick was a suspected terrorist, and guilty of nothing more than illegal weapons violations, very mundane stuff. And nothing that my federal marshal status puts under my jurisdiction. As you pointed out earlier I'm not a regular federal marshal. My jurisdiction is very narrow. I have no legal status on nonpreternatural crimes, but on preternatural crimes I have jurisdiction all across this country. I don't have to wait to be invited in." I know I looked smug when I finished, but I just couldn't seem to help myself. O'Brien was being pissy, and pissiness should be punished.

O'Brien looked like she'd bitten into something bitter. "This is my case."

"Actually, O'Brien, it's everybody's case now. Mine, because federal law gives me the jurisdiction. Zerbrowski, because it's a preternatural case, and that means it belongs to the Regional Preternatural Investigation Team. Truthfully, you have no jurisdiction on the murders. They didn't happen on your turf, and you wouldn't even have known that Heinrick was involved if we hadn't shared information so freely with you."

"We played fair with you," Zerbrowski said, "play fair with us, and we all win." His voice was almost normal. He'd lost that frightening bass.

She pointed a finger at me, rather dramatically, I thought. "But it'll be her name in the paper."

I shook my head. "Jesus, O'Brien, is that all this is about? You want your name in the headlines?"

"I know that cracking a serial murder could make me a sergeant."

"If you want your name on this case, fine," I said, "but let's worry more about solving the case than who's going to get credit for it."

"Easy enough for you to say, Blake. Like you said, you don't have a career in law enforcement. Getting credit for this won't help you, but you'll still get the credit."

Zerbrowski pushed away from the wall where he'd been

leaning. He touched the files on the edge of the table. He opened one just enough to pull out a photo. He half-slid, half-threw the picture across the table at O'Brien.

It was a splash of shape and color. Most of the color was red. I didn't look too hard at it. I'd seen the real deal, I didn't need a reminder.

O'Brien glanced down at the picture, then looked again. She frowned, and almost reached out for the photo, then stared harder. She concentrated on the image. I watched her try to make sense of what she was seeing, watched her mind rebel at making sense of it. I saw the moment she saw it, on her face, in the sudden paleness of her skin. She sat down slowly in the chair on her side of the table.

She seemed to have trouble looking away from the picture. "Are they all like this?" she asked in a voice gone thin.

"Yes," Zerbrowski said. His voice was soft, too, as if he had made his point and wouldn't rub it in.

She looked up at me, and it looked like a physical effort to pull her gaze away from that photo. "You'll be the darling of the media again," but her voice was soft, like it didn't matter.

"Probably," I said, "but it's not because I want to be."

"You're just so damned photogenic," her voice had held a hint of her earlier scorn, then she frowned and glanced down at the photo again. She seemed to hear what she'd just said, and with that awful, hideous photo sitting in front of her, it seemed the wrong thing to say.

"I didn't mean . . ." She rallied, and put back on her angry face, but it seemed more like a mask to hide behind now.

"Don't worry, O'Brien," Zerbrowski said, and he had his teasing voice back. I knew enough to dread what would come out of his mouth next, but she didn't. "We know what you meant. Anita is just so damned cute."

She gave a weak smile. "Something like that, yes," she said. The smile vanished as if it had never existed. She was all business again. O'Brien never seemed to get very far from business. "Seeing that this doesn't happen to another woman is more important than who gets credit."

"Glad to hear we all agree," Zerbrowski said.

O'Brien stood up. She pushed the picture back towards

Zerbrowski, doing her best not to look at it this time. "You can question Heinrick, and the other one, though he doesn't say much."

"Let's have a plan before we go in there," I said.

They both looked at me.

"We know that Van Anders is our guy, but we don't know for sure that he's our only guy."

"You think one of the men we have here helped Van Anders do this?" O'Brien motioned towards the picture that Zerbrowski was tucking away.

"I don't know." I glanced at Zerbrowski and wondered if he was thinking the same thing I was. The first message had read "we nailed this one, too." *We.* I wanted to make sure that Heinrick wasn't part of that "we". If he was, then he wasn't going anywhere, not if I could help it. I really didn't care who got credit for solving the case. I just wanted it solved. I just wanted to never, ever have to see anything else as bad as that bathroom, that bathtub, and its . . . contents. I used to think I helped the police out of a sense of justice, a desire to protect the innocent, maybe even a hero complex, but, lately, I'm beginning to understand that sometimes I want to solve the case for a much more selfish reason. So I don't ever have to walk through another crime scene as bad as the one I just saw.

# 57

HEINRICK WAS SITTING behind the small table, slumped back in the chair, which is actually harder than it looks in a straight-backed chair. His carefully cut blond hair was still neat, but he'd laid his glasses on the table, and his face looked younger without them. His file said he was closer to forty than thirty, but he didn't look it. He had an innocent face, and I knew that was a lie. Anyone who looks that innocent after thirty is either lying, or touched by the hand of God. Somehow I didn't think Leopold Heinrick was ever going to be a saint. Which left only one conclusion – he was lying. Lying about what? Now there was the question.

There was a Styrofoam cup with coffee in front of him. It had been sitting long enough that the cream had started to separate from the darker liquid, so that swirls of paleness decorated the top of the coffee.

He looked up when Zerbrowski and I entered. Something flickered through his pale eyes: interest, curiosity, worry? The look was gone before I could decipher it. He picked up his glasses, giving me a blank, innocent face. With his glasses back on, he came closer to looking his age. They broke up the line of his face, so that the frames were what you saw first.

"You want a fresh cup of coffee?" I asked him as I sat down. Zerbrowski leaned against the wall, near the door. We'd start out with me questioning Heinrick to see if I got anywhere. Zerbrowski made it clear that I was up to bat, but no one, including me, wanted me alone with Heinrick. He had been following me, and we still didn't know why. Agent Bradford had guessed that it was part of some plot to get me to raise the dead for some nefarious purpose. Bradford didn't know, not for sure. Until we knew for sure, caution was better. Hell, caution was probably always better.

"No," Heinrick said, "no more coffee."

I had a fresh cup of coffee in one hand and a stack of file folders in the other. I placed the coffee on the table and made a show of arranging the pile of folders neatly beside it. His gaze flicked to the folders, then settled serenely back on me.

"Had too much coffee?" I asked.

"No." His face was attentive, blank, with a touch of wariness. Something had him worried. Was it the files? Too large a stack. We'd intended it to be too large. There were files at the bottom that had nothing to do with Leopold Heinrick, Van Anders, or the nameless man that was sitting in another room just down the hall. It was impossible to have a military record with no name attached, but somehow the dark-haired American had managed it. His file was so full of blacked-out spaces that it was almost illegible. The fact that no one would give our John Doe a name, but they would acknowledge he was once a member of the armed forces was disturbing. It made me wonder what my government was up to.

"Would you like something else to drink?" I asked.

He shook his head.

"We may be in here a while."

"Talking is thirsty work," Zerbrowski said from the back.

Heinrick's eyes flicked to him, then back to me. "Silence is not thirsty work." His lips quirked, and it was almost a smile.

"If sometime during this interview you want to tell us exactly why you were following me, I'd love to hear it, but that's really secondary to why we're here."

He looked puzzled then. "When you first stopped us that seemed to be very important to you."

"It was, and I'd still like to know, but the priorities have changed."

He frowned at me. "You are playing games, Ms. Blake. I am tired of games."

There was no fear in him. He seemed tired, wary, and not happy, but he wasn't afraid. He wasn't afraid of the police, or me, or going to jail. There was none of that anxiety that most people have in a police interrogation. It was odd. Bradley had said that our government was going to just let Heinrick go. Did he suspect that – know that? If so, how? How did he know? Why wasn't he the least bit afraid of spending time in the St. Louis jail system?

I opened the first file. It held grainy copies of old crimes. Women Van Anders had slaughtered in foreign countries, far from here.

I laid the photos out in front of him, in a neat row of black and white carnage. In some of the photos the quality was so bad that if you hadn't known you were looking at human remains, you'd have never guessed. Van Anders had reduced his victims to Rorschach tests.

Heinrick looked bored now, almost disgusted. "Your Detective O'Brien has already shown me these. Already marched out her lies."

"What lies would those be?" I asked. I sipped my coffee, and it wasn't bad. It was fresh, at least. As I sipped, I watched his face.

He folded his arms across his chest. "That there are fresh murders here in your city like these old ones."

"What makes you think she's lying?"

He started to say something, then closed his mouth tight, his lips a thin angry line. He just glared at me, pale eyes bright with anger.

I opened the second folder and began laying out colored photos just above the old black and whites. I laid them out in a line of bright death, and watched all the color drain away from Heinrick's skin. He looked almost gray by the time I sat back down. I'd had to stand to reach the ends of the table, to lay out the photos.

"This woman was killed three days ago." I got another file out of the stack. I opened it, and fanned the photos on top of it, but didn't put them with the stack. I wasn't a hundred percent sure I'd be able to match the photos back to the right crime. They were supposed to be marked on the back, but I hadn't marked them personally, so I didn't want to risk it. Once you get into court the lawyers get damned picky about evidence and stuff.

I pointed to the file pictures. "This woman was killed two days ago."

Zerbrowski stepped forward and handed me a plastic baggie with a handful of Polaroids in it. I tossed the baggie across the table so that it slid by him, and he caught it automatically before it hit the floor. His eyes were very big when he saw the top print.

"Those women died last night. We think there were two victims, but truthfully we haven't finished putting together the pieces, so we're not a hundred percent certain. It could be more, or it could be just one woman, but that's an awful lot of blood for only one woman, don't you think?"

He laid the baggie of Polaroids carefully on the table, so that they didn't touch any of the other photos. He stared at all the pictures, his face gone death white, his eyes huge. His voice squeezed out like it was an effort to breathe, let alone talk. "What do you wish to know?"

"We want to stop this from happening again," I said.

He was staring down at the pictures, as if he couldn't look away. "He promised he would not do it here. He swore that he could control himself."

"Who?" I asked, softly. Yeah, the government had given him a name, but that was the same government that wouldn't give our John Doe one.

"Van Anders," he whispered the name. He looked up, and there was surprise underneath the shock. "The other detective said you knew it was Van Anders."

Great. Nothing like giving your suspect more information than he's giving you.

I shrugged. "Without eyewitnesses it's hard to be certain."

Something like hope sparked in his eyes and he started regaining some of his color. "You think this might be someone else? Not Van Anders?"

I riffled through the files again, and Heinrick flinched. I found the thin folder with the picture of Van Anders and the two women. I flashed him the picture. "Van Anders with the victims from last night's slaughter."

He winced at the last word, and the color that had been seeping back into his face drained away again. His lips looked bloodless. For a second I thought he might faint. I'd never had a suspect faint on me before.

His voice was a hoarse whisper. "Then it is him." He laid his forehead on the table.

"Do you need some water, something stronger?" I asked. Though truthfully, black coffee was as strong as I could give him. There were rules about giving liquor to suspects.

He raised his head, slowly, but he looked awful. "I told them that he was crazy. I told them not to include him."

"Told who?" I asked.

He sat up a little straighter. "I agreed to come here against my better judgment. I knew the team was assembled too quickly. When you rush such a task, it ends badly."

"What task?" I asked.

"To recruit you for a mission."

"What mission?" I asked.

He shook his head. "It doesn't matter now. Some of our people got you on tape raising a man in a local cemetery. He did not look alive enough for what my employers wished. He looked like a zombie, and that is not good enough."

"Good enough for what?" I asked.

"To fool people in the country that their leader is still alive."

"What country?" I asked.

He shook his head, and a ghost of a smile crossed his lips. "I will not be here long, Ms. Blake. Those that employ me will see to it. They will either work to free me soon, with no charges, or they will have me killed."

"You seem calm about that," I said.

"I believe I will go free."

"But you're not sure," I said.

"Few things in life are certain."

"I know one thing that's certain," I said.

He just looked at me. I think he'd said more than he'd planned to say. So he was going to try not to say anything.

"Van Anders will kill someone else tonight."

His eyes were bleak when he said, "I had worked with him years ago, before I knew what he was. I should not have believed him that he was in control of his rage. I should have known."

"Are your employers just going to leave Van Anders here to butcher more women?"

He looked at me then. Again, I couldn't quite read his expression. Determination, guilt, something.

"I know where Van Anders is staying. I will give you that address. I know that my employers would wish him dead now. He has become a liability."

447

We got the address from him. I didn't hurry out after it, because unlike the movies, I knew I wouldn't be allowed in at the capture. Mobile Reserve, St. Louis's answer to SWAT, would be the ones running the show. When you have people that can go in with body armor and fully automatic weapons, the rest of us are just out-classed.

I opened one last file and showed him the man they'd crucified against the wall. "Why did you need Van Anders to do this? Not his kind of kill."

"I don't know what you are talking about."

He was going to deny it, fine. Even if we could have pinned it on him, I doubt we could have kept him long enough for a trial. "We know you and your team did this. We even know why." If Bradley was telling the truth, I did know.

"You know nothing." He sounded very sure of that.

"You were ordered to kill him because he ran. Ran away from people like you, and people like Van Anders."

He looked at me then, and he was worried. He was wondering how much I knew. Not much. But maybe it was enough. "Whose idea was it to crucify him?"

"Van Anders's." He looked like he'd swallowed something sour. Then he gave a small smile. "It won't matter, Ms. Blake, I'll never see trial."

"Maybe not, but I always like to know where the blame goes."

He nodded, then said, "Van Anders was so angry when we shot him first. He said what good is a crucifixion if the person isn't struggling." He looked at me with haunted eyes. "I should have known then what he meant to do."

"Whose idea were the runes?" I asked.

He shook his head. "You've gotten the last startled confession you shall get from me."

"There's still one thing I don't understand." Actually, there were lots of things I didn't understand, but it's never good to appear con-fused in front of the bad guys.

"I will not incriminate myself, Ms. Blake."

"If you knew what Van Anders was capable of, then why bring him along? Why make him part of the team, at all?"

"He is a werewolf, as you have learned from what he does to his victims. There were those who believed you were a shape-shifter, as well. We wanted someone that could manage you without risk of infection, if you fought us."

"You were planning on kidnapping me?"

"As a last resort," he said.

"But because Balfour and Canducci didn't like my zombie, the plan is off?"

"Those names will do for them, but yes. We had reports that you could raise zombies that thought they were still alive and could pass as human. My employers were very disappointed when they saw the tape."

I owed Marianne and her coven a thank-you note. If they hadn't gotten all witchier-than-thou on me, I'd have raised a fine, alive-looking zombie, and I might even now be kidnapped, and at the mercy of Van Anders. Maybe I should send Marianne flowers, a card just didn't seem to be enough.

I tried some more questions, but Leopold Heinrick had given out all the information he was going to give. He finally asked for a lawyer, and the interview was over.

I stepped out into the main area, and it was in chaos. People yelling, running. I caught the phrase, "officers down." I grabbed Detective Webster of the blond hair and bad coffee. "What's happened?"

O'Brien answered for him. "The Mobile Reserve Squad that went out to pick up Van Anders – he cut them up. At least one dead, maybe more."

"Shit," I said.

She had her jacket on and was digging her purse out of a drawer. "Where's Zerbrowski?"

"He's gone already."

"Can I catch a ride?"

She looked at me. "Where to? I'm going to the hospital."

"I think I need to be at the crime scene."

"I'll take you," Webster said.

O'Brien gave him a look.

"I'll be at the hospital later. I promise."

O'Brien shook her head and ran for the door. Everyone was leaving. Some would go to the hospital. Some would go to the crime scene and see if they could help there. Some would go sit with the families of the downed officers. But everyone would go. If you really wanted to commit a crime in any city, wait until there's an officer-down call, everyone drops everything.

I'd go to the scene of the crime. I'd try to help figure out what went wrong. Because something had gone very wrong if Van Anders had taken out an entire squad from the Mobile Reserve. They're trained to handle terrorists, hostage situations, drugs, gangs, biochemical hazards; pick your nastiness, and Mobile Reserve can handle it. Yes, something had gone terribly wrong. The question was, what?

# 58

I'D SEEN ENOUGH of Van Anders's handiwork to be prepared for the worst. What I saw in the hallway wasn't even close to his worst. Compared to the other crime scenes, it was almost clean. There was a uniformed officer standing next to the window at the end of the hallway. The window was almost completely free of glass, as if something large had been thrown through it. I turned away from the thought of one of the city's finest plunging to his death. Other than the window, there wasn't much else.

A sprinkling of blood on the pale brown carpet in the hallway. Two blood smears on the wall looked almost artificial, overly dramatic on the off-white walls. That was all. Van Anders hadn't had time to enjoy himself. One officer was dead, maybe two, but he'd just had time to kill them. He hadn't had time to cut them up. I wondered if that made him angry? Did he feel cheated?

There was a trickle of police in the hallway, but the sound of voices from the open door of the apartment was as murmurous as the sea. A sorrowful, angry, urgent, confused sea.

The apartment was pristine, untouched. There had been no fight inside. All the trouble had started and ended in the hallway.

Detective Webster had come up with me. He was still in the doorway, because there wasn't room to walk into the room. Every homicide has more cops than you think it needs, but I'd never seen a crowd like this. It was nearly wall-to-wall people like at a party, except that every face was grim, or shocked, or angry. No one was having a good time.

Zerbrowski had called my cell phone in the car on the way there. Everybody was wanting answers; answers, about the monsters, answers that he couldn't give, because he didn't fucking know. His quote, not mine.

I debated on whether to yell for Zerbrowski or call him back on his cell phone. I don't usually mind being short, but this time I couldn't see through the crowd, and I sure as hell couldn't see over it.

I glanced at Webster. He was damn near six feet. "Can you spot Sergeant Zerbrowski? "

Webster suddenly looked even taller. I realized that he'd been slumping, artfully, the way some tall people do, especially if they got tall early and didn't like it. Standing with his shoulders back, and trying to gaze across the crowd, he was at least six one, maybe an inch more. I'm usually a pretty good judge of height.

"He's on the far side of the room." He suddenly seemed to shrink, shoulders rounding, almost like his spine compressed before my eyes.

I shook my head, and said, "Can you get his attention?"

He got a mischievous grin on his face, a look that Zerbrowski and Jason had made me dread. "I could put you on my shoulders, then he'd spot you."

I gave him a look that wilted the grin into a smile. He shrugged. "Sorry." But it was the kind of sorry I'm used to, the one Jason always gives when he's not sorry at all.

Either Zerbrowski is more psychic than I thought, or he was trying to get away from the man who was dogging him. It was one of the Mobile Reserve officers in full combat black, body armor still in place, but he'd lost his helmet, his mask, and his eyes were wild. The whites kept flashing like a horse's when it's about to bolt.

Zerbrowski saw me, and the look of relief on his face was so pure, so happy, that it almost scared me. "Officer Elsworthy, this is Anita Blake, Marshal Anita Blake. She's our preternatural expert."

Elsworthy frowned, blinking a little too rapidly. It was as if it took longer than it should have for the words to filter through and have meaning. I'd seen enough shock to know the symptoms. Why wasn't he at the hospital with the rest of his squad?

Zerbrowski mouthed, "Sorry," to me.

Elsworthy blinked at me, his brown eyes didn't even look like they were focusing, as if what he was seeing was somewhere inside his head. Shit. A moment ago he'd been yelling at Zerbrowski, now he was staring at things that we couldn't see. Probably reliving the disaster. He was pale, and there was a light dew of sweat on his face. I was betting he would be clammy to the touch.

I put my face close to Zerbrowski, and spoke low, "Why isn't he at the hospital with the others?"

"He wouldn't go. Said he wanted to ask RPIT how the hell a werewolf can grow claws when it's still in human form."

I must have reacted to the question, because Zerbrowski suddenly gave me a look through the rims of his glasses. "I told him it wasn't possible for a shifter to gain claws while still in full human form. Was I wrong?"

I nodded. "A shifter has to be really powerful to be able to do it. I've only known a handful that could do partial change while they pretty much looked human."

Zerbrowski lowered his voice even more, "It might have been good to know that before they busted in on Van Anders."

"I thought a minimum of one person from each squad went down to Quantico for the big preternatural class and lecture."

"They did."

I gave him a disgusted look. "I don't go around assuming that I know more about the monsters than the freaking FBI."

"Maybe you should," Zerbrowski said softly.

The way he said it took the heat out of my words. I couldn't really get angry with Elsworthy standing there blinking like an innocent come to slaughter.

"Is it hot in here?" Elsworthy asked.

Actually, it was, too many people in too small a space. "Detective Webster, take Elsworthy out into the hall for a breath of air, would you?"

Webster did what I asked, and Elsworthy went without a single complaint. It was as if he'd used up all his anger before I got there, and now all that was left was the shock and the horror of it all.

Zerbrowski and I stayed in our little corner. "What went wrong?" I asked.

"I've been yelled at by Elsworthy, but even better, Captain Parker. He's waiting at the hospital for me to get my ass down there and explain to him how the hell Van Anders was able to do what he did."

"What exactly did he do?"

453

Zerbrowski dug his ever-present notebook out of his jacket pocket. The notebook looked like it'd been rolled in the dirt, then stepped on. He riffled through it until he got to the pages he wanted. "Van Anders cooperated completely when they came in. He seemed surprised and didn't know why anyone would want to arrest him. He was handcuffed, patted down, and the two tactical officers, Bates and Meyer, led him out into the hallway, while the rest of the squad reformed and made sure the rest of the apartment was clear." He glanced up at me. "Standard procedure."

"So when did it stop being standard?"

"Then it gets a little confused. Meyer never came back on the radio, at all. Bates started yelling, officer down, and something about, he's got claws. Elsworthy and another officer got out the door in time to see Van Anders clear enough that they both swear he had claws but was in full human form." Zerbrowski gave me a look. "Truthfully, I was ready to think Elsworthy, and . . ." He turned a page of his notebook, "Tucker, were seeing things."

I shook my head. "No, it's possible." I shook my head again and fought the urge to rub my temples. I had a headache starting. "The lycanthropes that I've seen do this, the claws just whip out. It's like having five switchblades suddenly appear. There wouldn't have been anything for the officer, Bates, was it? to see."

"Meyer, Bates is still alive."

I nodded. Names were important. It was important to remember who was dead and who was alive. "Van Anders stabbed Meyer. When the claws shot out of his fingertips, he used them like knives."

"Apparently Kevlar doesn't stop lycanthrope claws," Zerbrowski said.

"Kevlar isn't made to stop a stabbing attack," I said, "the claws acted like blades."

He nodded. "Van Anders used the officer as a shield, held him on his claws like a . . . puppet, is what Elsworthy finally said."

"He should have gone to the hospital with the others," I said.

"He looked fine when I got here, Anita, honest. I don't blame them for not forcing him to go."

"Well, he doesn't look fine now."

"We can give him a ride to the hospital when we go."

454

I looked at him. "Why do I think that we are going to the hospital for more than just a show of moral support?"

"You're just perceptive as hell tonight."

"Zerbrowski," I said.

"I told Captain Parker that I'd be right along once Marshal Blake showed up."

"You bastard."

"He's asking questions about the monsters that I don't have the answers to. Maybe Dolph would, but there is no way I want him to be here. We managed to quiet down the worst of what happened in the interrogation with your furry friend, but if Dolph loses it in a public setting . . ." He just shook his head.

I agreed with him. "Fine, I'll go with you to the hopsital and see if I can answer the captain's questions."

"Ah, but first ya gotta see this." He was actually smiling, and it wasn't a place for smiles.

"See what?" I asked suspiciously.

He turned without a word and led the way down the hallway towards the empty window. Webster had taken Elsworthy in the opposite direction so that they stood as far from the window as the hallway allowed. Good for Webster.

When we were close enough, my eyes started looking at something besides the window. There were two neat bullet holes in the wall near the window at the end of the hallway. Mobile Reserve's weapons can go fully automatic at the flick of a switch, but they're trained to do it one bullet at a time. With two officers down, and a monster on the loose, they'd remembered their training.

Zerbrowski motioned the uniform back, so we had some privacy. There was almost no glass on the carpet, because it had all gone outside.

"Did Van Anders throw someone through the window?"

"He threw himself," Zerbrowski said.

I stared at him. "We're twenty stories up, even a werewolf isn't going to walk away from that kind of fall. It may not kill him, but he'll be hurting."

"He didn't go down, he went up." He motioned me closer to the window.

I didn't like the window. It had a very low sill, almost low

455

enough to step through. That gives a better view, but without glass in the metal frame, there was nothing but empty air between me and a very big fall.

"Careful of the glass, and don't look down. But trust me, Anita, it's worth leaning out just a little, and looking up. Look at the right side of the window."

I placed a hand against the wall and found a place in the metal that was glass free so I could get a grip. The air was beating against me, like eager hands ready to snatch me away. I'm not afraid of heights, but the idea of falling from them, well, that I'm afraid of. I fought the almost irresistible urge to look down, because I knew if I looked down I might not be able to look out the window at all.

I leaned out, very carefully, and at first I didn't understand what I was seeing. There were holes in the side of the building, all the way up, as far as my eyes could follow. Small holes at regular intervals.

I eased myself back in, carefully, watching for glass as much as a fall. I frowned at Zerbrowski. "I saw the holes, but what are they?"

"Van Anders did a Spiderman on them. The sniper and observer were set up on the opposite side of the building. There was nothing they could do."

I felt my eyes go wide. "You mean the holes are where he shoved his hands into the building, and climbed up?"

Zerbrowski nodded, and he was smiling. "Captain Parker was screaming that he didn't know werewolves could do that either."

I glanced back at the window. "Captain Parker isn't the only one that didn't know. I mean they have the strength, but they get cut and scraped and break bones even. They may heal quickly, but it hurts them." I looked up at the ceiling as if I could still see the upward march of holes. "Being shot would have hurt like hell."

Zerbrowski nodded. "Will he need to see an emergency room, a doctor, something?"

I shook my head. "I doubt it. If he's strong enough to do a partial change, then I'll have to assume that his healing abilities are on the high end. If they are, he'll be healed within a couple hours, maybe less. If he changes form, when he's human again, he'll be good as new."

456

"They've put the word out to all the emergency and urgent care places, just in case."

I nodded. "Can't hurt, I guess, but I don't think you're going to catch him that way."

"How are we going to catch him, Anita? How do you catch something like this?"

I looked at him. "Did you ask the upper brass what they thought of using werewolves to track him?"

"They vetoed it."

"I think you might find them in a more receptive mood now."

"You think your friends will be nice on a leash for me?"

"I was really thinking I'd been holding the leash." My phone rang, and the sound made me jump. I flipped it open, and it was a voice I didn't recognize. I don't talk to the chief of police all that often.

I did a lot of yes, sir, and no, sir. Then the phone was buzzing, and I was left with Zerbrowski staring at me. "Were you talking to who I think you were talking to?"

"They've issued a court order of execution for Van Anders."

Zerbrowski's eyes were wide. "You are not going after him alone."

I shook my head. "I hadn't planned on it."

He looked like he didn't believe me. I actually had to give him my word I wouldn't try to pop Van Anders without backup. I'd have backup. The police chief had told me over the phone that they'd go along with the werewolf tracking idea. I'd have backup – if I could persuade Richard to give them to me.

I asked for some plastic evidence bags and raided Van Anders's dirty clothes drawer. I used gloves, not to keep my scent off them, but because I didn't want to touch anything that had touched Van Anders's body. I sealed the clothes in the bag, and hoped it would be enough to help the werewolves track him. We'd come back and start around the foot of this building. Van Anders might have climbed up, but he had to come down somewhere.

Zerbrowski drove me, Officer Elsworthy, and himself off to the hospital, so Captain Parker could yell at us both. Bates had died on the operating table.

Zerbrowski had to take the tongue lashing, because a sergeant

457

doesn't outrank a captain. I took it, because I smelled the fear on Parker. I didn't blame him for being afraid. I think we were all afraid, every single person in the hallway. Every person in the apartment. Every policeman, and woman, in town should have been afraid. Because when something like this happens it's still the police that have to clean up the mess. Well, the police, and your friendly neighborhood executioner. We were all afraid, and we should have been.

# 59

I met Richard at his house. We sat at the kitchen table where we'd sat so many weekend mornings. He drank tea. I sipped coffee. He wouldn't meet my eyes, and I didn't know what to say.

He caught me off guard by starting, "If you'd stuck to my morals, Asher would be dead right now, or worse, trapped in Europe with that monstrous bitch."

I was pretty sure that "monstrous bitch" was Belle Morte. "That's true," I said, and I tried to keep my voice neutral. I wanted to get down to business and ask Richard to loan me some were-wolves, but it didn't usually work well to approach Richard head on. It didn't take much to offend him. I needed his cooperation, not another fight.

"I don't understand how you could let them feed off of you, Anita." He finally looked up and his perfectly brown eyes were filled with a pain and confusion, so raw, that it hurt me to look at them.

"It's hard for me to cast stones anymore, Richard."

"The *ardeur*," he said.

I nodded.

"I can't let you feed off of me either."

"I understand that," I said.

He searched my face. "Then why are you here?"

Had he really thought this was going to be some tearful reunion, some plea on my part to get him back in my bed? Part of me was pissed, part of me was sad, none of me had time for it.

"The werewolf that's been raping and killing women here got away from the police today."

"I haven't seen anything on the news."

"We're trying to keep it quiet."

459

"You're here for business," his voice was soft.

"I'm here to keep other women from dying."

He got up from the table, and I was afraid for a moment that he'd leave, but he took the tea cozy off the teapot and refreshed his mug. "It's not one of my wolves, Anita."

"I know that."

He turned, and there was the first hint of anger. "Then what do you want from me?"

I sighed. "Richard, I love you, I may always love you, but I don't have time for this fight, not right now."

"Why not now?" he asked, and he was angry.

I opened the file folder and took out the first photo. I held it up so he could see it. He frowned, narrowing his eyes, then finally his mind made sense of it, and total disgust filled his face. He turned away.

"Why are you showing me that?"

"He's killed three women here and over a half-dozen in other countries. Those are only the ones we know about. He's out there right now picking a new victim."

"I can't do anything about that."

"But I can, if you'll give me some werewolves to help track him."

He looked at me then, then away, because I still had the photo showing. "Track him, you mean like a dog?"

"No, most dogs won't track a shape-shifter, they're too scared of them."

"We're not animals, Anita."

"No, you're not, but in animal form you have the nose of one, but you still have the brain of a person. You can track and think."

"Me, you expect me to do this?"

I shook my head, and laid the photo down on the pile. I stood and spread the pile out across his table. "No, but Jason would, and Jamil would if you asked him to. I'd say Sylvie, but she's not well enough to do much of anything."

"She challenged me, and she lost," Richard said. His eyes kept flicking to the photos on the table. "Get those off of my table."

"He's out there right now, about to turn another woman into so much meat."

460

"Fine, fine, take Jason, take Jamil, take whoever the hell you want."

"Thank you." I started gathering the photos up.

"You didn't have to do it this way, Anita."

"What way?" I asked, shutting the file over the gruesome photos.

"Harsh. You could have just asked me."

"Would you have said yes?"

"I don't know, but those photos are going to haunt me."

"I saw the real deal, Richard, your nightmares can't be worse than mine."

He moved in one of those blurs of speed and grabbed my arm. "Part of me thinks they're horrifying, just like I'm supposed to, but part of me likes the pictures." His fingers dug into my arm, bruising. "Part of me just sees fresh meat." He let a growl trickle out from between his even white teeth.

"I'm sorry you hate what you are, Richard."

He let go of me so fast, I almost fell. "Take the wolves you need, and get out."

"If I could wave a magic wand over you and make you human, purely human, I'd do it, Richard."

He looked at me; his eyes had bled to wolf amber. "I believe you, but there isn't a magic wand. I am what I am, and nothing will ever change that."

"I'm sorry, Richard."

"I've decided to live, Anita."

I looked at him. "I'm sorry, I don't understand."

"I've been trying to die. I'm not going to die anymore. I'm going to live, whatever that means."

"I'm glad, but I wish you sounded happier about the choice."

"Go, Anita, you've got a murderer to catch."

I did, and time was not on our side. But I still hated leaving him like this. "I'll do what I can to help you, Richard, you know that."

"Like you help all your friends."

I shook my head, gathered up the folder, and went for the door. "When you want to talk, and not to fight, give me a call, Richard."

"And when you want to talk, and not catch murderers, you give me a call."

461

We left it at that. But I didn't have time to hold his hand, even if he would have let me. Van Anders was out there, and there were so many people he could hurt. What was a little emotional desolation between friends compared to getting Van Anders off the streets?

## 60

JASON AND JAMIL stayed in human form, while Norman and Patricia stayed in wolf form. I'd seen Norman in human form before, but I couldn't put a face on Patricia. She was just a big shaggy wolf, pale, almost white. We had to put the two pony-sized wolves on leashes. Today of all days I did not want the police seeing a giant wolf running loose on the streets. I was thinking they'd be in a shoot-first-ask-questions-later sort of mood.

I'd unzipped the two bags that I'd collected from Van Anders's rented apartment. The wolves sniffed it, growled, and on the end of leashes, they tracked him from the sidewalk around his apartment building, and all through the city, and finally to a mall.

The police had been watching the airports, the bus stations, the highways. Van Anders was sitting in the freaking food court of Eastfield mall. He'd piled his hair up under a billed cap and added a cheap pair of sunglasses. As disguises went it was okay. Besides, I couldn't complain, much. I was wearing a billed cap with my hair up under it, and sunglasses. I hate it when the bad guys copy. I was also wearing a baggy T-shirt, and baggy jeans with my Nikes. Short as I was, I looked like a thousand teenagers wandering any mall in America.

I'd deputized Jamil and Jason. They stayed out of sight, but warned me that he'd smell them sooner or later. I'd already flashed my badge at mall security. I'd made the decision that we wouldn't call the police, and we wouldn't try to evacuate. I had a court order of execution. I didn't have to give him a warning. I didn't have to do anything but kill him.

It was mid-afternoon, so the food court wasn't too busy. That was good. There was a group of teenagers at the table nearest Van Anders. Why weren't they in school? At the table next-closest to him was a mother with a baby in a stroller and two toddlers. Two toddlers, neither of them in baby seats, but running free, while she tried to help the baby eat soft-serve yogurt.

Van Anders was still more than fifteen feet from the rampaging toddlers. The teenagers were frightfully close, but I couldn't figure out how to get them to move. I was working up my nerve to wind my way through the daytime moms and kids, when the teenagers got up, left their trash on the table, and walked away.

Van Anders was as isolated as I was going to get him here in the mall. I wasn't willing to let him escape again. He was too dangerous. I made the decision in that moment that I would endanger all these nice people. That the mother with her yogurt-smeared baby, and the two screaming toddlers were going to have to take their chances. I was fairly certain I could control the situation well enough to keep them out of it, but I wasn't *completely* certain. All I knew for sure was that I was going to take him, now. I wasn't going to wait.

I had my gun at my side, safety off, round-chambered long before I got to the table with the mother and her children. I had my federal marshal badge hanging out over the pocket of the large T-shirt, just in case some brave civilian decided to try and save Van Anders.

I had the gun up and pointed as I passed the woman's table. I think it was her soft gasp that made him turn. He saw the badge, and he smiled, taking another bite of his sandwich. He talked with his mouth full. "Are you going to warn me not to move, tell me to freeze?" He sounded Dutch.

"No," I said, and I shot him.

The bullet spun him out of his chair, and I fired again before he'd hit the ground. The first one had been rushed; not lethal, but the second one was a solid body shot.

I fired into his body twice more before I got close enough to watch his mouth open and shut. Blood blossomed from his lips, and turned his blue shirt purple.

I circled wide, so I could get a clear head shot. He lay on his back and bled, and managed to cough blood, and clear his throat enough to say, "Police have to give warning. Can't just shoot."

I let out all the breath in my body, and sighted on his forehead just above the eyes. "I'm not the police, Van Anders, I'm the executioner."

His eyes widened, and he said, "No."

I pulled the trigger and watched most of his face explode into an unrecognizable mess. His eyes had been bluer than in the photos.

# 61

BRADLEY CALLED ME at home that night. Strangely, after blowing a man's brains out in front of a lot of suburban moms and kids I just wasn't in the mood to go into work. I was already tucked into bed with my favorite toy penguin, Sigmund, and Micah curled beside me. Usually Micah's warmth was more comforting than a truck-load of stuffed toys, but tonight I needed that choking grip on my favorite toy. Micah's arms were wonderful, but Sigmund never told me I was being silly, or bloodthirsty. Neither had Micah, but I kept waiting for it.

"You made national news, and the *Post-Dispatch* is running a front-page picture of you executing Van Anders," Bradley said.

"Yeah, turns out I was across from a camera store. Lucky me." Even to me, I sounded tired, or something more. What's more than tired? Dead?

"You going to be alright?" he asked.

I pulled Micah's arms closer around me, snuggled my head against his bare chest. I was still cold. How could I be cold under all these blankets? "I've got a few friends staying with me, they'll keep me from getting too morose."

"He needed killing, Anita."

"I know that."

"Then what's that tone in your voice?"

"You haven't gotten to the part of the article where the three-year-old boy is having screaming fits about me killing him, like he saw me do to the bad man in the mall, have you?"

"If he'd gotten away . . ."

"Just stop, Bradley, just stop. I made the decision before I moved on him that the witnesses' psyches weren't as important as their physical safety. I don't regret that decision. Much."

"Okay, I'll just talk business then. We think Leo Harlan is best

466

known as Harlan Knox. He's worked with some of the same people that employed Heinrick and Van Anders."

"Why am I not surprised?" I said.

"We tried the number he gave you. The answering service says he's canceled his contract with them, except for one message."

I waited for it.

"You're not going to ask?"

"Just tell me, Bradley."

"Okay, Here goes. 'Ms. Blake, sorry we didn't get to raise my ancestor. In case you were wondering, he is real. But under the circumstances, I thought discretion the better part of valor. And the assignment has been canceled, for the time being.' Do you understand what he means about the assignment being canceled?"

"I think so, I think he means the deal was called off. It got too messy. Thanks for checking, Bradley."

"Don't thank me, Anita, if I hadn't tried to get you onto our payroll as a federal agent, you might never have come to the attention of whoever hired Heinrick."

"You can't keep blaming yourself for that, Bradley. It's like spilled milk, clean up the mess, and move on."

"The same goes for Van Anders."

"I always give better advice than I take, Bradley, you should know that by now."

He laughed, then said, "Watch your back, okay?"

"I will, you, too."

"Bye, Anita, take care."

I was in the middle of saying, "you, too," when he hung up on me. What was it about working for law enforcement that gave you such bad phone manners?

Nathaniel came into the bedroom with the copy of *Charlotte's Web*. "It was in the kitchen, and it's got a second bookmark. I think Zane, or somebody has started reading it."

I cuddled tighter in against Micah's body, and he held me, his arms warm and fierce as if he could squeeze the bad feelings out of me. "Let them get their own copy," I said.

Nathaniel smiled. Micah kissed the top of my head. "Who's reading tonight?" Nathaniel asked.

"I will," Micah said, "unless Anita wants to."

I buried my face in the crook of his arm. "No, being read to sounds just about right tonight."

Nathaniel handed him the book and climbed into bed. I wasn't sure if it was the warmth of both of them under the covers, or the sound of Micah's deep voice as he read, but slowly, I began to be warm again. I hadn't read *Charlotte's Web* in years. I was overdue. Overdue for so many things that didn't involve guns or killing people.

# 62

DOLPH IS STILL on leave, but I'm working on arranging a get-together between him, his wife, and their son and daughter-in-law. I don't know if there's anything to talk about, but Lucille, Mrs. Dolph, wants me to try. I'll try.

Richard seems to have some peace. Not enough peace for us to date. But hey, I'm just thrilled that he's no longer suicidally depressed. At this point, I want him healthy and happy more than I want him with me.

Asher, Jean-Claude, and I have an understanding. I guess, you could say we're dating. You wouldn't think that dating two men simultaneously would be a first with me, but two men on the exact same date at the exact same time – that's new.

Stephen and Gregory's father is still in town. Valentina and Bartolomé asked Jean-Claude's permission to kill him. Jean-Claude said okay, as long as Stephen and Gregory agree. Stephen's therapist thinks it would be healthier if the boys handled it themselves. Gregory's comment had been, "Oh, we get to kill him ourselves."

"That's not what I meant," Stephen said.

The two of them are still arguing about how to handle their childhood nightmare come to town. I'm with Valentina and Bartolomé on this one. Kill his ass. But I won't take the choice away from Stephen and Gregory, not if their therapist says it'll do more damage. God knows they've had enough damage in their lives already.

But because they haven't been able to satisfy their debt of honor, the two child vampires are staying in St. Louis. Besides the debt of honor thing, I think Valentina doesn't want to be anywhere near Belle Morte when she goes up against the Mother of All Darkness. Me either.

There are nights when I dream about the living dark. As long as I sleep with a cross on I'm okay, but if I forget, she haunts me. I'd get a cross tattoo if I wasn't afraid it'd burst into flames.

The Mobile Reserve has me on their list of civilian experts. They'll call if they need me. Captain Parker was wicked pissed that the feds' latest update on the preternatural wasn't so updated. The FBI just doesn't have enough friends that are monsters. If they did they'd know more.

Larry is back in town all duly trained to be a federal marshal and vampire hunter. The wedding is set for October. Tammy is threatening to have me in the wedding. Some friends they are.

We're still reading *Charlotte's Web*. "The Crickets sang in the grasses. They sang the song of summer's ending, a sad, monotonous song. 'Summer is over and gone,' they sang. 'Over and gone, over and gone . . .'" Some people think that's a sad chapter, but it's always been one of my favorites. Summer is over and gone, but autumn is here, and next month is October with the bluest skies of the year. For the first time in years, no, scratch that, for the first time ever, I had someone to hold my hand and go walking out under those blue skies. Richard and I had always planned to do it, but he had his job, and I had mine, and we never made the time. But now I have Micah. And I'm learning that you have to make time for what's important. You have to fight to carve little pieces of happiness out of your life, or the everyday emergencies will eat up everything.

When we finish *Charlotte's Web* Nathaniel wants to read *Treasure Island*. Sounds good to me.

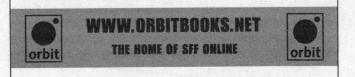